The Bluebird Brooch

By

Rosemary Noble

Developmental editor – J L Dean
Cover Design by Kate Sharp
Cover Image - Shutterstock

This is a work of fiction. Unless otherwise indicated, all the names, characters, businesses, places, events and incidents in this book are either the product of the author's imagination or used in a fictitious manner. Any resemblance to actual persons, living or dead, or actual events is purely coincidental.

All rights reserved © 2022 Rosemary Noble
Aldwick Publishing

For mothers everywhere

A woman's choice is often no choice at all.

She was so evidently the victim of the civilisation which produced her, that the links of her bracelet seemed like manacles chaining her to her fate. - Edith Wharton

Peggy

She's coming. I can feel it in my bones. It won't be long now. There is so much to tell her, but my voice is silent. I can only love her and find a way to guide her. She needs to know the truth.

Prologue

1854 London - Susanna

The mattress he promised was of goose feather, with sheets of crisp white linen. And the house my bed should rest in? A snug apartment somewhere not far from Regent Street. War and pestilence have put paid to that. I hate to admit, but my brother was right. Essie – well she was always righteous, her voice a snag-toothed saw grating in my head. And yet, if a woman of a certain age can never say yes to love, what good is life?

My brain has spun in circles to find another solution. With money so short, I have no option but to make my own way. A lone woman, bereft of love and family, I must discard all that I have to forge a new life.

'That you have brought yourself to this!' Essie holds out her plump arms to take Amelia Rose. 'Your brother and I agreed to bring her up as our own, though it will be hard enough with another mouth to feed.' Her ice-blue eyes snap with a mixture of resentment and forbearance rather than sisterly warmth. She used to have such a sweet face. Eight children and a husband who has never lived up to expectation have soured her. My heart sinks for my sweet babe. Does Essie think I want this? There is no other way.

'I'll try to send money when I'm settled. Write to me via the Post Office. Let me know your new address in Liverpool.' I glance at the packing cases piled in the corner of the room before my eyes drift back to my baby's face, hoping to implant her image in my brain. She yawns, her pink gums make my breasts tingle. 'There, there, my love. Aunt Essie's your mama now.' I plant a dozen tiny kisses on Amelia's cheeks, until she begins to mewl with hunger. Desperate to cling on, instead I hand her to Essie who opens her blouse with a sigh of resignation.

'When do you leave?' Essie asks.

'They travel tomorrow. I must be there today to take up my duties. I'm only grateful that Mrs Billington found me this position.'

Essie nods, 'You are lucky to retain her support. Most employers would have cast you out without a reference.'

I sigh deeply. 'My lady is not one to turn her back on those less fortunate.' I cannot help the slight tone of annoyance in my voice. I brush it aside and force myself to a more compliant note. 'Essie, I want to leave my recipe books with you. Please give them to Amelia on her wedding day.' My eyes beseech her.

The corners of Essie's mouth droop further. She disapproves of my conduct and has turned my brother against me. They prefer to model their morals on those of our dear Queen and Prince Consort. Essie has even begun to dress her hair after Victoria's fashion, but I fear her brittle locks cannot compare. I attempt a smile. 'I'm begging you. If she needs me…'

'She won't, Susanna. We know our duty. Amelia has latched onto my breast, look. You have no reason to stay.' As Essie's youngest daughter, Harriet, begins to cry from the nest of cushions beside her, Essie snaps in irritation, 'You'd best leave.' She turns away from me, her mouth set in a thin line and my eyes smart at this renewed rejection.

How many times had I begged James and Esther to accompany them to their new life in Liverpool? She was always keen enough before to accept my help with her brood. Now she turns her nose up at me, preferring martyrdom.

I jut out my chin and stand firm. 'Very well, but I am leaving this small box with the books and the copy of my father's portrait for her.' I leave no room for argument. 'May I kiss her one last time?'

I am scarcely out of the room when my heart splinters to hear Essie murmur loud enough for me to hear, 'Rose, we'll call you Rose. Harriet, say hello to your new sister.' I steel myself from running back to drag my daughter from Essie's breast. How could she not let Amelia keep the name her father gave her?

'Robert for a boy, Amelia for a girl, Susanna, promise me.' I did promise him. My daughter's name is the only thing she owns. One day, God willing, I will send her the bluebird brooch to pin on her wedding gown, but for now I dare not. It may yet keep me from starvation. It will be the last thing I sell.

As I close the heavy wooden door behind me, my heart shatters. The thick woollen shawl drawn around my face, protects me from onlookers as icy raindrops mingle with my tears.

Chapter One

May 2019 – Sussex Coast

The train doors slide open with a welcome whoosh. Laura side-stepped the shabby giant with his vacant stare. Always first on the train with his grabber poised to collect the left-over Metros, cardboard coffee cups and sweet wrappers, passengers had given up attempting to smile at him years before.

Keen to get home, Laura left Bognor station without noticing the newly planted tubs with their spindly geraniums and straggly lobelias, an attempt to soften the bleakness of the concourse. The town shops were closing, cafés too. Nothing much happened even in summer, until the bars began to fill and girls half her age, clad in skimpy dresses, no matter the season, tottered down to the nightclub on the pier.

Onward through the Edwardian arcade, she crossed the road towards the broad promenade, pausing to look at the sea and breathe in the scent of salted air. The final homeward stretch always calmed her after a hectic day at college. The shifting colours, the water occasionally mirror-like, more often roaring its way over the pebbled beach, reminding her of a stormy scene from a Turner painting.

Today, the green of the sea was offset by a band of navy close to the horizon. Tiny white sails punctuated the sky. A race must be underway. Despite the stiff breeze, great blobs of cloud hung motionless in the blue sky, whipped cream morphing into a gloomy grey.

Laura hugged herself with a new sense of pride. Her boss had been full of praise for what she had achieved in the year since her promotion to Head of College Library Services. She needed to hold onto that boost after yesterday's hammer blow.

As faint spots of rain sprinkled her face, Laura quickened her pace.

The flat was perfect, just yards from the sea, two bedrooms, although the second 'guest bedroom' could only be described as dinky; enough for a small child. She had resisted decorating the room so far, but imagined friezes and soft colours, cute curtains rather than the harsh slatted blind, and a nursing chair. There had to be a nursing chair. But that was before Jake had left his note. A note, a solitary, skimpy note, after ten years. It was true that things had not been good lately between them, but she had never imagined him walking out.

Reaching her front door, Laura registered the lack of Jake's red sports car in the parking space, a stark reminder of her new status. She turned her key in the lock. A couple of letters lay on the mat. She picked them up and threw them on the small pine table in the lobby, before walking into their open-plan kitchen/living room and drew a deep breath. His things were gone. No Xbox on the coffee table, no iPad plugged into the wall. Laura walked into the bedroom, drawers open and emptied. The wardrobe hung now with her clothes and his empty hangers.

She had done her crying last night, now she felt empty, hollowed out at his betrayal, without even the decency to face her. Laura had never considered Jake a coward. A macho rugby player, brimming with a sense of self- importance, it turns out he was unable to brave her scorn.

Laura poured a glass of wine from the fridge. She had devised a plan, a night of self-indulgence. First, she was going to scrub all evidence of his presence from the flat, next she would cook up his favourite Vietnamese spicy pork and noodles and eat it all by herself and then she would turn on Netflix and find something she wanted to watch. Goodbye to Die Hard, The Matrix, farewell to James Bond and Star Wars. Part of her, the child yearning comfort part of her, longed for one of her father's classic videos such as Terms of Endearment, something Jake would have rolled his eyes at, if she had ever dared to suggest it. She could hear his voice, 'What century were you born in, girl?'

Later, with the taste of chilli and ginger on her tongue, she sipped at a second glass of wine. She snuggled up on the sofa, a packet of chocolate digestives beside her and picked up the remote control, scanning her mind for all those films on her to be watched list. The first one up on the menu was Lion. Dev Patel with his dark, brooding looks, the antithesis of Jake. Yes, that would do nicely. Laura pressed the OK button.

Chapter Two

On autopilot, following a wine induced sleep, Laura began her usual morning routine, always in a rush to make the train. At least she did not have to prepare breakfast for Jake, nor hunt for his favourite shirt in the wardrobe. That niggling sense of freedom again. She grabbed the letters from the lobby, stuffing them into her bag before hurrying to the station. The 07.16 was standing at the platform - no delays or cancellations, one small mercy.

After rummaging for her season ticket, she picked out the two envelopes. The first was an invitation to visit a car showroom for a test drive. Laura screwed it up before a cold feeling settled on her. Jake had taken his car, her only means of transport and the funds in her bank account low from the inevitable flat purchases. Shopping she could manage, there was a supermarket within yards of the station, but visits to her father, Sunday lunches in one of the many country gastro pubs, the music festival she had booked in Dorset, all were off the cards without a car. Laura's world shrank to what was doable by train. She shrugged, telling herself she would get by.

She extracted the other letter, a slim white envelope, franked with no post mark. She turned it over, an unknown solicitor's name printed on the back. Laura crumpled both letters and threw them in the nearest litter bin. Some invitation to invest in a dodgy scheme, no doubt. Jake was always getting those.

She pushed at the train door button when a thought struck her. Had Jake advised a solicitor to demand that she sell the flat already? Laura's mood nose-dived. Why hadn't she thought all that through last night? His leaving could render her homeless. Returning his share of the deposit and paying the mortgage on her salary was a non-starter.

Laura turned and rushed back to the litter bin to extract the letters, grabbing them both before heading for the nearest train door as the conductor was about to signal departure. With her heart thumping, she made her way to her usual seat. 'Sophie will help,' she mumbled to herself as she sat down.

Her travelling companion further up the line was a solicitor and had proffered advice several times before when asked. They had met five years before. Tall and blonde, Sophie stood out in a crowd of flustered passengers when their train stopped at Billingshurst because of some obstruction further up the line. It was the kind of announcement that all commuters dreaded.

'I am sorry to announce that the train will be held at this station for at least an hour, maybe more. We have no more details. Southern Rail apologises for any inconvenience.'

Laura's fellow passengers had groaned in frustration as the heating shut down and cold seeped in, turning their feet to ice within minutes. With an important meeting scheduled for ten o'clock, Laura looked at her phone, the digital screen blinked 8.30. The minutes ticked by. She wondered if there were any buses for the last few miles of the journey. People began to leave the train and Laura picked up her bag to follow. Perhaps they knew something. Several passengers huddled in the ticket hall, but an air of resignation told Laura buses were not forthcoming. She scanned the platform for a station buffet. A large, strong coffee was required pronto. Nothing, nada, zilch. The day was getting worse until she noticed the woman with a phone to her ear.

'Yes, Billinghurst Station. You can pick me up? Great, thanks, Tony. How long? Fifteen minutes? I'll be out front.'

Laura screwed up her courage and walked over. 'You're not going to Horsham, by any chance?'

A sunny smile greeted her question. 'Sure, do you want a lift?'

Laura nodded in relief. 'Yes, please.'

A train friendship had begun that morning and thereafter they had sat together on their morning commute, never meeting elsewhere, but it was the nearest thing Laura had to an intimate friendship outside of her relationship with Jake.

'Gosh, you look rough. How are you this morning?' Sophie asked, settling into her seat at Arundel.

'I've had this letter.' Laura extracted it from her bag.

'You haven't opened it.' Sophie looked quizzical as she took the crumpled envelope.

'Jake walked out on me. I'm gutted to think he may want me to sell up immediately before I've scarcely had time to rid the flat of the smell of his aftershave.'

'It's too soon and anyway you have rights.'

Laura's mood lifted a fraction. 'That's good to know.'

Sophie pursed her lips. 'I hate to say it, but he never treated you well.'

'No don't. I'm beginning to understand. It's because we'd been together forever. He was all I knew, my first and only boyfriend.'

'By the sounds of it, he kept you for himself. You should have been having a ball instead of stuck with one guy. A controlling one at that.'

It was difficult to argue with this point. The scales were falling from Laura's eyes. More and more instances of the way Jake had put himself first were creeping to the surface of Laura's mind.

'You want me to open this?' Sophie's voice punctured Laura's reverie.

'Yes, so I can watch your expression. If I open it, I'll only cave into whatever he wants.'

'No, you won't. It may not be my area of expertise, but I'll help you get the better of him.' Sophie leant across the table to squeeze Laura's hand.

Laura returned a wan smile of thanks. She hated the thought of losing her flat. Was it possible to find a way of keeping it?

Sophie tore open the envelope and scanned the letter. Laura watched her eyebrows rise and her mouth open slightly, then smile. Not the reaction she had expected.

Sophie laughed. 'It seems your immediate worry may be over.'

'What? He's giving me the flat?'

'No, you may have come into an inheritance.'

Laura's mouth dropped open. She shook her head. 'That's impossible. Dad's my only close relative and he was alive and kicking the last time I heard.'

'Aunt Edith, it says here. Edith Swain.'

'Never heard of her, it must be some mistake. This solicitor has mixed me up with another Laura Grey. It must be a common enough name.'

'It has your date of birth and your mother's name, Jeanette Winters.'

The shock of hearing her mother's name glued Laura to her seat. 'Jeanette was her name. Do you know I didn't even remember her surname?'

Sophie drew her eyebrows together. 'How could you not remember?'

'She died before I knew her. Dad worked away so much that he palmed me off on a nanny before he became a serial philanderer. I was brought up by strangers and then several step-mothers, none of whom cared a jot.' Laura shrugged, she had long learned not to dwell on her childhood and never discussed it. An inheritance – visions of antique clocks, Victorian vases or a dresser covered in blue and white china, floated through Laura's mind. Please let it be worth something, maybe a diamond necklace.

'What's this inheritance? Will it pay Jake off?'

'It doesn't say. Just asks you to get in contact as a beneficiary.'

A beneficiary. A word which could mean anything, but then it could be mean everything. Laura uttered a silent prayer as Sophie handed her the letter.

'It's inviting me to go up to Grimsby. Where is Grimsby?'

'Somewhere up north, I think.'

'North? We've always lived in the south-east. I assumed Mum was born here. I suppose I should feel sad that someone has died but I honestly have no idea who she is.'

'You must go. There will be papers to sign, proof of identity required, that sort of thing. Apart from that, don't you want to know something about your mother's side of the family? It sounds like a great opportunity. Give the solicitor a ring when you get to college. He will know more than he's told you in the letter.'

Laura nodded, a thoughtful expression on her face. Who was Edith Swain? The question intrigued her. After Jake's betrayal an adventure would be cool.

Ignoring two texts from Jake demanding that they talk, Laura waited for lessons to end before phoning the solicitor. She closed the door to her office and keyed in the number. The call was answered by a woman with an unidentifiable accent, not one she associated with 'the north', but distinctive. Laura had spent a couple of minutes looking up Grimsby and saw that it was a town on the southern side of the Humber River in North Lincolnshire. She was quickly put through to the writer of the letter, a Mr Dewsbury.

'Ah yes, Miss Gray. At last. We have been searching for you for a few weeks now. Can you confirm that I am speaking to the daughter of Charles Gray and Jeanette Winters.'

'Yes, but are you sure it's me you want? I've never heard of a Miss Swain.'

'She was your grandmother's sister on your mother's side. Did she never tell you about her?'

'My mother died when I was two.'

A slight pause before he began to stumble through his commiserations.

Laura interrupted. 'No, don't worry, Mr Dewsbury, It's a long time ago.'

'Didn't your grandmother mention her, either?'

'My grandmother? I've never met her. I assume she died years ago.'

'Oh, my dear Miss Gray, she's still alive. We tried her first, but she couldn't help us.'

Laura's blood chilled. 'I have a grandmother?' Her words were no more than a whisper. 'My father never breathed a word.'

'Ah yes, your father. He's difficult to get hold of too. Never in the country and doesn't answer his mobile.'

'Tell me about it,' Laura replied. 'He is renowned for not taking personal calls, from me, anyway.'

'Your grandmother lives in a nursing home. Has done so for a few years apparently. Would you like the address?'

Laura scribbled it down, her mouth dry with annoyance. What possible excuse did her father have for not telling her she had a living grandmother?

The solicitor gave her a moment to collect herself before continuing. 'We are proceeding with probate now that we have identified you. It's not a complicated will. Apart from one small bequest, you are her sole beneficiary. However, we would like you to come up here to decide what you want to do with the house. We need to take copies of your birth certificate, passport, driver's licence and a utility bill or something like that. That should be sufficient.'

House, an actual house. Laura suddenly had difficulty breathing and sank onto her office chair.

'Miss Gray? Are you still there?'

'Yes, sorry. It's half term in ten days. Would that be soon enough?'

'Of course. How about four o'clock on Tuesday the 28th? That should give you enough time for the journey. You can stay in the house. It's comfortable, if a little outdated. I'll get the electricity turned on for you.'

'Thank you.' Laura put down the phone, stunned. All the questions she had intended to ask forgotten. She had a living grandmother and a house.

She stared at the piece of paper. Storrington. Her grandmother lived in Storrington. Years of loneliness when she had a living relative less than thirty miles from her childhood home in Guildford, and fifteen miles from her flat on the coast. But how on earth was she to get there? She sighed. Another thing I need to sort out, she thought, a set of wheels. She had no idea what kind of car she wanted, or the costs involved, but it appeared she may soon have the funds to buy one.

Remembering Jakes's earlier texts, Laura replied – *Talk 1st week in June.*

His reply was short. *Why so long? Decisions to make.*

Hers was briefer. *Sorry, will be away.* She kicked herself - sorry. It was him who should be apologising. Laura turned off her phone.

Having fruitlessly searched for buses to Storrington that evening, Laura decided that a train to Amberley and a taxi to Storrington was the best option, but would no doubt cost an arm and a leg. Bringing Sophie up to speed the next morning, her problem was solved when Sophie offered a solution.

'Why don't I take you on Saturday. Jim's playing tennis in the afternoon. If you get a train to Arundel, I can pick you up and bring you back. I'll happily mooch around Storrington. It has some pleasant shops and cafés.'

'As long as I pay for your petrol.'

Sophie acquiesced. 'Did you ring your father to ask him why he was keeping you in the dark like that?'

'He's in Japan this week. I texted that we need to talk. He hasn't got back to me.'

By the time Sophie collected Laura from the train on Saturday afternoon, Laura had still not heard from her father, hardly unusual. With three other children, two ex-wives as well as a current one, he was used to dodging texts.

Sophie dropped Laura off outside The Nightingale Care Home. 'Will an hour and a half be enough? You can always text me if you need longer?'

'Or shorter. I have no idea what I'm going to find. She may be ga-ga.' Laura waved off her friend, feeling that this could be a mistake. If her grandmother had never bothered making contact before, perhaps she would not be interested in her granddaughter now. Maybe her father had been protecting her. She should have phoned ahead to find out the lie of the land. Nobody liked surprises.

Rolling her shoulders to ease the tension, Laura pushed the buzzer to request admittance. Behind the glass door stood an elderly lady, wafer thin, dressed in mis-matched clothes while cradling a doll, her eyes staring out with a blank expression.

'Don't mind Bridget.' A gentle voice said through the intercom. 'Just don't let her out.'

Laura heard a click and pushed the door open to slide through, closing it swiftly behind her.

A woman exited a nearby office. 'Mrs Winters, you say. Wow, no visitors for three years and then two in the space of a fortnight.'

'Two?'

'Yes, the other was a man in a suit. He tried asking her questions, but she just shook her head. I say, you're not her granddaughter, are you?' Laura nodded.

'Oh, my goodness. She is going to be over the moon.' The cheerful, black assistant manager, Heather, according to her name badge, beamed with delight, the warmth of her eyes matching the warmth of her smile. 'Such a lovely lady, your grandmother.'

'What's wrong with her?' Laura began to relax.

'She had a stroke, poor love. Her husband said it was when her daughter died. He tried to look after her himself until it got too much. She's been with us for five years now.'

Laura's brain hurt with this new information. 'Are you telling me that my grandfather is alive too?' she asked.

Heather looked askance. 'Oh no, dear, he passed three years ago. Since then, no one's visited apart from the doctor. Look, I'll take you to her room.' Heather trotted off down the corridor with Laura in tow.

Heather opened the door of room eight and Laura blinked at the contrast between the dark corridor and the sun streaming in the westerly facing windows. The assistant's squat body jiggled up and down, surprisingly light on her toes. 'Peggy, you have a visitor.'

Laura peeped around Heather's back and smiled at the iron-haired old lady, whose dark amber eyes looked sharply at her, before a lop-sided grin drew her lips into a grimace of concentration, 'L- l - l - l,'

'Peggy understands everything but can't speak. Ask her questions she can nod or shake her head to,' Heather whispered.

Laura drew a chair up and sat down. 'You know it's me, don't you, Granny.' The word sounded strange to Laura. 'Is Granny, okay?' Peggy nodded. Her right hand was rooted to her lap but the left one reached unsteadily to Laura.

'Is it because I look like Mum?' Laura knew that it was, without Peggy's nod. She had a framed photograph of her mother taken when Laura was a baby. Long black hair caught in a chignon, two shades darker than Laura's, piercing blue eyes, heart-shaped face, a slight dimple in her right cheek when she smiled. Strangely, there was little resemblance to her grandmother. Peggy had an angular face with high cheek bones, threads of dark copper in her straggly eyebrows hinted at a once handsome woman.

Laura took her grandmother's left hand in hers, envying her long slim fingers, though gnarled and knobbly with age. Laura's hands were square and too small, she had always hated them.

'I would have come before but I didn't know you were...'

Her grandmother tapped Laura's hand with her left thumb and attempted to smile again.

Heather, who remained in the doorway said, 'Peggy, would you like to show Laura your album?' Peggy nodded vigorously. 'She loves her album. We look at it every week, don't we, sweetheart?' Heather crossed over to a cupboard and reached for a battered, red photo album sitting on top. Laura took the well-thumbed album from her and began to turn the pages, strangers peeping out from history. She stopped at one photograph.

'Is that you and Edith?' She pointed to a young woman with fair curly hair and a child of around ten on a promenade. Peggy nodded. 'I can't see much of a likeness, maybe around the mouth. She's quite a bit older than you.'

Peggy held up five fingers twice, wincing with the effort of straightening them. A graduation photograph followed by a blank page and then a wedding photograph. A grown-up Peggy arm in arm with a slim balding man. They looked so stiff and formal. Peggy dressed head to toe in a white figure-hugging gown, her hair hidden by a veil and circle of daisy like flowers, her new husband in a dark pin-striped suit.

This was Grandpa. He featured in a few other photos, always suited, even on a beach with Laura's mother as a baby. Another sitting with a pipe in an armchair with a toddler sat beside him, Grandpa obviously loved his daughter. His eyes feasted on her. There was not a single photo of him smiling at the camera. He was always turned towards Jeanette. Laura could only imagine how bereft he was when she died. How could her father keep her from her grandparents? Laura frowned. The first colour photographs of Jeanette growing up surfaced on the next page, making her heart flip. Photographs of the mother she had longed for, but no memory of her remained, not so much as a glimmer.

Laura turned more pages and her heart twisted further. A young woman, her mother, stood behind a settee, her hands on the shoulders of the older seated women, one of whom was nestling a baby in her arms.

'Is that you, holding me?' Another nod from Peggy. 'With Edith? She met me?' The woman, then around seventy years old, stared directly into the camera with pale blue-grey eyes, her mouth slightly open. It was as though she were speaking to the older Laura. *'I'm here, we don't know each other, but I'm here.'*

'You know she's left me a house?' Laura felt a pressure on her fingers. Peggy looked at her and the expression in her cloudy eyes grew gentle, warm, understanding. Peggy pointed at herself. 'It was your house too, the one you grew up in?' A slight nod of agreement.

'I wish I could have visited while she was alive.' Years of missed opportunity gnawed at Laura. 'I'm going up there in ten days, is there anything you want me to bring back?' A tiny lift of the shoulders spoke of Peggy's indifference. Everything was too late.

Before Laura left to meet Sophie half-an-hour later, she asked Heather why she thought Peggy had not given up and died.

Heather observed Laura with something between bemusement and compassion. 'Peggy may look frail, but she's tough mentally. Goodness knows why. I am pretty sure Peggy's hung on to meet you. Every time we looked in the album, as soon as we came to that photo of you, she would try to say your name. You are her reason to live.'

Laura shivered to think of the missing years when she and Peggy could have been together. Her anger with her father threatened to boil over. 'What was my grandfather like?'

'Mr Winters? He looked after her for years, you know.'

'But what was he like?'

'Percy was always a little stiff to my way of thinking, but he always insisted Peggy had the best care.'

'Peggy must have been heartbroken when he died.'

An odd expression passed over Heather's face. 'It was strange, she seemed almost relieved. Perhaps that he was no longer having to get a taxi over to visit her. He was very grey and drawn towards the end.'

'What killed him?'

'A massive stroke. Ironic when you think about it. At least he didn't linger.'

Not like Peggy, you mean. Laura left the words unspoken.

Chapter Three

Laura stared at the flattish countryside where vast fields of bright yellow oil-seed rape led the eye north to the slim, tall, flame belching chimneys of an oil refinery. She glanced at the map on her phone, Killinghome, not far from Grimsby now.

Her emotions balanced on a hair thin wire. Mainly anger. Anger at Jake and her father. Jake, for abandoning her after ten years for the daughter of an ageing wealthy baronet, so one of his mates had informed her after bumping into her in the supermarket.

'Where did he meet her?' Laura asked.

'She came to the rugby club with her cousin who was going out with Luke, the new fullback, not long after you stopped coming. She's about twenty, pretty in an insipid way but she doesn't have your style. We call her Georgina the limpet.'

'Why?' Laura suspected she knew the answer.

'She hangs onto his every word. I don't like clingy women.'

If only he knew. Laura understood exactly what Jake was doing, replacing her eighteen-year-old self with a new clone. Poor girl.

Twice Jake had sent her a link to an estate agent with a vaguely threatening emoji. Taking Sophie's advice, Laura had changed the locks on the flat and begun to dread Jake's texts. If the talk with the lawyer worked out, she could tell Jake to take a running jump. Until then, she would hold her fire.

Then there was Laura's father. How many times had she run through their only phone conversation since his return from Japan?

'Daddy, I've inherited a house.'

Pause. 'Oh, have you?'

'Yes, Aunt Edith's in Grimsby. How come you never told me about her, or the fact that my granny's still alive?'

'Is she?' He attempted to be surprised. 'I thought she would have died by now.'

The conversation went downhill from there. Daddy's first excuse was that he did not want Laura having to visit sick and elderly grandparents when she was still grieving for her mother. Laura could almost understand that.

'But I would have loved to know my grandfather,' she countered. 'He wasn't ill.'

'He blamed me for your mother's death. He wanted to take you from me. Even sent a solicitor's letter. I never spoke to him after that.'

'What! Why would he blame you?'

A few hums and haws down the phone before. 'All right, I admit it. Your mum phoned me to ask me to come home that night. But something urgent came up and it cost me an extra thirty minutes, that's all. In the meantime, she called her parents who phoned for an ambulance. The hospital said it would probably have been too late, even if I'd not delayed.'

'Why did you never think to mention this before? What did Mum die of, exactly? You said it was pregnancy complications.'

'An ectopic pregnancy. Her fallopian tube burst. I'm sorry, Laura. I didn't even know she was pregnant. Anyway, after your granny's collapse, the threat of trying to take you from me disappeared.' He gave a wry laugh. 'They'd never have won. I would have fought them all the way.'

He would too. Laura knew he would never step away from a battle. Had he been only thirty minutes late? How many times had she heard her father promise to be home by a certain time, only to see him arrive an hour or even two later? Laura wondered what kind of words had passed between her grandparents and her father. He could be quite aggressive when he was under pressure. Laura did not bother to tell her father about Jake. It was still too raw for his indifference.

The train passed from countryside to town. Laura looked at her phone. It was on time giving her an hour to kill before the appointment. Time for a cup of coffee and an explore. Strange to say that this was the furthest north she had travelled in England. Holidays were always taken abroad, her father preferring the Caribbean or Tuscany and Jake the Far East or southern Europe. Laura had gone on school trips of course, the Isle of Wight, various London museums and once a field trip to Slapton Sands in Devon. That was the extent of her knowledge about her own country. Her history degree field trips had taken her to Ireland and Europe.

Laura had researched Grimsby before her journey. Once the largest fishing port in the world, it had begun a downward slide in the mid twentieth century. The article she read had blamed overfishing, the Icelandic Cod Wars and problems when joining the EU concerning fishing rights. There appeared to be controversy over whose fault it was. However, the journalist writing the article pointed the finger squarely at the British government for allowing fishing quotas to be sold abroad, the only country in the EU to allow that. Chemical industries and wind energy had taken its place, a positive outcome Laura hoped. She suspected wiping out an entire industry led to a great deal of resentment and unemployment.

As she stepped down from the train, a cool easterly wind nipped at her bare legs. The station was in the centre of town and Laura quickly found herself in what was probably once a marketplace. An ugly red brick building loomed to her left which she assumed was a museum or municipal building. Walking onward, she was surprised to find Wilko in bold letters above the door. The shop masked a pleasant open area where an ancient church stood surrounded by trees and grass. She stared at the Wilco in disbelief. It was the definition of ugly in an otherwise pleasant if non-descript town centre.

'It's an eyesore, isn't it?' A middle-aged woman stopped beside her.

'That's such a lovely church. Why hide it behind that monstrosity?' Laura recognised the woman's accent from the telephone conversation with the solicitor's receptionist.

The woman shrugged, 'Planners, eh? They've wrecked the town. It's not a patch on what it once was.'

The same was said of Bognor Regis. Laura offered a smile of sympathy. 'Perhaps you could direct me to a decent coffee shop.'

The café the woman had recommended was in Abbeygate, a small, covered alley of genteel shops. Posh frocks and posh prices, Laura thought. The kind of places that come and go. Perhaps these boutiques would be lucky. A smiling face greeted her at the counter, then the same accent. Laura could not put her finger on it, so unlike Yorkshire, a stone's throw away across the Humber, according to the map. She ordered a latte and a piece of carrot cake, hoping it would be moist, and found a free table in the window. A local newspaper lay discarded on the chair. Laura picked it up and began to flick through. Crime and drugs appeared all too frequently; she skimmed through to the back to look at the adverts. What kind of house had she been left? A modern box, a terrace or a pretty cottage? A quick glimpse told her that terraces were in the majority and the prices staggeringly cheap. It was best to keep her expectations low. If it allowed her to buy Jake out, that was all she cared about.

After nibbling the cake, which was acceptable, and drinking her coffee, Laura walked the short distance to Town Hall Square and the solicitor's office. Suddenly nervous, she entered and was greeted warmly by the receptionist who took her straight through to meet Mr Dewsbury.

'Ah, Miss Gray. At last.' A balding middle-aged man rose to shake her hand. I hope the journey was not too arduous?'

Laura shook her head. 'Long, but all the connections worked.'

'Glad to hear it. Do you have your birth certificate and passport etcetera?'

Laura opened her bag. She had them safely in an envelope. He took it from her hand. 'I'll get my secretary to make copies.' He picked up the phone while Laura scanned the office. Nothing unusual, a bookcase full of law books against the far wall, two filing cabinets, an oil painting of a sailing ship over a fireplace. The secretary interrupted her musings.

'Would you like a tea or a coffee, Miss Gray?' she asked as she took the documents.

'No, thank you. I've just had one.'

As the door closed behind her, Mr Dewsbury passed Laura a letter. 'Your aunt left this for you. Read it later if you like.'

Laura took the letter, although weighing nothing, it lay heavy in her hand. 'This is all such a surprise to me. I have found the last ten days quite unnerving.'

'Did you meet your grandmother?' His pale blue eyes crinkled at her in sympathy.

'I did. She's lovely. I just wish… I suppose you hear all sorts of sad stories in your line of work,' she sniffed, annoyed at herself.

Mr Dewsbury turned to his desk and picked up a will. 'Apart from a small bequest to the next-door neighbour who did her shopping and other bits and pieces over the last couple of years, Miss Swain left everything to you.' His studied business-like manner allowed Laura to recover her equilibrium. 'That's the house and all effects plus a sum of money, not large, but around sixty thousand pounds.'

'Oh!' Laura was taken aback. 'I didn't expect that.' Why had she never considered a monetary bequest? That amount of money solved all her immediate problems.

'As wills go, this is a straightforward one. We applied for probate immediately. These things can take a while, at least six months. But I'm pleased to say we pressed a few buttons.' He winked. 'And I hope we'll get it through earlier, a few weeks ahead of schedule. If we take your bank details now, we can arrange to transfer the money as soon as it arrives.'

Laura's hand shook as she handed him her bank card. This was all too good to be true, a burden of worry lifted from her shoulders. I am independent, she thought, no need to go cap in hand to Dad, and Jake can go hang. She was free.

'I'm surprised she had so much money. I understand she never married.'

'Her fiancé, who died in World War Two, left her his house as long as she took care of his widowed mother. After the mother died, Miss Swain rented the house out until a few years ago. I sold it for her about ten years ago. She chose to train as a nurse in the war and worked until she was sixty with a pension enough to live on. Over the last few years, she spent little, I gather.'

'That's a shame. These days women go travelling. I suppose she rarely left the town.'

Mr Dewsbury shook his head. 'Apart from the occasional visit to her sister, I believe she didn't. Anyway, I have the house keys for you. You may as well stay there while you sort out what you wish to keep. Keep a record of anything you sell for probate, although it's more likely you will have to pay for house clearance. If you decide to sell the house, I can handle the sale.'

'Dare I ask how much you think it's worth?' Laura tried not to appear greedy.

'Just under sixty thousand. It needs work and house prices here...'

'Are cheap, I saw the adverts in the paper.'

'I hope you aren't disappointed.'

'I am grateful that she thought of me. It couldn't have come at a better time. My boyfriend walked out so now I can buy him out.'

'That must be a relief. Look, you're my last appointment. Would you like a lift to the house? We'll collect your documents on the way out. I just need you to sign the paperwork and we can be on our way.'

They drove through the town and into a road which crossed the railway line. After passing rows of terraced streets, they turned left into Buller Street. The name gave away the date of construction, Boer War, General Redvers Buller. Laura's fascination with historical facts had always bored Jake, but then he had no time for history. 'Give me numbers every time.' he had said. 'Numbers mean money.'

'It's that one,' the lawyer said, pointing to a small, brick terraced house in need of a good lick of paint. Laura clutched the keys as she hauled her bag out of the car and gave her thanks to Mr Dewsbury. She stood on the path as the car disappeared up the street before plucking up courage to walk the few steps through a pocket handkerchief garden towards the flaking blue door. Laura inserted a Yale key and twisted. The solid unglazed door opened smoothly. She felt like an intruder in the narrow hall as her eyes adjusted to the gloom. A straight steep staircase lay ahead, hooks for coats on the wall to her left. Dropping her bag, Laura took off her thin summer jacket and hung it up, before rummaging for a sweater in her bag, feeling like a trespasser in a stranger's house.

A door lay to her right, she opened it and walked in. Tiny, square and darkened by the heavy drapes at the window, Laura walked over to draw them letting in light and warmth. It was obviously a sitting room. Red patterned carpet, grey moquette three-piece suite, pretty watercolours on the wall. Not untasteful, it shouted 1980s. The sight of a gas fire in the hearth and a radiator on the wall was a relief; Laura had half-expected the house to be heated with coal.

Moving on, she walked into a room near the stairs, it had been used as a study. Bookshelves lined the wall facing the door, together with a small oval painting of an old man wearing something peculiar on his head. Dressed in a white smock, he looked like an inmate from an asylum, although too well-fed. His face sported an enormous handlebar moustache, a grey beard to match almost covering a squat nose. Any mouth he possessed, disappearing into the thicket of hair. It was both humorous and ugly in turn. Laura shuddered to think of having it on her wall.

Next to it was a framed newspaper photograph, the paper behind the glass almost translucent and yellow with age. The headline - Grimsby Skipper Awarded Medal for Bravery by Norwegian King - sat in bold type above the grainy, informal image of a family group taken outside a terraced house. Laura picked it off the wall to take a closer look. It was dated September 1930. George Webster, Louise, Edith, Doris Swain was written in faded pencil above the people as though they were likely to forget.

George, balding and stocky wearing a collarless shirt, braces with trousers nestling somewhere not far below his armpits, had his arm thrown around his wife who matched him in shape. Both beamed with pride. Louise's left hand lay on Edith's shoulder. Not a hair's breadth existed between Louise's shapeless cardigan and Edith's waistless tunic. The closeness between them oozed from the image. Edith, perky and clearly intrigued by the camera stared out just as she had in the photo with Laura as a baby, an intelligent curious child. Doris, her pregnancy with Peggy not quite hidden by a baggy maternity smock, stood as though not part of the family. Her overly thin face and sideways glance, made her look shifty and uncomfortable.

What a contrast between the stout, happy couple and a nervy, plainly discontented daughter. Laura wondered what the story was. There had been little attempt to smarten up, other than the women taking off their pinafores, no doubt. Laura imagined a reporter and photographer turning up on the doorstep, and the family's consternation at finding themselves in the spotlight. Strangely, the article under the photo had been snipped away, presumably so it would fit in the frame.

Laura found it disconcerting to think these strangers were her ancestors. She could see no similarities in the faces of her great, great grandparents, nor her great grandmother. They remained unknown. A connection without connection.

A narrow, netted window over a desk looked out onto a long wall dividing the houses and a passageway to a postage stamp of overgrown grass. On the desk were other photographs Laura recognised from her grandmother's album. She took out her phone to snap pictures for Peggy. There had been no images of the house anywhere in the album. She then pulled out a couple of desk drawers, the smallest contained photographs, ancient leather-bound notebooks and bundles of letters. A woman's life, her family's life. Laura knew she would have to go through them. Burning them would be a betrayal of her newly discovered relatives. Maybe they would give her an insight into their lives.

A door led on to another room on the left, a narrow kitchen-diner. A deal table sat in a bay window looking out onto the brick wall. The kitchen cupboards also screamed eighties, modernised on Edith's retirement with her lump-sum no doubt, it was now in need of urgent refurbishment but, Laura was pleased to think not too expensive. Apart from the wall she would knock down between the study and front room, there was less work than she had first thought. She stopped herself. What was she thinking? No way was she going to move to Grimsby, even if this house were twice the size of her flat for a third of its value. She walked on; one more door lay ahead. A lobby to a wet room. Now this had been recently done. Perfect for an unsteady elderly lady to shower in safety.

Back in the kitchen and dying for a cup of tea, Laura opened a couple of cupboards and found an unopened box of tea and a loaf of fresh bread. That surprised her. She opened the fridge to find a pint of milk and some butter. How thoughtful. She was just about to fill the kettle when she heard a doorbell ring. It was either someone trying to sell something or some busybody checking up on an empty house, no doubt.

Neither - a warm smile greeted her when she opened the door.

'You must be Laura. I'm Netta from next door. We've been looking after the place.'

'Should I thank you for the milk and butter?'

The woman, slim with platinum blonde hair and probably older than she appeared at first glance nodded. 'Your aunt was a lovely lady.'

'Come in,' Laura said. 'I was just about to put the kettle on.'

'No, that's okay, thank you. I came to invite you round for supper. There's nowhere decent to eat around here and I notice you don't have a car.'

Laura was astonished. Strangers in Sussex did not invite people to dinner as a rule. She must have looked unsure because the woman piped up, 'We have a proposition to put to you and you'll want to hear about your aunt.'

That was true. 'Of course, thank you. I would love to come.'

Chapter Four

March 1920 – Doris and Louise

Doris turned the key in the lock and pushed the door, the smell of paint, distemper and newly laid linoleum increased her nausea.

'Ted's done you proud, love,' her mother commented. 'He didn't have to do all this you know.'

'What do I want with this big family house, Mam? It's not as though John is …'

Louise rubbed her daughter's back. 'He'll get better, Give him time.'

'I don't like it, Mam. I'd rather live with you. Go back to the way things were.' Doris trailed after her mother as they inspected the downstairs. 'I'll never be happy here. I can feel it in my bones.'

Louise sighed. 'We can't go back to the way things were. The last few years have taught us that. So many bright young men lost.' Her voice caught in her throat. She coughed to clear it. It was a constant effort trying to keep Doris from falling apart when her own heart was no more than a dry twig ready to snap. 'The baby, think of the baby, dear.'

Doris glanced down at her bump while her heel ground an indentation into the brown linoleum. Her face when she looked up chilled Louise. 'I don't want this baby without Harry, Mam. You'll have to look after it.'

'You don't know what you're saying, Doris. That's new mother nerves talking. As soon as you look at it, you'll feel different.'

'Will I, Mam? I feel like my life has ended before it's barely begun. Even Ted can't stand to be around his own son. That's why he's bought this house, so he won't have to listen to John sobbing at night. This is no house for a child.'

Louise sank onto the brown leather settle beside the unlit range, the burden of her daughter's wrecked life too much to bear. I did this, she thought. I told her to honour her marriage vows. If only John had stayed missing in the asylum a little longer. If the child had been born, Harry would have felt honour bound to stay with Doris. He was a good man underneath all the bravado. But Louise had made her daughter write to call it off, couldn't bear the gossip, the name-calling. A woman deserting her husband in the hour of his greatest need to go off with a fancy man – who could forgive that?

Louise breathed deeply. 'Is it too late?'

Doris stared down at her mother, her mouth twisting. 'Aye it's too late. He's gone, left the dairy, left the town with another woman, a spinster. Someone without a husband returned from the dead.'

'I'm sorry, love. If only we could go back. I was wrong, too crushed. Everything came at once. But the baby will be born soon, and I promise that I will do anything you need to help look after it.' Louise hefted herself up from the settle and put her arms tight around her daughter. A few months before, Doris would have nestled in, now her body felt stiff, unyielding.

'I want to go back to work, Mam, as soon as I can. I won't stay in this house tied to John, day and night. I need my friends. You owe me that.'

'If that's what you want, love. The baby can stay with me as much as you want, but when you see it ...'

'I'll see Harry, the man I was meant to be with. Harry, the man I love. Why did I let John grind me down with his proposals before he left? Couldn't bear to leave me without marrying, on and on he harped. Now, he doesn't even remember who I am. If only you had warned me against marrying a soldier.'

'But Harry was a soldier.'

'For a few weeks until they took his arm off after the Somme. Mam, have you looked in John's eyes? They're haunted almost dead with the horrors he's seen. I do feel sorry for him, I do. But...' What was there left to say? A shroud of hopelessness settled on Doris's face.

Louise hugged her daughter tighter, guilt souring her throat. A grammar school educated man working in his father's business had been a good catch at the time. It was true she had encouraged Doris to accept. The tension in her daughter's shoulders relaxed a fraction. Then there it was, unmistakable, the baby kicked against Louise's stomach and her heart flipped, she fell immediately under the spell of her first grandchild. The grandchild she never thought she would have.

Chapter Five

May 2019 – Laura

With her hair still damp, Laura tapped the shiny brass knocker on the pristine red door. A younger version of Netta answered. Same dyed blonde hair though shorter, spikier, wearing blue jeans with designer slits and a crop top, she made Laura feel ancient in her tailored slacks and patterned blouse, work wear she had thought suitable for meeting a solicitor. She should have changed into jeans.

'Come in. I'm Netta's daughter, Gina, and this is my fiancé, Sean.' A skinny guy bearing a broad grin joined her. They made way as Laura walked into a large open-plan space.

Yes, she thought, this is what you could do next door. Light and airy with sanded floorboards and pale grey furnishings, it immediately felt modern.

'Mam's just serving up. Come through.' They walked into the back room, a shiny space of brushed stainless steel and granite tops. A bit too spaceship for Laura's liking. 'Sit yourself down, please.'

Laura sat at the glass table while Netta dished out pasta and Bolognese sauce into wide bowls. It smelt heavenly. Once they were all seated, Laura sank her fork into the rich beefy mixture. Her stomach began to grumble in earnest. It was nine hours since she had snatched breakfast before her train north.

While Sean poured out wine, Netta asked if the food was to her liking.

'Absolutely, Italian's my favourite. That and Thai.'

'Your aunt enjoyed my pasta. I always cooked an extra plate for her.'

'Thank you for looking after her so well,' Laura replied. 'I didn't even know she existed until I received the letter from the solicitor.'

The other three faces displayed shock. 'That's awful!' Gina said. 'Fancy not knowing your own flesh and blood.'

'It's complicated.' Laura did not wish to explain. 'But I wish I could have known her. What's this proposition you wanted to put to me?'

'What are you intending to do with the house? Will you live in it?' Netta asked.

'No, my job is two hundred miles away. I'll have to sell.'

Gina's face lit up. 'Can me and Sean buy it? We're getting married next year. Mam's going to give us the money your aunt left her, together with what we've saved, as a deposit. We'd give you the asking price.' Her words came out in a rush, eager, breathless.

'Really? Are you sure?' Laura's hesitancy was not because she wasn't delighted at the easy solution this proposal offered, it was because this house, unlike the one next door felt like a home should, full of warmth, love and laughter. Maybe it was her imagination, but Edith's house felt like love had died an early death, a bit like Laura's childhood home where mothers, stepmothers and siblings took temporary residence before deciding to do a flit.

'We'd take all the bedroom furniture too. You would only have to clear downstairs.'

Better and better. 'I like what you've done here.' Laura smiled. Maybe this young couple could add the joy that Edith's house lacked.

'Sean did it. He's in the trade.'

'Well, if you do as good a job on my aunt's that will be fine.'

'So that's a yes?' Gina almost jumped out of her seat in excitement.

Laura nodded, beaming at the girl's enthusiasm. 'Now that's settled. Tell me about Edith. I brought this photo. Do you know the story?' Laura took the newspaper article in its frame for her bag.

Netta picked it up and nodded. 'Edith's grandfather rescued a Norwegian fishing crew, I believe.'

'Wow, that's something to be proud of.'

'It happened more times than you'd think. Fishermen always looked out for each other.'

'Her mother doesn't look happy there.'

Netta pursed her lips. 'I remember Edith telling me her mother worked hard all her life for little reward. Some people cope with that and make the best of it, don't you think?'

Laura nodded again. It was beyond her limited knowledge.

'Edith told me her father was shell shocked in the first war. It was a difficult marriage, and her mother became a glass half empty kind of person.'

'Oh, that's so sad.' Suddenly the connection Laura had lacked before began to click into place. These were real people with lives full of joy and sadness.

Netta handed the photo back. 'Edith was a sweetheart with a great sense of humour. She never complained. We thought the world of her. She was born in that house and wanted to die there, but…'

'I understand,' Laura put her hand over Netta's. There's only so much a neighbour can do.'

Netta nodded. 'In the end, Edith needed more care than any of us could give.'

Laura was heartened to hear how this kind family had set up a bed for her downstairs and Sean had converted the decrepit coal store and toilet into a wet room, so that her final two years could be lived in comfort in the house she had known all her life.

'She always insisted on paying us, you know. She had a carer who helped too. When she couldn't cope anymore, she went into St Andrew's Hospice for the last few weeks. It's very nice there. They look after you well,' Netta reassured Laura.

'I'd like to visit to say thank you. Is it nearby? I really need to sort myself out a car.'

'My brother works at Grimsby Motors. He'll look after you. What sort do you want?' Sean asked.

Laura looked at him wondering how to answer. 'Reliable, small, maybe four or five years old.' She knew little about makes and models. Jake was the enthusiast. Of more importance was price.

While Gina cleared the dishes and Netta made coffee, Laura began to go over calculations in her mind. She had a new credit card in her own name since the previous weekend. It had a limit of six thousand pounds. It should be enough to pay for a reasonable car, together with her savings of a few hundred. Within months, she could pay it off.

Laura smiled at Sean. 'I can't afford more than five thousand. If you think he can sort me out a car for that, I'm happy for you to phone him.'

'I'll give Mick a bell,' Sean replied, taking his phone out of his pocket.

A minute or two of chat and Sean turned to her and said, 'He'll pick you up on the way into work tomorrow at 8.45.'

Laura nodded. 'I suppose.'

'Don't worry, he'll look after you. He won't sell you a dud.'

Back in her aunt's house, Laura's head was spinning from a few glasses of cheap red wine and the feeling she was on a racetrack. A fortune, a house, a sale and a car within twelve hours, none of it began to make sense. She had intended to spend two days in Grimsby. Call a house clearance firm, find an estate agent and be on the train home by Thursday. Why? She had no need to be back at work until Monday. Maybe she would drive back on Saturday, visit her granny on Sunday to tell her about the trip and take the extra couple of days to do the clearance properly, giving herself chance to explore the area.

Early next morning she was picked up by Mick, a clone of his brother but dressed in a sharp suit. The same designer stubble, although his darker hair gave him a swarthier appearance.

'Sean's over the moon,' he said, as he shot off, far too fast for Laura's liking, before slamming on his brakes at the end of the road.

'He doesn't mind the prospect of living next to his mother-in-law?' Laura asked, as they turned into Ladysmith Road.

'Nah, she's all right is Netta. Gina's very close to her mam since her dad scarpered.'

It seemed no time at all before they turned into a motor showroom. Laura could have walked it in ten minutes.

Mick showed her several cars, blinding her with meaningless words about horsepower and engine sizes. Finally, she pointed to a car and asked to have a test drive. She liked the colour. It reminded her of the Mediterranean on a summer's day, a deep blue but with a hint of green.

'It's almost six years old and an automatic,' Mick warned her.

'I've driven automatics, I like them better than manuals.'

The contempt on Mick's face made her giggle. He recovered in time to give her lots more meaningless statistics before fetching the key.

The sun was fighting the clouds as Laura turned left into the road following Mick's directions. The car handled perfectly as far as she was concerned. They drove up to some woods and turned left again. Once past two roundabouts they crested a hill and turned right to come face-to-face with a wide estuary. Mick then directed her towards the pier and a promenade beside a long sandy beach. I can drive here myself and then walk, thought Laura, already deciding to take the car. I need insurance, something else to sort out.

'When can I pick the car up?' she asked.

'Friday morning. We'll give it the once over, it's due an MOT and a valet.'

She hadn't quibbled at the price; it was cheaper than the other cars he had shown her.

She walked back to the house, mentally compiling a list of things to do. Car insurance, speak to her aunt's lawyer about the house sale, arrange a clearance company to take the downstairs furniture, sort through what she wanted to keep. With a car she could take things with her when she left. Making decisions on her own was new, empowering. Her phone pinged, Jake, an incoming text. Her good mood nose-dived. He could wait. She decided not to read it until later while her fingers itched to delete it.

After phoning Edith's lawyer to ask him to deal with the sale and sort out the change of ownership of her flat, she phoned an insurance agent. The quote was horrendous, despite ten years of accident-free driving on Jake's policy. Thank goodness she could just about afford it, although it would max out her credit card.

The lawyer had asked if she had read Edith's letter and she had to admit that she had not. Now she took it out of her bag, noticing the crabby handwriting. Thank you, she mouthed before opening it. She knew little about Edith as yet, but this woman had done her the most enormous favour. She wished she could have met her before she died. Smoothing the single sheet out, she read,

My dearest Laura,

I have few regrets in life, other than not marrying my sweetheart before he died. One is not meeting you again. My lawyer tells me he will find you, but I should have asked him before I became too decrepit. I hope that my bequest will make your life easier. You may already be married, if not, I hope you find yourself an honourable man like my Gordon, someone who will protect and care for you, who always has your best interests at heart, a strong but gentle man.

 I wish my ashes to be scattered in the Garden of Remembrance at the crematorium. You can collect them from the Co-op Funeral Home. I will always be a Grimsby lass.

 I phoned Peggy every week, she will miss that. Look after her.

 There is something else you can do for Peggy. My grandmother, Louise, always had a melancholy about her after her mother, Rose, disappeared when she was five years old. It always upset us girls because Granny Lou was the one who brought us up while our mother worked. Louise wasn't like the other Victorian grannies; she was warm and funny but sad too. There are lots of papers in my desk; read them. My neighbour tells me that everything is on the Internet these days. I wouldn't know. Perhaps now is the time to solve the mystery and let your Granny die peacefully.

 I'm ready to join my Gordon now. His death during D Day was my greatest sadness, but I didn't let it destroy me. My grandfather was a Webster. They had to be strong to survive at sea.

 Be happy, Laura.

 Your loving aunt,

 Edith

Laura read through the letter twice and then looked at the date. It was written only three months before she died. Her brain at ninety-eight must have been as sharp as a woman's half her age. She detected strength and determination in her words despite the shakiness of the handwriting. It left her with so much to think about.

 Picking up the old photograph frame which she had left on the table, it was Doris who looked unhappy whereas Louise seemed cheerful. Now there was another link in the chain – Rose. It scrambled Laura's mind trying to work out the number of greats involved in the relationship. A fortnight ago, the only female relative she had was her mother, Jeanette, and now it stretched back in time what, a hundred years, no it must be more. The mystery sounded intriguing, but now was not the time. The first puzzle was how to phone her grandmother.

Chapter Six

Grimsby 1919 - Louise

The keening began low like a cow in labour then rose higher and higher to a prolonged scream and then a 'Nooo'- which froze their blood and stilled fingers which had been darting at speed through the strands of the nets. Each of the women in the braiding shed had a husband, brother, son or fiancé fishing the North Sea, more than one. In Louise's case two. Hands rigid by their sides, they stood silent, uncertain, unwilling to move. It was best not to know. With knowledge came sorrow, heartache, despair.

It could not last. The sound of boots on cobbles, the heavy door, shut against the cold easterly winds, scraped open on its hinges. Eyes fixed on whoever walked through the door. Hearts thumped, nausea rose in their throats and then the voice, rushed, anguished.

'It's Theban, hit a stray mine. All lost.'

Arms clutched at Louise as she fell to the floor, a new keening, her own, bounced around the walls, filled the space with pain so intense, the other women, hard-bitten women, shivered, toes curling inside their boots, knowing it could have been them, but wasn't – this time.

'Does George know?' Louise's voice cracked and broken, her face a sodden mess already. Someone passed a rag.

'No. We'll try and get word. His boat is somewhere near Iceland. I've arranged for a cart to take you home.'

Home, what did that mean anymore? Somewhere to lay her head, would she ever sleep again?

Later, home meant somewhere to howl, somewhere to burrow her head into her son's pillow, sniffing, desperate to soak up any remaining scent of him. Louise longed to curl in a ball and never unwind, let the damp, dark earth swallow her whole as the cold sea had swallowed her boy and refused to spit him out.

There's something about losing a child that's different from any other grief. It was knowing that she must live out her life counting each of his missing birthdays and wondering about the life he should have lived. It was not holding his children on her knee, nor ever loving those children that might have been. It was also knowing that she was not there to protect him. It was knowing that he had died calling out for her and she had not answered; that she had let him down.

And the grief for her boy unleashed the grief for her mother whom she had never been allowed to mourn. Pent-up for fifty years, renewed waves of loss crashed over her for what she needed now was her mother's comfort. She begged for those arms which had held her so tightly, begged for the tiny kisses covering her face, begged for the lullaby which had soothed her to sleep, begged for the warmth of her, the smell of her, the love.

Instead, there was torment as the screams of her drowning son, merged with the cries of her mother amidst an argument so loud that five-year-old Louise had wrapped herself amongst the mops and brushes in the broom cupboard, hiding from the sound of a fist meeting flesh, of more screams, of doors slamming of boots trampling, then the utter loneliness of silence and not knowing. Where did her mother go? Why did she disappear? Why had she left her?

Louise lay on Bertie's bed, oblivious to anything other than all-consuming pain. She needed George, only he had the trick, the right words, the whatever it was that cut through the dark days, the black nights that had dogged her life. In the end it was Doris who had patiently hovered, vainly tempting her with morsels of food brought by well-meaning neighbours. Doris who had mourned her husband missing in the war and now her brother. Doris who also needed her mother and was ignored.

'Mam, I'm in the family way. It's Harry's. Mam, I need you? What am I going to do?'

'Do?' Louise raised herself up, sour and filthy from days of selfishly giving into grief. 'Why, you'll keep it, of course. We'll name him Albert if it's a boy. There'll be a way to stop tongues wagging.' There was no blame only a sliver of hope.

Chapter Seven

Grimsby 2019 - Laura

Laura had not seen a handset in her grandmother's room. She picked up her mobile and dialled the care home. Heather answered on the second ring.

'Hi, it's Laura Gray. Does Peggy have a phone in her room?'

'Only an old pay as you go.'

Laura snorted in surprise. 'Can you give me the number please.'

'It won't be charged. It hasn't been used since her sister died. Let me plug it in. If you give me your number, I'll phone you back when it's charged. I need to check the balance too. You might need to add some money.'

How on earth was Laura to do that? 'Who used to do it, do you know?'

'Your aunt's neighbour, I believe. She bought it and set it up before posting it here.'

Laura gave Heather her number, while silently thanking Netta for her ingenuity.

It would be a one-sided conversation for sure, but she bet her grandmother had lived for those phone calls and she intended to stand in for Edith.

Laura decided she needed caffeine and walked over to the cupboard where she had found tea the night before. Yes, there was a jar of granules which were not yet sticking together in a gloopy ageing mess.

With a cup of strong coffee in her hand, she summoned up courage to open Jake's text.

'Took estate agent to value flat. Locks changed, embarrassing. Flat on market by end of week unless u get Daddy to buy me out. Jake.'

Empowered by her aunt's advice, she replied, *'Flat not going on market. Contact my lawyer.'* She copied the number down.

Ping – *'Why do u need a lawyer? My colleague can sort out legal stuff.'*

'No way, José,' she muttered to herself. She wanted someone on her side.

Laura didn't bother to answer the text. She sipped the coffee and waited. It had lost its flavour. Goodness knows how old it was.

Ping – *'Why a Grimsby lawyer?'*

She smiled and deleted the text. The phone rang, it was him. She blocked his number and then flicked through the photos on her phone deleting each one he appeared in. No more floppy white blonde hair that she had once loved to sink her fingers into, no more chiselled chin, although the chiselling was less defined in later photographs, his once lean body showing signs of incipient flabbiness. As for those pale blue eyes, she decided they lacked depth and there were definite indications of bags forming beneath.

Her WhatsApp trilled. She turned off her phone, leaving it on the table to walk upstairs with a roll of black bin bags.

Time to tackle an old lady's wardrobe and think about the quest that Edith had set her. It sounded vaguely exciting. From having no family other than her absent father and half-brothers, she had been gifted a set of ancestors, possibly with a murky past. If nothing else, it would give her something to focus on over the quieter summer months. All her holiday plans had drifted away in the debris of Jake's betrayal.

Laura was all packed up to head home by Saturday morning. She had paid for the ground floor furnishings to be cleared. Her car was laden with the contents of the desk drawers, that painting of the odd-looking man, a few dishes she had taken a shine to, a box of old jewellery, including a brooch labelled with her name, maybe worth nothing but pretty. Everything else was either left for Gina or had been deposited at charity shops. Friday had been hectic, collecting the car, picking up her aunt's ashes to take to the crematorium and watching with a lump in her throat, as they scattered them in a circle beneath a tree. Once a vibrant lady, now white dust, stark against the bright green grass. Laura hoped that rain would disperse them quickly. She hated to think of them being trampled by uncaring feet.

In the evening, Laura had taken Netta and her family out for a fish and chip supper on Cleethorpes pier to say thank you.

Netta came out to say goodbye as Laura placed her rucksack on the back seat.

'Thanks again for everything, Netta. You've been an amazing help and a wonderful neighbour.'

'We look after our own.' Netta brushed aside the compliment. 'Did you manage to sort out the Satnav?'

'I did, although it was a steep learning curve, all those knobs to twist. Far easier on a phone.' Laura had thrown the instruction booklet on the floor in disgust but had then pulled herself together and persevered until she thought she understood how it worked.

'I've made you a sandwich for the journey.' Netta handed her an overstuffed packet. 'Perhaps you'll come back for the wedding and see what Sean has done to the place?'

'Aww. That's so nice of you. They're a lovely couple. The clearance company promised to pick up the boxes on Monday. Is that okay?'

'Don't worry. I'll be here. Have a safe journey.'

Laura waved cheerio to Netta. Without her, she would have stumbled around trying to sort everything out. This was a town she did not know and yet, it had been her family's home for at least a century, with people who looked out for each other. Strangers who did not hang back to offer help. She looked forward to returning.

Chapter Eight

It was good to be back in her own bed. Laura stretched before rising to take a quick shower. Work began the next day and she had loads to do. For a start there was next to no food in the house. Netta's fulsome picnic had kept Laura going, but a shopping trip was urgent, as was the visit to her granny.

Her first phone call to Peggy had been awkward despite confirmatory interjections from a care assistant, *'Yes, Peggy's nodding her head and smiling.'*

Something had to be done about that. Laura's decided to finish unpacking the car while thinking through the problem. She placed all the paperwork in a cupboard vacated by Jake's clothes, stacked the dishes in the kitchen and placed the painting on the top shelf of the wardrobe after taking a photo for her phone. By the time she had finished, a solution popped into her mind.

After a quick trip to Tesco, Laura set off to drive over the Downs. No matter what time of year, nor whether by car or train, she loved the scenery. Today, in early June, the sun picked out every shade of green as she drove along the road. Young beech leaves shimmered as they rippled in the breeze. Gardens full of roses, clematis and laburnum rioted in a tangle of colour.

Did Heather ever have a weekend off? Laura wondered, thankful to see her smiling face. This time she was grasping a female resident in a slow twirl around the lobby and crooning a song Laura recognised vaguely. The woman smiled as though lost in a world of memories as she danced. Heather noticed Laura and settled the old woman into a chair.

'Did you enjoy that, Gladys? We'll have another dance later, my love. Let me see to this lady now.' Gladys nodded and waved at Laura.

Laura waved back as Heather walked over to her.

'Hi Heather, I've been meaning to ask. Do you, by any chance, have Wi-Fi?'

'Do we have Wi-Fi?' Heather laughed. 'You should see the amount of Amazon parcels we get delivered each week. Some of our residents spend their days browsing for books and films to buy.' Seeing Laura's mouth drop open in surprise, Heather cocked an ear. 'Can you hear that?'

Laura listened. A Beethoven concerto was playing down a corridor to the left.

'Alexa, play this, Alexa play that.' What would they do without it?'

Heather walked with Laura down the corridor towards her grandmother's room, pointing out the eager internet users on the way 'That's Google Hub playing the cricket scores there; Guy's looking forward to the world cup. Marge over there likes to listen to The Archers on Alexa.' Heather pointed to the room next to her grandmother's. 'Bob prefers his sixties music.' The strains of a loud guitar drifted through the shut door.

'I had no idea.'

'This is a wealthy area. A lot of our residents are cash rich but lonely at home where relatives have stopped visiting or live too far away. They prefer to come here, with their meals cooked for them and then they lock themselves in with their new-found toys. Talk about teenagers being glued to their gadgets.' Heather frowned. 'It would make me laugh if it didn't make me cry. I used to book singers and pianists to entertain them, not so much now. Our dementia patients still love a sing song.'

'How about my grandmother?'

'She will come to the lounge if we have a choir at Christmas and there's a lady flautist who comes occasionally. She likes her.'

'So, my grandmother must miss out.' Laura frowned.

'She does, poor thing. She arrived here when things were just beginning to change. I often think if she'd had her stroke now, her speech may have improved with all the therapists they use to help patients. Back then, Peggy seems to have been written off. I'm not sure why. She learned to walk again, enough so she could get to the toilet and shower. But arthritis hasn't helped her. We try and do armchair exercises with her. The doctor sent a physio to draw up an exercise regime.'

'That's good. Can you show me so I can do them with her? I have brought an old iPad with me. Maybe she can learn to use it. What do you think?'

'It's worth a go. I'll find you the Wi-Fi code.'

Heather opened her grandmother's door. She was sitting by the window staring into the garden with overt longing. Laura sighed. Peggy deserved better than being locked into this loneliness and silence.

'Would you like to go into the garden? Heather, can you help me get her into the wheelchair, please.'

With help, Peggy managed to stumble from the chair to the wheelchair. Laura had imagined that neither of Peggy's legs worked, but apart from wincing, Peggy managed the few steps. Was it true that she had been written off by her stroke? Could she have recovered completely with proper therapy? Laura burned with indignation at the thought.

They sat together underneath an arbour looking out onto borders filled with deep blue iris and columbine, yellow, pink, white bonnets dancing in the slight breeze, while Laura told Peggy of her journey north.

'I have photos,' she said. 'They're on my phone but you won't be able to see them in this light.' Laura decided to send them to the iPad.

'Granny, there's a painting I've brought home from Grimsby. It's of a very strange looking man in a funny hat. Can you remember it?' Laura asked.

Her grandmother nodded and tried to speak, but the sound was unrecognisable. Laura fished a laminated sheet she had made in college out of her bag and laid it on her grandmother's lap. Her granny stared at it and a tear formed in her eye. Her left finger drifted towards it, hovering over the letters and numbers. *Cook* - she tapped. Slow but definite, followed by a grin.

'Has no one given you a sheet like this before?' Laura asked. Her grandmother shook her head. Laura's brain refused to accept that such a simple idea had been ignored. She tried to dampen down her anger and turned back to the question in hand.

'Cook,' Laura repeated. Her grandmother nodded, a twisted smile but a light in her eyes. 'Cook, that's his name?' A shake of head. 'His job?' A nod. 'Was he a relation?' A slight shrug of her shoulders. 'You're not sure?' Another nod. It was a start.

Back in the room, Laura set up the Wi-Fi on the iPad with the code Heather had left. She created an email address for Peggy and sent her the photos. The pictures of the seafront at Cleethorpes brought the biggest smile. Laura demonstrated how to use FaceTime but realised her grandmother had difficulty holding the iPad. She needed a stand, not this delipidated cover which keeled over in two seconds. Finally, before she left, she installed Spotify. She loved the thought that Jake's family account was being used for her granny. She wondered if he would realise.

'What music do you like, Granny?'

Laura had left the alphabet card on the trolley beside her chair. Peggy closed her eyes, memories floating around her head before she tapped the word – *Day*.

'Doris Day?' Peggy nodded.

'I'll start a play list for you.'

Laura left with the sight of her gran's left foot jiggling to '*Move Over Darling*' and the broadest lop-sided smile imaginable.

***

Peggy

More than twenty years I have waited. Two decades of longing and wondering would she care? Would she return once she had satisfied her curiosity? Did she feel the connection we have? If only I have enough time, if only I could talk.

I listened intently while Laura talked about Netta and her family and how helpful they had been. I nodded along, delighting in my granddaughter's chatter. I loved the garden but the most beautiful sight of all was the girl sat beside me, the image of my daughter and her father before her. A precious afternoon full of the scent of mock orange and the sound of her voice. If I could have stretched this afternoon into days, into years - but my time is limited. My body is weak though my heart is full.

Laura has opened a chink to the modern world. I knew it existed. I watch it on the television. How I miss my books, my music, my crosswords. My husband read to me from his newspapers, played my favourite records. Luckily, they were his favourites too. Heather does her best, but it can never make up for everything I lost. I tried to write with my left hand, but the results shamed me and eventually arthritis meant I couldn't hold a pen.

The door opened. Heather poked her head through.

'Is there anything you want? A nice cup of tea, maybe?'

'Whisky', I tapped on my alphabet, oh, the look on her face! It's made my day.

Chapter Nine

Laura

It was obvious now that Laura looked at the painting. A squashed chef's hat. Fancy being a chef with those huge mutton chop whiskers. Food hygiene inspectors would have a field day. Laura opened her laptop to do a reverse image check. She brought up TinEye.com and uploaded the image of the cook to the site – nothing – hardly surprising. Laura remembered the notebooks amongst her aunt's papers, perhaps one of them would give her a clue. She walked to the cupboard in the bedroom to rummage through the documents.

Several well-thumbed, A5 sized, red leather notebooks with Susanna's Recipes on the flyleaf lay amongst the jumble of letters. Who was Susanna? Laura selected one and carefully opened it. Inside, handwritten recipes were interspersed with the odd note, the neat copperplate writing in ink now faded from black to brown. Laura took it into her sitting room to peruse. She began to turn the pages with interest, noting the old-fashioned ingredients – isinglass for a strawberry fool, a fish soup using perch. This had to be before the advent of cheap sea fish. Laura thought back to her brief research into Grimsby. When had the docks been built? The late 1840s rang a bell. As she turned over one page a piece of paper fluttered onto the rug by her feet. She picked it up. Her heart skipped a beat, it was a letter, despite the evenness of the handwriting, it was written in a hurry, some words squashed, some letters flamboyant with capitals strewn around willy-nilly. She forced herself to read it slowly.

Lowther Castle – Westmoreland
October 21st 1841.

My dear Susanna,
I regret I have not had the time to reply to yours of the 14th of July until this day. I have been so busy that I can scarcely leave the kitchen. We have twenty to dinner almost every day and an enormous quantity of servants

to feed. I am happy to hear you are well and I hope your new job may suit. It will keep your hand in and employ your time.

There followed a recipe for the perch soup which Laura scanned past to read the final paragraph.

James has informed me of his having succeeded Lavagne (Laura had difficulty deciphering the letters of the name, presumably a French chef). *I hope this place may suit him and he may remain there. Write to me as soon as you find time. It is always a pleasure to hear from you.*

Your affectionate father,
J Thornley

Such a formal letter to a daughter but here were real names to work with. James was presumably the cook's son, was it also his father's name? Laura decided to chance it. Typing in James Thornley cook on her phone, the first hit had her gasping. No, surely not! How could it be this easy, this intriguing? There was another hit further down which took her to a site called Waterloo 200 – descendants' stories. Her hands were shaking as she typed in the name and there it was, the same image, her painting. How could that be? Was there more than one painting? Could hers be a copy? The one on the screen looked more assured, cleaner, the features finer.

She had to tell someone, the only person who mattered. Would she answer?

***

Peggy

The contraption lit up and started playing an irritating noise. My carer, Betty, picked it up, swiped it with her finger, saying, 'You have iPad now?' Laura's image flickered large on the screen as she handed it to me.

'Granny, you'll never guess. I've found out who he is, the man in the painting.'

48

I peered over the screen, and it showed my image too, a horrible, distorted version of me. I shuddered, itching to turn it off, but curiosity made me nod at Laura. Sweet child, she looked so excited.

'His name is James Thornley and he worked for all sorts of interesting people, including the Duke of Wellington. He was at the Battle of Waterloo, Granny. There's even a book about him. I'm going to order it.'

She prattled on and I kept nodding while my mind worked overtime. This was more stimulation than I've had in years. Laura gave a final wave before the screen went blank.

'I charge iPad for you?' Betty asked in her sweet, accented English.

I shook my head and settled it in my lap, the small icons taunting me. What are they? I tapped one with my left index finger and the image changed. Safari – what's Safari? A search box appeared on the screen. Oh, yes, I know what a search box is. My husband spent hours on his PC. I used to watch him tapping away into his computer, his back towards me, the resentment of his lost retirement increasing the rigidity of his shoulders as the years passed.

There's no keyboard. How do you search without a keyboard? Betty noticed my puzzlement. She is patient, unlike some of the other staff, and she's younger, more savvy. I remember that word from my teaching days. I imagine her real name, Elzbieta, so much prettier. That's what I would call her if I had a voice.

'You want to do search?'

I nodded. She tapped the search box and a keyboard appeared as if by magic. I breathed out slowly and began to type, clumsy, unsure, one fingered – James Thornley cook - just as Laura described. Betty stood over my shoulder, then showed me how to make the search work. She pressed an arrow, which she called -Enter- and the screen changed again. There it is. I sat back, overcome with amazement, hooked.

The stroke left my thinking brain intact while it my destroyed speech and some movement. I squinted at the screen through the cataracts filming my eyes. Betty bent down, did something with her fingers and the print grew larger. I read. I am reading. What else can this machine do? Are there books? How I miss books! Since I stopped being able to hold one and read the tiny print, my life fractured further than I thought possible.

Chapter Ten

Laura ordered the book from Amazon. She had no idea if this James Thornley was an ancestor, but she was fascinated that she had ended up with a painting and his letter. The information from the website mentioned Apsley House in London. Googling it, she noticed that Waterloo Day was to be held there in two weeks' time. In a fit of impulsiveness, she decided to book a ticket as her doorbell rang. Laura glanced at the clock, seven, a strange time for someone to call. Putting aside her laptop, she walked towards the door, her heart sinking as she caught Jake's shadow in the part-glazed door and half-remembered agreeing to meet him around now. Should she pretend not to be here? She saw the letterbox lift and his eye met hers.

'I've left my cricket gear in the cupboard. I need it.' Reluctantly she opened the door. He strode in, looking around, the swagger in his shoulders undiminished while scanning the bedroom. 'Whose is the car?'

'It's mine,' Laura's voice flattened, she attempted to hide her displeasure. His shoulders relaxed and he wore a thin smile.

'Has Daddy been subbing you again?' A note of scorn in his voice. 'It must have cost you a few thou'.'

'No, I came into an inheritance.'

'You never mentioned that.' His eyes narrowed. Was he accusing her of something?

'An aunt, I didn't know. It's not much, enough to buy you out after you left me without so much as a warning.' Laura's attempt at staying calm faltered.

A sulky grin passed over his face. 'You'd have made a fuss.'

A fuss! Furious now, Laura opened the cupboard under the stairs, scrambled at the back for his sports bag and thrust it at him. 'I expect that's everything and you won't be back.'

'Don't let's part on bad terms, Laura.' The sulkiness grew more apparent.

'You can't betray me and think I'll forgive you. Even you can't be that obtuse. Please go.'

He dropped the cricket bag and grabbed her wrist. She tried to shake him off, but he held tight. 'Don't be like this. We had ten years together. Let's still be friends.'

Seriously, he was asking to be friends? Turning her face towards him, anger bubbling in her throat, the expression in his eyes warned her. She forced the tension in her body to release. 'Very well, Jake. But please leave, I've had a very busy week and I'm exhausted.' She smiled, 'Good luck with the cricket matches.'

'Answer my calls, right?'

Laura nodded and he let go of her wrist, before kissing her lightly on the lips. His breath stank of beer. Laura attempted to turn her head, but he held her face between his hands and stuck his tongue into her mouth while she squirmed. He dropped his hands and grinned before picking up his bag.

'Speak soon, Laura.' More of a threat than a promise. What was going on? As soon as the door closed, she bolted it and sank onto the floor. Her phone pinged – the sound of an omen. Smiley face, a number she did not recognise, she shuddered. He must have a second phone. Why had he decided to play this game?

There was an unlocked phone in the drawer, the one they had used abroad. Shaking, she stood and dug it out, rooting around until she found the original sim card to swap it with the one in her phone. A call to Tesco Mobile to change her number followed. While Jake loved to talk about his amazing ability with tech, he never gave her any credit, but technology was key to her work, and she had picked up far more than he knew. Two could play at this game.

Laura brought Sophie up to date on the train the following morning. They had just left Christ's Hospital by the time she got around to Jake's visit. Sophie's expression changed to a frown.

'Log every contact from now on. Don't respond to texts but keep all the messages he sends you. If he becomes threatening, you may have to seek an injunction.'

'He's got a new girlfriend. What does he want with me?'

'Has he? Perhaps she's seen through him. He's always sounded controlling and maybe can't bear to let go. Who knows?'

'This all sounds overdramatic.'

'It's not worth analysing beyond understanding he sounds like a narcissist with possible psychopathic tendencies. Accept he's a danger to you. Never open the door to him. Get a chain fitted.' Sophie's warning filled Laura with trepidation.

It was on Laura's mind all day. As she walked home along the prom in the late afternoon, the June sunshine had brought people out to enjoy the fine weather. Silhouettes of bathers paddling, mere streaks of black against the sparkling shoreline, the splashes and cries of children carried from three hundred yards away in the breathless air. A mother and son walked hand in hand a little further ahead. They were humming a nursery rhyme, his overlarge, brightly patterned wellington boots slapping against the concrete. Laura's heart twisted with longing.

She sat down on the low wall, trembling as one last pleasure plane droned above, disturbing the still air. For the first time in her life, she was afraid to go home. Sophie's advice was sound. A chain for the door became Laura's number one priority.

A thin jiffy package from the Book Depository lay on Laura's door mat when she arrived home from work a day later. Laura dropped her bag on the table and opened it eagerly. A small, slim hardback sat inside; on the flyleaf a stamp 'withdrawn from Wiltshire Libraries'.

'Their loss, my gain,' Laura exulted, her heart thumping with excitement. Half of the book was taken up with an introduction by Elizabeth Longford, the remainder was an interview of James Thornley by his employer, Lord Frederick Fitzclarence. Someone else to google. There was no doubt James Thornley had moved in exalted circles. A quick check revealed the peer to be one of the many illegitimate sons of William IV.

'Wow, employed by a Duke, an Earl and the first cousin of Queen Victoria. I wonder if he ever cooked for her?' Laura was catching up with the series, Victoria, on TV. She imagined James as the cook in Buckingham Palace, what was his name? Francatelli, that was it. A quick search revealed that the famous signor also sported a very fine set of whiskers. 'I wonder if they knew each other?' she mused.

What could she cook for herself this evening? A carbonara would be quick. Laura went into her bedroom to change into some jogging pants, as she kicked her shoes under the bed, she picked up the other phone which was charging. She must let her family know her new number. It was her father's birthday on Friday, and she was expected to trek up to Guildford for the annual celebration.

Three missed calls and two texts.

Are you and Jake coming on Friday? Dinner at eight - Melissa – her latest stepmother.

Wish your father happy birthday – no name – smiley face.

A cold finger ran down her spine despite the innocuousness of the message. Laura itched to delete it. Who else would look at it as anything but pleasant? An old boyfriend wishing her father well. She threw the phone back on the bed, her stomach turned to jelly.

Returning to the kitchen, Laura reached for a bottle of rioja and a schooner, a small wine glass would not cut it. A few sips and she began to calm down. The other item in the post was the fortnightly librarian's situations vacant leaflet. She tore off the plastic wrapper, idly wondering if there was anything in Grimsby. Jake would not bother her there. A vaguely interesting job in Doncaster but at far less money, was the closest. Jobs were scarce, austerity had crippled budgets, she was lucky to have the one she had, and how could she desert her grandmother now that she had found her? After making herself a quick cheese and pickle sandwich to soak up the wine, Laura texted Sophie to say that she was driving tomorrow and would not be on the train. Storrington was only three miles off her route home; she would take the book to show granny after work. She settled down to read.

Chapter Eleven

Peggy

Laura arrived as Betty handed me a plate of the oh, so predictable tuna sandwiches cut into small manageable squares. The weekly menus are scored on my brain. My granddaughter gauged my distaste.

'Is the food okay in here?'

I shrugged my shoulders, but she sensed my frustration.

'What kind of food do you like?

Something with flavour, something exciting. My body may be failing but I still have my senses. I pointed to the weekly menu on my side table. She picked it up and read.

'Is it the same every week?'

I shook my head and raised three fingers.

'It repeats every three weeks? It seems quite bland.'

I nodded slowly and sighed. I know they do their best and it's all carefully monitored for dietary purposes, but I'm bored with cottage pie and lamb hot pot.

'I'll have a think. Maybe I can bring in something each time as a treat. I love cooking. Perhaps I inherited this guy's culinary genes.'

Laura produced a small book from her bag with a flourish. She read out a few marked sections while I chewed my sandwich. After I finished, she wiped my hand with a tissue and handed me the book. I looked at it. Years ago, I would have devoured it, but its importance has waned. I pointed to the iPad which she swapped for the book. I tapped on an icon called notes and a message I had typed painstakingly for her next visit – *Tell me about yourself – your love life, your hopes, your dreams.*

Consternation clouded her eyes. I reached for her hand and nodded, attempting a reassuring smile until she calmed. I sensed a sadness in her, my prayers for a happy childhood I feared had fallen on barren ground. She stared at me; a tic throbbed momentarily close to her left eye before she smoothed it away.

She began slowly, carefully, unwilling I suspect to upset me. I tapped her hand, attempting an encouraging smile. She swallowed and then it began to pour in a torrent of words as though she had never opened up before. A deeply controlling boyfriend, an emotionally absent father, an ambition to succeed in her work but above all, and this unspoken, a longing to be loved. When she mentioned the phone messages and how she felt threatened, I reached for my sheet and spelt out - bring phone, keep here.

Laura looked puzzled by my interruption. I saw her glance at the carriage clock beside my bed. Yes, you spoke for twenty minutes about yourself. No need to feel guilty, I have nothing but time. Loneliness, I fear, has been Laura's constant companion. I know what that feels like. Well, no more. I observe an almost imperceptible lift to her shoulders. Her eyes clear. Can she feel the connection we have, have always had? An invisible thread stretching down the years since I last rocked her tear-torn body to sleep. I tapped out my instruction again.

'What will you do with the phone, Granny?'

Keep safe – I tapped. She nodded, accepting without question. Relief uncreased a fine line in her brow. I'm on your side – I tapped. She nodded and smiled.

'Someone in my family who's on my side. That's a first.' Laura laughed.

She may have said it as a joke, but I felt the edge of bitterness in her words.

'If he sends a text, don't read it. I'll show you how to reply with a smiley face. That should keep him off my back. Are you sure you don't mind?' Laura asked.

That worry line returned. I will read the texts and find a way to protect her somehow.

The door opened. Betty held my bedtime hot chocolate. She noticed the intensity in Laura's face and her normal smile turned to concern. I shook my head, and she made a tactful retreat.

Ten minutes after Laura left, Betty returned with a fresh drink.

'Your granddaughter upset,' a question mark in her voice.

I nodded and began to tap – *Ex boyfriend* – I struggled for the word. I have heard it on TV, seen a programme about it. Ah yes – *stalking her*.

Betty looked puzzled 'stalking' - she pronounced it as it is written with a short a. I shook my head. Her puzzlement continued. I opened my mouth to try and force the word out st -or, I try. A brainwave – I lifted my left hand and flapped it slowly like a big bird – st-or.

'Stork?' Gradually Betty's expression cleared. 'He stalking, like chasing?'

I nodded, furious with this unknown Jake.

Chapter Twelve

Laura

Laura arrived at the Guildford house a little after six on Friday. Her father arrived soon after.

'So, you and Jake have broken up? Good job.'

'He found someone else, left me a note, didn't even have the courtesy to tell me in person.'

The look of sympathy on Melissa's face scarcely mitigated her father's next comment.

'He probably got bored. How long had you been together, seven years?'

'Ten.' Laura glowered at his crassness. Melissa's perfectly arched eyebrows shot up.

'Lucky for me I can't afford another divorce,' her father joked, looking at his wife.

Why had Laura expected support, even anger, on her behalf? Her heart could be broken for all he knew.

'You've met your grandmother, then?' He changed the subject.

'Yes.'

'Can you believe it?' He turned to Melissa. 'She had a stroke twenty odd years ago and she's still alive. I actually liked the old girl. Couldn't stand the husband. Always interfering, nothing was too good for his girl. I was glad to see the back of him.'

Laura seethed. 'It would have been nice to have met him, so I could make up my own mind.'

'Trust me. You wouldn't have liked him. How about a martini to get us in the mood to celebrate?' His expression warned against pursuing that argument. He always does that, she thought, closing down any discussion he didn't care for. How did Melissa stand it? She was no fool. Of her stepmothers, Laura almost liked her. Slim with sleek blonde hair and high cheek bones, she epitomised the elegance of Laura's other stepmothers, but appeared less self-centred, less vacuous, perhaps even more understanding than her predecessors.

The only thing to come out of the weekend was an offer to join them on holiday in Tuscany. Laura studied the details. An old watermill in the mountains, nothing much around but a river and waterfall for her seven-year-old brother, Christopher, to play in and Laura to keep him company. She could imagine the scenario. Her father would stay for seven days maximum and then demand that Melissa drive him to the airport. Melissa, if anything like her previous stepmothers, would spend a few days trailing the smarter shops in the nearest large town while Laura babysat her brother. If Laura refused the invitation, they would take a nanny.

'I'll think about it,' Laura said to avoid any attempt at arm twisting.

Half of Laura did not want to bother catching the train up to London the following Saturday. She had had enough of trains during the week. However, in a fit of excitement, she had booked for *Wellington Day* at Apsley House two weeks before and it seemed a shame to waste the ticket. What else was she going to do in the middle of this damp and disappointing June? Her visit to see her father the weekend before had left her dispirited and irritable, compounded by the text that had been waiting for her at home.

Did u wish ur Daddy happy b'day from me?

Laura itched to get the phone out of her flat. It lay in the drawer each evening daring her to pick it up. What Granny would make of it she could not imagine.

The copy of the book which she had skimmed and the earliest recipe book, dated 1837 lay in her rucksack. She took the book out before stowing the rucksack in the overhead tray. But as the train began to move, she found herself unable to focus. 'I have to get on with my life,' she repeated to herself for the umpteenth time. This quest to discover what was behind the papers she had inherited was surely a diversion. As unwelcome as her father's advice was, he was right. She was in a rut, she had to make new friends, get 'out there', become someone interesting. The thought terrified her, and she pushed it away, taking down her bag and fishing out the journal in the hope that it would divert her from her own inadequacy.

1837

My seventeenth birthday and Papa has sent me this perfect notebook. I wish he could have given it to me himself. Mama wrapped it with the most beautiful paper decorated with roses and tied it with a pink ribbon which I can reuse for my hair. It was so thoughtful of her. Papa will send me recipes so that I may build a repertoire in case I should need it. Meanwhile, I shall write something about myself.

My life is ordinary, occupied as I am with looking after Mama and helping my sister-in-law, Essie, with her growing brood.

I live with Mama. We miss Papa so much when he is absent, as he has been so much throughout their marriage, first in Spain through the Wars, later in France during the Waterloo Campaign for the great Duke. Now he is in such high demand for house parties all over the country, that we see him only for days at a time. Mama tries not to be lonely, but I see her looking out of the window each day, her hazel eyes haunted with longing.

What do I wish for myself? I would like a little excitement to lighten the days and to see more of the world than this square mile around the parish of St George's, Hanover square. Mama says I should not like the world. Too much dirt and filth, too much noise and bustle. She has grown used to quiet, rarely leaving our rooms this last year or more.

It seems strange that the only excitement in my life occurred in the months after I was born, before I knew anything. I was born at Apsley House. Which grand visitors did my father welcome there while I lay in my crib below stairs? To think that the Duchess once patted me on the cheek and gave my mother a sovereign towards my dowry. I still have it, although I doubt that I will ever marry. Mama needs me. She never complains that my father quarrelled with the Duchess and left his position and has lived the last years with uncertainty. Now my brother, nine years my elder, inflicts the same on his wife. He cooks for the Duke of Buckingham. There are lavish parties, no expense spared. Jim says that the Duke lets money slip through his fingers like water through a sieve. He wonders how long the Duke's money will last and what will happen then.

What excitement could I wish for, I wonder?

Although the copperplate handwriting was beautifully neat, Laura found the curlicues and flourishes awkward and painstaking to read. However, she felt drawn to Susanna. Young and with a father often away from home, she presented similarities with Laura's own life.

She read on. There were shorter entries, amid the recipes for cabinet pudding or how to make short crust pastry, often only one line about herself. A dreary catalogue of days spent caring for her sickening mother with occasional bouts of Essie's children clambering over their aunt, while their mother rested with her new infant. Laura really hoped that Susanna's life would become more than this litany of self-sacrifice. She was sure that the first letter mentioned a job.

As the train reached Clapham Junction, Laura reached for her rucksack to replace the journal. Her eyes were beginning to sting from deciphering the elaborate handwriting.

Immediately Laura stepped off the train, the buzz of London grabbed her. She followed the crowds out of Victoria station and set off to walk to Apsley House. Her phone told her twelve minutes. The tube was scarcely quicker and always heaving. Better the bustle and noise of the streets. She tried dreaming herself back to the early part of the 19th century. Hansom cabs taking the place of taxis, pedestrians dodging horses and carts on streets which lacked pavements, the manure steaming in the heat of the day until swept up by men whose clothes beneath their leather aprons reeked with the stink of ordure. Hawkers of everything from caged birds to ribbons and buttons, mingling with the flower girls, coffee stalls, and pie men. Laura let her ears fill with imaginary cries until an overhead jet engine on its way to Heathrow brought her back to earth.

The pathway bordering Green Park offered some respite from the traffic: buses, taxis and cars gave way to Saturday morning joggers. She wished she had time to linger at the newish memorial to Bomber Command. No one could say it lacked grandeur, it fitted the scale of the Wellington Memorial on the opposite side of the road. Crossing the busy junction first to the Wellington Memorial and then over to Apsley house, Laura noticed a small crowd gathering to watch the morning's re-enactment in the small courtyard.

An officer and four soldiers in green uniforms, of the period, she assumed, were waiting to perform a drill. Hardly the event of the season, it attracted few tourists, mostly of the middle-aged variety. The officer began to bark out instructions and explanations as the soldiers shifted their rifles into different positions, his words almost drowned by the roar of traffic.

Out of the corner of her eye, Laura caught the glance of a lone male in the crowd. She sensed his eyes lingering on her. Trying to ignore him, she looked down at the programme she had printed the evening before.

A minute later a voice in her ear whispered, 'They have a reconstruction of the battle next, using vegetables to show the positions,' his accent faintly northern.

Despite trying not to, she giggled. 'I have the programme and underlined it as one to miss,' she said, attempting to dampen down the stranger's interest.

He was not put off. 'If you don't fancy that, there's a demonstration of battlefield surgical techniques if you're not squeamish. I imagine it will be graphic.'

At this point in her life, Laura was not prepared to be told what to do, especially by someone who looked as geeky as this guy.

'I expect I could handle that,' she said, before realising that she had been bounced into it.

'Hi, I'm Daniel.' He stuck out his hand.

Laura took it, his handshake pleasingly firm. She glanced down, noticing the fine red hairs beyond the fraying cuffs of his faded checked shirt. 'Laura,' she replied. 'I'm mostly interested in the house, but I suppose I can spare a few minutes for the surgery demo'.'

'No problem, although I have toured the house before. Wellington fascinates me.'

'That's why I'm here. I've just been reading a little book about Wellington's cook.'

'James Thornley. Yes, I have come across it. An odd little book, isn't it? He used to be mentioned on the audio tour until they changed it.'

'Oh, that's a shame. I have his daughter's journal in my bag.'

Daniel's eyes widened. 'I never knew such a thing existed. Is it published? I'm sure such a thing would have appeared in my literature search.'

'No, it was left to me. I shouldn't think it's been read recently. Or ever,' she added as an afterthought.

He curled his tongue over his lips to moisten them. 'I don't suppose you would show me over a cup of coffee?'

'It's quite boring what little bit I've read, very domestic.'

'I'd still like to take a peek.'

'Why are you so interested?'

'I'm an historian. You never know where a new piece of evidence may lead.' Laura looked doubtful but accepted the answer. 'My area of interest is on social unrest in 19th century England. I'll read anything contemporary for an odd snippet of commentary for my research. I'm a part-time lecturer at UCL, hoping to make it full-time one day. Look, why don't I take you for a coffee?'

'Well, perhaps after you've shown me the house.' His eyes lit up as he steered her towards the entrance. What had she let herself in for?

Daniel was a surprisingly competent guide and good company. Laura warmed to him as he pointed out which paintings and artefacts were worthy of interest while her mind boggled at the richness and beauty of the rooms.

'Look at the gilding on the ceiling, it's so delicate!' she cried as they entered the splendid Piccadilly Drawing Room. She would love to see it unmuted by the blinds at the windows, the yellow-papered walls gleaming in full sunlight.

'Wait 'til you see the Waterloo Gallery. Victorian bling hardly begins to describe it.'

By the time they reached the gallery, her eyes were dazzled by the magnificence of every room, from the yellow and red walls, once covered in silk damask, the silver gilt place settings and ornate furnishings.

'I can't believe this. It must have taken an army of servants to keep it all clean and sparkling. The Duke certainly had some ego to fill it with so many memorials to himself, don't you think?' Laura burbled, her admiration for the house vying with a sense concern for the lowly paid and overworked housemaids.

'In those days it was expected. The people of both Britain and Europe were extremely grateful to Wellington and his achievements were widely vaunted, a celebrity idol in every sense of the word.'

'I can see that. I wonder why James Thornley really resigned from his service. An argument about his overordering meat seems trivial. To be steward here – well unless you were going to Buckingham Palace, it couldn't get much better than this for a servant.'

'The Duchess was a fairly unaffected woman. She didn't take to society and she and Wellington weren't well suited. It may have been a simple clash of personalities. Are you ready for that drink yet?'

'Yes, but I must buy a guidebook first and after this I want to visit St George's in Hanover Square.'

'Okay, we'll walk along through Mayfair. There are some cute pubs, no Costas that I can think of until we reach Burlington Square.'

Easy going, acquiescent, unusual qualities to Laura's mind, Daniel was the polar opposite to Jake. But she didn't want him to get the wrong idea. She was not ready for a new relationship.

'This is one of my favourites.' He guided her into Shepherd's Tavern after several minutes walking.

'I love it,' Laura said, settling herself into a seat in the corner as she admired the dark wooden floors and walls. 'I shouldn't think it's changed much since it was built.' She picked up a menu. Her stomach was grumbling, hours having passed since a quick slice of toast that morning.

'Do you fancy sharing a plate of nachos? They're pretty good here.' Daniel second guessed her.

'Exactly my choice but I'll pay.'

'If you insist. I'll have a pint too, please.'

Laura crossed over to the bar to order drinks and food. She picked up a leaflet saying that the pub had been a favourite with RAF crew in the war too. History oozed out of the walls, and she wondered if James Thornley had ever stopped here on his route from Apsley House.

The nachos when they arrived were crisp and spicy. Daniel and Laura tucked in; conversation forgotten in the face of delicious food.

'That was so good. I wish I could get nachos like that where I live.' Laura said, wiping her mouth on her serviette.

'Where's that?' Daniel asked.

'On the south coast.' Laura had no intention of being more specific at this stage.

Not giving up, Daniel asked her about herself. The perfect entry to let him down gently.

'I'm a college librarian in Sussex and just out of a long-term relationship. It came as a bit of a shock and it's going to take me time to get over it.'

She saw the flecks of disappointment in his brown eyes before he perked up. 'Time will help. It's been three years since my girlfriend walked out on me. I didn't want to take a chance with anyone else and I had no luck with dating websites, but...' he paused. 'Now I feel the time is right.'

'Let me show you the notebook.' Laura wiped some grease off her fingers, keen to move the conversation on.

After wiping his hands clean, he handled the leather-bound book with the delicacy of an academic used to primary sources. 'Susanna was a relative, yes?'

Laura shrugged. 'Honestly, I don't know. I was unaware of her before finding these books and some letters together with a painting of James at my great aunt's house.'

'Books, letters– there's more?' The excitement in his voice amused her.

'At least three notebooks and loads of letters. I haven't had time to put them in order as yet.'

'I'd love to help you with your research. My contract is almost over for this term, so I have time and I still have access to resources.'

Laura bristled slightly. He was muscling in on her project. 'My term's almost over too.' Not quite true and she had to work for part of the summer holidays.

'Two heads can't hurt, and family research is time consuming, you can get sent down false trails quite easily.' He smiled at her. 'I'd love to photocopy the notebooks too.'

'I'll think about it, okay? Are you on WhatsApp?'

He took out his phone and asked for her number. Her phone pinged a few seconds later. She finished her cappuccino and stood. 'I must get going. Nice meeting you, Daniel.' Laura took the notebook to stuff into her bag, aware of his forlorn expression.

'Do you know your way to Hanover Square?' he asked.

'I'm sure I can find it on my phone. 'Thanks, she smiled. 'I'll be in touch.' He grinned and she relented. 'Maybe I'll copy the notebooks for you.'

On the train home, she mulled over her day. Susanna and her father were beginning to take shape in her mind; It helped to see the setting for Susanna's early life, not that she would ever have set foot in the grand rooms of Apsley House. James, as Steward, would probably have known every inch of the house before it was extended a few years later. It would have been his job to ensure everything ran smoothly, that the other servants obeyed his instructions. No mere cook, this man, but at the top of his game and working hard for his family, it must have been a huge risk to resign his position over a disagreement with the Duchess.

The church on Hanover Square had been something else too. Built in the early 1700s in the Palladian style, it was not only a beautiful example of Georgian architecture, but also the church of the nobility. This place, where James had probably been married and his children christened, boasted church wardens that were dukes and earls. Wooden plaques commemorated them just below the gallery. It was a Who's Who of the great and the good. Laura had picked up a leaflet as she was leaving. She took it now from her bag and smoothed it out. It described St George's as Handel's Church. She read through the descriptions of those who had married there – Lady Hamilton, Benjamin Disraeli, Shelley, George Eliot, the pioneer aviator, Amy Johnson-. The list went on. *And James Thornley*, she thought. *I have to find if there is a link with my family.*

It was time. Looking up ancestors would be her next project, but should she work backwards or forwards and how much time was it going to take? How much time did granny have left? At her age, who could know? Laura took a slurp of the coke she had bought at Victoria and looked around the crowded carriage. Saturday afternoon and she was on her own amongst a crowd of happy, smiling people.

She took out her phone and googled Daniel Steventon (thank the Lord for a reasonably unusual surname) – yes, there he was, a bone fide academic. She glanced through the papers listed against his name, he was obviously serious about his work. He must have tidied himself up for his university photo, shorter hair, an open-necked shirt, clean shaven. A pleasant open face, she concluded.

Closing Google down, her fingers hovered over Whatsapp. Damn it, why not? She began typing –

Hi Daniel, Wd be grateful for your help. Cd u look up James and his family, 2 children, James and Susanna (born 1820) – don't know abt her brother, but nine years older. He married Esther, lived near St George's Hanover Square. I'll track backwards from my granny.

Laura hit send before she could change her mind. The reply was swift

Happy to. Be in touch.

Laura relaxed, something new to tell Granny. She looked forward to seeing her tomorrow to try and find out if she knew any more about the family.

By the time Laura arrived at Storrington the next day, she had taken out a free trial on Ancestry.co.uk and entered Edith's name in the search box only to be inundated with results. She also had a present in the car, a Bluetooth speaker, an impulse buy from Sainsbury's that morning. The audio on the old iPad was rubbish. Laura had already created a Spotify playlist for Peggy and filled it with the music of the forties and fifties. Her mind played with ideas for simple things to brighten up Granny's life, making up for lost time and the empty years of mindless TV. The next thing on the list to organise were audiobooks. Would Granny have the concentration to cope with a long book? Laura hoped so. What type of books would she enjoy? Another thing to ask, the list becoming endless.

Daniel had messaged her to say that he had found James Thornley's birth and marriage certificates. The father's family had originated from a tiny village in Northamptonshire. Questions buzzed around Laura's head. What had made them travel to London? How had his son become a cook sufficiently well known to cook for the most important General in the country?

Chapter Thirteen

Peggy

You look happier – Peggy spelled out the words on her sheet as Laura sat down in the chair opposite.

'I have brought you a present.' Laura removed a small, black plastic box from her shopping bag. 'Can I have your iPad?'

While she tapped away on the machine, Laura grinned like a Cheshire cat. I can't believe how she makes my heart sing again after years shrivelling to the size of a pea. After plugging in the box and more tapping on the iPad, her smile broadened into a laugh.

'You're going to love this, Granny,' Laura looked up and waved her index finger in the air like a conductor with a baton.

A moment of silence before the room filled with a rich and wonderful sound, it was like being thrown back into a dance hall with his arms tight around me. My love, how I miss him.

'Here's another present. Don't worry, Heather has agreed I can bring you some treats.

Laura took two pots out of her bag. 'This one is a Moroccan salad. Do you want to try it?'

I nodded. She scooped my dinner plate, with its cold lumps of congealing roast potato, off my lap table and taking a spoon she dipped it into the salad. I opened my mouth like a baby bird, and she placed some of the mixture on my tongue. It was akin to the Mediterranean on a summer's day. I tasted lemon and the slightest hint of garlic and chilli, as my mouth crunched on chickpeas, sultanas and feta cheese. Blessed jewels of flavour. She handed me a tissue as the room continued to fizz with the strings of Mantovani. I twirled on feet as light as air in my memories. How many years since I have walked rather than hobbled, let alone danced? The music changed to Begin the Bequine - I wished I could at least hum along.

Laura gave me another spoonful of the salad, but my appetite is so small, that I waved her away as she tried for a third time.

'Shall I leave the tropical fruit salad for later?'

I nodded, smiled and tapped - *food of gods*- on my alphabet sheet.

'I've created a list of 100 songs for you. If there's more you want, let me know next week. You can also listen to books. Would you like to try?'

My heart skipped. Would I? How many times did I lose myself in a book or a concert to still the yearning in my heart? But no amount of Hardy or the Brontës ever made up for the longing to feel his skin on mine once again, his lips nuzzling my neck while I drank in the smell of his hair, spicy from the shampoo he used.

I tried with Percy, tried so hard to love him but after a couple of years I gave up. He knew something had changed but we never discussed it. What could I have said? He idolised Jeanette always, and she followed him around like a moth to a flame.

Laura was waiting for an answer. What to ask for? If I had one wish before I died it would be to listen to Under Milk Wood read by Richard Burton. Percy tried reading it to me once, but his voice had no magic, no understanding. In the end I read it for myself, painstakingly, the tiny print stroking the images back to life, while trying to capture Burton's intonation in my memory.

I nodded to Laura, commanding my heart to still. She handed me the alphabet sheet which had fallen on the floor – *Under Milk Wood*, I tapped, a tremble of excitement in my fingers. She nodded, turned to the iPad and showed me. It was there – Richard Burton, I pointed to it and instantly the music stopped and a few seconds later his honeyed tones leapt from the speaker. We listened to the opening lines together. I felt her fingers tighten in my crooked hand.

'Wow! The language, it's so poetic. I never knew! I love the description of a moonless night as bibleblack.'

Quietly and companionably, we listened longer until her fingers twitched at the passing of the minutes, and I knew there was more that she needed from me. Tomorrow I will listen again and remember. I will hear him speaking these magical words as we sat by a river with a picnic of cheap white wine and apples. His accent more pronounced than Burton's, no less mellifluous. My heart continued to ache until Laura interrupted my thoughts. She paused the recording.

'I want to find out about your family, but I have no birth dates. When was Edith's birthday?'

It is a small price to pay for the pleasure she has brought me. 2. 5. 1920 - I tap.

'May 2nd 1920,' Laura repeated, fiddling again with the iPad. 'Bingo! I've found her.'

She showed me but I couldn't see until she did that trick with her fingers to make the words larger.

'Look Edith Swain, born Grimsby, parents John Swain and Doris Webster.'

Good God is there nothing private anymore?

'What about you Granny, what's your birthday?'

Despite myself, I tap 14. 7. 1930. Laura tried typing in Peggy Swain but found nothing. I shook my head at her and tapped out - *Margaret*.

'Oh, of course. That's your real name!'

I nodded but never remember having been called that since the vicar spoke it in church and I thought that's not me, maybe I should leave now, but I stayed.

'Here you are, Granny, your birth record.'

I stared at it, more childhood memories than I could shake a stick at. Who was left to remember now that Edith had gone?

Laura fiddled some more. 'Is this your marriage record?'

My head snapped up. No, I don't want to look. Tired - I tapped -Talk about you.'

Laura spoke about her trip to London and a young man she had met, saying, 'He's only a friend.' A friend can be everything or nothing. Will she know the difference? I want to scream, 'Don't waste your life on the wrong man, sweetheart.' I remain silent - my life, my mistake.

Taking her cue as my head began to nod, Laura showed Betty, who had arrived with a cup of tea, how to set up the music before she left. I longed to lie on my bed and let myself drift away to the orchestra strings of Mantovani. Betty turned down the sound and my eyes began to droop. I have difficulty picturing his face after sixty years, but taste and smell have not faded. I wonder if he's still alive. Maybe. He is my age and I have survived; God knows how. What if he has forgotten all about me?

Chapter Fourteen

Laura

July turned brighter, drier than an indifferent June. Laura had been busy at work, preparing for the new academic year with a plethora of management meetings and training days scheduled. She now jumped at invitations to spend a few nights out with female colleagues at leaving-do bashes. With no Jake at home to complain, she was beginning to have fun with little spare time to think of her "project", as she called it.

Sunday afternoons were spent in the care home garden tempting her grandmother with Laura's tastiest food. Heather advised against anything too spicy, so Laura stuck mostly to Greek and Italian recipes. Granny looked less frail than she had seemed on that first visit. A sparkle often cut through her filmy eyes, though Heather told Laura that Peggy was becoming more demanding.

'As soon as we go into her room, it's iPad this, iPad that. You've unleashed a demon. Once I forgot to charge it overnight for her and she glared at me all morning.'

'I'm sorry, Heather.'

'Don't be. We're all thrilled that she has something to occupy her days. That new cover you bought for the iPad, works well on her lap tray. She likes listening to classical music too. Why don't you make her another playlist? I'm sorry that we never thought to find her an old iPad before. Your grandfather gave us the impression that she had lost interest in anything but the TV.'

Grandfather was still a mystery. Those few photos in the album, the marriage record on the Ancestry website were all she had. Heather had thought him caring, her father disliked him. What was the truth? Laura decided to ask Peggy on her next visit.

The sun was warm on their backs as Laura sat on a wooden bench next to her grandmother, having pushed the wheelchair around the circuit of flower beds. She covered her grandmother's knees with the travel rug, before adjusting the position of the wheelchair so that Peggy could reach the plastic beaker of cranberry juice.

Laura began with an innocuous statement. 'Grandpa was a teacher like you.'

Barely a nod in reply. 'Did he teach English too?' A shake of the head. Laura thrust the alphabet sheet at her grandmother. Peggy tapped – *maths*.

'You met working at the same school?' There was a staff photo of them both in the album. A nod, then a turn of the head away from Laura.

'Do you miss him? Is that why you don't want to talk about him?'

Her grandmother turned back with eyes devoid of warmth. She opened her mouth to try and speak. 'S-st.' Frustration made her slap her left hand on the plastic glass, sending it flying.

Laura bundled up paper tissues and mopped at the mess. The juice had smeared the laminated sheet. As she wiped, Laura felt her grandmother's cool, clammy hand touch hers. She pointed at the sheet and Laura passed it to her. Peggy spelt out – *stop*.

Laura had no chance to ask her why or anything else. Her phone began to trill.

'Excuse me, Granny. It's Daniel, that guy in London I told you about. Hi Daniel, it's a bit difficult to talk right now, I'm with my granny.'

'Hey, Laura. How are you getting on?' He ignored her delaying tactic.

'I've done nothing lately, been too busy.'

'Well, I've been making a family tree for you. So far, I have the cook, his father, two children and nine grandchildren. I need to know if any relate to you.'

'Wow, I feel guilty for having done so little.'

'Are you busy next weekend? I could come down, and we can make some real progress. Have you sorted out all the papers?'

Laura's mind scrambled with excuses until she saw the query in her grandmother's eyes. This was who she was doing it for. 'Yes, that sounds great. Why don't you stay in the spare bedroom? We can spend the weekend on research?'

'Wonderful. I'll book a train leaving around ten on Saturday morning.'

'Text me and I'll meet you at Bognor Station.'

'Looking forward to it.'

Laura relayed the conversation to her granny. 'Hopefully we can get some answers as to why your grandmother was so sad. Edith wrote that you wanted to know.'

Her grandmother tapped the name – *Louise*.

'That was your grandmother's name?' A nod. Laura remembered the name from Edith's letter and the photograph.

'I'll look into her.' An unrelated thought occurred to Laura. 'Did you get any more text messages from Jake?' The relief in not being plagued by his messages was enormous.

Granny nodded then spelled on the sheet – *no more*.

'What happened? Why did they stop?'

Tap – *take me back*.

Back in the room Peggy pointed to a drawer where Laura's phone lay on top of a jumble of tins of talc and bars of soap, the detritus of a dozen Christmases. Had her grandfather parcelled them up and left them here? The wrappers were faded and torn, any fragrance long since lost.

'Do you want these?' Laura asked as she tipped the contents onto the bed.

Peggy shook her head.

Laura swept them into the rubbish bin before turning on the phone. Little battery remained, enough to read the latest messages. She clicked on the last one and her cheeks flooded with embarrassment. How could he do that? Laura turned towards Peggy. 'Oh, Granny, I don't know what to say. I've never felt so ashamed.'

Her grandmother appeared to be choking. Strange gurgling noises bubbled from her throat. Laura hit the buzzer on the wall beside the bed for help before she realised that Peggy was trying to laugh. Laugh! How could Peggy laugh when she'd been sent that photograph with the caption 'Remember what this is for, hon?'

Laura scrolled through the previous texts, expecting bland questions and smiley faces in reply.

Jake presumably -*Still thinking of u*

Who are you?

Jake - *U know me*

Stop it now

Jake - *U know u still want me*
Prove who you are.

'Those other texts were from you? You used the stylus to reply? You must have, the keys are too small. You were goading him?'

Tears of laughter trickled from Peggy's eyes. She nodded. Laura looked at the date of the photo, six days ago. The phone died and that dreadful image disappeared.

Betty, the care assistant, arrived. 'What you need, Peggy?' She smiled at Laura until she noticed the phone in Laura's hand. Her smile faded. 'He sent new message? Bad man, your boyfriend.'

'You knew about this?'

Betty nodded. She could hardly look at Laura until she too chuckled.

'What's been going on?'

'Peggy show that photo to me.' Betty wagged her finger at Laura. 'Not good to send to old lady.'

'Of course not. I'm mortified.'

'Not understand that word. My husband, he work for phone company. I ask him about it. He know what to do. He find number. It belong company, B...' Betty hesitated, searching for the name.

'BJC - he didn't use a pay as you go?'

Betty looked perplexed.

How stupid could Jake be? Did he think Laura would be too cowed to complain? She flushed. It was true, she had been cowed. Instead, she had left her grandmother to deal with her problem. She needed to grow a pair, as they so subtly say. 'What happened?'

'My husband speak to boss, show him messages. Say old lady frightened. Boss phone company. They say something like displin... I don't know word, sorry.'

'Disciplinary action?' Betty nodded.

Laura sank onto the bed, her head mulling with the consequences for Jake. Had he been sacked?

On the train the next day, Sophie exploded with exasperation. 'You're not responsible. He brought it on himself. You can't send a dick picture to a sick old lady and not be held to account. For heaven's sake, Laura.'

'But what if he's destroyed his career? Is it my fault?'

'No, it isn't. Look, I have contacts in BJC, let me do a little digging. I'll be discreet.'

'I'm worried that if he's been sacked, he'll take it out on me too.'

'If he does, we'll get an injunction. Honestly, if this happened a few days ago and you haven't heard anything, then I wouldn't worry too much. He's probably skulking with his tail between his legs.'

Sophie was on the platform, when Laura hurried down the steep stone steps to catch her return train home.

'Final warning.' She said as Laura caught up with her. 'My contact couldn't wait to spill the beans. Your Jake isn't much liked by the female clerks, it turns out. He's very full of himself and not averse to sly sexual harassment. They were delighted that he's been pulled down a notch.'

'What's that mean?'

'Any further complaint and he's out. You're home and dry, my friend.'

So, if he tries anything and I make a complaint, he's sacked.'

'You've got it.'

'He will never risk that. It was his dream job.' A weight lifted from Laura's shoulders. Laura smiled her thanks. Once seated on the train, she told Sophie about Daniel's forthcoming visit.

'You really think he's going to be satisfied with the spare room? Frying pan to fire springs to mind.' Sophie's mouth curled in amusement.

'Daniel's sweet.'

'For goodness' sake, Laura. Now is not the time to take on a waif and stray. Tell him, no long-term commitment, then have your wicked way with him. You deserve some pleasure.'

'Sophie, you're outrageous.'

***

Peggy

Meanwhile, Peggy's heart was singing that her granddaughter was shot of that unworthy young man. So eager to make a fool of himself that she had not had to consider how to tackle him. Putting aside Laura's questions about her grandfather had been trickier. One day they would resurface, but she pushed thoughts of Percy aside.

Peggy turned to the old newspaper photograph which Laura had reframed and placed on the cabinet beside her chair. Her mother, Doris. Peggy could feel every ounce of regret that had resulted in that pregnancy, another child to tie her to John, another shackle in the chain. Edith, her beloved sister, bright eyed with the promise of a future, just not the future she had envisaged for herself. George, the grandfather, dead within a year of that photo and before his time, mourned by all, loved by all, hoping for a grandson to replace his beloved Albert. Then there was Louise, Granny Lou, Peggy's mother in all but name. Despite the crackly paper, the lack of a pinafore and the turban she always wore, this was exactly how she remembered her.

Laura would never know these people, never know their stories, their secrets, their hopes and dreams. Peggy remembered what they had chosen to tell, knew other things because she had lived through those times. Her eyes settled back on Granny Lou. How the ghost of Rose, the invisible great grandmother, had coloured her childhood as she lay cuddled on her grandmother's squishy lap. A time of warmth, a time of love.

'This is the lullaby my mother used to sing to me just before she disappeared. I'm brushing your hair the way I brushed my mother's, though your hair is the colour of conkers and hers was buttermilk, so long, it fell to her waist, soft like a butterfly's wing. She ground lavender flowers into the water when she washed it. I've always loved the smell of lavender.'

Granny Lou's hands smelt of the lanolin she coated her hands with after braiding fishing nets for hours in her kitchen. They were so rough that she wore cotton gloves when dressing and undressing Peggy.

The Skye Boat Song. Hadn't Peggy sung the same lullaby to Jeanette - *Speed Bonny Boat Like a Bird on The Wing* – hadn't she heard Jeanette sing it to Laura. Down the ages from mother to daughter through five generations in a straight line. The words may have changed but the music and sentiment remained. Rose was in their memories, in their DNA. If Laura could find out what had happened to her it would be a miracle but a sweet one.

Chapter Fifteen

Peggy

Life with mother was always a clash of wills but it was Granny Lou who won the battle for me. I never understood why Mother fought me until later in life and our conflict became my penance.

We could never depend on father to provide for us. Some days he coped but more often he stumbled through life like a shadow fading in the grey light of the North Sea. He was there, then again, he was not. War can do that to a man, especially a war like his. He volunteered with his mates, one of the Grimsby Chums, full of optimism, full of dreams, my granny once told me with a pained look in her watery eyes. He had married my mother on the brink of departure for the Western Front. She had two days of marriage with a man in his prime before he returned - a ghost, a spectre haunted by memories. We woke to his screams and Mother's soothing murmurs. That did not always work and then heard cries of pain which she did her best to muffle, but she could not disguise her bruises. He never looked her in the eye the next morning – his shame unmanned him further.

As a child, I never understood why she did not leave. I determined that I would never have anything to do with a violent man. *Love deserted the house before Edith was born*, I overheard my mother once whisper to her friend. I always suspected that I was an accident, a compensatory quick fumble with someone mother met at work, a married man maybe. My mother's eyes were grey and my father's, hooded always with pain, I remember as a dull blue – mine are more brown than green, a weird mixture of neither.

Mother skirted around my father like a spoonful of oil in water, touching only at the edges. She cooked for him, washed and mended his clothes, took any money he earned on his better days, but I never saw a kiss, nor a hug, not so much as a fleeting caress of a finger on hand or cheek. Occasionally he looked at her the way men do. If she caught his look, her shoulders would droop, and her lips turn down. At the time I could not understand why. I learned later.

Silence reigned in our house. Father hated noise of any kind. He always had a book in his hands, but rarely turned the page. We children learned not to cry, nor to laugh when he was around, and it became easier to speak in whispers whenever inside. I learnt never to be loud or extroverted. It was something I worked hard to overcome at university, but it always remained beneath the surface. In those days, I escaped into books and schoolwork. My bedroom became my haven.

Father never drank as many men did to lay their ghosts. I remember one man, I think his name was Norman, filthy, pitiful, wrecked; always drunk on meths, if he could not afford whisky. Mother would cross the road to avoid him, saying, 'Thank heavens for small mercies.' I knew what she meant.

Edith and I scarcely registered with father. He took no interest in us, rarely spoke of us other than to say to Mother, 'At least we have no sons to sacrifice.'

Mother worked at the dairy in the street behind our house. I think it kept her sane. Eight hours of work and laughter until she returned to her purgatory. I used to watch her walk down the alley behind the house, arm in arm with her friend, Mabel. They would hug each other at our gate, smile and wave goodbye, then Mother turned. Her shoulders began to droop, her smile fixed to one of resignation and her steps slowed as she walked down the path. It was hard for us children to be part of this other life, the one she loathed.

Everything changed the week war was declared. Father retreated to his chair, morose and shaking, one minute muttering, and whimpering the next. I was thankful that the holidays were over, and I could return to school. On the first day of term, I arrived home from school sometime after four, still jittery because of the practice air raid siren that morning. The awful wailing sound we learned to ignore in the first year of that war and later learned to dread. I lingered, knowing that Edith would be at work as a filing clerk for the council. I would be on my own with Father.

Unexpectedly, Granny Lou greeted me at the door. I loved Granny Lou, having lived with her as a baby until I slept through the night, and then each weekday until I began school. Grandad was dead by then and she welcomed the company. Poor Grandad, he had coughed his way to death by the time I was one. The ciggies did for him. All the deckies smoked. You would see them in town in their blue suits, a wad of cash in their pockets and a fag between their fingers until it was time to sign back on for another three weeks at sea.

We had haddock for tea that day. It lay wrapped on the table in greaseproof paper tied in string, enough for two days at least. As she fried it, I asked where Dad was. It was not that people kept secrets so much as they avoided telling the truth.

'He's gone away for a while.'

'Where?'

He needed some peace. The hospital will look after him.'

'When will he be back?'

A shrug of her shoulders as she turned the spitting fish in the pan. To distract me Granny Lou began to retell the story I loved most when I was younger, how Grandad had rescued her from her ugly sisters, so I always thought of him as Prince Charming and my granny as Cinderella. Although I could never imagine her bunioned feet in a pair of glass slippers. I played along, pounding her with questions, braver, more demanding than when I was younger.

'How ugly were your sisters? Did they have warts on their noses?'

'No,' she snorted, turning the fish in the pan. 'They weren't really my sisters. They were cousins but I was told to call them sisters. Our fathers were brothers although you could never tell. My father was a bear of a man, all brawn and muscle from his work as a fireman on the railways. While their father was skinny and slightly stooped. My stepmother moaned more than once that her daughters took after their father's scrawny build, while she had curves in all the right places.'

'And how cruel was she? Did she lock you in the cellar?'

'Your imagination is working overtime,' Granny Lou plonked the fish on my plate. 'We had no cellar. Hattie's cruelty lay in words.'

'Was your stepmother mean to your dad as well?'

'There's the thing,' she said, dishing up a plate of fish for herself. 'She mooned over my father, flicking her long dark lashes in his direction when she wanted something. He was putty in her hands when he saw those turquoise-coloured eyes; 'Of course, Hatty, whatever you want, Hatty,' he would say. As soon as he was out of the way, those eyes became ice, and I missed my mother all over again. I wish I could remember her face.' She sniffed before taking a forkful of fish.

'Do you remember anything about her?'

Granny chewed on her fish looking wistful. After swallowing, she said, 'Mam let me brush her hair. I had to be careful not to tangle it. I remember it as a long rope of butter yellow silk like Rapunzel's in the fairy tale.'

'I wish I had her hair.'

'So did I, dear. It smelt of lavender. My mother's hands smelt of cocoa and marzipan from working in the family shop, the scent so good, I wanted to lick them. Whenever I slice a Battenberg cake, it brings tears to my eyes soon as I smell that almond paste. I remember my father once joking that Mam's eyes were buttons of chocolate. She was the only one of her family to have brown eyes. He made it seem something to be ashamed of.'

I think this was the first time I understood the story as more than a fairy tale. Granny Lou lost her mother one day, gone, just like my father. Would he come back? I began to feel sorry for myself even though Dad's presence in the house was unnerving. He was still my dad. Before I could ask anything else, Mam walked through the door and shooed me up to my bedroom. Conversations needed to be had and they did not include me.

Nothing was said of Dad again. It was as though he had never existed, never lived with us. I asked Edith, of course, but she had just started going out with Gordon and she told me it was best to leave it.

'You don't want him back do you, Peggy?'

'But people just don't disappear.' I grumbled, not liking a mystery.

Chapter Sixteen

Peggy

It took time for the atmosphere to change. Granny moved in and took charge of running it which, once rationing began, was a boon to mother who had no time to queue. One day a radio appeared, and the house filled with music and mother began to sing, jolly songs, daft songs. She began to smile at us, rather than frown for making too much noise. It confused me so I hid away with my books, the noise suddenly too raucous. I could not concentrate. Once you discover the magic of reading, it never leaves you. I was entranced by the Greek myths at the time. The big argument came when I won a scholarship to the grammar school.

'No,' said Mother. 'You need to leave school and earn a living like your sister. I have no money to spend on uniforms and other fripperies.'

'You stopped me from going. Don't stop Peggy. Please, Mam.' Edith cut in.

'What's the point? She'll marry someone who can look after her if she has any sense.'

'Like you did,' I retorted. She slapped my face. Rather than cry, I surprised myself by saying, 'I want to be a teacher.'

Mother's face dropped. 'Leave home for a training college? Girls need to stay near their families.'

'I can find a teaching job in Grimsby.' I was begging her to listen.

'Pipe dreams!' she scoffed. 'Girls from round here don't become teachers. Anyway, you'd have to give it up when you marry. What's the point?'

'Maybe I don't want to marry.' What I dared not say was that the example she and father had set had put me off marriage. I was no fool.

Mother's eyes screwed up with fury. 'You're eleven and far too young to know what you want. Forget grammar school. You are not going.'

I ran to my room and threw myself on the eiderdown while plotting how I could get her to change her mind.

The argument raged for days. Edith had begun her nurses training with Gordon away at war. 'If I had the money, I would pay for you.' she told me, 'But I'll earn a pittance until I qualify.'

Just when I thought I could never win, Granny Lou stepped in. 'If you want to lose Peggy, you are going the right way about it, Doris. Think about that.' She said it softly, without any threat, but it brought mother up short.

She looked at me and I saw fear in her eyes. This mother, who never had time for signs of affection, loved me. For the first time I saw it. Regret for my lost childhood, for the years she had not really known. She was afraid of losing me before I could begin to love her. In those few seconds I saw the years of suffering and the pain of her lost chances. If only we were not destined to repeat our mothers' mistakes.

She nodded. 'Go then, Peggy. We'll manage somehow.'

Should I have launched myself into her arms, covered her face with kisses of gratitude? It was too late for that. 'Thank you, Mam. I'll make you proud.' It was Granny Lou I kissed.

I worked hard for Granny Lou, for the faith she had in me. When other girls in my class began to doll themselves up on the off chance of catching the eye of an American serviceman, I kept my head down. When Gordon died, I worked harder, unable to bear Edith's pain. I was fifteen when the war ended, never been kissed, never set foot inside the Gaiety Ballroom – the only thing that mattered was that school certificate.

By that time Granny Lou was failing. The war had taken it out of her. The lack of coal to keep the fire and range heated, the rain drenched queueing for bread and a scrawny piece of beef skirt, or sausage more bran than pork, played havoc with her chest. A simple cough turned into a hack that never seemed to leave her. 'What I wouldn't give for honey and lemon with a dash of whisky,' she grunted, between spasms of rattling discomfort, her wrinkled hands pressed into her chest as though it could relieve the pain. Honey and lemons were a distant memory and whisky was unaffordable in those last dreary months of the war. Everyone was tired and hungry. If we had not had the weekly parcel of fish which magicked its way to us from one of Grandpa's old ship mates,

I think Granny would have succumbed earlier. Frying fish always put a smile on her face.

I owed her so much that I spent all the hours I could with her in that final summer. I'm sure she knew it would be her last, her swan song she called it, as we trailed around the boating lake, happy to see the end of barbed wire, and children paddling in the pool near the sand pit once more. We rested in the shade of one of the brick grottos and she told me the story which had plagued her life.

'I was born in Liverpool. All I can remember is my mother's family. Large, noisy and full of life. So many cousins, though I can't remember all their names. Grandpa had been a confectioner and one of my uncles ran the shop. My mother worked there. It was full of the most delicious treats, a wonderland of tastes and smells. He supplied all the best hotels and cafés. I remember hovering at the counter unable to choose between the marzipan, toffee or chocolate bonbons.'

'Oh Granny, don't make me jealous. It's so long since we've tasted any of those,' I said.

She patted my hand before continuing. 'Granny Essie, a fearsome woman, looked after me while Mam worked, just like I looked after you. Her little house heaved with children, but she mostly ignored us. We were all a little scared of her, so we looked after each other. I was never lonely.'

She plucked a hanky from her bag and dabbed at her eyes. I was surprised to see tears. I had never known her cry; she was always one of those indomitable women who got on with whatever life threw at them. I took her liver-spotted hand in mine, feeling both the callouses and her declining strength.

'Maybe I shouldn't tell you this but there's no one else. I don't want to trouble Edith or your mam; she's got enough on her plate. But you, one day you may find out the truth. Perhaps someone will come looking.' She stared out towards the sea, though we could not see it from where we sat. It was like looking into the past and the future all at the same time. There was longing there, a hunger for something.

'One day, we left Liverpool on the train and never returned. I was nearly six years old. I never saw any of them again and I don't know why.'

'Who left, Grandma?'

'There's the thing. It was Dad and me, my Aunty Harriet and her two daughters, Flo and Minnie. Minnie died of the diphtheria when she was ten.' Granny Lou hacked into her handkerchief before continuing.

'Mam disappeared a week or two before we left, and I was taken to live with a stranger until one day my father came for me and took me to the station where we met Harriet and the girls.' Granny Lou paused and swallowed. 'For nearly seventy years I haven't known what to believe. Did Dad elope with Aunty Harriet. I've always assumed he did. But why take me? Why not leave me with Mam? Harriet and her daughters shut me out. We'd always got on well before, but they acted like it was all my fault, like I was to blame somehow. Maybe because I never accepted it.'

'Oh Gran, that's terrible. Didn't you ask your father when you got older?'

'When we were on the train, he told us we were never to speak of my mother or Uncle Alf again. Alfred was Harriet's husband. We all had the same surname because they were brothers. As far as anybody was concerned, we were an ordinary family, and we must not say different. But I always felt that didn't include me.' Granny Lou sighed and I stroked her hand before she continued.

'They were glad to get rid of me when your granddad came to my rescue. Harriet had died by then, of a growth in her stomach. My father gave me a brooch to wear at my wedding, said it belonged to my mother. It will be yours to wear one day. That's almost the only time he mentioned her. He was ailing by then, his lungs clogged from stoking engines. I remember him saying how a man should have a son but what did he have but useless daughters. It was the pain talking – he was frightened after losing Hattie. Flo cared for him after her mother died and they shut me out.

'I saw Flo with one of her grandsons a few months ago but she crossed the road to avoid me.' Granny Lou sighed long and hard. Sorrow dulled her eyes. I leant against her, the scent of camphor mingling with the damp of the grotto.

I considered asking if she believed she would meet her mother again in heaven until I remembered her antipathy towards the church after her son died. She had cursed God for that more than once in my presence.

'Why do you think Flo blamed you?' I asked cautiously, wondering if I were overstepping the mark.

'Because over the years, I've come to think that maybe Dad and Harriet were escaping some shame, not theirs, but my mother's. I have this awful feeling that she abandoned me to run off with Alfred. Why else would Harriet's daughters shun me?'

I sat in the scruffy grotto, feeling the dank walls closing in, overwhelmed by the sadness Granny Lou felt after so many years. I hated Grandma's parents for hurting their daughter and wished Granny hadn't told me because I didn't know what to do with her sorrow.

'When I die, will you make sure my obituary says, "Louise, daughter of Rose and Thomas White of Liverpool?" That way someone may find me after my death. It's the only thing I ask.'

I did as she asked though Mam grumbled at the extra expense, but I offered to pay out of the shilling she let me keep from my Saturday job at the Tudor Café. No one ever did come asking.

Chapter Seventeen

Laura July 2019

Laura had dismissed Sophie's recommendation to take Daniel to bed, intending the weekend to be business-like. Daniel was no more than an acquaintance, albeit helpful and generous with his time.

The solicitor's letter had brought good news that morning. Probate had been granted allowing the flat to become hers. Jake had been paid off and the sale on the Grimsby house was progressing. All being well, the exchange of contracts could go ahead in the middle of August.

The train was on time and began to disgorge its passengers. While the town needed the hordes of Londoners who had visited in their thousands, decades before, only a trickle remained. Laura stepped back to let them through the barriers, her eyes scanning the platform. Daniel's height made him stand out. Laura smiled and he responded with a wave. When he stood in front of her it was clear he had made an effort, his hair neat and short, face freshly shaven with the merest hint of stubble, clean blue jeans and a new T shirt replacing the check shirt of their previous meeting - modern, understated.

'You look smart,' Laura could not help herself, surprised that he had scrubbed up so well.

'Big day, yesterday. I had an interview for a new job, which I aced. You see before you a permanent, full-time lecturer.' He beamed with pride.

'That's fantastic. Well done.'

'I have a bottle in my rucksack. Perhaps we could celebrate this evening?'

She grinned. 'I have a meal all planned. Is it white or red?'

'Prosecco.'

'Perfect, I can't wait. Let's get it in the fridge.'

The sun shone, catching the strawberry blond glints in Daniel's hair as they ambled out of the station and down through the shopping precinct towards the seafront.

They strolled through the crowded Saturday market and over the road onto the promenade. The tide was out, leaving the stunted pier high and dry, but families were out enjoying the warm weather. Some children were building sandcastles in the square of sand separated from the pebbles by a low wooden fence.

'This reminds me of Filey, apart from the cliffs. It needs cliffs.'

'It does,' Laura agreed. She pointed to the southwest. 'Those faint hills beyond Selsey are on the Isle of Wight. That's the closest you'll get to cliffs.'

'I like it though.' He turned to her and grinned. 'I checked; this place gets the record for the most sunshine in the UK. It must be like being on permanent holiday.'

Laura grinned back, the breeze wafting a strand of hair across her face. 'I'm really interested in what you've found out so far. I left all the papers on the coffee table this morning. They're in a total mess. What's the best way of getting started?' Laura attempted to turn the conversation to the task in hand.

'It's best to be methodical. We'll put the letters into date order and marry them up with the dates in the notebooks.'

Laura nodded. 'It sounds like a long job.'

'Rushing it is the worst thing you can do. I'll log everything onto the laptop because I'm hoping that there's something worth writing a paper on. We could do it in joint names.'

'No, Daniel. I'm only interested in finding out about the family. You must have any credit for your research, though I'm worried that it won't be worth your time or interest.'

'Let me be the judge of that.'

Back at the flat, Laura took her Italian coffee pot and placed it on the hob to work its magic. With the prosecco safely in the fridge and the salmon steaks marinating in her own special mixture of herbs, spices and white wine, she asked Daniel about the family tree.

He switched on his laptop and asked for her Wi-Fi code, then extracted some documents from a clear plastic wallet. 'I've printed out copies for you.'

He smoothed out a sheet with a printed tree. 'Here's James, Wellington's Steward, below is son James, and daughter Susanna. James married Esther in 1832, the next line is all their children with dates of birth. I haven't found any marriage certificate for Susanna.'

Laura studied the tree, counting the children. 'Nine kids! Gosh, there's a Rose, right at the end. Why have you got that bracket linking her with Harriet?'

'Because I think they were twins. I couldn't find Rose's birth record, but they are the same age on the 1861 census.' Laura scarcely listened, her mind on Rose.

'Could she be the missing Rose?' Laura's face shone. 'Will you forward it to me please?'

'Sure. You'll have to explain about the missing Rose. Here are the census records for 1851 and 1861. It shows the family moved to Liverpool at some point between. James, the elder, died in 1854 in London of cholera. There was a huge outbreak at the time. Maybe the family thought it safer to move away.'

'You mean like the series on TV. Victoria's dresser who married Francatelli the cook, she died of cholera.'

Daniel frowned. 'Total fabrication. It made a good plot line, I suppose.'

'Wasn't there a doctor who discovered the source to be a single water pump?'

'John Snow, yes. That bit was true. He's a personal hero of mine. The research he did to uncover the source was meticulous.'

Laura shivered. While watching the programme, she had never considered a possible connection. She felt herself being drawn into the story of her family,

'How far have you managed to go back?'

Laura took her phone and showed Daniel the photo from the newspaper. She pointed to Louise. 'This is Rose's daughter. Rose went missing sometime when Louise was a small child. I traced everyone back to Louise but didn't have time to look for Rose.'

'Where was Louise born?'

'It says Liverpool on the census.'

'That's it, then. You are related to James Thornley.'

Laura beamed, surprisingly proud of being related to a man who a few weeks before was unknown and a stranger. 'Thanks for your help. I'm very grateful because you have saved me loads of time and I have something exciting to tell granny. But she will demand to know what happened to Rose.'

'That's a big ask. Are you going to pour that coffee?'

It was bubbling away filling the flat with a rich aroma. Laura opened her cake tin and cut two slices of the carrot cake she had made the evening before. She brought coffee and cake back to the table where Daniel's forehead creased with concentration as he searched for Louise's birth record. He reached out for the coffee and took a sip. 'Found it. That's good coffee by the way. Yes, bingo. She was born in 1872 to Thomas White.'

'No mention of the mother?'

'We would have to apply for the birth certificate for the mother's name.' Daniel turned towards her, smiling, his pale, almost grey eyes crinkling with mild excitement before sinking his teeth into the cake. He groaned with delight. 'Oh! This is delicious.' Crumbs coated his mouth and a smear of orange icing, lingered on his lips. Laura handed him a paper serviette before she disgraced herself by wiping them away with her own. Her cheeks flamed to see the look of gratified surprise on his face.

'Sorry,' she mumbled. Why had she done that? His geniality was unnerving.

'I suggest we tie the family tree up this morning before we tackle the letters and diaries. Is that okay with you? It shouldn't take too long.' Daniel tactfully avoided her confusion.

After two hours of puzzlement and frustration, Laura offered to make a cheese omelette for a late lunch. A forest of scrunched white paper lay on the floor.

'That would be great,' Daniel said. 'This has been one of the most complicated searches I've done.'

As Laura whisked eggs and grated cheese, Daniel recapped what they had found. 'Louise is on the 1881 Grimsby census with parents Thomas and Harriet White, sisters Minnie and Florence.'

'Could it be a lie? In her letter, Edith says Rose was Louise's mother and we found Thomas and Rose on the 1871 census in Liverpool.' Laura dripped oil into the pan and threw in some chopped mushrooms which began to sizzle.

'We also have Thomas and Rose's marriage record. I'm checking the father of Florence White. Yes, this could be it. The same year as Rose was born.'

'Twins again?'

'No, different months and it gives the father as Alfred White. Same surname, different first name. Strange.'

Laura came and stood at Daniel's shoulder to look at the screen. As her breast grazed his shoulder, he turned to grin.

Laura stepped back, her face flushing. 'I need to check the mushrooms aren't burning.' Hurrying back to the hob, she poured the beaten eggs into the pan and scattered the grated cheese on top. As the omelette began to cook, Laura chopped fresh parsley.

'It's a nuisance that they're such common names. It makes the search twice as long. Could Thomas White and Alfred White be the same person. That doesn't make sense.' Daniel continued his search.

Laura placed the omelette under the grill to brown the cheese before sprinkling the parsley on top.

Daniel sighed with irritation before walking over to Laura who was slicing the omelette onto plates with some salad leaves and a tomato salsa.

'That smells so good,' he said, as she snipped some fresh coriander over the tomatoes.

'Can you take the knives and forks while I carry the plates?'

Daniel took them and rushed to move his laptop out of the way.

'Rose was only sixteen when she and Thomas married, poor kid. I'd love to know the story. That could be why my grandmother thought Louise was sad. She obviously lost her mother at a young age. I wonder what happened. Rose must have died.'

'TB, cholera, childbirth for a woman. They were dangerous times without medical help.'

Laura poured two glasses of white wine as Daniel picked up a fork and placed a slice of omelette in his mouth. 'I can see now that you inherited your culinary genes. I wish I ate like this every day. This is so tasty.'

'That's true, isn't it? James, who cooked for nobility and royalty was what, my six times great grandfather,' she said, counting on her fingers.

'I can't wait to taste tonight's meal.'

She hid a smile as she slid a forkful of omelette into her mouth. 'Do you fancy a swim this afternoon? The tide should be coming in. You did bring your swimming trunks?'

'I did.'

'You can change while I clear the dishes.'

'Sounds like a plan.'

Following a refreshing swim and shower and with a fine evening promised, Laura began to set the table on the decking in her tiny courtyard garden. While she prepared the meal, Daniel began sorting through the papers she had dumped onto the coffee table that morning. He hummed some unrecognisable song as he worked. Laura heard him catch his breath once or twice.

'Have you found something interesting?'

'Maybe. Let's eat first.'

The meal was simple, poached salmon, new potatoes and sugar snap peas, followed by Eton Mess and cheese. Nothing that took long to prepare. Daniel had texted that he never ate meat, but fish and dairy were not a problem.

'Do you always eat this well?' he asked, as he tucked into the mixture of cream, meringue and fresh fruit.

'It's better having someone to cook for.'

'I normally stick something in the microwave. This is amazing.' He put down his spoon on an empty dish. 'Can I beg a second helping?'

She sipped her wine while he ate, enjoying watching him devour her dessert.

After clearing his plate for the second time with a sigh of delight, he said, 'I found a letter to Doris which explains how the notebooks ended up with your aunt.'

'Doris was Louise's daughter. Why don't you read it while I fetch the cheese?'

They both stood. Daniel handed her his dish, the soft skin of his fingers grazing hers before she carried the crockery into the kitchen. Laura placed a Somerset Brie, some mature Cheddar and a wedge of Stilton on the cheeseboard together with a bunch of black grapes.

'Shall I open the Prosecco?' He opened the fridge.

'Absolutely. We must toast your new job.'

Laura carried out the cheese, biscuits and fresh glasses to the table. Daniel popped the cork and poured the bubbly.

'Best of luck. I hope it's everything you dreamt of.' Laura clinked her glass to Daniel's, avoiding his eyes. She was still unsure about jumping into something she was not ready for.

Once seated, he produced the letter he had mentioned earlier. 'It's dated May 1950.

Dear Doris, I was sorting out the house after mother died and I found a box in the attic labelled for Louise. It's just a box of papers, so maybe of no interest but I thought you should have it. Cousin Malcolm.'

'That explains how the papers ended up with her daughter, Edith. What else have you discovered?'

'Apart from the notebooks, there are more letters from James Thornley, the last dated 1853. The remainder begin in 1855 and are sketchy by the look of them. They're from Susanna to her sister-in-law, Essie, one every year until 1870.'

'Perhaps Susanna died in 1870. Does it say where they are from?'

'Brighton to begin with, although she says she moves to the city sometime in the 1860s. Presumably that's back to London. I don't think we can assume she died in 1870. Something else could have changed.'

'But what?'

'Look at what else I found. Daniel handed Laura a yellowing card with copperplate writing, the ink faded from black to brown.

> *Mr and Mrs James Thornley*
> *Invite you the wedding*
> *Of their daughter, Harriet, to Mr Alfred White*
> *And afterwards, to the engagement*
> *Of their daughter, Rose, to Mr Thomas White*
> *On July 15th, 1870, 10.00 a.m.*
> *At St Bride's Church, Liverpool,*
> *Wedding breakfast at the bride's home*
> RSVP Mrs Esther Thornley

'I think this explains so much.'

'Wow! Harriet, the twin sister married Alfred. So, Thomas and Alfred could be brothers. You know, I can't believe two sisters seemingly married two brothers. Was that even legal? Then Harriet and Tom go on to have what we call a blended family these days but very strange for that period unless Rose died, and Alfred too.'

'So, what do we know and what do we need to find out?'

Laura studied the card some more. 'Harriet and Rose both married in 1870. Rose and Alfred disappear, and Harriet and Tom end up in Grimsby with the children. I want to know what happened to Rose and Alfred and why the others moved to Grimsby. How about you?'

'Yes, but there's something else bugging me about Rose and Harriet. I want to show you the first letter from Susanna in the later sequence.' They left the remains of the cheese outside. Back in the house, Daniel picked up the top letter from the pile and read it out.

'*Dear Essie,*

You will be pleased to know that I am settled and have work as a cook in the Little Brighton Hotel. Father's contacts worked wonders here. I am sending you what I can afford. Take care of our family. I beg you for news. Your grateful sister, Susanna.

'It sounds innocuous, doesn't it?'

'Yes,' Laura agreed cautiously. She sensed Daniel was about to expound on his theory.

'Why is she sending money? She's a single woman. Why the words *our family*. Why is she grateful?'

Laura shook her head.

'I should check their birth records again. Maybe there's something I missed.' Daniel looked up at the darkening sky as though running an idea through his mind. 'It's a long shot. Where's my laptop?'

Ten minutes passed. Laura took the time to clear away and put the coffee on. Research excited Daniel, that much was clear.

'Yes!' His shout almost made her drop a cup. She walked over to sit down beside him. 'I don't recognise that site you're on.'

'It's called FamilySearch.org and great for baptismal records. I checked Harriet's and Rose's baptism records because I haven't found Rose's birth record. If they were twins, they would have been baptised on the same day, don't you think?'

Laura nodded again.

'Well, it appears not. They were baptised three months apart, Harriet in London and Rose in Liverpool. Either Harriet or Rose was not the daughter of James and Essie.'

'You think one of them was Susanna's daughter? That's why her notebooks stop in 1854. Did she leave them for her daughter?'

'Let's check the final entry.'

Laura picked up the last notebook and thumbed through to the end. 'It's dated September the tenth 1854.' They both read the entry.

My beloved Papa has left us. God have mercy on his soul, I pray he may at last find peace. I take to my bed within the month. Eternal Father save us.

'When was Rose baptised?'

Daniel checked the date, 'November the fifteenth.'

'That's a very cryptic entry but I think we can read between the lines. Poor Susanna and poor Rose.' Laura drew a diagonal dotted line between Rose and Susanna on Daniel's family tree. They both stared at it. Laura took Daniel's hand and squeezed gently.

'Thank you,' she said. 'You've helped solve the first part of the mystery. Rose and Harriet were cousins not sisters. Susanna gave her daughter to her sister-in-law to bring up. What a saint Esther must have been to add another mouth to the family when she already had so many.' As much as Laura was desperate for a child, the thought of, what was it, eight, nine children with no washing machine, no constant hot water and an outside privy, made her knees tremble.

Chapter Eighteen

Liverpool 1870 - Essie

I should never have agreed to taking Rose. It's not that she's trouble herself, she never has been. Rose has her mother's temperament. Quiet, dutiful, industrious until Susanna's head was turned by a handsome, strutting major, with no thought for her self-respect, for her future, for the shame it brought to her relatives.

I caught a fleeting glimpse of him once, tall, blonde moustaches, ram rod straight in his scarlet jacket and gold collar and cuffs. For a moment, I could see why Susanna was bowled over, until horror overtook me that he was leaving her father's apartments at ten on a Sunday morning, when I knew Papa was out of town. That scoundrel passed me on the stairs, looking quizzical at my horrified expression, then a curling, arrogant smile lit his face. It's the wink that I could never forgive. How dare he? My heart pounded at the disregard for Susanna's reputation.

I wrote to her father, what else could I do? That he did not cut her off disgusted me. What honourable father could countenance such behaviour. 'I would not deny my daughter her one chance of happiness,' he wrote back. 'The Major is a good man, separated from his wife and trying to divorce her. You know how difficult that will be. He has promised to take care of Susanna. If you think I did not have my doubts, I did.'

I refused to let it rest. When next I saw him, I brought it up again.' Think how it reflects on us,' I said. 'My daughters may be shunned.'

'You have too high an opinion of your position in society, dear Essie.'

His remark cut me. 'Our dear Queen…'

'Is a saint in your eyes, I know. If only you could see what your betters get up to behind closed doors. Do you think that all the dukes and earls, and even princes do not have mistresses, and highborn ones at that? Our so-called betters are only better at holding on to their money and reputations.'

I sickened at his words, refusing to listen to any more of his slurs.

Never let it be said that I would speak ill of the dead, but who was right and who was wrong?

It was no surprise to me that Susanna was eventually left with an unwelcome present and without means of taking on her responsibilities. No that was left to me and her brother. For two pins, I would have let Rose go to the foundling hospital, but Jim, still raw from his father's death, persuaded me to offer her a home. It wasn't the child's fault that her mother had become wayward, and her father was killed doing his duty, Jim told me.

'He should have made provision for the child,' I argued.

'True enough,' Jim said. 'But she's my niece and my father's grandchild. He would want us to bring the poor little waif into our care. Almost his dying words to me were, 'Don't let harm come to the child.' We will do our duty, my love.'

All my huffing and puffing could not dissuade him. He might think what was one more child in the house, but a man never sees the extra work, the extra burden. At least we were moving away from wagging tongues.

Rose takes after her father in looks, those dark, soulful eyes and hair like honey. The trouble is I quite like the girl but never dared to show it. I searched for signs of her father's arrogance or her mother's flightiness but never once saw either. Somehow instead, they tainted my own daughter, Hattie. I wondered did nursing both babies contaminate my daughter. Could poison pass through a mother's milk? Jim told me I was being irrational. But the idea took hold in me, and my resentment of Rose and her mother sometimes boils over. All Susanna has to do is write a letter once a year and send a little money. It's me that deals with the everyday battle of wills, not between Rose and me, but Hattie. My daughter could have been so different, if not for Rose, I'm sure.

Hattie was a difficult baby. Colicky and clingy for those first months. She took time to settle, always demanding my attention but that paled into significance after Rose arrived. Somehow, Hattie sensed a rival. From a crotchety baby, she turned into wailing, querulous tyrant. I was already exhausted by constant childbirth and the move to Liverpool. For two pins I would have handed Rose back but by then it was too late.

From a tyrannical baby, Hattie turned into a jealous, spiteful child as Rose's scars can testify. The burn mark from the iron held to her face has never properly healed, even after six months. I never believed Hattie's story that she tripped, though Rose did not dispute it. I caught the warning glance flashing from my daughter's eyes and the look of fear that crossed Rose's face as I smeared butter over her cheek.

Rose could have been such a beauty, but now, the red puckering turns people away with distaste. I tell her to cover her face with a shawl when we walk to the shops. Jim wanted to take his belt to Hattie, but the little minx wept so much that he melted. At least he threatened Hattie with a similar injury if she ever did such a thing again. Hattie is too vain to risk that.

Jim took her to work in the shop after that and I kept Rose here with me, a reversal of how things were. We could not risk questions about Rose's face. She was too popular with the lady customers.

A part of me knows that Hattie attacked Rose because she was jealous and pestered me to let her work in the shop. Hattie hates being with me, hates my attempts to school her in domesticity. She won and it angers me. The truth is she needs a husband to school her because no words of mine have any effect. We keep a constant eye on the girl because of her threats to run away to find excitement. 'Excitement!' I tell her. 'You would soon find yourself in the gutter and don't expect us to take you back.'

Tonight, Jim brought her home in such a temper. 'Find her a husband,' he said. 'She's attracting the wrong kind of clientele, men of dubious character. And now she's begun fluttering her eyelashes at married men with their wives in tow. I'm losing business.' A cardinal sin in both our opinions. 'You've been too lax with her, Essie.'

'Lax! That girl has had more slaps than all my other girls,' I retorted. Perhaps, but I didn't say this out loud, if you had taken notice of any of our daughters instead of filling your head with half-baked ideas and expensive new recipe ideas, most of which don't ever make it onto the shop shelves, you could have helped tame the girl. My grumpiness wasn't helped by the pain in my legs, which seems worse every winter. I sighed. We are both getting older. Jim is almost sixty, a mirror image of his father in his last years, apart from the hazel eyes which he must have inherited from his mother. We are both tired. Hattie leaving home to become someone else's problem would lift a huge weight from my shoulders for sure.

I spent a sleepless hour or two thinking how I could find a man of the right sort. Hattie needs a man, older, wiser, with sufficient income for her not to work, at least not in mixed company. Perhaps a sober, church going man, who would offer guidance and if not taken, chastisement. There's an idea. I'll take her and Rose to church this Sunday and ask around. Maybe I'll find a husband for Rose too, one willing to accept a good housewife and overlook her other imperfections. I'll write to Susanna and demand money for a dowry for the girl. It's only right after all that we've done for her.

Jim liked my idea. 'Do you think in a few years, I can leave the shop to our eldest boy, and you can stop being a perpetual baby-sitter to children and grandchildren?'

'Nothing would please me more. But how would we live? There's never been money to put away.'

'I've a hankering to teach. I am going to look at setting up a school for the culinary arts.'

I was surprised. This was certainly one of his better ideas. 'In Liverpool?' I asked.

'Yes, but any whiff of scandal would put paid to that idea. I have an idea for a class teaching the finer points of domestic arts to young ladies of good character.'

'All the more reason to get Hattie settled. But what if she refuses to marry the man we choose?'

'There is always banishment to my cousin's farm in Wales. I hear he's in need of a companion to his sick wife and some help with milking the cows.'

Hattie milking cows – no way on God's earth would she accept that. Marriage it is then.

Chapter Nineteen

Laura, July 2019

Laura woke to find the sun streaming through the window. What time was it? She picked up her phone. Ten o'clock. Good grief, they would not have much time before her afternoon visit to Peggy. Daniel was already up and about. Laura could hear him stirring in the kitchen.

After a quick shower, she joined him for coffee.

'You are so beautiful.' His attempted rendition of James Blunt's song made her giggle rather than cringe. She knew he wanted her to invite him to her bed, but it was too early, despite what Sophie tried to suggest.

'Come on, I'll make breakfast. Fried, poached or scrambled eggs?'

'I could get used to this. Scrambled would be lovely.'

While Laura fried up mushrooms and tomatoes before beating the eggs, she found herself humming and realised that it was a long time since she had done something so normal and so relaxed. She felt Daniel's arm slip around her shoulder.

'I do miss the smell of fried bacon. It's the one thing I miss about not eating meat.'

'I have some in the fridge.' She gently shrugged off his arm.

'You are a temptress, but that I will decline. If I fall off that particular wagon I may never climb back on.'

It would be so easy to slide into a relationship with Daniel, he was kind, gentle, smart, more attractive than at first sight and she knew he wanted her. However, she held back and asked, 'Do you fancy a pub lunch? I visit my grandmother on Sunday afternoons, but I can leave it until later?'

'I'd like to meet her.'

'I'm not sure you would. She lives in a care home and is disabled; she can't talk.'

'I'm good with old ladies. My granny always said so. I'd like to meet her. Let's have that pub lunch first and then you can drop me off at the station after.'

'If you're sure?' Laura was mentally racking up a list of ticks for Daniel. This one was huge.

After breakfast, the first thing they double checked were the baptismal records for Florence and Minnie. Both had Alfred listed as the father. Daniel checked the death records for Alfred and Rose, nothing appeared.

'That's so strange. I can understand one missing, but both?'

'We're going round in circles. Let's leave it there for the moment and begin on the notebooks.' Daniel replied.

Laura could not refuse. She knew he was itching to get stuck into them. While Daniel worked through the first notebook, Laura picked up the letters from Susanna's father. The first was dated in April 1840. With the recipe for a curry, of all things.

'I didn't realise they had curry powder as far back as 1840.'

'India, Laura. The East India Company would have been importing it.'

'It says that he's working at the London Tavern. I thought London pubs just cooked pie and mash at that time. It sounds a come-down for him.'

'Why don't you Google it? I think you will be surprised.'

The Wikipedia article made her eyes open wide. 'My God, it's an enormous Georgian mansion.' She read on, 'A large dining room with Corinthian columns, numerous public and private meeting rooms and just look at the list of notable meetings. It reads like a who's who of radicalism, the great and the good of British society. A revolution dinner with Tom Paine and Joseph Priestly, Marc Brunel for the inaugural meeting of the Thames Tunnel, Frederick Douglass – Farewell Address to the British People. I've just been reading about him in a novel.' Laura sat back in disbelief.

'Many of those were before your ancestor's time, not Douglass. He was a former slave, American abolitionist, wasn't he?'

'I don't care. It just makes me feel part of something big, something important and I know James wasn't just a cook. Today, he'd be lauded as a celebrity chef.'

'Dickens wrote about the London Tavern in Household Words.'

Laura was on a high. She logged onto her work account which gave her access to the *Household Words* resource. After a few minutes she found the article and began to read. 'Eugh – they had a whole wine cellar for keeping turtles. Can you imagine it?'

'No self-respecting Victorian diner would forego his turtle soup.'

'It sounds disgusting. Are you discovering anything worthwhile?'

'As you said, it's very domestic. Susanna takes a job with a widow. Quite a lowly role as cook in a fairly small household, I should imagine.'

'While her father and brother led exciting lives. Women had it hard, didn't they? All of this history has been lost to the family. I'm proud of James, but that pride didn't permeate down through the generations.'

'Families struggled to get by. The son may not have lived up to his father.'

'Anyway, I have so much to tell Granny. Are you hungry? I'll ring the George and Dragon in Houghton to book a table.'

A couple of hours later, Laura drove down Bury Hill towards Houghton.

'Wow!' That's some view,' Daniel exclaimed looking over the expansive Arun Valley.

'Isn't it lovely? My journey to work is one of the best things about living where I do. In winter, the valley is often flooded, and the train ride is like gliding through a Scottish loch.'

Hanging baskets of pink geraniums brightened the old flint walls of the picture postcard pub.

They found an outside table looking down across the Sussex countryside, a patchwork of green and gold. Almost the only building in sight was a small church spire peeping through the trees.

'That's the South Downs Way over there.' Laura pointed at two heads bobbing through the barley. 'One day, I'd love to walk it.'

'You would like Yorkshire,' Daniel replied. 'The Dales, the Wolds and the Moors. Perhaps I can take you walking there.'

'Perhaps.' Laura preferred a non-committal reply. It was too soon to encourage him.

Daniel chose the fillet of plaice. Laura looked longingly at the roast loin of pork but stuck to a goat's cheese and caramelised red onion tart to make Daniel feel comfortable.

'This is a lovely pub.' He sipped his pint. 'The beer's good too.'

'We are spoilt for choice in Sussex, and they all seem to do amazing food.'

'Tell me about your granny.'

'She's sweet. It's difficult, her not being able to talk, but we get by with the help of an alphabet chart and the IPad. I know she likes music and books. Communication is just so slow; I'd love to know what she's thinking; I have a sneaking suspicion that she has a wicked sense of humour.' Laura proceeded to tell him about the messages from Jake and the photograph he sent. Daniel choked on his drink.

'Your ex sent you that! What a jerk.'

The food arrived. They stopped talking, first to admire, then to tuck in.

'Delicious.' they chimed.

It was no more than a ten-minute drive to the care home where they found Granny sitting in the garden eating a cone of ice cream.

Laura introduced Daniel. 'You'll never guess how much we've found out.'

As she recounted their discoveries, Peggy watched her granddaughter. She seemed more animated, less jittery, happier.

It was only when Laura told her that Rose was Susanna's daughter, that Peggy sat up and took notice.

'You suspected Harriet and Rose were cousins already, didn't you?' Laura looked disappointed.

Peggy nodded. She indicated her alphabet card which Laura passed to her. *Rose – what happened?*

'Did Louise never find out?'

Peggy shook her head.

'That's awful. At least I knew my mother died.'

Her granny began tapping again. *Find out.*

'We will, Granny. I'm not sure how.' Laura's brow creased until Daniel spoke.

'The trouble is none of the letters will tell us. They end when Rose marries. It may require a trip to Liverpool. Even then, we'll be clutching at straws.'

'We could do that. Holidays are coming up and I have no plans. I need to sign some papers for the Grimsby house sale. We could go there on the way. What do you think, Daniel?'

'Great idea. I could show you York too.'

'We have a plan.' Laura smiled at him unaware of the fluttering of alarm in her grandmother's heart. 'We need to be making tracks. Daniel's train leaves in half an hour.'

'Is there a cloakroom I can use?'

Laura explained where the nearest one was. After Daniel walked inside to search for it, Laura asked. 'What do you think, Granny? He's nice, isn't he?'

Peggy nodded before tapping – *Don't rush.*

'I've learnt that lesson.'

Peggy wished she could put voice to her feelings. *Have you, Laura? Be careful my love because I'm not sure he's right for you. I watched hope flare in his eyes and my heart twisted. It's possible you could break his heart or be swept into something you may not be able to escape. I can tell Daniel is smitten but the reservation in your eyes belies your words.*

The last time I gave that warning it did not turn out well.

Chapter Twenty

Peggy

When my daughter brought Charles Gray into our home, I hoped it was a passing phase, mere infatuation. I saw through his rebellious youth act to something darker beneath. That he preyed on women was a given. I suffered his pretend flirtation with me, still an attractive woman approaching my fiftieth year with misgivings. It was the way he acted around any woman. No, there was something worse. He lacked empathy, it was all about himself, his needs, his wants.

Percy loathed him on sight, making his feelings plain, which put Jeanette on the defensive. I tried to be more subtle. Would it have made a difference, had we ignored how we felt? Would she herself have seen him for what he was, had we not tried to tell her? I now doubt that. The next thing we heard was that she had moved into his squat, somewhere in Chelsea and then nothing. Silence. Percy charged up to London to speak to the university, but she had stopped attending lectures. None of her friends seemed to know much or they refused to say. It was in the days before mobile phones. Charles had graduated from his art college, and they refused to give out his parents' address. We had no option but to sit and wait it out. The agony of that year was indescribable.

When she wrote to say that she was married and pregnant, I was almost grateful. Imagine that; grateful that she had thrown away her chance of a worthwhile career. It took days to calm Percy down. She had given no address, probably because she knew what her father's reaction would be. She was after all, his reason for living, his princess, the apple of his eye, those expressions grated on me for their banality, but they described exactly how deeply Percy felt.

While I tried to bring Jeanette up to be an independent, free-thinking woman, Percy also wanted her to succeed, but within his mould. We pressed her to consider teaching as a career. Small wonder she wanted – needed to break free. I did not realise at the time how completely she rejected the path we had imagined for her.

The call which summoned me still gives me nightmares. 'Your daughter has miscarried and wants you.' His voice cooler than it should have been. I travelled to London in a state of panic, but it was anger that sustained me when I saw how they were living. Some grotty artist's studio; paint everywhere, a mattress on the floor, scarcely any food in the cupboard. She, too thin, exhausted from working in a bar so that they could eat. I begged her to come home. When she refused, I turned on him, told him he needed a job; that he would end up killing her with neglect.

He played the struggling artist, as though he were an undiscovered genius and showed me his work trying to win me round. I would happily have broken those paintings over his head. However, Jeanette's eyes beseeched me to co-operate.

As I trawled through the stacked canvases, I agreed that he had talent. He could paint but they lacked passion, were too self-aware, too controlled. Try advertising, I suggested, earn some money to look after Jeanette. I stocked the tiny kitchen with food and prayed for the first time since childhood to the God I had stopped believing in years before.

Laura knows nothing of this, than goodness. After Jeanette's second miscarriage when she almost died, Charles, in an uncharacteristic moment of guilt took my advice. The doctors told him she should not try for another baby for a couple of years and by the time Laura was born five years later, Charles had an established career. In the meantime, I tried to suggest she finish her degree. 'Oh Mum, don't try to foist your ambitions on me,' she told me. She was working in a vegetarian café, part waitress, part cook. 'This suits me. I enjoy cooking, believe it or not.'

It took me years ti understand that Jeanette adored Charles from the moment she met him until the day she died. I have learnt to be thankful for that. For all the heartache Charles caused us as parents, Jeanette was happy in her marriage. She saw his faults and continued to love him.

While Percy never forgave Charles. I tried for the sake of their precious family. But then our beloved daughter died from her final ectopic pregnancy. Charles allowed me to take Laura home for several weeks until he could arrange childcare. I longed to be part of Laura's life and took immediate retirement, a few months earlier than planned; my dreams for the future blown away on the winds of fate.

But Percy must take matters into his own hands. He let all the resentment of those twelve years since his daughter ran off with Charles Gray, fester in his mind. When I found out that he had informed social services that Charles was an unfit parent and applied to the courts for custody, my anger boiled into something uncontrollable which almost destroyed me. They said it was an aneurism which could have struck at any time. But I know what I know. Thirty years of living a lie, was that not penance enough?

By the time I awoke, Laura was gone from our lives. It's only now I can make amends to Jeanette by helping her daughter.

I cannot count the number of letters Percy sent to Charles begging to see Laura, always returned unopened. Percy scoured the Internet looking for her once she left school, but by that time, it seems she had passed to another man's control.

I knew Percy blamed my stroke and its consequences for not having won his case. He looked after me through duty, putting up with a myriad of carers traipsing through his home. Edith offered to take me. With my lump sum and her money, we could have bought a bungalow and he would have been free to follow his retirement dreams. But he had taken out Power of Attorney and refused me access to my money. Without speech or the ability to write, I was at his mercy.

Was I grateful for his sacrifice, did I love him for it? No, because he did it out of guilt and duty rather than love. That duty turned to something darker in the final year before I ended up in here, releasing us both from torture I knew towards the end he was waiting, hoping for me to die, to free him. Did I fear that one night he would allow his growing resentment with the poor hand he had been dealt, to press a pillow over my face? Sometimes. I saw the possibility in his eyes. I watched the battle raging within him and was powerless to prevent the outcome. It was a prison sentence for us both. What was it that prevented him from taking that final step? Was it fear? Was it the God he did believe in? Was it cowardice? Who can tell?

For twenty-five years I have waited to know Laura again. Time now is short. I want her to discover who she is, who she can be, to be braver than I was.

Chapter Twenty-One

Laura

Back at home, Laura began to tidy the flat. Several empty bottles lined the worksurface and the recycling box overflowed with empty cartons. Pleased with how the weekend had gone, she poured the last of a bottle of red into a glass before taking the rubbish outside to the bins.

The coffee table looked empty since Daniel had persuaded her to let him take the notebooks and the letters prior to 1854 back to London with him. 'The progress I can make will be much quicker now that I have time. You still have a week before the end of term,' he had said. Laura thought about it and agreed; she wanted the answers quickly for Peggy's sake.

Laura picked up the remaining letters and flicked through to find there were two sticking together. She gently prized them apart. One was not in the same handwriting as the others. It appeared to be the last in the sequence and smudged with what she took to be teardrops. Laura put down the remaining letters and began to read.

1870
Dear Tom,
Now that you and Rose are married, I feel that I must pass on these papers to you. You may decide to destroy them. I have always kept them secret from my husband and from Rose. Susanna wanted her to have them at some point, but I am not sure that should happen. Rose has a sweet disposition, but who knows? Her mother had the same disposition as a young girl, but she became wayward as she grew older. In my opinion it is best that Rose continues to believe her mother died in childbed.

Laura gasped. She glanced at the signature, Esther. How could she write these things? She reached for her wine and took a gulp before continuing.

I enclose, as promised when you agreed to marry Rose, the money that Susanna sent as a wedding present, together with the bluebird brooch she sent for her sixteenth birthday. Rose thinks the bauble belongs to me, but it is now yours to do with as you wish. I believe it was a present from Rose's father, a soldier who died three weeks after she was born. You may keep it for Rose's daughter or sell it. It probably has little value.

I have done my duty by Rose. We are grateful that you agreed to take her on with her disfigurement and knowing her history. I hope she does not betray your generosity.

Esther Thornley

Laura sat in disbelief. What a cruel letter and what disfigurement was she writing about? 'Oh, Rose,' she whispered, 'I need to find out what happened to you. You can't be written out of history like this. I hope something good happened, I really do.'

Laura ran to the bathroom to throw cold water on her face. After towelling it dry, she crept into the bedroom and lay on the bed until her eyes closed. Her mind on Essie and Rose, wondering what Essie had done. It sounded like she had sold her to Thomas.

'I thought you were a saint, Essie, to bring up Rose along with all your other children,' Laura said to herself. 'But now – what a grade one bitch!'

It was still daylight when Laura woke. The time on her alarm clock read eight thirty. Her throat felt dry and as she reached for the water beside her bed, her glance rested on Edith's jewellery box. Something clicked in her brain. She sat up and emptied the contents on her bed. There it was, the old brooch she had rescued from Buller Street, silver-coloured, set with turquoises and pearls – shaped like a bird. She clasped it in her hand. Had Thomas given it to Louise to wear on her wedding day? Had Doris worn it, Peggy even? She screwed up her eyes trying to remember Peggy's wedding photo, but the image was hazy.

Laura took the brooch into the kitchen and searched for a suitable dish, lined it with some aluminium foil and sprinkled on bicarbonate of soda before pouring on hot water to soak away the grime of decades. After gently rubbing the brooch with kitchen paper, the silver began to gleam. To be certain of its age and value, she needed to take it into a jeweller's.

At lunchtime on Monday, Laura walked into town through the park, dodging the students who liked to congregate there. There was money in Horsham, closer to London, close to Gatwick airport and home to insurance and chemical headquarters, the town centre bristled with wealth. West Street lay beyond the Swan Walk shopping centre. Laura chose a long-established jewellery shop.

The first shop assistant directed her to an older man. He took the brooch and studied it without using a magnifying glass.

'Victorian silver. To be honest, this kind of jewel isn't popular these days. The silver is worth a little. I could give you scrap value.'

'I'm not selling, thank you.' Laura had to resist snatching the brooch back. The man shrugged and turned with a fixed smile to address a nervous young man standing in front of a case of engagement rings.

During the journey home that evening, Laura considered her options. A trek to London on a weekday would require a day's leave; more jewellery shops, why should they prove any different? Petworth was full of antiques shops, but mainly furniture. What about Brighton? It was ages since she had been, and she could try to find out about the Little Brighton hotel mentioned as Susanna's address in the earlier letters. That sounded like a plan.

Laura scoured the letters that evening for more clues. Each one was a plea for news. Had Esther replied? She hoped so as she imagined Susanna living a lonely life, working hard to earn money to send to her child and wrapped in sadness for the family she had lost. Laura's hunger for her own child became more acute. Occasionally snippets of Susanna's life emerged, she wrote of being extra busy because of the Brighton races, of a tram accident and once of the terrible kidnapping and beating of a child. Her pleas for news of Rose in that letter were heartrending – *Please say she is safe. My heart bleeds for the parents of that child, not knowing what had befallen him. Life without your child is a life worse than death.*

The letter was dated 1859 when Rose was five years old. The pain in Susanna's words screamed from the paper. Were those blotches more tear stains? Laura began to well up and a sudden emptiness threatened to crush her. Reaching for her phone she began to call Daniel, then stopped. She FaceTimed her grandmother instead. The response was almost immediate.

'Hi Granny, I needed to see a friendly face.'

A wave and a nod.

Granny do you remember a brooch? I have it here somewhere.' Laura scrambled for her bag and pulled it out of the tissue paper before holding it up to the screen.

Another nod.

'Did you wear it for your wedding?'

More nods.

'It belonged to Susanna. She sent it to Rose for her wedding. A family heirloom, maybe. I'm going to try and find out more in Brighton on Saturday.' Her grandmother began to tap a message. Knowing how long it would take, Laura waited silently. The strength of connection she felt with the old lady surprised her at times.

Something old, something new.

'Something borrowed, something blue,' Laura finished for her. Her grandmother's lips curled in a way Laura recognised as a smile. 'I have several letters from Susanna. I'll bring them on Sunday to read to you. Night night.' She blew a kiss at the screen and closed it down.

A thought struck Laura. Surely Edith and maybe her grandmother had read through all the letters. They knew what was in them, knew about the brooch, knew about Rose and Susanna. Were they playing games with her? The only mystery was what had happened to Rose. But there was something more behind it all. Laura struggled to pin it down. Perhaps a chamomile tea would help her see things more clearly. While the kettle boiled, Laura began to go over everything she had found out since receiving the first letter from the solicitor. Edith could have simply left her the house and the money, but she also left her a puzzle. Was it some kind of test? Was her grandmother in on it? She certainly knew James was a cook although that was the extent of her willingness to be forthcoming.

'Agh!' Laura hit her forehead. They wanted her to find out about the family for herself. Of course! Once Laura had the bit between her teeth, they had hoped she would carry on, but why? What else was she meant to find? Was it just a way of binding her to her grandmother or were there other secrets? If they had wanted to play these games, why wait so long? Why not try to find her earlier? Or had they?

Laura poured the tea and decided to play some soothing music to ease her muddled brain. It felt like flies were buzzing around inside her head. She stroked the brooch, thinking of the generations of women who had worn it on their wedding day. Had her mother worn it? Laura could not remember a photograph of her parents' wedding. It was hardly something that stepmothers cared to display. That was worth asking her father about. She sat for a while, sipping her tea to Katie Melua on her Spotify Playlist, then curled up on the sofa and slept again.

On Saturday she caught a train to Brighton. An hour later she stepped out from the station turning left towards the North Lanes, a familiar path. How many student afternoons had she spent window shopping amongst the alternative delights of vegan shoes or Indian bracelets and cheesecloth shirts. It seemed a lifetime ago now. Heading south, she skirted the Royal Pavilion and entered the touristy narrow streets of the southern Lanes where antique shops abounded. After two false starts, she found a shopkeeper in Meeting House Lane who gave her confidence that he knew his stuff and was not ready to palm her off with an offer to buy the brooch for scrap. The man, in his mid-fifties, could have walked straight out of an episode of *The Great Antique Hunt* programme on TV, tweeds, moustache and the unmistakeable reek of pipe tobacco.

'Nice.' His eyeglass firmly in place, he examined it inch by inch. 'It has a London hallmark, dated 1853.'

Laura breathed slowly out. This proved it came from Susanna.

'Typical early Victorian romantic jewellery.'

'What do you mean?'

'It would be given to a sweetheart, a love token. It was made by a reasonably competent London jeweller. Do you have the box?'

Laura shook her head.

'That's a shame. Do you see these stones?' He pointed to the bird's eyes. Laura nodded. 'Those are blue sapphires, from Ceylon - Sri Lanka now – most probably.' He squinted further into the stones. 'They're flawless. They alone are worth something.'

'I thought they were chips of blue glass.'

He looked up and laughed, showing tobacco-stained teeth. 'No. You would expect the brooch to have been made out of gold, a jewel this good. It screams class, but it's understated, almost as though the purchaser didn't want to attract attention. Do you know where it comes from?'

'I believe it was given to my five times great grandmother by her lover or fiancé, although I doubt she ever had a ring.'

'That would make sense. I suspect she was of lower status. He wanted to give her something she would keep rather than be tempted to sell. Who was the lover?'

'I have no idea, other than that he was a soldier who died in 1854.'

'Do you know which regiment?'

Laura wracked her brains, trying to picture the letter, unsure why it was important. 'No, I'm sure none was mentioned. Why?'

'My other interest apart from jewellery is military badges.' He indicated a range at the back of the tiny shop. 'Do you know what month he died?'

'Sometime in October, I should think.' Laura thought back to what she had read. Rose was born a few weeks after her grandfather died in September and was baptised in mid-November after her father died. 'Late October probably,' she offered.

'Oh, that could make a big difference to the value, but you would need proof – provenance we call it.'

Laura was perplexed. The dealer was enthused.

'Was it possible that he died in the Charge of the Light Brigade on October 25th? There were quite a few regiments involved. This was no ordinary soldier, don't bother with privates, or sergeants, this was someone of standing and private means.'

It all sounded too fanciful for Laura. Other than the hospital at Scutari and the work of Florence Nightingale, her knowledge of the Crimean War was limited to cause and political outcomes.

'I could find a buyer if you can prove who bought it.'

'No, thank you. It will never be for sale.' Laura took the brooch with thanks for the information, neglecting to ask its value and left the shop. The story of Susanna's love life had become fascinating but still a sideline.

The central library was back towards the railway station. Laura stopped on the way for coffee and a sandwich at one of the many cafés in the Lanes. Sitting outside in the warm sunshine gave her time to mull over what she had learnt. What did it matter if Susanna's lover had been in the Charge of the Light Brigade or any other of the battles? The important thing was that he cared enough about Susanna to give her a precious jewel and that she had not sold it when he died, preferring to keep it for her daughter.

Susanna must have faced an impossible choice. To bring up a child alone in those days would have been virtually impossible without funds. Had Susanna known the value of the brooch? She had the choice to sell rather than give Rose away, but how long would it have kept them from starvation? Was the loss of her reputation so grave that she had to disappear? From what Esther had implied in that dreadful letter, it seemed so. There were so many unanswered questions; Laura wondered whether she would ever find all the answers.

The Jubilee library had opened a few years before Laura began as a student in Brighton. A modern glass structure, it was light and airy with a buzzy atmosphere, so different from the enforced peace of her college library. She headed for the reference section to request street directories of the 1850s. She chose one for the year 1859 and carried the slight volume to a table.

Laura thumbed carefully through the thin paper to find the right section. Strange, she sat back in her seat, there was no mention of the Little Brighton Hotel. She took directories for the preceding years, nothing. Googling the Little Brighton Hotel only brought up one in Wallasey. Where was that? Another search and Laura felt the hairs on her neck stand up. It lay across the Mersey from Liverpool, almost within spitting distance and next to New Brighton.

If the hotel existed back in the 1850s, could that mean that Susanna lived close to her daughter but never visited her? It made sense that she would want to be nearby, but there was no indication from any of the letters that she had attempted to make contact or even watched her from a distance. More investigation required and that journey to Liverpool moved up the list.

Chapter Twenty-Two

Peggy 2019

Laura handed me the brooch before picking up the photograph album.

I wore this brooch in a state of denial, my mother wore it in misguided hope. My sister never wore it, neither did my daughter. I want Laura to wear it with joy and pride and love.

She is beginning to find out the truth, there is so much more to learn. I have thought about this over the years. Laura deserves to know her background to avoid making the mistakes I made but she needs to find out for herself. I look at her, the image of Jeanette, knowing that I failed my daughter. I must not fail Laura.

I first thought that Jeanette clung to Charles because she knew that our marriage was a lie. I should have been truthful with her, should have been braver. Truth cleanses, allows you to make the right choices. When we deceive ourselves, we betray those we love. Only Granny Lou lived an honest life, she had a happy marriage. I would love to know what happened to Rose, to Susanna, but more than that I need Laura to know the truth about her parents and about me.

'Yes, I can see the brooch on your wedding dress. I never noticed it last time. Did my mother wear it too?' Laura cut into my thoughts. Just as well, I was becoming maudlin.

I shook my head. She looked puzzled. I reached for my alphabet sheet and tapped - Ask your father.

'I will. I don't understand why she wouldn't wear it.'

I watched as the penny dropped.

'You weren't there, were you?'

I shook my head slowly. She saw the sadness in my eyes, and I reached for her hand, squeezing as hard as my strength allowed. She nodded. I could see the battle in her brain. Despite his neglectful ways, Laura loves her father and craves his approval. Unless he starts being honest with her, he will lose that love. I never wanted that. When I die, which will happen soon enough; I can't bear that Laura has no one to lean on. She will fall back on someone like Daniel, a sweet man, but will he ever be enough?

Had I chosen differently, there may have been aunts, uncles to nurture her.

Chapter Twenty-Three

Peggy

Everyone said we were suited, but Percy and I, we disappointed each other. He fit my plan to marry after six years of teaching. I thought I was marrying someone safe, a good provider, someone who shared my love of music, theatre and books and who regarded me as though I were some kind of Madonna. Why did I ever want to be regarded as such?

I discovered later that he was marrying to avoid his innate loneliness. He longed for children as he had longed for childhood friends. He thought me fit to be the mother of his children.

How did we both get it so wrong? We should have remained friends. But in the late 50s, women did not have 'friends of the opposite sex' without stirring tongues. It became expected that we would marry, and I fell into that expectation until I could not see how to escape. That was until I was handed it on a plate. A stark choice – Love on a Shoestring or Cold Comfort Farm. If only I had realised. If only I had been brave enough.

Percy did not believe in sex before marriage; it was after all before the advent of the pill. He had been in the army, albeit a desk job, and so it was a shock to find him a virgin on our wedding night. I assumed there would have been experiences. Naturally, I had not told him about mine, other than saying I once had a fiancé, short lived as it turned out.

My mother thought the sun shone out of Percy's backside. A proper gentleman she called him. That we would not live close enough for her to babysit appeared not to trouble her at all; another mark against her for all the arguments over the years. She wanted to organise the wedding, but I was having none of that. 'Why won't you let her?' Percy asked. 'It will make her happy.' Percy siding with my mother should have made me run a mile. 'I want a simple wedding,' I told him. I held out for a registry office wedding in Lichfield, although Percy preferred a church. I told him that I would rather spend the money on a honeymoon in Italy, thinking he would jump at the chance. 'But women like to feel special on their wedding day and I would like to see you in a beautiful white dress walking down the aisle to stand at my side,' he replied. I thought he was being romantic, whereas he was displaying his orthodoxy.

Why did I let him win?

There was a point the night before the wedding when I knew I was making a huge mistake, that I should have cut and run, but all that money had been spent, his money. My mother had none. A church in Grimsby, a choir, flowers, two maids of honour and a buffet lunch booked at the Tudor Café for twenty guests clouded my senses. How do you disappoint so many people? All that week I had been living a lie, telling myself that the life Percy was offering was the one I wanted; half of me believed it and I quashed the other half.

I walked down the aisle on the arm of a cousin, Malcolm, whom I barely knew, hating every moment of the pretence and hypocrisy. I had given up believing in God during my university years. When Percy slid the ring onto my finger, I felt trapped. No doubt I smiled; no doubt I laughed, but if someone had taken the trouble to look into my eyes, they would have seen me weeping inside.

I met Percy's mother for the first time at the wedding. He spoke of her without love so much as respect. Disgusted of Tunbridge fitted her perfectly, a thin austere widow with disapproval as her raison d'être. He had talked of breaking free of his childhood, of creating a new life for himself and I believed him. When it came down to it, he reverted to type, her type. The type that said cleanliness is next to godliness, that you persevere no matter what, that you never give in to weakness. 'Til death do us part'.

As for the honeymoon in Brighton, the less said the better. He had booked a guesthouse where the landlady proudly displayed her list of rules. Those included being out of the room between ten and five, one bath a week, which had to be booked a day in advance, no food or drink to be brought in for illicit midnight feasts. A honeymoon of fumbled whispers rather than gay abandon.

I pleaded with him to abandon the trip or to blow caution to the wind and move to a hotel, but he had spent more on the wedding than we could afford. So, we ate fish and chips in the rain on the seafront, rather than forking spaghetti Bolognese in Bologna. We drank warm beer and Babycham in a seedy pub akin to a Graham Greene novel, rather than sipping limoncello on a balmy night in the Piazza Navona in Roma. We listened politely, in saggy deckchairs, to an amateur brass band rather than being transported by opera in Verona. He made love with urgency and no finesse designed to get me with child, whereas I was already with child, though neither of us knew.

In later years he made me visit doctor after doctor to find out why I failed to conceive again. I never told him it was his problem and he never bothered to find out.

We found a way to live together. He squandered what love he was able to give on Jeanette, leaving me the dregs. I tried, how I tried, to make it work during the first few years. I learned to cook and sew, the qualities he realised, rather belatedly to my mind, that he expected in a wife. Order above everything. I remember the horror on his face when he returned from work one day to find paint daubs all over the kitchen, or the time Jeanette and I made chocolate cup cakes with smears of chocolate covering our faces and his mother's tablecloth. What displeased him the most was that we laughed at his displeasure.

When we moved to Sussex, I left my few friends with regret but gracefully, willingly. I threw myself into childcare as long as the evenings were mine to fill with music and books.

The late sixties came as a shock to Percy. I greeted new freedoms with delight, shortening my skirts, sewing kaftans out of colourful psychedelic rayons, growing my hair longer, straighter. I even sported a bandana as I learned the words to Sergeant Pepper. I refused to comply with his ideas of womanhood, just as I refused to abandon my studies because it upset my mother. Quiet rebellion came easily to me. It was the core of my childhood.

We should have divorced then, but I had no income and no legacy from my mother who died around the time of the first moon landings. It was a new, exciting era and I was drowning in boredom until I applied for a job teaching English when Jeanette advanced to secondary school.

Those years were the happiest of my marriage. I was fulfilled by teaching in a way I had forgotten. Rising to head of department in my late forties, Percy and I settled into a routine of getting by together. He began to talk of his retirement plans; a flat on Worthing seafront appealed to him. While I was making a list of all those places I wanted to visit, things

I wanted to see. When we sold our four bedroomed house in the Sussex Downs, I intended to take half the money to buy somewhere with Edith, maybe in Scarborough, unless I could persuade her to sample France. I bought CDs to refresh my French and signed up for an OU course. He never suspected my intentions.

He gave up on sex when I hit the menopause. Sex was for him only of interest in the biblical sense, as a means of procreating children. Poor Percy - if he only knew. He considered I had failed him. Instead of disabusing him, I took a lover, a warm and generous widower, a teacher. Once a week, after inventing yet another staff meeting, we would make our separate ways to his semi-detached in south Arundel and make incredible, guilt-free love. Jeanette was at university by then and I did not care if I was caught. I was sure that she was enjoying herself with her arty student friends just as I was.

And what about Jeanette? At first sight I knew. Those wisps of black hair, blue eyes the colour of cornflowers, that tiny dimple, all of these made my heart sing with joy to know that **he** had given me this perfect gift. After Percy left the maternity hospital, I sobbed with joy and loss. Each day she lived was that same mixture of wonder and pain. My mother knew. I took Jeanette up to Grimsby for my mother's sixty-fifth. She took one look at her beautiful granddaughter and hissed, 'How could you?' I laughed at her before saying, 'It's all down to you, Mam.'

I confessed everything to Edith during one drunken night at the Dolphin while mother babysat. 'Find him, Peggy,' she advised. 'You shouldn't live this lie.' She offered to be a go-between for letters. I realised how much I missed my sister. We had drifted apart after I left for university, but that evening we reconnected. She became my compatriot and then my best friend. The letters never found him. It seems he had dropped off the face of the earth and I knew it was my fault.

That was the night she told me what had happened to my father.

'Mam received his death certificate a month ago.'

'What? It's almost twenty-five years since he left. Where was he?'

'He had a breakdown.'

'You don't say.'

'Yes, this was far worse. He stripped off all his clothes and jumped into the dock. They took him to hospital in Lincoln.'

'Did he stay there all those years?'

'No, they sent him to work on a farm near Mablethorpe.'

'But why didn't he come home after the war?'

'You're not going to believe this. He met a land girl twenty years younger than him and it turns out that he stayed with her on a cottage at the farm. She sent a letter to Mam after he died, with the death certificate so Mam could claim his pension.'

Edith told me my face was a picture before we both burst into uncontrollable laughter. We were so pleased that Dad had experienced some joy in his life. If only Mam had done the same. Maybe she would have been less keen to destroy my chance of happiness.

Had I never married Percy I would have been content. Edith and I would have moved in together at some point, two spinsters and a love child but with sufficient income to travel and enjoy all that we wanted. Jeanette was mine; I could never have given her away. With Edith's help, we would have muddled through.

As retirement approached, that dream of living together took shape.

Chapter Twenty-Four

Laura 2019

Laura spent an evening filling blanks in her family tree. Eager to start with her grandmother, then going backwards in time, she had ignored her mother. Laura added her mother's birth in Lichfield of all places, another place to visit one day. She included her marriage but left her death out of the record. There were too many difficult circumstances bound up with it.

Discovering that her mother was a honeymoon baby, she thought it sweet, imagining her grandparents saving themselves up for the big night. Although it was odd there had been no further children. Much to her amazement, she discovered that her own parents married much earlier than she had imagined. Her mother was nineteen and her father twenty-one. That was crazy. She immediately phoned her father to ask why, leaving a message as the call went to voicemail.

He phoned not long after she had returned home the following evening.

'Hi, Daddy, how are you?'

'What? Fine. Why are you asking about when your mother and I got married?'

'I'm working on the family tree, and I noticed you and Mum married in Scotland in 1978. I was wondering why so young and why Scotland? I know that Peggy wasn't there. Did your parents attend?'

'No. We wanted a quiet affair.'

'But why Scotland?'

Silence.

'Daddy, why Scotland?' Laura was determined to get answers.

'Because it wasn't legal in England to get married without consent at that time.' He was annoyed, his answer clipped. 'Look, drop it, Laura. It's ancient history.'

'No. Please, I want to know. You hardly ever mention Mum's name. I feel as though I know nothing about her. Why did you elope?'

Silence again. She could hear his breath struggling to contain – what? Anger? Sorrow?'

'She was pregnant, okay. There I've said it. She lost him at five months. It was very painful, and I don't want to discuss it anymore. I blame your grandmother for this. She should have left things alone.'

'She can't even talk, Daddy, and she never hinted at this. Stop blaming her. I almost had a brother and you never thought to tell me?' She heard an intake of breath down the phone, then a weary sigh.

'Two. Your mother had difficult pregnancies. It was a miracle you were born.'

'That's so sad. I had no idea. I wish you would talk to me about Mum.'

'It's ancient history, Laura. Forget it, can't you?'

'Not to me. It's my history.' Laura cut the call, recognising her father's closed tone. Why was he unable to talk about things that mattered to her?

She grabbed her keys, deciding to go for a walk.

The summer evening was perfect for a stroll. As Laura reached the seafront and turned left, she forced herself to concentrate on what was around her. Cyclists mingled with joggers and the occasional skateboarder. Walking past the pier, the smell of fish and chips permeated the air. Unusually there was no breeze. The windfarm far off in the distance near Worthing stood out more than usual, the rays of evening sunshine picking out each turbine so that they looked like a row of miniature lollipops.

Laura walked as far as the holiday camp and then turned left towards the park. It was quiet at this time of the evening, although diners were still sitting outside the new Italian café. Laura stopped to order a tuna ciabatta and cappuccino.

The conversation with her father had unsettled her. Her phone began ringing.

'Exciting news, Laura.' Daniel's voice crackled down the phone.

'Where are you? You're breaking up.'

'Sorry, I'm walking down the road.'

A siren blared into Laura's ear. 'What news?'

'It seems Susanna met a soldier in Portsmouth. Government House hosted a large party for the great and the good in August 1850 and help was required in the kitchen. Her father invited her to assist.'

'Why would a soldier have been interested in her? She was considered an old maid by then. I bet he took advantage of her.'

'You sound extra judgemental. Is anything wrong?'

'Sorry, Daniel. I'm not long off the phone to my father. We had a bit of an argument.'

'Do you want to talk about it?'

'No, I really don't. Did she name the soldier?'

'She calls him x. It's almost as though the entries were written in code. There are references but nothing explicit, although you can feel her excitement. I'll send you the transcript.'

'Great, I look forward to reading it. This soldier was probably killed in the Crimean War.'

'Possibly, that would work, assuming he was killed.'

'Maybe the Charge of the Light Brigade even.'

'How do you work that out?'

'I found a letter, saying he'd died three weeks after Rose was born.'

Laura went on to tell him the rest of her discoveries.

'You've been busy. Well done.' Was that a slight tone of patronisation in his voice? She hoped not.

Another siren and then loud conversation from passers-by interrupted him.

'Sorry, Daniel. You're breaking up. I have to go.' Her food and coffee arrived. While she ate, her phone pinged. It was the transcript. She decided to read it later. The food was too good not to savour.

Laura walked back the same way. The sky on the horizon was turning a shade of dusky pink as the sun began to set over the trees in West Park. Walking was the best cure for solving problems, she decided, feeling almost serene until she caught sight of her father's unmistakable red Jaguar outside her flat.

She stood motionless for a few seconds, vaguely surprised that he even knew the address. The car door opened, and he stepped out, looking towards her, trim in a lightweight cream linen suit, grey hair slightly thinning, handsome for a man in his early sixties.

'Laura,' he called.

She began to walk towards him, her mouth dry as she approached.

He kissed her lightly on the cheek which she accepted without comment and unlocked the door to her flat before ushering him in.

'Would you like a coffee? I don't have any beer.'

'I like what you've done here,' he said looking around. 'You have a flair for colour and texture.'

Pleased by the rare compliment, Laura turned away to put the kettle on, waiting for him to get to the point of his visit.

'I thought it was time we talked. Laura, I know that I've been a fairly useless father, but I want to change.'

'Really!' She slammed two coffee mugs onto the worksurface. 'Milk?'

'Please. Mind if I sit?'

'Help yourself.' Spooning instant Nescafé into the cups, she took a carton of milk out of the fridge.

'Did you know when your mother died that you went to live with Peggy for several weeks?'

Involuntarily, she spun around and said, 'What? I thought that's when she had her stroke.'

'No, that came later.' His voice was gentle, a tone she never associated with him. 'Come and sit down. I'll tell you everything. I thought it best for you not to dwell on things, but I can see now that I was wrong.'

She left the coffee and sat opposite on the sofa, leaning forward, her hands clasped tightly, eyes fixed on his.

'You were distraught, of course, when your mother died. I was too, believe it or not. I hadn't been a very good husband to begin with, I admit that. It was Peggy who put me on the right path. She made me get a job. I found I was rather good at it and, after you were born, I set up my own business, working all hours. I never cheated on Jeanette. All those meetings, trips away it was all for you and your mum.'

Laura nodded, suddenly desperate to believe him.

'I didn't want Jeanette to have another child, I knew it was dangerous and offered to have the snip. She was on the pill and refused. I had no idea that she'd come off it. She hated being an only child herself and wanted you to have a brother or sister. We argued about that before she died.'

'Was it my fault?' Guilt made Laura rock backwards on the seat.

'No, no. Of course not. If anything, it was Percy's fault.'

'Why?'

'He spent her childhood telling her that only children missed out. She often overheard him telling Peggy that as a mother she had failed by only producing one child.'

'That's awful.' Laura's heart reached out to Peggy.

'Jeanette and her father had a complicated relationship. He projected all his hopes and dreams onto her, smothering her to excess. As a teenager she tried to rebel. I was part of that rebellion and happy to go along with it. I hated the man. But all the time she was begging for his approval.'

'A bit like me then.'

He looked at her surprised. 'What do you mean?'

She shrugged. 'You ignored me but …'

'I went too far the other way. Yes.' He threw his hands in the air. 'I admit it. You think me self-centred, unfeeling.'

Laura nodded. 'Are you surprised?'

'That's what my wife tells me.' Her father paused before taking a deep breath. 'Melissa has given me an ultimatum. I change or she leaves.' He ran his hand through his hair and puffed out some air. 'I find that I love her.' His voice caught in his throat. After a pause to gain some equilibrium, he carried on. 'I'm going to change, Laura. The business is up for sale and I'm retiring to spend more time with my family. All of you.'

'Wow! I hardly know what to say.' Laura sat back. 'How can you be sure you won't be bored to tears?'

'I'll keep my hand in. Take some consultancy work, but I'll work from home. Flying here, there and everywhere has lost its appeal.'

'Okay.' Laura's tone displayed a measure of scepticism.

'You don't believe me? How can I prove it? I'm turning over a new leaf and that means I'll tell you whatever you need to know.'

Laura was quick to take him at his word. 'Why did you cut Peggy out of our lives? She's amazing.'

Her father told her about the social services letter, about his phone call to Peggy and how she claimed to have known nothing about it.

'I decided to take you home on the evening Peggy had her stroke. Percy told me she was unlikely to survive. Doubly heartbroken and screaming for Mummy and Mou-Mou, it tore me up to listen to your cries. I had no idea how to console my baby girl.'

'Mou, Mou? – that's the name of my doll, the one I slept with every night until you sent me to that awful school.'

'Mou Mou was your name for Peggy. I bought you the doll after I took you home. It was the only way of pacifying you.'

Laura sat open-mouthed, turning the information around in her brain. 'Oh God, it's like Rain Man.'

'What is?'

'That film with Dustin Hoffman playing an autistic guy. Charlie, his brother, discovers at the end that he had early memories of his brother, Raymond, before he was removed to an institution.'

'You don't remember Peggy?'

'No, but there's this huge connection between us and I feel she's always trying to look after me.'

'I thought she was helpless, scarcely more than a vegetable.'

'You have no idea.' Laura's voice grew cold. 'You made no effort to find out. She loves music and books. We FaceTime and she protected me from Jake, more than you ever did.'

His face showed bemusement. 'What did Jake do?'

Laura told him and he roared with laughter, not the reaction she expected. It broke the shutter which she had erected between them, and she found herself joining in.

'I'll get the coffee. It's getting late. Why don't you stay in the spare room tonight?'

'I'd like that. Thank you. Do you think Peggy will agree to see me? I want to thank her for what she did.'

Laura considered it. 'I'll take a few hours off in the morning. If you give me a lift to college tomorrow, we can go via the home as long as we get there after ten. You can apologise to her then.'

He raised his eyebrows. 'Apologise?'

'For the many years you kept us apart. Can you imagine how that felt for her?'

Chapter Twenty-Five

Laura's father's meeting with Peggy had been fascinating to watch. They observed each other warily at first until her father, prompted by Laura, grasped Peggy's left hand and shook it fleetingly. After a minute or two of inconsequential and one-sided small talk, Charles finally opened up about how he had felt when Jeanette died. Peggy fixed her eyes on him, darting occasional glances at Laura, a slight smile pulling up her lips. When her father did eventually apologise for keeping Laura from Peggy, her grandmother sighed, two decade's worth of tension released in a single breath.

'I want Laura to come to Italy next week, a week to learn how to be father and daughter all over again. I've neglected her for too long.'

Laura was surprised and pleased that he had admitted it, but Peggy reached for her alphabet strip.

Why?

'Why what? Why do I want her to come?' Her father had asked.

Peggy shook her head.

'Why did I neglect her?' It was her father's turn to glance at Laura.

Peggy nodded her head vigorously and reached for his hand.

He looked uncertain. Laura waited for an answer. His shoulders took an unaccustomed slump. If Laura had been asked to describe her father's character, she would have said brash; confident verging on cool calculation, charming but that only skin deep. She thought him incapable of real feeling. Watching him with her granny, that one single question appeared to dispel that view. It took the following week in Tuscany to answer it.

***

Melissa looked genuinely pleased to see Laura when she arrived by hire care at the isolated mill.

'I'm so pleased you made it.' They stood in the dark kitchen while Melissa brewed up coffee. Despite the windows to the front and back, the thick walls closed in. The only sound being the water trickling outside the mill along a drying riverbed.

'This place is way off the beaten track. Why on earth did you choose it?' Laura waved her phone around in a fruitless attempt to find a signal.

'Partly that.' Melissa pointed at Laura's phone. 'The Wi-Fi is almost non-existent.'

'Did he know?' Laura could never imagine her father agreeing to that.

'Not at the time.'

Laura cocked her head to one side. 'You took a risk.'

'I thought it necessary.'

'He told me that you threatened to leave him.'

'Yes, I did. I love Charles, but he's his own worst enemy. These last few years, I need an appointment to spend any time together. The company has consumed him. He needs to slow down and learn what's important. Three months ago, he had a health scare. I told him that no one puts hotshot advertising executive on a tombstone, it needs to say husband and loving father, and he's not.'

'Not to Christopher?'

'Not to any of his children, especially you and Christopher. The others won't see him or return his calls. They have new stepfathers and gave up on Charles several years ago. But you and Chris need a father, don't you?'

'Tell me about the health scare.' Laura sat at the wide table, her legs a little wobbly. Staring at the fruit bowl with its abundance of fat peaches, nectarines and grapes, she reached out to take a grape to moisten her mouth, her hand shaking.

'It was a panic attack, nothing more. At the time, we thought it could be his heart. It scared him. It scared me for that matter.'

Laura breathed out slowly. 'I thought I was past caring about Dad ignoring me, but I'm not. If there's any hope of repairing our relationship, I will grab it. That's why I came.'

Melissa poured the coffee and sat next to Laura, squeezing her shoulder. 'There's nothing more important than family. I want Chris to have a loving big sister and I want to be your friend as well as your stepmother.'

Laura turned to face Melissa, her eyes glistening. 'I think I might enjoy that.'

'Now that you've got rid of that awful Jake, we're going to have a great week. I want you to spend time with your dad, go for walks, talk everything through, get to know each other.'

The breakthrough with her father came on a walk in the mountains while Melissa and Christopher played hide and seek around the stone ruins on a deserted hilltop. As Laura and Charles ambled along a wide gravelled path overlooking meadows and distant villages across a deep valley, Laura asked her father if he had worked out the answer to Peggy's question.

'It's something I've thought hard about ever since. I suppose there are a mixture of reasons but no excuses. I could talk about my own childhood. My father wasn't a warm character, and my mother was too under his thumb to protest.'

'I remember them a little. We only visited once a year.'

'It's all I could handle. But that should have made me more determined to be a better father to you. When your mother died, I had that opportunity, but I handed it over to others. Mistakenly, I thought women, strangers it turned out, were best suited to that role and you were so needy.'

'Was I?' Laura had little recollection.

'Every night when I came home and every weekend, you turned on the tears and refused to let me out of your sight.'

'I could have been only three or four years old!'

'I know, but I felt incapable, resentful. I made excuses not to be there. When I married, Helena, I thought she would take over, be a mother to you, but you hated her and made your feelings crystal clear. Do you remember how naughty you were, running away, throwing things, biting her?'

Laura stopped mid-step and turned to face him. She shook her head. 'I have no memory of that at all. Is that why you sent me away to school at seven?'

'Helena, thought you might harm the baby.'

'Do you mind if we sit on that log? I feel sick.' This news came as a revelation. After a while, she said. 'I didn't know I had it in me to rebel.'

He laughed. 'Oh yes, it took two years for the nuns to quell that side of you. Helena dreaded the end of every term and in the end, she couldn't take it anymore.'

'So, I broke up your second marriage?'

'To be honest, it wasn't working. I was away for days and there were affairs. I married her to be a mother to you, but I found that I didn't like her very much.'

'I was right there. You should have trusted my instincts. Did you marry number three for the same reason?'

'Good God, no. By that time, you had become a timid little thing, biddable but with no character, nothing to say. I scarcely noticed you.'

'Who was to blame for that?'

He shook his head, bewildered. 'I just thought you had grown out of your anger. Do you remember I sent you to summer camp one year to toughen you up, but you returned even more withdrawn?'

Laura barked with derision. 'Listen to yourself! You sent me to a convent, even though we're not Catholic. Did you not question why I seemed so unhappy there?'

'Are you telling me they abused you?' His eyebrows knitted together.

'Not abuse, rather a slow pernicious clamping down of my spirit. The nuns undermined my self-confidence at every point. I already felt unloved, but learnt there how unworthy I was of love to the point I found it difficult to make friends.' Laura took a deep breath to calm herself. 'Next you complain that I'm not tough enough. What did you expect?' She stood facing him, her hands balled into fists.

He stood too and put his arms around her stiff body. 'I'm sorry. I had no idea. Helena recommended the school. One of her friends had been there.'

'Don't blame her. It was your job to find out.' Laura moved out of his embrace.

'I've made every mistake in the book, haven't I? My father sent me away at six to toughen me up. I hated it. I thought girls' schools may be less harsh for some reason.' He sighed. 'I should have asked more than I did. I rang the school to check how you were settling in after the first week. They told me it was best to let you find your feet.'

Laura snorted. 'Hmm. You're not the only parent they fooled. I remember three of the older girls running away. They lasted three days on the run, before they were brought back by the police. I think that was the point when I gave up hope of being rescued and served my time. I thought of Jake as my rescuer when I met him.'

'But you were at university by then.'

'Yes. It's strange, but it's taken me years to break out of the walls I had built around myself. I mistakenly thought that he kept me safe.' Laura stepped aside and swung her arms out, twirling around in the bright sunshine. 'I'm learning to be free. Free of that awful school, free of Jake, and maybe free of my anger with you.' She pointed at her father; a question mark remained.

He flailed, searching for an answer. Laura's voice flattened, 'I don't get what Melissa sees in you. She's way too nice for you.'

'You're right. I don't deserve her, or you, but I promise things will be different. I know I've been a disastrous husband and parent.'

'You have.' Laura scowled. 'I want to give you another chance, though. What does that say about me? I'm too soft, too trusting? Well, I've turned over a new leaf too. I'm learning to say what I want.' She kicked the gravel with her left foot, dust swirled around her white trainers.

'Let's make a fresh start, Laura. Please.'

She looked up at him. He was still handsome, but the coldness in his eyes had lessened. Genuine concern for her was not there yet, but she saw glimmers of it. 'Tell me, why did you saddle me with stepmother two, the clotheshorse, throughout my teenage years?'

'Julia? Sheer eye candy.' He shrugged. 'She looked good on my arm at business events, and she was great in the sack.'

Laura snorted with laughter. 'Well, I suppose your taste in women is as bad as my taste in men. That's something we share.'

He joined in laughing. 'I'm liking your honesty. Although, I have to say that both your mother and Melissa rather disprove your theory.'

No one could say that her father did not try after that. They swam in the sparkling cold water beneath the weir near the mill, played ball games with Christopher in the grass beside the river, ate pizza, the most delicious Tuscan sausages and slivers of pecorino cheese. They drank bottles of rich red Chianti and, once Christopher was in bed, talked long into the night on the terrace lit by coloured solar lamps entwined in the orange trumpet vines.

One night a violent thunderstorm hit as Laura prepared for bed on the third floor of the mill. The thunder echoed around the mountains and through the forests. The lights went out plunging the mill into darkness. She stood outside the bathroom feeling disorientated when she felt a small hand creep into hers.

'Hi, Chris. Did the storm wake you?'

'I'm frightened, Laura. Can I sleep with you?'

'Of course, you can. Hold my hand, watch the step.' She guided him into her bedroom and pushed him towards the large comfortable bed. He clung to her as the thunder clapped around the mill and streaks of lightning flashed across the bare window. She felt his warm slim limbs cuddling into her and her heart began to heal. Tears slid down her face as she stroked his back. 'My little brother, Christopher,' she whispered to herself, as his snuffles turned into sleep.

On the final day of her stay, her father set up an easel to paint the mill and Laura began to understand the change that was taking place. She sat idly with her feet trailing in the water, watching the breeze play amongst the leaves of the trees opposite. A jay shrieked from a far hillside. Looking down, she noticed tiny fish gathering around her feet amidst the patchwork of white rocks scattered along the riverbed. If they were nibbling, she could not feel it. Christopher came down to sit beside her. She pointed out the fish and giggling, he dipped his toes into the water too. She put her arm around his shoulders, and he lay with his head resting on her arm. Melissa walked over to sit in a deck chair a few feet away. No need for words.

Chapter Twenty-Six

Laura dozed in the car while Daniel drove towards Liverpool from York. After picking up Daniel in Guildford on the way north towards Grimsby, he had commented not only about her tan but also that she seemed less uptight. That much was true. Italy had done her good, laid some demons.

Netta still had a set of keys for the house and had switched on the fridge for them, stocking it with milk and wine. A fridge magnet secured an invitation to join her family for supper.

'I'm pleased about that,' Daniel scanned the empty kitchen. 'Where were you thinking of sitting?'

'I have a couple of camping chairs in the boot.' Laura tossed the keys to Daniel. 'I'll pour us a wine if I can find glasses. I may have given them all to a charity shop.'

Opening a cupboard, she found two, along with two plates, bowls and mugs. Thoughtful Netta again. Had she also made beds? If not, Laura had told Daniel to bring a sleeping bag. There were beds enough for him to choose from.

They were already merry when they knocked on Netta's door after polishing off the wine.

'This is a celebration.' Sean said, popping a bottle of cheap champagne as they walked into the kitchen/diner. 'It looks like we will be the proud owners of next door by the end of the month thanks to you, Laura.'

'You've done me a favour, Sean. I'm happy for you. Meet Daniel, everyone.'

Three hours and free flowing drinks later, Daniel helped Laura over the wall between the properties and they fell back into the house.

'Loads of beds,' Laura pointed up the stairs with her head swimming.

Laura woke, fully dressed, on top of a counterpane of a double bed in the middle bedroom. Daniel lay beside her, also fully dressed. She had no recollection of climbing the stairs, nor choosing which room to sleep in. Her mouth felt sour. Slipping her feet over the edge of the bed, she fiddled with her jean's pocket to find her phone, knowing she had an appointment with the lawyer at eleven o'clock. Seven, plenty of time for a shower and coffee. Laura glanced at Daniel and smiled. It had been a great evening. Maybe she was ready to take their friendship to another level.

'We're coming into Liverpool. Can you keep an eye on the satnav while I keep my eyes on the traffic?'

'Gosh, I was sound asleep.' Laura rubbed her eyes and looked around at the unfamiliar scene, built up, industrial, busy, so different from the remnants of her dream.

'You were mumbling about chianti and pecorino. Do you fancy Italian tonight?'

'Mmm yes, sounds good. I must have been dreaming about Tuscany. I hope Melissa is keeping Dad to his promises.'

'Families, eh! Although mine sounds normal compared with yours. Parents still together, a sister I get on with.'

The city apartment hotel Laura had booked was in a modern block not far from the docks. Once they had manoeuvred into the underground car park and picked up their keys, they took the lift to their room.

'This is fine. In fact, I'm impressed.' Laura walked through the large kitchen diner to the lounge area. 'We even have a balcony. Mind you it looks out onto the street, hardly Greek island stuff.'

'The bedroom's okay too. Do you want to try the bed?' Daniel winked.

Since that first night in Grimsby, they had slipped into a comfortable sexual relationship. No strings, they both agreed. Daniel was a kind and considerate lover. Laura decided not to think of the future and see how their friendship progressed.

'Later, what I need now is to stretch my legs.' Laura unpacked some basics she had bought after an overnight stay in York. 'We could do with some milk. It was too warm to bring what we had.'

'Spoilsport.' He put his arms around her and kissed her. 'Let's go then. I confess I am itching to see what becoming a Unesco World Heritage City has done for Liverpool. The last time I came here as a child it was fairly rundown.'

'This is seriously impressive,' he said a few minutes later, as they walked along the regenerated wharves. 'I had no idea of the scale, and Albert Dock is only one of several.'

'Do you know, I had this impression of northern England being all grime and industrial buildings, but York and Liverpool just go to show that's not true.'

'Post-industrial heritage centres are the new industry – tourism, along with shopping. Though it glosses over the poverty beneath the surface. Bars and art galleries in old warehouses don't make up for what we have lost in terms of our manufacturing tradition. Sometimes I wonder if all this gentrification will become its own white elephant.'

'Time will tell, I suppose.' Laura stopped at a bronze sculpture of a cart horse and read the inscription. She looked around at the wide-open spaces of what had once been a busy dockland, imagining the carters and thousands of horses moving goods arriving from all over the world. All gone; the dirt, the smells, the bustle, the din of industry making way for joggers and wine bars.

They walked to the river and watched the colourful ferry ply its way across the Mersey. Laura's family had lived here, but she felt no connection. There had been a tacit agreement not to discuss the research on this trip until they reached Liverpool. Now they were here. It was time to find out what had happened to Rose. Laura crossed her fingers. Had Susanna stared over this river from the other side, a lost soul mourning the daughter she could not visit?

Returning to the apartment hotel, they asked at reception for Italian restaurant recommendations and were directed to Villa Romana, around ten minutes walk.

Walking in, it was as far away from a modern high street Italian as could be. Red and white checked tablecloths, dark walls and a low ceiling with a traditional trattoria appeal. The buzz of early evening diners was always a good sign, unless it meant they were fully booked. Laura worried that they would be turned away, but a smiling waiter directed them to a small corner table and handed each of them an extensive menu.

After they had ordered, Laura asked, 'Should we work on a plan of research for tomorrow?' Daniel shrugged in a non-committal manner which surprised Laura. She ploughed on. 'How far have you got with the notebooks?'

'Almost finished. I've annotated them for you. I found some nuggets for my research amongst them. Susanna worked as a cook for a Mrs Billington, a widow with an interesting network of friends.'

'How so?'

'She was a friend of certain individuals seeking electoral reform. There's no indication that Susanna was aware of her interest, but the later notebooks contain dinner menus for evening parties together with lists of some of the attendees and dates. Some of the connections I was surprised by. It will take time to unpick, but I can certainly write a paper on the subject.'

'I'm pleased about that. I was worried you were giving up your time unnecessarily.'

He cocked his head. 'You don't think I have an ulterior motive? In any case you're paying for this jaunt. I feel like a kept man.'

Laura had insisted on paying. 'Believe me, I intend to get my money's worth out of these research skills of yours.'

The waiter arrived at that moment with a bottle of red wine which he opened with a flourish and offered Daniel a taste. He took a sip and smiled his approval.

As the waiter poured the wine into both glasses, Laura asked Daniel, 'Did you find a name for Susanna's lover? I read her description of their Portsmouth meeting that you sent before I went to Italy. Between the lines, you can imagine how smitten she was.'

'No, she never names him. You would need to find which regiments were stationed in Portsmouth when they met, track down where they were in the Crimean War and find casualty lists. It will take some work.'

Laura thought about it and decided not to bother at this stage. 'He's not my priority. All he did was donate to our gene pool. If he had lived, I doubt he would have married her. Rose is the one I am interested in, Susanna to a lesser degree. How can we use tomorrow to find Rose?'

'Let's not discuss that tonight.'

Really! Laura frowned, frustrated with his reticence but then the waiter arrived with Laura's dish of lamb cutlets marinated in garlic, mint and lemon. It looked and smelled delicious. She was pleased she had chosen to ignore Daniel's sensibilities this time, although his dish of penne with smoked salmon in a dill sauce looked enticing. They tucked in and grinned, pleased they had taken the hotel's recommendation.

Laura left the hotel with Daniel in a buoyant mood the following morning. They walked at a brisk pace through surprisingly empty streets towards the library. As they progressed towards the library knots began to form in Laura's stomach. The search could end here, either in fruitless disappointment or in added excitement. A sudden doubt hit her; what if they found something awful had happened to Rose? Maybe even murder? How would she tell her grandmother?

The library was a magnificent pilastered Victorian building, jaw-dropping in size and a grandiose statement on the wealth and power of Liverpool in the nineteenth century. Laura stood in admiration before Daniel took her hand and led her through the main doors.

'It was bomb damaged in the war but had a major refurbishment a few years ago. Oh wow!'

The grand Victorian outside did not prepare either of them for the stunning glass roof cascading light onto an open central staircase.

'It's magnificent. I could happily work here,' Laura whispered as they searched for directions to the Archives and Family History Section on the third floor.

'Oh, Daniel. It says we need an appointment. Have we come all this way for nothing?' Laura's heart sank at the thought of a wasted journey.

'Find a seat, we have an appointment. I did some research while you were away. I know exactly what we want.'

A broad smile lit his face which perplexed Laura. Was this why he had been so reticent the evening before? They walked towards a free table and sat down. Daniel opened his laptop bag and shuffled inside while Laura watched with a mixture of impatience and curiosity.

'I found this article in the British Newspaper Archive.' He handed Laura a print-out which she took with trembling hands.

Custody of a female child was granted today to Mr Thos White of Milton Street following his wife's disreputable behaviour. Sir Benjamin Potts pronounced that he had no option but to dismiss her counter claim. July 1878. Liverpool Daily Post.

Laura's heart hammered in her chest. 'It doesn't mention Rose by name, but this could be it, couldn't it? The date seems right. Oh Daniel, how could you keep this secret?' Her voice rose amidst glaring looks from nearby users.

He grinned and whispered, 'Let's cross reference with the magistrate's records. I have pre-warned them.'

While they were waiting for the documents to be brought to them by a member of staff, Laura thought she would do a search for the New Brighton Races mentioned in one of Susanna's letters and asked Daniel to log on to the newspaper database.

'That's odd,' she said to Daniel a few minutes later.

'What is?'

'I can't find any mention of a racetrack near New Brighton.'

'The nearest one is Aintree and that's on this side of the river.'

'People wouldn't stay in New Brighton for racing at Aintree, then?'

'I doubt it. Do you have the letters with you?'

'Yes, they're in my backpack.' Laura took them out. 'It definitely says Brighton Races.'

'Well, it can't have been New Brighton. It must be the one in Sussex.'

'I'll check the letters for the child kidnapping she mentioned in 1859 in Brighton.' Laura rummaged through the letters before pulling one out. 'Here it is - a butcher's child was taken and horribly tortured.' That's bound to have been reported.'

Every search term she tried failed to bring up any results for the place or the date. Daniel tried and failed too. They were both shaking their heads when the assize documents arrived. While Laura searched the court minute book to find it contained no further details beyond names, date, and judgement. Daniel scanned the loose papers.

'Read this one first, it's the plea from Thomas White. Here are your answers.'

Laura took it, eager to read what her ancestor had stated.

My wife, Rose White, was found in the home of my brother engaging in an illegal act on Sunday last. She is no longer fit to be a mother to my child.

So short, so damning, totally without emotion; yet very few facts. What did he really feel? Laura could get little sense of the man. Was he hurt or angry, surely both? She turned to the second document and her heart stopped. This was Rose, was it in her own handwriting?

If it please your worship, I am a good mother. I love my child and know that she misses me. If my husband will not take me back, let me keep my daughter, I pray you. I will bring up my child to be honest and God fearing, so help me God. I have the offer of a home with my cousin while I work in his shop. My child will want for nothing.

It was a silly argument that made me run from my husband's house. My husband kept a secret from me which I had the right to know. I left the house and ran to the woman I thought of as my sister. Being away from home on an errand, her husband, my brother-in-law, invited me in to wait for her. After hearing of the argument, he began to comfort me. My cousin returned home a few minutes later. I beg you to believe me that an illegal act did not occur. My husband has refused to listen to my explanation and denied me my child.

'Wow!'

'Patriarchy, eh!' Daniel said.

'It sounds like Alfred made a pass, welcome or unwelcome do you think?'

'Who knows?'

'And yet, Harriet ran off with Thomas and all the children. Maybe once Thomas won custody of Louise, Alfred threw Harriet out for snitching on Rose.'

'I'll see if Alfred applied for custody of his children.' Daniel grabbed the laptop and began to search the newspapers.

Laura reread the plea. 'The secret she mentions - perhaps she found out Susanna was alive. Do you think she found the letters?'

'Maybe.'

Laura picked up the letters to look through them again, searching for any clue she had missed.

Daniel interrupted her reading. 'Found it. *An arrest warrant for Mrs Harriet White formerly of Addison Street, has been granted for the abduction of her children. She may be living with, Mr Thos White, her brother-in-law.*'

'Whoa! That changes everything. How did they get away with it?'

'Fairly easy I should think, with no telephones and no internet. Even if a telegram had been sent to every force in the country, it wouldn't be difficult to hide in a crowd, especially a melting pot like Grimsby. People were pouring in from everywhere.'

'Poor Rose and Alfred too. They both lost their children. It makes me think that Harriet was a snake in the grass.' Laura took out her phone to take images of the pleas and was struck again by the emotion in Rose's statement. It shone through each line in contrast with that of her husband. 'Do you think Harriet and Thomas planned it and Alfred was also a victim? Perhaps Harriet made the story up about catching them in an illegal act.'

'You can't make suppositions like that.'

'You can't as an academic, but I can.'

'Petulance doesn't change things, Laura.'

She huffed. 'What's the next step then, Doctor Steventon?' She could not help the sarcasm in her voice but then regretted it. It was not his fault. Something had unsettled her.

'I'm not sure. We didn't find Alfred or Rose in any other records for the 1870s. We should check later records, I suppose.'

They spent a fruitless hour on Ancestry.co.uk checking the British census and death records. Midday came and went, with Laura's stomach beginning to grumble loudly. I'll return these court records, then we should grab something to eat.'

The assistant at the desk signed the documents in and then asked if Laura had found what she was looking for.

'Partly. I'm trying to find out what happened to a distant grandmother. After this court case she disappears completely.'

'From Liverpool?'

'Yes, but then from anywhere in the UK.'

'That's not unusual.'

'Oh?' Laura frowned, a question in her eyes.

'When people wanted to disappear from Liverpool, they got on a boat, mostly to America. She could have worked her passage as a servant, if she couldn't afford to travel as a passenger.'

'I can't believe we didn't think of that! I suppose I thought that lone women didn't do that kind of thing in Victorian times.'

'You'd be surprised?' The assistant's broad Liverpool accent emphasised the last syllable and a childhood image of Cilla Black flitted through Laura's mind as she returned to Daniel.

'Why are you grinning?'

'Because we missed an obvious clue. Let's have something to eat and I'll tell you.'

'You and your stomach. I'm amazed you are as slim as you are.'

'I enjoy my food, Mr Beanpole. Shall we see if there's a tapas bar somewhere. Then I really want to fit in a visit to the Catholic cathedral. I've seen pictures and it looks amazing.' Laura's mood was jaunty after their successful morning and this exciting new lead.

Chapter Twenty-Seven

Liverpool 1878 - Rose

A breeze from the Mersey whipped the shawl from Rose's face as she passed the library, giving barely a glance at its grandeur. It was a long trek from her brother's house to the Dale Street Magistrate's Court, but every step closer, the sweatier her palms became and the drier her mouth. Beads of perspiration trickled down her back in the heat of the late afternoon. She longed for someone to hold her hand but yet again she was on her own. Her brother would not leave the shop, her supposed parents feared the loss of their respectability, and Alfred? She should have been able to rely on him.

It was a kiss on the cheek, yes, more than a brotherly kiss but hardly a lover's kiss. Tender, affectionate, lingering, like being rescued from drowning. The discovery that her mother lived and had always loved her, made her run blindly to Hattie's after that bitter argument with Tom. Why Hattie? Rose could not face Esther, the betrayal too deep.

Rose tripped on a loose paving stone and was caught by passing workman. She tried to thank him, but he hurried off disturbed by her face. After almost a decade she knew the look, the catch of breath, the superstitious shudder. The only person in the world who appeared not to notice was Louise, darling Louise, the most precious thing in Rose's life. She could put up with anything, would lay down her life in an instant for Louise. Today was all about Louise, she had to persuade the magistrate to let her keep her or at least let her see her daughter, but if he were to look at her as that man had, would all her pleas be for naught? The anxiety made her sick, all week she had been unable to eat, barely able to keep down a sip of tea. She stumbled again, hearing the quarter hour chime from somewhere nearby. She was too early. Rose paused to catch her breath, leaning on one of the great stone lions outside the law courts. How had it all come to this?

Hattie, the other cuckoo in the nest, along with herself. Hattie, misunderstood by her mother who sought to tame her when she was untameable. Growing up, Rose had trailed after her mercurial sister, in awe of her confidence and ambition. Hattie would only ever be happy marrying the dashing prince of her childhood dreams, instead, Essie had forced Hattie to marry Alfred, hoping he could control her daughter, whereas he became her slave. Alfred idolised his beautiful, delicate butterfly. Rose knew Hattie could also be a wasp, primed to sting at will. Which is why Alfred was too afraid to speak the truth to the magistrate. 'If I write to the magistrate telling him what happened, Tom will tell Hattie. You know how furious that will make her. It may go even worse for you.' The fear in his eyes caused Rose to bite her tongue, she could not afford another enemy.

The truth was that Hattie was an actress, she played any part which suited her. A wife who fluttered her eyelashes at her husband but stuck her tongue out behind his back, a loving mother to her children who was not averse to a sharp pinch when they displeased her. Rose had seen it all, borne the brunt of her moods and disgruntlement throughout her life. What disturbed Rose most was the light of triumph in Hattie's eyes when she had caught Alfred kissing her. The scream of anger, the pummelling fists, the cries of treachery were all for Alfred; the smirk was for Rose.

It must be time. She could not afford to be late. Rose looked up and caught sight of Tom marching past.

'Tom,' she shouted, her voice a bird's breath against the cacophony of the busy street, cartwheels against cobblestones, the whinny of horses, even the whistle of a train departing Lime Street station. She fell back against the smooth, cool stone, dizzy with the effort of making herself heard. Where had it gone wrong?

She had been happier than she deserved to be. Tom, so strong and vibrant, her a mouse beside him. He had been tender on their wedding night. She had been ashamed of her face and drawn a napkin over it. 'I am an engine fireman,' he'd said. 'I've seen far worse burns.' For that, she loved him.

Thinking back, he had changed towards her after the loss of their baby boy six months before, dead before he was born. Tom so wanted a son. He turned away from her in his grief, got drunk and stayed drunk for a day and a night while she sobbed alone in her blood-soaked nightgown. Essie, who was looking after Louise, sent Hattie round to be nurse. At first, Rose had been grateful, surprised by her care. Hattie brought her warm water to wash, found her a clean nightgown and made some nourishing soup, encouraging Rose to sleep though her distress. By the third day, her head muzzy with sleep, she had felt well enough to leave her bed and stumble into the kitchen, ravenous for something more than soup. The sight of Hattie in her shift and robe stopped Rose in her tracks.

'Have you been staying here?'

'I have, I was worried about you.'

'But Tom?'

'He stayed with a friend, Bill, or maybe Bob.'

Rose did not recognise either name. She tried to shake the fuzziness from her brain, it was like a fog had descended. Why had she slept so long? 'But I heard his footsteps.'

'You were mistaken. That was Alfred, he wants to know when I'm coming home. If you're well enough I will leave today.'

Rose knew enough to recognise the sound of hobnailed boots, boots that Alfred did not own. Since then, Hattie had been so sisterly, so concerned with Rose's health that she had dismissed her suspicions, but they had flared back since Hattie had run to Tom with her false tale of treachery.

The dizziness subsided but the nausea returned. It was time to go, Rose had ten minutes or less to reach the court. If only she had not chosen to look in the unlocked box or read the letters. It was impossible to weigh the joy of finding her mother against the loss of her child. But then she had compounded her mistake by running away after the argument. The thought that Tom had only been persuaded to marry her for money was eating at her. Money had changed hands. Money she knew nothing about. Any tender words suddenly meant nothing. And where was the brooch? The last time she had seen it, Hattie was wearing it on her wedding dress, and yet it belonged to Rose, the only relic of her mother and her unknown father. Had Tom sold it? He had refused to say and when pressed, he lashed out. But the brooch meant nothing now. As Rose stood panting at the door of the Magistrate's Court, she cleared away the debris of the argument. She was here for Louise. She took a gulp of air before walking through the door. 'Please God, let me have Louise.'

Five minutes was all it took to turn hope to despair. All Rose could remember was the cold disdain, the clipped tones of the Magistrate's dismissal of her plea. She rushed after Tom to beg him to reconsider.

'Please, Tom. Take me back. It doesn't have to be like this. I can't live without Louise.' Rose began to sob.

'No, it's settled.' He drew her into a recess, shamed by her tears.

'What's settled? It needn't be. You know nothing happened between Alfred and me. He was kissing my bruised face, the bruise you gave me. Remember.' Rose grabbed Tom's hand and put it to her cheek, still purple above the 'red ridges of her scar.

'It's settled, Rose.' The glinting aquamarine eyes gave the veiled figure away. Rose knew the voice anyway.

'What's she doing here, Tom?'

'I may have been called to give evidence.' Hattie's spiteful voice jarred.

'What evidence? You know it's lies.' Rose turned back to Tom. 'My love, I think I may be …'

Hattie interrupted, smothering Rose's words. 'It's all settled. Time to go now, Rose.'

That word again. What was settled? Rose looked at them both. Tom's eyes slid away, Hattie's expression unseeable, but her hand rested on Tom's arm. Possession he accepted by moving his hand to hers.

'Oh. So that's the way it is. You think you can step into my shoes. You can never be Louise's mother. Don't you see Tom, Hattie has only ever loved herself. Hattie, are you really willing to lose your own girls? Alfred will never let them go.'

Alfred must be warned. He would stop this. Rose turned to leave. A foot sneaked from under Hattie's dress and tripped Rose. She fell, banging her head against the wall and blacked out.

When she came too, she found herself sitting on a wooden chair, an usher fanning her frantically.

'Where am I?'

'The Magistrate's Court, Ma'am.'

'Where's my husband, my sister?'

'I'm sorry. You were on your own when I found you.' The usher's tone both sympathetic and shocked.

'I must talk to the magistrate. My husband lied. Please, where is the magistrate? Call him for me, I beg you.'

'I'm afraid he's left for the afternoon.'

'No, no, you don't understand. They're going to steal our children.' Rose felt the room sway, the usher's voice faded, the walls closed in and darkness returned.

Chapter Twenty-Eight

Laura 2019

At home the following evening, having dropped Daniel off at Guildford Station, Laura thought over the conversation in the car. While she drove down the M42 after Birmingham, Daniel had itemised all the available information they had discovered. Thanks to the assistant in the Records Office, they discovered on Ancestry.co.uk that a few days after the warrant for Harriet's arrest, her husband Alfred had set sail for New York.

'When you think about it,' Daniel said, 'it makes sense for Thomas to escape in the opposite direction. Most people would have expected them to head for America.'

'Wasn't there a telegraph by that time across the Atlantic?'

'Yes, but they could have travelled under false names. Travel documents at the time were just a single sheet of paper and, I imagine, easily forged. But they didn't go that way. It was enough for Alfred to think they had.'

'Perhaps they got someone to plant that idea in Alfred's mind.'

'It's strange we didn't find Alfred in the US census, maybe he didn't stay there.'

'The classic wild goose chase.' Laura said. 'I feel so angry with my - whatever great grandfather he was. Fancy doing that to his own brother.'

'The thing that I can't get over is that Rose travelled in the opposite direction to Melbourne. Why on earth did she go to Australia?'

'Perhaps a ship left for Australia at the same time as Thomas and Harriet went missing. Alfred decided to search in New York and Rose in Melbourne. It seems far-fetched, I know.'

'You think they were working in concert?' Daniel shrugged. 'Now who's coming up with wild theories?' Laura turned her head to laugh at him, feeling vindicated. 'I think my theory about Harriet being the main culprit still holds water. She ran off with Thomas and Rose's child, leaving her husband. I can't imagine doing that to a cousin.'

'You just don't want to put all the blame on Thomas.'

'What I don't understand is why Thomas took Susanna's notebooks and letters with him. It seems odd. They must have been travelling light with three children and all their belongings. Why take up more space?'

'Just be thankful they kept them, otherwise we would never have met.'

She turned and grinned. 'That's true.'

Later that evening in her flat, Laura read the court pleas again. The phrase *'My husband kept a secret from me which I had the right to know* struck Laura as the key to everything that happened after. What if Rose had found the letters and she thought Harriet had the brooch? Perhaps she suspected something was going on between them.

She reached for her phone, keen to share her theory with Daniel. He answered to the throb of background music.

'Where are you?'

'In a pub. It's Saturday night and there's a band playing.'

'Oh!' Her excitement faltered and loneliness set in. What was she doing in a flat on her own amongst dusty old papers when she could be enjoying herself in London?

'I did ask you to stay for the weekend.'

'Yes, I know. I wish I had now.'

'I'll go outside so I can hear you.'

'No need. I'll phone tomorrow. Enjoy the music. Bye' She cut the call; her mood altering from euphoria to disappointment.

Why was she doing all this research when she could be living life instead of trying to find out about people who lived a hundred and fifty years ago? It was ten o'clock on a Saturday night in a sleepy seaside town and she was on her own. Maybe it was time to set all this aside. She had found out why Rose had disappeared. Tomorrow she would tell her grandmother the story and that would be the end of it.

Laura woke up out of sorts after a restless night. She was back at work the following day with the start of a frenetic term looming. A week of enrolment followed by inductions and research workshops left little time for relaxation. She loved her work with the students. It was time to begin concentrating on that and to make sure she filled her weekends with fun things. She would visit her grandmother after lunch, tell her what she had found and then put all this aside.

Daniel phoned as she was getting out of the shower.

'Do you fancy coming up to London next weekend for a free concert?'

'Great. Shall I come straight from work on Friday?'

'Sure. Was there a reason you phoned last night?'

'No, no reason. See you around six on Friday. I'm looking forward to seeing your place.'

'That just about gives me enough time to clean up.'

Laura grinned imagining a flat piled high with books and papers.

Chapter Twenty-Nine

Liverpool 1870 - Harriet

You can't call Alfred handsome. His hair is thinning and his eyes muddy. His skin is pockmarked and his gait awkward from perching on a bank clerk's stool for hour after hour. Mama says Alfred has brains and a future, while Tom only has the brawn that comes from being an engine stoker and everyone knows how many accidents there are on the railways. Her tone is dismissive.

Give me brawn any day. I shake off Alfred's attempts at compliments with a shrug and tap my toe in impatience, but his moonlike gaze fixes on me until I shudder at his narrow ink-stained fingers clutching a cup of Mama's delicate china. I imagine him in twenty years shrinking into his stool, never having had an ounce of fun, never leaving Liverpool. Whereas his brother, who won't be a fireman for ever, will be driving his mighty locomotive across this great country of ours. Maybe he will take me with him. How I would like to see the sights of London.

When Rose enters the room with a plate of biscuits, I don't care for how Tom turns and smiles at her. Mama says I'm jealous because I was weaned too young to make way for Rose. No. I may envy her buttermilk curls but not her cow-like brown eyes. I liken mine to the topaz in the jeweller's window, pale blue with a hint of green. They would go far better with buttermilk than my dark brown locks.

'Please give Alfred a biscuit, Rose,' I say. 'Did you know Alfred, that Rose is an excellent cook? Everything she makes tastes divine, unlike me. I burn the simplest of things.' Mama scowls at me as I say this.

However, Alfred does not shift his gaze which is unnerving. I cast my eyes to the floor as though to inspect the scratched wood. I've never learnt how not to be a coquette. Maybe there is a disadvantage in that.

'I haven't seen your brother in church, Mr White,' I say.

'Half-brother, my mother died not long after my birth.'

That explains why they look so dissimilar. The second Mrs White I imagine as a beauty, the first a narrow-hipped blue stocking. Pah! I can't see the point of books.

'How long have you lived in Liverpool, Mrs Thornley? Alfred asks, turning towards Mama. I take my chance to flutter my eyelashes at Tom who almost drops his biscuit.

'Since 54, but my husband has been looking to retire from his shop and let our son take over. We'd like to see our youngest girls settled first.'

This is news to me, and I look up in surprise only to catch sight of globules of tea caught in Alfred's thin moustache.

Tom is helping himself to a second of Rose's biscuits and turns to look at me grinning. 'Thank you for the recommendation, Miss Thornley. The biscuits are delicious.' His gaze makes my stomach flutter. He knows the effect he has on me.

Rose sits on her chair with her hands in her lap, demure, prissy, obedient as ever. She would suit Alfred, if only he could see it, but he can hardly bear to look at her. If only the accident hadn't marred her face. It was hardly my fault that I tripped over the foot stool when taking the iron to the fire. It could have been me.

Rose lives in this family on sufferance and I know my mother has tired of her responsibility. I suspect Mama is weighing up which brother will take her. Only let it not be Tom! I could never forgive that.

I do not trust my mother's wiles. To strangers she may appear soft and motherly but to us children, she is a veritable crosspatch. None can gainsay her. Even our Papa can testify to that. I suspect a new impatience. What scheme does she have in mind?

Chapter Thirty

2019 - Peggy

'That's the whole story, Granny. Harriet and Thomas ran off to Grimsby with the children, leaving their respective spouses, who then disappeared to the opposite ends of the earth.'

Would this have satisfied Granny Lou? I thought back to our conversations in the weeks before she had died seventy years before. It's strange how those are somehow easier to remember than the days which preceded this. At fifteen, my senses were alive to everything, now they are dulled by my stroke and the daily indignities of staying alive. I could have given up long before, turned my face to the wall, refused to eat, but clung on to see Laura again, wanting her to discover the truth about her mother. I feel so tired, so weary.

Maybe I drifted off before wincing from the pain in my stomach.

'Granny, are you alright?'

I felt Laura's hand on my arm, opened my eyes and smiled. She is so good, visiting me most Sundays. How could I have fallen asleep? It was happening more these days. What had we been talking about? Yes, Lou's parents, that was it. Something surfaced from way back, some little detail. I struggled to remember. Why did Lou make me put that death notice in the newspaper? Who had she wanted to find? It was there in the back of my mind as pain gripped me again.

'I should go and let you rest.'

No, no, don't go. I shook my head and caught Laura's arm with my hand.

'Are you sure?'

I nodded, desperate to keep Laura close by. If only I could remember what I needed to tell her.

To fill the void in conversation, Laura asked, 'Did your Grandma Lou ever talk about Harriet? What was she like?'

I cast my mind back. Now that's something I did remember. I reached for my alphabet sheet and tapped out - *sly* then *cruel* and *vain*.

'That chimes with what I thought. I'm surprised she gave the brooch to Louise.'

I shook my head and tapped – *dead*. Granny Lou had described nursing Hattie to the end and begging her to reveal what had happened to Rose, but Hattie told her it was too long ago, to forget it.

Laura nodded. 'Poor Louise. It must have been so hard being brought up by a woman like that. At least Thomas did the right thing by giving the brooch to his own child not to one of his stepdaughters.'

A flash of memory, some spark flew across the remaining synapses of my brain. Lou and I had been sitting in Grant Thorald Park at the end of Buller Street not long before she died. The pigeons were crowding around for food, but it was the end of the war, bread was in short supply and the birds were left to peck desultorily at the grass. Lou talked about feeding the pigeons with her mother the day she disappeared. I searched in the depths of my mind for that conversation and out it popped, my grandmother's voice as clear as though she were sitting beside me.

'My mother was poorly every morning that week before going to work in the shop. I remember begging her to take me out on the Sunday to the park. She was pale, almost grey but she smiled and kissed me. Her breath smelt sour, but she put on a brave face and was cheerful for a change. I have always treasured that memory.'

Why had it never occurred to me before? Rose was pregnant when she disappeared. Lou, rather than thinking her mother was dead, had believed she may have a sister or brother somewhere. That's why she insisted on the notice in the newspaper after she died. How lonely she must have been all those years. Like me, like me.

'Granny, you're crying. You seem so sad today.' Laura grabbed a tissue to wipe my eyes. My finger taps urgently on the card. Laura looked down.

Rose baby find.

Laura shook her head, perplexed. I tapped again.

Find baby.

'You're saying Rose had another baby?' I nodded, encouraging Laura. She must understand.

'Before she disappeared? No? - after she disappeared? How do you know?'

I mimed being sick.

'She was pregnant when she split with Thomas?'

I nodded again – *Find baby.* Why was it so important? I don't know but something was telling me it was imperative.

'How do I do that? Even if I find the birth then it will mean tracking the child through generations,' Laura's tone sounded harsh, exasperated. 'This research takes hours, you know.'

Find baby I pleaded.

'Granny, I've done everything you asked, but I'm going to be busy at work. I don't have time.'

Something in me broke. A dam shattered. Pain engulfed me. Not just mine, Lou's, Rose's, even my daughter's. It flooded my eyes, my nose, my throat, left me gasping for breath. All the stoicism I had cultivated through years of my disability peeled away and left me bereft, helpless, in pieces.

Laura stood aghast. 'I'm going to fetch help.' She fled from the room.

I prayed that she would return, that I hadn't driven her off with my nonsense.

Chapter Thirty-One

Laura

Laura was horrified that her harsh words had had this effect and remonstrated with herself. Where was the harm in pandering to an old lady? She should simply have agreed to Peggy's request. What harm could it do? It just meant more precious hours on the laptop.

She found Heather in Reception talking to another relative. Laura managed to catch Heather's eye, communicating that she needed help. Heather excused herself and wandered over.

'Is something wrong, pet?'

'Granny's beside herself. I've managed to upset her. I'm not sure how to calm her down.'

'I wanted to speak to you. We had the doctor out on Friday. Have you noticed how her legs have swollen?'

'No, her blanket's covering them.'

'He thinks her heart is under pressure. We need to humour her, keep her calm. Betty reported that she was crying the other evening. It was to do with something on the TV, that Long Lost Family Programme. Do you know what's going on?'

Laura shook her head. 'She wants me to find her grandmother's brother or sister. She became quite agitated, and I think she's in pain.'

'Sounds like a possible urinary infection. I'll get her tested. Let's see if we can cheer her up, shall we? Maybe make a nice cup of tea, hey?'

Peggy was calmer when Laura returned although her face was blotched and her eyes red.

'If something like this happens in future, ring her bell.' Heather pointed to the alarm around Peggy's neck.

'Sorry, I should have thought. I panicked.'

'What's upsetting you, Peggy? Let's wipe your face and make you more comfortable. Do you need the toilet?'

While Heather dabbed at Peggy's face with a wet wipe. Laura went to fetch tea from the dining room down the corridor. Betty was pouring over the patient logs, a pencil poised over tick boxes.

'So much paperwork.' She looked up and smiled. 'Peggy, she happy today, yes?'

'Not really.'

Betty's face dropped. 'So sorry. She lovely lady, always tries to smile at me.'

'Heather said she was upset earlier in the week.'

'Yes, I hold her hand. She watch television. Young lady trying to find her father, very sad.'

Laura poured tea into the spouted beaker for Peggy and made a cup for herself. 'Thank you, Betty. I'm glad she has you to look after her.'

The conversation had given Laura an idea, a possible shortcut.

As Laura helped Peggy with her tea, she asked if she had heard of DNA. Peggy nodded as tea dribbled down her chin.

'I thought if you do a DNA test and someone else related to Rose had already done one, we might find an answer more easily. What do you think?' Laura could see the cogs turning in Peggy's mind. The confusion cleared and she nodded with enthusiasm.

'Look, I keep getting emails offering deals on DNA tests.' Laura picked up her phone and scrolled through her emails. 'Here's one. Summer sale, DNA test only fifty-nine dollars. It's American. Shall I go for it?'

Peggy held two fingers up.

'No, we only need to buy one.'

Peggy pointed at herself and then Laura.

'There's no need for us both to do one. I'll get the same results as you, except for my father's side and I've no wish to know his relatives.' Laura stopped. She had two other half-brothers out there somewhere. One day, one of them may come looking for her. She had memories of both as annoying boys, but children change. Look at Christopher. 'Okay two tests.' She took out her credit card to order them. 'Next time I visit, in a fortnight, we'll do them. Very simple. It will be fun.'

Peggy smiled, almost for the first time that afternoon.

On the train the following morning Laura told Sophie about her investigations into the history of the brooch. 'It turns out that Grandma thinks Rose was pregnant when she split from her husband.'

'But you think Rose read the letters and discovered her mother was alive? I have to say I'm on Daniel's side, speaking as a lawyer. I need evidence.'

'I know, there is none. I would need to find some connection between Rose and the letters. All I know is that she left for Melbourne a few days after Thomas left Liverpool.'

'What did you say the address was on those letters?

'To begin with the Little Brighton Hotel, Brighton, then a hotel in Elizabeth Street. I checked on google, there's an Elizabeth Street in London with lots of hotels listed.'

'And you've checked Brighton in Sussex and the one on the banks of the Mersey?'

'Yes, no joy at all.'

'Have you ever visited Melbourne?'

'No, why?'

I should take a look at google maps, if I were you.'

Laura screwed up her face but took out her phone, typed in Melbourne, Australia into maps. When it came up, Sophie said, 'Look to the south.' Laura did and her jaw dropped.

'Oh my God!' She turned her face to Sophie's, her mouth hanging open. 'Have you been there?'

Sophie nodded, 'Brighton, Victoria, famous for its colourful beach huts. Also, there's an Elizabeth Street in central Melbourne.' She smiled in a knowing way. 'That could be construed as evidence, M'Lud.'

A prickle began in Laura's lower spine. Sparks of renewed interest flashed behind her eyes. A list of things to check formed in her brain. Had Susanna reunited with her daughter? She ached for that to be true.

Chapter Thirty-Two

Susanna 1854

Three days and her heart was still pierced with hot needles. The pain would never lessen, how could it? In six weeks, she had lost her father to cholera, her lover to the war and now Amelia Rose. Essie may call her whatever she wanted, but Amelia Rose would always be her name.

Susanna held her employer's baby to her breast, her milk feeding someone else's little one. This stranger's child could never take Amelia Rose's place. The sustenance he drank rightly belonged to her daughter. He may be a usurper but as his gums latched onto her nipple, the free-flowing milk betrayed her. She glared down at his tiny mouth which should be Amelia Rose's. Attempting to curb her resentment, she stroked the skin of his cheek, silk under her coarse fingers.

Bitterness surged through her veins. All those years when her father had served the greatest in the land had not helped him at the end. His death was quick but unpleasant. He had begged her to leave him, to think of her child. She had refused, staying with him to the end, a cotton rag around her face, hands scrubbed raw with soap, her only protection against infection. When the end came and his body had been removed for a pauper's burial, she had taken to her bed for a week, unable to imagine her future without protection. Her lover's wife had long tentacles and her sting would be merciless. Susanna's prayers for his safe return fell like tears on tainted ground. Escape from England became her only reality.

She wiped the baby's face as he dropped off her breast into sleep. Adjusting her clothing, she laid him in his crib then peered out of the portlight as the steamship skimmed the sea. England was no more, not so much as a speck of land to be seen. In eighty days, God willing, she would enter a new life in a new land where her culinary skills would be in demand, and her father's credentials were sure to guarantee her work, enough to provide something for Amelia Rose. Could she hope that one day she may see her daughter again? Unlikely, but Essie had promised her a letter each year. She would live for those letters.

Chapter Thirty-Three

Laura - Mid October 2019

Autumn arrived early. On the south coast, September often heralded a return to summer after a blustery August. A regret that the beginning of term coincided with the advent of warm calm days, offset by twilights of smoky-pink skies over opalescent seas was tempered only by the photo opportunities which Laura looked forward to on her evening walks along the promenade. This year, however, September had determined the end of summer and a swift change to colder weather.

Laura was in her courtyard garden where she had coaxed a bright red dahlia into flowering, despite an ongoing battle with slugs. Pink and white geraniums nestled in pots and would most likely flower all winter if guarded from frosts. Swaddled in a thick jumper, she perched at her garden table, a bulb catalogue open at a page of tulips. She tried to decide whether to go for yellow or wine-coloured flowers. The yellow would brighten the dark corners of her garden, but her eyes were drawn to the almost purple blooms in the picture standing like stately glasses of ruby port.

Daniel was not coming down that weekend. He was thrown into the deep end of university life. He had also been working on his paper based on her notebooks, which she was looking forward to reading and which, according to Daniel, promised her some surprises. They had settled into an easy, companionable relationship.

Laura was unsure what love should feel like. Her mind played around with images and tastes. If she were describing her boyfriends as food, Daniel would be a warm syrup sponge, perfect for comforting her on a cold winter's day, whereas Jake? Her mind struggled to find an analogy. Ah yes, an overdone steak, the meat too tough with chips soggy rather than crisp. A memory from a childhood birthday kicked in. The 1990s steakhouse version which looked tempting in the photo but always too much when it arrived. Laura chuckled, pleased that she had moved on. The question was how would she describe her perfect man? That needed a lot more thought. She doubted Daniel would ever fit the bill.

A chill settled over her and she decided to make a cup of coffee. While the kettle boiled, her phone pinged with a new email. She poured her coffee and sat on the sofa to check it.

A slight pounding gathered in her head – maybe it was the results of the DNA tests she had sent off six weeks ago. Her research had come to a full stop again. Yes, she had discovered that the Brighton Races in Victoria had indeed been running since the 1850s and a Little Brighton hotel had been in operation at the time, but that was it. No record of Rose giving birth, no remarriage, no death record – a complete blind alley, so this was the last chance of putting the mystery to rest, of healing her grandmother's heart.

Laura had sensed a desperation in her grandmother over the last few weeks. Was it a feeling that time was running out? Water tablets had reduced the swelling in Peggy's legs and her urinary infection cleared up with anti-biotics, but she complained of coldness in her hands and feet. Laura hoped there would be some magic in the results to cheer her.

She clicked on the email. Yes, the results were available. Had Peggy received her own email? Laura decided to drink her coffee and head for Storrington so they could check together.

Chapter Thirty-Four

Peggy 2019

'This is it, Granny. Are you ready? I'm keeping my fingers crossed we find something, but you know it's a long shot, right?'

Peggy nodded, her tongue snaking between her dry lips as she watched Laura tap the link.

'Oh, wow! We have some results. It says here your geographical origins are seventy-one per cent English, ten per cent Scottish and nine per cent Scandinavian. That's interesting. I wonder where the Scandinavian comes from. The rest is a mixture of European and Middle Eastern. Possible matches - let's see. The nearest one is an Alfred John Thornley who is a first cousin, once removed. I wonder what that means. Shall I look it up?'

Peggy tapped her left hand on the armrest and jiggled her left foot with impatience. She had already worked it out. First cousin said it all.

Laura gawped as she peered at the diagram, sharing it with Peggy. 'I think it's saying that your mother and this man were first cousins. One of his parents was Louise's brother or sister. I don't believe it. How old is he for goodness' sake? He must be ancient.'

She looked at her grandmother whose head was bobbing. 'I think we have found Rose's baby.' Laura did a little jig then threw her arms around Peggy to hug her. 'We ought to celebrate. I wish I'd bought a bottle of champagne.' Laura sat back down.

Peggy pointed to her cupboard.

'You haven't got a secret bottle stashed away, have you?' Laura wandered over to it and pulled out a bottle of whisky, a glass and a mug. 'Wow, how did you get this?'

Peggy tapped – *Heather* – and tried to grin. Once Heather knew her preference over sherry, she had made sure she always had a bottle of Scotch.

To his credit, the one thing that Percy had done before he died, was to ensure there was money in her care home credit balance. It must be dwindling now she was being bought whisky. That was another thing to ask Laura. She needed to speak to her solicitor to check on the money situation. Her house sale funds must be running out by now. Percy had always refused to discuss anything to do with their finances. Peggy had resented the power her husband had over her once the stroke took away the ability to look after her own accounts but there was nothing to be done.

Peggy could not fault his choice of care home, nor how she was looked after, but it drove her mad wondering if at some point, she could be thrown out through lack of funds.

'Here you are, Granny. Oh, I should have asked, do you want water with it?'

Peggy shook her head. The glass was a sherry glass which she could clasp in her left hand. Be thankful for small mercies she thought, not for the first time. She sipped, letting the honeyed liquid seep through her old bones.

'I'll check this Alfred Thornley's timeline if it's not protected.' Laura put down her mug and searched for a few seconds. 'Found it. It has hardly any people. Gosh his father was sixty when he was born which makes Alfred eighty years old. His father was called Alfred too, born in 1879, that works, doesn't it? Alfred's mother was...' Laura paused and blinked. 'So that's why I couldn't find her. He has her name as Amelia Rose Thornley, her maiden name, no birth date, but her death is listed as 1884. She died when her son was five years old in somewhere called Ballarat.'

Granny Lou lost her mother when she was five and her brother was the same age when he lost her. If Lou had known she would have been even more heartbroken. That was sixty odd years of not knowing about each other. Peggy dabbed her eyes with a tissue from the table beside her chair.

Laura interrupted Peggy's thoughts. 'There's no father listed for young Alfred which is strange. Let me check the birth records.'

A couple of minutes passed before Laura said, 'Nothing for Alfred Thornley born in 1879, let me try something else. Okay, found it. Thomas Alfred White born to Amelia White, father deceased, Melbourne, 1879. This guy, your cousin, has no idea, has he? He and his father have the wrong surname. Why did Rose change her name and say Thomas was deceased? Was she covering her tracks?'

Peggy took another sip of whisky to hide her distress. Laura posed all these questions about some distant relative but to Peggy, Rose was almost close enough to reach out to. Her Grandmother had loved Rose so much that the loss had touched every fibre of her being. It lay heavy on her mind throughout her life and communicated it to her granddaughters, through words, yes, but mostly through the love that she showered on them as compensation. Granny Lou's loss felt as acute today as it had done eighty years before. This newly found cousin had a father who had suffered the very same loss. Peggy needed to know how it had affected him. It was time to pour salve on those wounds.

'Shall I message Alfred Thornley? What should I say? Something non-controversial to begin with, I can hardly say you should be called White not Thornley.'

Peggy shook her head and tapped on her sheet– *too cruel*.

Laura nodded and paused in thought. 'I'll write – Hi cousin, I'm writing for my grandma. Her grandmother was Amelia Rose's daughter, but we only knew her as Rose. Is that okay?'

Peggy nodded.

'He'll be able to trace Rose back through your family tree. I won't add his father's birth record to our tree just yet. He might be upset.'

Peggy nodded. *Oh yes, take things slowly, Laura. This could be a big shock.* Peggy paused then pointed at Laura and her phone, then tapped – *your results*.

'What, oh my DNA results, well they'll be more or less the same. I doubt my brothers will be listed, they're too young.' Laura clicked on the second email. 'That's odd. Mine has English as 65 per cent, then Welsh at twenty percent followed by a smidgeon of Scandinavian etcetera. I didn't know my father had any Welsh blood. Nearest relative is you, of course and then a few distant Thornley relatives. Nothing else surprising here.'

If Peggy was disappointed, she hid it. Time enough to dwell on that when Laura left. Meanwhile she had another task for her. She pointed to the same cupboard where the whisky was and tapped – *bag*.

Laura walked to the cupboard and peered in rummaging amongst folded towels before lifting out a beige clasped handbag. She held it up, 'Do you mean this?'

Peggy nodded and beckoned to her to bring it over. It was like a time capsule inside. How long since she had needed a handbag? A cotton handkerchief with an embroidered P; once it had been scented with lavender now it smelt of decay; a comb; a powder compact, with a pretty enamel flower on the cover; a purse containing a few coins, no notes, a driving licence and an old library card. Peggy unzipped the compartment in the lining and drew out a banker's card with an expiry date of 1992 and a solicitor's card. Yes this. Peggy tapped – *phone him.*

'Is this your solicitor?' Laura asked. 'What do you want me to say to him?'

Peggy spelt out, '*See him.*'

'You want me to set up an appointment? Should I be there too?'

Peggy nodded.

'It's half term in a week. I'll set something up.'

Peggy yawned with tiredness and relief.

After replacing all the items in the handbag and tucking the card in her pocket, Laura kissed her grandmother goodbye and left

Once she had gone, Peggy rang her buzzer. She felt exhausted. Betty arrived and Peggy pointed to her bed.

'A nice afternoon nap for you, yes?'

Yes.

Chapter Thirty-Five

Peggy

My school certificate results were too good. The promise of a degree in my beloved English Literature dazzled me and would not let go. I hungered for it. I saw before me a classroom full of rapt girls hanging on my words just as I hung on to Mr Watt's, my favourite English teacher.

'A primary school teacher isn't good enough for you now?' Mam said, scorn shredding her voice into spikes of resentment. The letter from school balled in her hand as she screwed it between her fingers. 'Four years away, not two? Edith has a good job, a nursing sister and she managed to train here. Why not follow her path?'

'Mam, I want this. I can apply to Hull, that's not far away. I could come home every weekend on the ferry.'

'She'll get a full grant so money's not a problem.' Edith's voiced soothed. She had acquired a steely softness in dealing with snappy patients. 'With my wage we'll manage.'

'It's not the money.' Mam scowled. 'It's …'

'What?' I said, ready for any arguments she could throw at me.

Her face crumpled. 'I'll miss you. What if you find someone, marry and have children and I never get to see them?'

This was emotional blackmail that my prepared arguments had failed to address. I stumbled for an answer.

'Marriage is not in my plan for now. I want to teach for six years at least before I have a family.' I conjured up numbers out of nowhere to mollify her but at the same time it was true. Twenty-eight was the perfect age for starting a family, I decided.

'I'll be sixty by then and retired. I can help you out.'

This was her truth and it horrified me. Mam had missed out on her daughters as children, packing us off to Grandma Lou. Now she wanted her turn and the thought made me shiver. I knew then that I would never return to Grimsby. I wanted my children to fly but Mam would only drag them into her stunted world. Her lack of imagination, of ambition, of love, was not what I wanted. I looked at her and pitied Edith. I was going to abandon them both and it was Edith who would bear the brunt of Mam's disappointment. Edith smiled at me, knowing what I was thinking. Her head nodded imperceptibly giving me permission and I grasped it. Mam seemed to think she had won a battle, but I knew she had lost the war.

I opted for Birmingham pretending that Hull had not accepted me. In fact, they were the first to accept me and with a pass not the distinction I eventually achieved, but that ship had sailed. Birmingham was far enough away not to come home other than for major holidays. Both Edith and Mam saw me off from Grimsby Station, both had tears in their eyes while mine sparkled with anticipation. I remember little about that journey which is odd because it was the first time that I had travelled further than a school trip to Lincoln.

Scunthorpe, Doncaster and Sheffield scarcely registered in my brain but for some reason I was struck by the oddly twisted spire of Chesterfield's church. I looked out for it on all subsequent journeys, a personal landmark.

By the time I arrived at New Street Station, I was between a bag of nerves and a firework set to explode in a fizz of coloured lights. I stepped from the train into post-war, damaged Birmingham. It was like stepping into a new country. I was used to bustle, but this was more purposeful and the accents as I moved slowly along the platform and out into the station were strange, unrecognisable.

I was swept up in the crowd as it sped towards New Street and dispersed, right, left but with the majority straight on to the shopping area I later would discover as Corporation Street. The university had sent clear directions and I checked my map. Turn left, look for the bus stop outside the Midland Hotel. It is amazing how something as prosaic as the colour of a bus can throw you. I wonder why it was, but a cream bus was as unexpected as Hull's yellow telephone boxes which I'd heard about but never seen. It somehow confirmed that I had grown up, become more sophisticated. I stepped onboard with my battered case in a fit of pride. Other students with university scarves draped languorously around their necks, sat with assurance. I longed to be like them.

The university was everything I had ever dreamt of. The gravitas of its redbrick buildings, the clock tower, the chapel and, of course, the library;

all surrounded by acres of green space, became a haven I never wanted to leave.

Revelling in the work, I joined the choir and discovered classical music. I claimed the pinnacle of my life was attending an afternoon concert at the Victorian Town Hall on a winter's afternoon and exiting to a noisy choir of starlings as they swooped home to roost on the rooftops, my university scarf draped around my neck, Edith's Christmas gloves keeping my fingers toasty.

Everything changed when Rhys arrived fresh from National Service two years into my degree. Ex-servicemen abounded on campus, but none had affected me. I never worked out why it was that Rhys stood out. Over the passing years, I have had time to dwell, but the answer eludes me. Call it electricity, call it magnetism. I saw him and my heart jolted, blood drummed in my ears, and I felt dizzy with some new possibility that had never occurred before. It was not that I had never gone on a date, never been kissed. I had and it had been pleasant, nothing more. But in that instant, I longed to feel this stranger's lips on mine, run my fingers through his thick black hair, drown in the blue pools of his eyes.

I looked away, confused and embarrassed by my sudden hunger, hoping that no one had noticed the flush on my cheeks. I felt a tap on my shoulder and turned and almost fainted. It was him.

'I've been looking for you.' His voice threw me. It was deep and sang in my ears.

'We d-don't k-know each other.' My voice, stuttering with surprise, grated on me. I wanted it to sing in unison, to delight, but it let me down. I heard only my flat, ugly Lincolnshire vowels.

'But we need to know each other, Cariad.'

'Why?' I knew my reason for wanting to know him but could not understand his.

'Because...' He smiled and took my hand. His was square, strong, his fingertips were hard on my softer ink-stained fingers. 'I believe you have the power to save me. You do know that, don't you?' His voice softened and I could only nod, the gift of speech having deserted me.

I don't think I ever really understood the reason for his words. I do know that I let him down. If only I had the chance to apologise.

Chapter Thirty-Six

Laura 2019

'Do you know anything about this solicitor?' Laura asked.

Sophie took the card from Laura's hand and glanced at it. 'Good grief, that's ancient. The area code is wrong.'

'Yes, it's twenty-five years old, so he may have retired by now.'

'Uh uh.' Sophie shook her head. 'He should have retired. He's an old stick in the mud, so I've heard, but honest. Why do you want to know?'

'My grandmother has asked to see him. He's her lawyer.'

'And he's never bothered to give her a card with the current phone number? Do you know why she wants to see him?'

Laura shook her head. 'I have no idea how she pays for the care home. It must be costing a fortune. I know something's playing on her mind.'

'Do social services or the NHS pay?'

'No idea and I ought to know. I'm her nearest relative. What if there's a problem? You hear horror stories about people running out of money. Perhaps Edith's money should have gone to Granny. I'll ring the home and ask.'

'Okay. Here's what you need to do.' Sophie took pen and paper from her bag and began scribbling. 'I'm writing a list of questions for you to ask this lawyer. Don't be fobbed off, although he may need a rocket up his arse. If he tries to put you off, tell him you'll need to consult with your lawyer. Give him this name, he's the best in the business.'

Once Sophie had finished writing the list, she handed it to Laura who read through it with mounting apprehension. 'I wouldn't want to be on the wrong side of you. It reads like an interrogation.'

'It is and you need to nail everything down. Be firm, concise and stick to the script. I've written a list of what he needs to bring with him to the meeting. I suspect that he will have been granted power of attorney, so he'll have copies of everything.'

Later that morning, Laura rang the home to ask Heather who paid the bills for Peggy's care.

'Your granny pays.'

'Is there any chance the money will run out?'

'We insisted she had funds to last five years, but I have no idea how much is left.'

'So, it could be running out.' No wonder her Granny was worried. 'Has her lawyer ever visited?'

'Not to my knowledge. No, wait. We had a letter from a solicitor when Mr Winters died, saying he would be looking after Peggy's affairs and to contact him if there were a problem.'

That sounded hopeful. 'Thanks, Heather. I'll look into it.'

Laura had butterflies in her stomach when she lifted the phone in her lunch break. Most likely she would get a secretary and be fobbed off, but she had reread the questions and was as prepared as she would ever be.

'I would like to speak to Mr Jackson Cole with regard to my grandmother, Mrs Margaret Winters.' Laura prided herself on her firm tone.

'I will check to see if he's available.'

Laura waited, fingers drumming on the desk, she took a sip of water to moisten her lips.

'Jackson Cole.' His voice was languid, unhurried, smooth.

'My name is Laura Gray. My grandmother, Mrs Margaret Winters, tells me you are her lawyer, and she would like to see you. I am ringing to make an appointment for you to visit her.'

Laura sensed his confusion in the length of time it took him to answer. 'Um, now let me see, Mrs Winters. Ah yes, is that the Mrs Winters who lives in the Nightingales in Storrington?'

'Yes indeed. Can you tell me if you hold power of attorney for her?'

'I do.' Wariness had crept into his voice. 'Her husband left me in charge of her affairs.'

'That includes financial and care?' Remain assertive she told herself.

'Not care, only finance. It was an everlasting power of attorney. They are no longer issued, but still valid. Is there something wrong?'

'No. Have you visited her recently?'

A moment of silence preceded his answer. 'Her husband told me that she wasn't up to visitors and not to bother her. She's incapable of making any decisions, isn't she?'

With ice in her voice, Laura replied, 'My grandmother's brain is as sharp as a tack. Can you tell me how she is paying for the care?'

He resorted to bluster. 'Look, Miss Gray. I'm not sure I am at liberty to discuss this with you.'

Laura cut in, 'In that case, I could advise my grandmother to seek a change in Power of Attorney. In the meantime, please make an appointment to see both me and my grandmother at the home and bring with you copies of all documents including any financial statements.'

Laura detected a slight tremor of annoyance as he said, 'I'll put you through to my secretary to make the appointment.'

With the appointment made, Laura replaced the receiver. Sophie would be proud of her; she was proud of herself. She had been firm and controlled and felt sure the lawyer knew she was not to be fobbed off.

The meeting was set for the Wednesday of half-term. Laura arrived early. She had warned her grandmother well in advance of the meeting time.

After giving her a kiss, she noticed that her grandmother was dressed in an old fashioned but smart navy-blue jacket and skirt. Her hair had been freshly cut and set, and she even wore pink lipstick, the image of an aging headmistress, stern, unrelenting, scary.

'My goodness, Granny, you look the business. What do you want to talk to him about?'

Peggy tapped – *money.*

'I thought that might be the case. I asked Heather who pays the bills and she said you do. Social services are not involved so you must have funds.'

Peggy looked relieved then tapped – *how long?*

'That's what we need to find out. I've asked him to bring statements. Don't worry. Heather tells me that if you have less than around £23,500, social services must step in to help, though that may not cover the full cost. By the way, did you get a response from Alfred Thornley? I forgot that a reply would come to your email not mine.'

Peggy nodded indicating for Laura to read it. Laura picked up the iPad.

'Oh, that's so sad. His father went to his grave not knowing anything about his father, not even his name. He writes that our contacting him after all these years has made an old man happy and he longs to know more. Where to start? It's going to be a long story! He hasn't said where he lives. I'll reply and ask.' Laura began typing 'Where are you?' as Heather opened the door to introduce a portly man in a slightly shiny three-piece suit. Laura pressed send before placing the iPad on the table and standing up to greet their visitor.

'Mr Jackson-Cole, thank you for coming. I'm Miss Gray and you know my grandmother.' Laura shook his warm flabby hand, flinching at the strong smell of tobacco mixed with sickly aftershave lingering on his clothes. Small flecks of dandruff littered his shoulders.

Peggy nodded once. He put his hand out to Peggy and sharply withdrew it taken aback by her withering glare.

Laura placed a chair directly in front of Peggy's. When he was seated, Laura said. 'Peggy wishes to know how much money is in her account and what assets she still has. To be honest, I'm unsure why this wasn't all gone through when my grandfather died. He must have left a will.'

'He did. As I said on the phone, Mr Winters told me not to bother Mrs Winters. I haven't seen Mrs Winters since she signed the Power of Attorney, shortly after Mrs Gray, your mother, died.' His head was turned to Laura as he spoke.

Peggy leaned over and rapped him on the knee with her left hand.

'My grandmother wishes you to speak directly to her.' Laura gritted her teeth.

'Yes, yes of course. I have the will with me. Shall I read it?'

Peggy nodded, an imperious set to her shoulders.

'While you read it, may I look at the Power of Attorney document?' Laura held out her hand.

The lawyer shuffled the papers and drew out the relevant document, beads of sweat forming on his brow.

'I can assure you Miss Gray, that I have looked after your grandmother's affairs to the best of my ability.' This resulted with another tap on his knee. He quailed at Peggy's glare.

Laura had to admit that the POA document looked genuine. Not that she knew what to look for.

'That's as may be.' Laura said, folding the document. 'But you have left my grandmother anxious about her future. How much money is left? We need to apply to Social Services in good time.'

The lawyer's mouth dropped open. 'You were concerned about that, Mrs Winters? I'm sorry, I thought you knew. I thought Mr Winters would have told you.'

Puzzlement settled on Laura's face. She looked at her grandmother who shrugged her left shoulder and shook her head.

'The rental from the properties you own mostly cover your outgoings. Together with your pensions, your investments and attendance allowance, your income is sufficient to leave your capital almost untouched. I have to say Mr Winters was a very astute man.'

Peggy seethed. Percy had spent hours on his computer looking at stocks and shares, but she had no idea that they owned more than one property. Damn him for not discussing it with her. In an instant her mood changed, and she began to laugh. It choked from her mouth, splurges of uncoordinated mirth which sounded like a car engine spluttering and failing to catch.

The lawyer jumped up in alarm until Laura told him that her grandmother was laughing, before saying, 'How many properties are we talking about, Mr Jackson Cole?'

'Two, the family home in Washington and a spacious seafront flat in Worthing.'

'That's Washington Sussex, not the United States, I assume?'

'What? Oh yes, of course.' He looked across at her to see if she were joking. 'The rentals come to two and a half thousand a month. Your grandmother's income covers the other fourteen hundred required for her to stay here.'

Peggy was less inclined to rap him on the knee for talking above her now that she knew she was safe from being evicted. She tapped out *-rich -* on her alphabet sheet.

'Well, of course, I wouldn't say that Mrs Winters, but comfortable yes. The will specifies that everything is yours.' This time he talked to Peggy, the tension in his shoulders had relaxed. 'I've drawn up a statement of your assets with current values.' He handed it to Peggy.

After peering closely at it, she offered it to Laura with a smile, before tapping out – *my will.*

'It remains the same as when you drew it up immediately after your daughter's death. Everything goes to Miss Gray here. There will be death duties, I'm afraid. But Mr Winters also set up a small trust fund for Miss Gray which matures on her thirtieth birthday.'

Laura sat in a state of shock, her eyes and ears disbelieving. The two properties alone were worth over a million. Suddenly Mr Jackson Cole appeared avuncular. Her initial distrust disappeared in a puff of his hideous aftershave. Until – a thought struck her. 'I'm a year off receiving this money from the trust fund, you say.'

'Yes, that's correct.'

'Did you know how to contact me?'

'Oh yes. Mr Winters left me your father's details. Your father asked me not to let you know until your thirtieth birthday. Something about an unsuitable boyfriend, a possible gold digger, he said. Puce began to fill his cheeks as he watched her eyes begin to glitter with anger.

Laura glanced at her grandmother whose eyes were sharp as daggers. They both knew what it meant.

'Thank you, Mr Jackson Cole. We will be in touch if we have further questions. You may leave the documents here for us to peruse at our convenience.'

'But...'

'No please don't speak unless you wish to hear what I really feel. I was twenty- five when my grandfather died, and my father had no right, and you had no right to keep it from me. Go, please.'

He murmured apologies as Laura hustled him to the door and closed it firmly behind him. She shot to the window, despite the cool damp weather, to rid the room of its stale smoke, sweat and chauvinism, before turning back to her grandmother.

'I could have met you three years ago. I guess I understand why Dad didn't tell me about the trust fund, although he could have told me in Italy. It can't have slipped his mind.' She slipped onto the floor beside Peggy.

Peggy stroked Laura's hair. There was so much she wished to say and cursed her inability to do so.

'My father didn't like Percy, but Percy must have cared about me to set up a trust fund. That damned stroke is to blame. I missed you Mou Mou.'

Peggy's heart broke to hear Laura call her Mou Mou. She blamed herself for the damage done to Laura. If she had told Percy that Jeanette was not his daughter, would he have been so possessive? Would he have fought so hard for Laura? Both men had treated the child as an object rather than a precious gift to be nurtured; each an emotionally inadequate man, tainted by their own upbringings. And she? When it came to it, she lacked the courage to seize her opportunity for love, and a man worth fighting for. Twice she had let him go. She could not let Laura make the same mistake, and yet she had so little time left. Her heart was becoming sluggish, time and her body lay heavier each day.

'I don't remember Grandpa. That's so sad. He must have loved me too. Daddy said he didn't like him. I find it so difficult to know what to believe.'

Peggy's iPad pinged.

'You have a new email. I wonder if it's from your cousin?' Laura sat up and reached for the iPad. 'Yes, it is. It says he lives in Tasmania. It must be nearly midnight there. He asks where we are and is desperate to know about Rose.'

Peggy reached for her sheet. *Go tell him.*

'You're joking. Go to Tasmania? He's a stranger.'

Tell him.

'I don't understand. Why on earth would you suggest me travelling thousands of miles to meet someone I've never met on some flimsy excuse such as this?'

Be brave – Peggy spelt on her sheet.

Laura shook her head in disbelief.

Take letters.

'But I can scan them and email them. I don't need to spend two days on an aeroplane and several hundred pounds.'

Christmas.

'Why?'

Because I want you to.

Chapter Thirty-Seven

Peggy

Peggy placed the iPad on her lap tray. Typing a long spiel on the tablet was going to be arduous enough without having to choose every word to convey what she needed. Time in this case was not her enemy. Those honours were given to her weak left hand, her failing eyesight and the tiredness which dogged her at any inconsiderate moment in the day.

Peggy was not given to self-pity. How could she have survived so long otherwise? Endless hours, endless days all borne with one aim in mind – to see Laura again, and to ensure the damage was righted. This letter had to be written, however long it took and however many false attempts.

My darling Laura,

Love your father, he is all you have. He may not be perfect but in his own way, he wants the best for you. Jake was no good, you found that out for yourself.

Don't accept second best. I did and I have regretted it every day since. Your grandfather and I were not suited. I should have left him years before. I was not brave enough to make the right choices in life.

Peggy sat back, exhausted as Betty walked into the room with her beaker of tea.

'You tired, sweetheart? Let me help you into bed.'

Peggy nodded. When she was settled, she pointed to the iPad.

'Yes, I know. You want that Milk Wood, don't you?'

Peggy nodded again. To fall asleep to Richard Burton was to fall asleep in the arms of Rhys. How many years was it since they had sat on the riverbank, his arms around her as she lay against him, shocked at the shadows of pain behind his eyes? He told her how he longed to recapture the innocence of their time at university, and she thought there was still a chance until he showed her the photograph. He was hiding away from the world and wanted her to hide with him. Peggy tried to draw him out of himself, to find out why, but his lips remained sealed. Instead, she encouraged him to read the book he had brought her. Dylan Thomas's magic worked on her then as it had ever since. If only it had been enough.

Peggy's head sank into the pillow as Rhys caressed her hair, as his lips breathed on her cheek. Where are you, my love? I know I let you down. Give me a few more weeks with Laura, then I'll be waiting for you.

Chapter Thirty-Eight

Laura

What a strange morning, Laura thought as she drove along the A272 out of Storrington towards work. First, her father neglecting to tell her she was wealthy and then, to top it all, her grandmother wanting Laura to set off on a mammoth journey to meet an unknown relative.

As she approached the Washington roundabout, Laura considered driving into the village for a scout around, but stupidly she had forgotten to ask for the address of the house she was to inherit. She had no memory of visiting it as a toddler and yet she had lived there for several weeks, apparently. While Washington would be convenient for work, Laura preferred living by the sea and on a train route. Still, bringing up a family in the country with the South Downs as a playground did have its attractions. The small matter of a partner Laura put to the back of her mind.

Laura turned left onto the A24 and headed up the dual carriageway towards Horsham, deciding to put property issues aside. Her thoughts turned to Daniel. Was she going to tell him about the money? Laura doubted he would care that much but neither was it any of his business.

Which brought her to Australia. As a sudden rain shower spattered her windscreen, Laura began to daydream about Christmas in the sun. A long winter lay ahead with journeys to work beginning and ending in darkness. This year, she could look forward to evening meals for one with wind and rain battering the windows behind the shuttered blinds. Idly, she listed the places colleagues had talked about from Byron Bay round to the Great Ocean Road. One day she would do it, but the thought of undertaking such a journey on her own was daunting. Was she ready to ask Daniel to go with her? She drove into the college carpark with her mind made up. Australia and a Tasmanian cousin could wait.

A week later Daniel asked Laura to move in with him in January. 'We could manage a small flat in Clapham, then travel down to Bognor at weekends', he suggested. She had somehow let slip that more money was coming her way, although she had not mentioned the amount or the timing, his eyes had lit up.

Laura could only describe the resulting conversation as awkward, telling her a lot about how she viewed their relationship.

'We get on together well, don't we? We like the same things, have similar interests.'

'Yes, Daniel. I enjoy being with you. We've had a fun few months, but this is a big decision and I'm not ready.'

'What will it take for you to be ready?' His eyes had pleaded with her, which only made her withdraw further.

'I like you, but is liking enough? Can't we leave things as they are? We agreed no strings.'

'But I thought we were really moving forward. What more do you want?'

How could she explain? 'Give me time to think, please. It's a gorgeous day. How about a drive up to the Trundle then walking down to West Dean for lunch? You'll love it up there, great views.' Her sidestep closed off the discussion, but for how long?

That night, with Daniel asleep beside her, Laura tossed and turned, sleepless with regret and guilt. The truth was, as much as she liked him, the relationship had not progressed beyond friendship and mutual interests. Was that enough? No, there had to be more. If she loved Daniel, she would move to the ends of the earth to be with him but even the thought of moving to London dismayed her. Was it unreasonable to want someone who would set her heart on fire?

As a rain squall hit the windows, she made the decision. It was time to end it. Daniel would take it hard, but it had to be done and face to face, this weekend. It was unfair to keep stringing him along.

Telling Daniel was the hardest thing she had done. She sensed the tears he held back, the hurt he felt.

'You're a great guy, Daniel. I have enjoyed these last few months, but...'

'There always has to be a but, doesn't there?'

There did and however she might explain her feelings, Daniel was not in a mood to understand. He caught an early train back to London.

Then came the email. Laura had sent emails to her grandmother, but she had never replied. Someone must have helped her. Laura sat curled up in her chair, the heating barely taking the chill out of the air, reading and rereading the first few sentences. The pain and disappointment seeping through each line wounded Laura to the core. It vindicated what her father had told her about Percy.

Laura imagined her mother growing up in a home full of unspoken resentment. No wonder she wanted to run off with the first man who asked her. Laura sighed deeply. Why was her family so dysfunctional, with history endlessly repeating itself? Somehow, she had to break the cycle. Was that what this email was all about? Was Granny warning her from falling into a loveless marriage? The morning's awkward conversation with Daniel hit Laura with renewed force. She ran to the tap for a glass of cold water to take away the sour taste. Her hands shook as she sipped before spitting into the sink and taking a longer gulp. These last six months, her memories and beliefs were constantly dissolving and reforming. Could she trust any of it? Finishing off the glass of water, she poured another one and returned to read the final paragraph.

'Never settle for second best, Laura. Always seize your opportunities. Don't do as I have done, howl at my missed chances. You are on the verge of finding yourself, be brave, my darling. Take risks. Have adventures. Find a lover who is worthy of you, who makes your heart sing with joy, rather than weep with loneliness.

Yes, she was warning her. Her grandmother had met Daniel three times. He treated Peggy with kindness, nothing more, unaware that he was under intense scrutiny. The thought made Laura bristle until she saw the funny side.

'Oh Granny, you are watching my back, aren't you? You don't need to worry. I'm not going to repeat my mistake. I have to be sure next time.'

Grabbing her coat and scarf, she decided to take a walk along the prom.

Only a few stalwart souls dragging along reluctant hounds passed her as she strode towards the pier with the strong wind ruffling her hood.

That last paragraph of the email tore away the fog which had been clouding her mind. While professionally she had been developing in confidence, her personal life was full of self-doubt. She needed to take control of her own destiny, not just let things happen. It was time to rid herself of her inability to make decisions, be clear in her own head about what she wanted and where her life was headed.

Turning to face the wind, she allowed it to rip back her hood and blow into her face, relishing the blast of cold air.

'That's it,' she said to no one but herself. 'I'm done with settling for less. Give me more.' She raised her voice. 'I want more.' The breeze whipped her words back and she laughed. 'Australia here we come, Granny. If you can't join me, I'll make sure you are with me.'

On the way back to the flat, Laura sketched an itinerary and a video diary in her mind for Peggy to watch her progress. 'I'll prove to her I can be brave,' she said, turning her key in the lock. 'It's time for a new me.'

A month later, she sat in the departure lounge at Heathrow waiting to board a Quantas flight to Melbourne via Singapore. Laura's stomach rippled with a mixture of nerves and excitement. She had been reading about the bushfires in Australia and had planned her route hoping to avoid them. At least she was flying away from rain, endless rain.

Laura had planned the detailed itinerary with her grandmother and given her a copy so she knew where Laura would be throughout her trip, together with a laminated map detailing her journey. Four days in Melbourne, five days in Tasmania, then Sydney for New Year's Eve and three days at one of Sydney's northern beaches, before catching her flight back on January the fourth, in time for the start of term.

A scratchy voice from the Tannoy announced boarding for the overnight flight to Singapore. Laura shuffled forward in the economy class queue with her passport and boarding pass clutched in her hand, praying that the crying baby in front was not going to be seated nearby for the long flight.

She took her window seat next to a young Swedish guy on his way to Melbourne for a term at the university. Blond, handsome, charming, the perfect travel companion and a bonus start to her holiday. The transcript of Susanna's notebooks may well lie unread on her kindle. They were

Daniel's Christmas present to her, bless him. A rush of guilt brought colour to her cheeks.

After the plane left the runway and began to fly over London, Laura watched the lights of the city, her hear beating with a spirit of adventure.

Chapter Thirty-Nine

Laura entered the arrivals hall at Hobart airport after her early morning flight from Melbourne. She was still buzzing from the four days spent in the city. What was not to like apart from the lingering smoke of fires to the north? The free tram system in the city centre, the public barbecues along the Yarra River to the east of the bridge by Federation Square, the restaurants and street artists to the west. A city designed for youth and fun.

But there were older glories too, like the State Library. The awe-inspiring main reading room with its giant cupola drowning the space with light and an almost religious fervour, left Laura breathless. She wandered the galleries, not so much looking at the exhibits as gazing pilgrim-like upon one of the seven wonders of the world. Outside, the forest of slender new skyscrapers contrasted with the solidity of its Victorian architecture; a city in constant renewal but remaining proud of its past.

Laura had happily wandered the streets sampling the culinary delights. Dazzled by the best pizza she had ever tasted in the café behind the temple-like GPO building, she ventured into China Town. A jasmine tea and a humble chow mein which she expected to be ordinary but was somehow spectacular, made her indulge in a fantasy of throwing up her life in England to move to Melbourne. She had watched the odd programme on TV about people who did that. Why not her?

Conducting the necessary pilgrimage to Brighton, brought the journey to Tasmania into focus. She was about to meet Rose's grandson while her expectation that he could add more to the story remained low. Laura had FaceTimed briefly with John before leaving England, 'I prefer to be called by my second name. No one knows me as Alfred.' he had stressed. But the connection was poor and the hour late and they jointly decided to discuss Rose when they met. That he and his wife had invited her to spend Christmas Day with them was unbelievably sweet. 'You can't be alone for Christmas; you are family and believe me, I have little enough family as it is,' John had told her.

It was with both a sense of loss and anticipation that she had boarded the flight that day. Hobart airport was tiny in comparison to Melbourne, though she had caught sight of a picturesque city, fronted by sparkling water and bounded by mountains, as they were circling the airport ready for landing. However, today she would be heading north, away from the city.

She left the terminal within minutes, no customs checks, other than a spaniel sniffing to see if she were carrying fruit, then crossed the road to pick up her car hire. Laura was pleased that she was wearing a sweater. The early morning temperature was cool, no more than sixteen degrees. Unlike her arrival in Melbourne when she had stepped off the plane from Singapore into a fiery forty-one degrees and a pall of smoke from bushfires to the north, utterly wilting by the time she made her hotel. The following day it had been eighteen degrees and the receptionist had shrugged when she commented on the change. 'That's Melbourne for you, sometimes it drops twenty degrees between morning and afternoon. We need cooler weather to stop the bushfires. Better still, we want rain.' Laura could not complain. The clamour for rain dominated conversations on the street, in the media and even the coffee shops.

After the formalities at the rental company, Laura set off into moderate traffic, but that soon decreased as she left the small town of Sorell, with its single-storey shops and verandas lacking the usual historical references one found in English Market towns. After passing through flat farmland, the road north undulated through scrubby eucalyptus. Laura did a double take at a signpost for Bust-Me-Gall-Hill, laughing with delight at a name so evocative of the early settlers struggling up these hills with a loaded bullock cart. That image was compounded by Break-Me-Neck-Hill a little further. She imagined them being named by ex-convicts set free to farm the land, forging a better life than they had ever known in England. The road was narrow but without traffic, and she made good time driving along a river for the last few miles into Orford.

'Oh, my word! Just look at that view!' Laura shouted, as the river morphed into ocean next to a spit of pure white sand. She stopped the car and swung open the door, taking a deep breath of the sweetest air. A bay of extraordinary beauty lay in front. Blue-tinged hills framed the north and east with a few white sails dotting the horizon. If this were anywhere in England on what had become a glorious, if slightly cool, summer's day and with a view like that, crowds would have been thronging, but here scarcely a car was to be seen.

Large beachfront houses on enormous plots lined the road. The only sounds that of birds; not the tweeting of sparrows, something different, songs she did not recognise but which instantly filled her soul with pleasure. Looking around, she saw a road sign leading off the highway, her destination. If this was where she was going to be spending Christmas, no matter that she knew these people only from a few emails and that single FaceTime call, she was thrilled. Why didn't they tell me they lived in paradise? Why have I only given myself two days here? Because it would have been rude to prey on their hospitality for longer, she reasoned. Yes, but this – Laura traced the bay with her hand, feasting her eyes, wishing once more she had an ounce of her father's talent for painting. No photograph could capture the extent of the wild beauty.

Chapter Forty

They were looking out for her. John and his wife joined her on the drive of their house.

'Welcome, Laura.' They greeted her in unison with the broadest of smiles.

'We're delighted you made that long journey. I'm afraid it's a bit beyond me now.' John, stooped and leaning on a stick, took her hand in his long tapering fingers and squeezed gently.

'I'm so happy to be here and that you invited me. You live in the most beautiful spot.'

'It is on a day like today. It can be a bit bracing when the winds and the rain pile in.' He took her bag and ushered her into the house. 'Molly has the coffee on, and she's made peanut cookies.'

Inside it was light, bright and modern with large picture windows offering a view of trees, with a sliver of blue ocean in the distance.

Molly, sprightly and a good ten years younger than her husband, brought a tray from the kitchen and placed it on a glass table. 'We wish you could stay longer but treat this as home while you're here. No standing on ceremony.'

'You're too kind.' Laura took the proffered coffee.

'No dear. You've travelled twelve thousand miles all to make an old man happy. I promised my father that one day I would solve the mystery of his family, but I was beginning to doubt. When you get to eighty and the decades have passed, it's too easy to give up.' His eyes glistened for a moment before he wiped them with a handkerchief from his trouser pocket. 'How does your grandmother feel about you coming all this way? I'm still not sure how we two are related.'

'It was Peggy who was most insistent. We know your grandmother was Amelia Rose, although we didn't know about the Amelia part until you contacted us. Rose was Peggy's great grandmother. That makes you her first cousin once removed. I have a family tree here.' Laura dug it out of her bag, knowing it would be the easiest way of explaining relationships. She detailed the potted history of the family from Rose and Harriet marrying the two brothers.

'But why did Rose end up in Australia with my father?' John asked.

'We think that Rose discovered that her mother was living in Brighton, south of Melbourne and left England to find her. A few months later, she gave birth to Thomas Alfred White. I think that was your father.'

John blinked at Molly who stroked his hair. 'This is all new information. Dad called himself Alf, but never knew he was also Thomas. I don't understand why his mother would give him both those names. The DNA result tells us Louise and my father were full siblings.'

It was a question Laura had asked herself several times. Could it be that Rose wasn't sure which of the brothers was the father, but she hoped it was Alfred? Laura heard Daniel's voice in her ear shouting, 'Where's the evidence?'

'After I found out about the court case, I wondered if her brother in law had taken advantage of her, but there's no way Rose would have given your father that second name if that were the case.' Laura was trying to work it out in her own mind. 'Perhaps she loved him.'

'It sort of makes sense, John.' Molly turned and beamed at Laura, greying blonde curls bouncing around her face. 'What happened to Alfred the elder?'

'He sailed for America the same week Rose sailed for Melbourne. We think he was looking for his children. He didn't stay there, though. I have no idea where he went next.'

'That one tiny piece of the jigsaw is worth your journey, Laura. My father didn't even know his father's surname. He had vague memories of his mother. He knew she was called Rose but not much else. Can you tell us more about her?'

Laura, chewing on a peanut cookie, smiled at Molly. 'These are really good,' she said, after swallowing. Can I have the recipe?'

'Do you like baking?'

'I do, in fact I think my love of cooking comes from Rose's genes.' Laura proceeded to tell her hosts what she knew of Rose and her antecedents. They sat spellbound and when, with a final flourish, she produced a copy of *Your Most Obedient Servant* from her bag to give to John, she was disconcerted to see his shoulders heaving.

'I'm so sorry. I didn't mean to upset you.' Laura passed a tissue to John from a box on the table.

'He's not upset,' Molly replied. 'He's overwhelmed. Not knowing where you've come from, not knowing anything about your family, it's difficult to describe. It's fundamental to who we are, isn't it? You've given him something he has been missing all his life.'

John finished wiping his eyes and leant across the table to grasp Laura's hand. 'Thank you. I wish I could share this with my father, but it's simply the best Christmas present anyone has given me. I don't know how to repay you.'

Laura coloured in embarrassment. 'It's the least I could do,' she mumbled. She tried smiling. 'I'd love to know about Rose's life in Australia. Do you have any clues? What happened to your father after Rose died? Did she ever meet Susanna, her mother?'

'I know very little. Look I need a walk after all this talk. I want to get my head around it. Would you like to join me?'

'He'll be taking you off to see his precious birds. Why don't you two go while I prepare lunch?'

'I'd love that, thanks Molly. Are you sure I can't help?'

'No, you'll be needing to stretch your legs after that journey and it's only a light lunch. We'll have a barbie this evening.'

Laura grinned. 'That sounds delightful. A barbie on Christmas Eve!'

'Get your sunhat while I find my binoculars.' John stood with a sigh of discomfort and shook his left leg. 'I'll be pleased to get my new knee in January.'

Back on the Tasman Highway a few minutes later, Laura exclaimed again at the view.

'The whole of the East Coast is one breath-taking view after the other. It's a shame you don't have longer to explore.'

'Were you born in Tasmania?' Laura asked.

'No, in northern Victoria. I came here after Vietnam where I learned most of my medicine in field hospitals.'

'A real live M.A.S.H.'

John's laugh was contemptuous.

'I'm sorry, you must be sick and tired of that comparison.'

'It took me a long time to get over Vietnam. Let's leave it there. Tasmania was the peace I sought, and it was even sleepier than it is now. It healed me.'

'I noticed that the roads were quiet when I drove up today, despite it being the summer holidays.'

Hobart's busy, Launceston too. Most people live in the cities, but we have places where the inhabitants are numbered in dozens rather than hundreds. That's how I like it. However, the population is beginning to grow. Some people are being driven here by climate change further north and tourism is bringing more.'

They crossed the road and walked to the sandspit. John raised the binoculars to his eyes scanning the shore. 'Do you see that one?' He pointed at what, to Laura's eyes, was a small gull. 'It's a Fairy Tern. They're endangered but we're keeping our fingers crossed for a good breeding season.'

'To my shame, I know little about birds. I was thinking earlier that I don't recognise any of the bird sounds. Isn't that a pelican?' Laura pointed, excited to see what was to her a more unusual bird.

'It is. We'll go for a walk tomorrow down the Old Convict Road by the river. Ash will enjoy that.'

'Ash?'

'Yes, he's arriving later after his night shift at the hospital. He followed in my footsteps working in A and E as a registrar.'

'That sounds like a proud father speaking.'

John glanced down at Laura with a frown. 'No, my son lives in California. I rarely see him or speak to him. The break-up with his mother was bad. My fault. We were too young. Ash came to us when he was fifteen. His mother was Molly's best friend, but she died of cancer. She made us guardians. Look there's a Little Tern, its wings are greyer than the Fairy Tern.'

'I think I recognise those. We have them in Chichester Harbour. That's so good of you to take on another person's child.'

John turned towards Laura, his mouth a thin line beneath his grey moustache. 'I would never leave a child to go into a children's home after what happened to my father.'

'I'm sorry, I didn't mean to upset you.' Laura sensed a lot of pain buried beneath the surface of his warm affability.

He stood in silence, binoculars trained on the sea before dropping them back on his chest, then sighed. 'I suppose I should tell you what I know but it's minuscule. Rose was found dead from exposure. She was lying in a street in Ballarat, the richest city of the empire at that time.' John drew in his lips. Laura could tell how this admission pained him. 'My father was almost five, a miracle he was found alive. It can get icy in Ballarat in July. Europeans think Australia is always hot but it's not true. Dad told me that she gave every morsel of food to him and wrapped him in her warmest clothes. When they found her, she had no identification apart from an old letter on her, no envelope. I found a newspaper report from a day or two after asking if anyone knew her. It quoted the letter.'

'What did it say?' Despite the sadness of the story, Laura's excitement was mounting.

John screwed up his eyes, Laura could feel how painful he found to talk about his father. 'It's engraved on my heart.' He took in a deep breath before speaking.

'Dear Essie, I am sending all that I can spare for Amelia Rose's dowry. I pray you have chosen a good man. I will be leaving my present employment in the city shortly. My health is beginning to fail. I seek a better climate and hope to start a teashop in a town northwest of here, called... Unfortunately, the town's name was too indistinct to decipher apparently. It ended, *your sister, Susanna Thornley.*'

'Wow! Rose did have the missing letter. I really hoped that she had found them. And where is Ballarat in relation to Melbourne?'

'About seventy miles but more west than northwest.'

'She was looking for her mother.' Laura's eyes smarted, she wiped her hand across them, pretending to shield them from the bright sun.

'Maybe so. I often puzzle about where this Susanna Thornley lived. I wish I could see the original letter. Anyway, my father was taken to the Orphan Asylum in Ballarat with the name, Alfred Thornley, and stayed there until he escaped at fourteen.' John rubbed his eyes before growling, 'He described it as an emotional wasteland with occasional bouts of violence. My father was a gentle, peaceful man. It something he cultivated after the horror of his early years.'

It was Laura's turn to stand in silence. She ached to give John a hug but sensed he would shrug her off. His pain was too intense, too private. 'Granny will be so upset to hear all of this.' After more silence, she ventured, 'her grandmother, Louise, missed her mother so much. I'm sure she kept hoping to discover what had happened. Yet Rose died so young. It's too sad for words.'

John turned to Laura and put a hand on her shoulder, gripping tight. 'If my father had known that he had a sister, he would have moved heaven and earth to find her.' The pressure in his fingers relaxed. 'Dad was treated in England for injuries during the First World War. He talked about the hospital. I think it was called Graylingwell. What a missed opportunity.'

Goosebumps travelled up Laura's spine. 'That's so spooky. Graylingwell is eight miles from my flat. It's just to the north of Chichester. I was there at a summer fayre a couple of years ago, there are still remnants of the hospital, although it's being redeveloped.'

'The world is full of strange coincidences. We think of it as large, but in many ways it's small and fate has more influence than we imagine.' John sighed then abruptly changed the subject, as though he had had enough of being maudlin. 'Let's go back, lunch will be ready.'

The table was set with salads, cold cuts and a quiche when they walked through the door.

'I forgot to ask if you were vegetarian, Laura.' Molly's eyes crinkled in concern.

'No, not at all, though I try to eat veggie at least twice a week.'

Molly's face cleared before she pounced on John and wrapped her arms around him. 'You'll never guess. I'm so excited.'

'What?'

'I had a few moments, so I went on Trove.'

'What's Trove?' Laura asked, perplexed.

'Our newspaper database. It has all the old papers going back to the year dot, around eighteen hundred or so. Come on, I'll show you.'

John and Laura wandered over to the table where a laptop lay open.

Tragic Accident screamed the headline. John sat down to scroll through the article and began to read out loud for Laura's benefit. '*On*

Thursday last, we are sad to report that a thirty-six-year-old male was crushed by a runaway wagon at the Eureka Mine. Alfred White, a recent immigrant from Liverpool...' John stopped reading, his hand shaking on the mouse.

'Shall I read the rest for you?' Laura asked. He nodded and moved over to sit on another chair. The article went into a long description of the accident which Laura staggered through, aware of John's distress, finishing with. '*He leaves a wife, Mrs Rose White and a two-year-old son. The mine owners have declined to offer compensation. Fellow workers have donated money for the funeral.* It's dated February 1881, The Ballarat Star.' Laura had to shake herself. 'I don't believe this. Alfred travelled from America to be with Rose and their son. How did I never find that out? What awful luck they had.'

Molly knelt beside John and grasped his hand. 'I'm sorry love, but at least we now know what happened.'

'I just want to be able to tell Dad.' John's voice trembled.

'He'll know.'

'I wish I had your faith, Molly. Dad struggled all his life; everything was against him until he met my mother. He was sixty when I was born, Laura. He married a poor widow with a young child to save her from destitution in the depression and they grew to love each other. What did I tell you? Kismet. He was a wonderful father despite having no money, but he could never bear to see anyone hungry. When he died at eighty, I was so disappointed. I wanted him to see me qualify as a doctor. I wanted him to be proud of me, to achieve what he could not.'

Molly stroked the thin wisps of his grey hair and clutched him to her before gently saying, 'Let's eat now. Laura must be starving after her early start.'

He nodded and turned to Laura. 'I owe you such gratitude for giving me closure. That's what this is, and it wouldn't have been possible without you.'

Laura grasped his hand. 'I wasn't sure about making this trip. My grandmother encouraged me. Sometimes I think she has a sixth sense. I'm so pleased I came.'

'So are we, Laura.' John bent to kiss the top of her head.

After lunch, John retired to his bed for a nap while Molly cleared away and stacked the dishes. Laura filled a bowl with water to wash up.

'It's strange, isn't it? All this time and the answer was out there if only we had known where to look.' Molly opened the fridge to pile in the leftovers. 'I think we should have a little ceremony later to remember Rose and Alfred. We'll pick some flowers from the garden and then take them down to the shore. I think John would like that, don't you?'

'That's a wonderful idea. I'll film it on my camera to share it with Peggy. I'm making her a video diary of my trip.'

'What a great idea.' Molly came over to her to give Laura a hug. 'Thank you, for coming to visit. It means a lot.'

A rush of affection overwhelmed Laura and she leant against Molly's motherly bosom. A mixture of the scent of roses and onions wafted from Molly's purple blouse; it seemed like a perfect combination. Laura closed her eyes until the slamming of the front door heralded a visitor. She opened them to see a man staring at her with surprise and wariness – his eyes glowering black with suspicion. Her skin prickled and goose bumps rose on her arm. She shifted her gaze to Molly who gave her a reassuring smile.

Chapter Forty-One

Unsettled, Laura moved to the lounge area and sat in a deep armchair, leaving the man she presumed to be Ash, and Molly to talk. She sensed hostility in the air. Picking up a magazine, *Tasmanian Living*, she began to flick through the pages while taking sideways glances at the two in the kitchen. Low voices kept her from hearing but the stiffness in Ash's shoulders and the earnestness in Molly's face pointed to a heated discussion. Laura heard her name mentioned at one point and he turned to catch her watching, his eyes smouldering, jet black wavy hair glistening from the afternoon sun streaming in through a side window. Laura's heart flipped. What was it about him? Perspiration began to trickle down her back as sun filtered through the large window to the north. Laura wafted the magazine across her face, before taking off her sweater and wiping her face with it. This was ridiculous. She was reacting like a schoolgirl to her first crush.

She looked away and stared out at the gum trees across the road trying to ignore what was going on in the kitchen. Tiredness from her early morning start and some lingering jet lag, forced her eyes to close for a few seconds. She meant to open them again, but seconds turned to minutes as she drifted off to sleep. When she woke, her mouth tasted claggy. She grimaced to find dribble at the side of her mouth and strands of hair stuck to her chin.

'You slept for a good half-hour. Do you feel better? I have a glass of iced water for you.'

Laura's eyes opened wide at the sound of his voice. He sat opposite staring at her, an amused look on his face. God, he was handsome. Dev Patel without the facial hair he lately professed. A long, straight nose, white teeth, boyish cheeks making him look younger than he probably was. She had not expected Ash to be of Indian origin, a mixture probably, but whatever it was it worked.

'I'm sorry I was less than welcoming earlier,' he said. I'm very protective of Molly and John. A visit from a stranger they met on the

Internet. You can understand my reservations.' He proffered the glass of water.

Laura took it, conscious of her dishevelled state.

'Molly's explained about the DNA test and so I come bearing apologies. Please say you forgive me. I'm Ashwin Macauley. Most people call me Ash.'

He pronounced it As-hwin which sounded like a breath of scented air stirring on a summer's evening. Had she fallen asleep and woken up inside a Barbara Cartland novel? Laura sipped the water to calm herself, peeking at him from beneath her lashes. It was that sheepish smile which undid her. She had an urge to brush her fingers against his lips. She coughed, sure her breath stank of onions and garlic. 'Laura Gray, pleased to meet you and apology accepted. Excuse me, I really must visit the bathroom.'

'I'll show you to your room. Molly said that she hadn't got around to doing that yet. I've put your bag in there already. Take a shower if you like.'

Was that an indication that it was more than her breath that stank? Pink flooded her cheeks.

He stood and held out a hand for her. Laura grasped it, firm, square with short clean nails. He pulled her up and she followed him towards the bedroom, his lean sinuous body taunting her. Ash opened the door for her into a neat guest room, the small double bed made up with crisp white sheets; fluffy grey towels lay on a silvery throw. He pointed out the ensuite, grazing her hand as he left saying, 'Welcome.' Her skin burned at his touch.

Laura stood looking at the door after he left, thinking the only thing I have said to the most gorgeous man I have ever met is, for want of a better phrase, I need a pee. I should have my head examined. But she did need the toilet urgently. Grabbing her sponge bag, she marched into the bathroom.

Laura emerged from the bedroom smelling of peach scented soap, her hair of almond shampoo and her mouth of minty toothpaste. She wore her least creased trousers and a lavender shirt, the backpacker's dressed-to-kill options were limited. John and Ash were chatting but before she could join them, Molly demanded her presence in the garden to select flowers for the ceremony.

'John's delighted with the idea. He wants to do it soon, before the barbie needs lighting. I thought a mixture of English and Australian flowers to signify their journey from England, don't you?' Laura nodded. 'Shall we go for muted colours or something vibrant?'

'Vibrant. I'm guessing that they didn't have much colour in their final days.' Laura mused. 'There are so many flowers here I am unfamiliar with, but you also have ones I do recognise.' Laura stood in the sunshine, the temperature a more familiar eighteen degrees. 'I love the way the tones blend into each other. You have a painterly eye.'

'Thank you. That's the effect I was aiming for. John has his birds; I have my garden. It may not be large but it's enough for me. We used to have a wooden beach shack here for summer use. When John said he wanted to move permanently, I insisted we have a house with enough land for me to create a garden. It's taken me ten years but I'm getting there. The climate here is perfect for English flowers as well as native species.'

'I've never had a garden, just a tiny courtyard with some decking. We always had a patch of grass as a child, but Dad never had time and his wives displayed no interest. What's this plant?' Laura pointed to a bush with yellow flowers.

'Grevillea. It's native.'

'That's perfect, together with that one.'

'Waratah, also native.'

'I love it, so showy. I can imagine it as a corsage for an elegant ballgown. Was Ash's mother Indian?' Laura couldn't help herself. It slipped out.

'Priya, yes. She was so lovely, gentle, caring. I adored her.'

'And his father?'

'Australian. It was tragic; James died in a boating accident when Ash was ten. The poor boy was so lost when he came to us. John was great, took him fishing, got him interested in birds and medicine. I just made sure he had lots to eat and oodles of affection. He's the child I never had.' Molly's eyes crinkled with regret.

'I'm surprised he's not married with those looks.' There it was again. She did not mean to let the words leave her mouth. They slipped out.

'He was.' Molly looked at Laura speculatively. 'We never liked her, but you don't interfere. She was a vamp, is that the right word? Led him a merry dance. I knew she was seeing other men, but Ash didn't want to believe it until he had no choice. He was heartbroken. He finds it difficult to trust attractive women which is why he was so suspicious of you. I like the scent of this apricot rose. Shall we include a couple in our bouquet?'

Laura bent to sniff. The rose was divine - sweet and strong. It allowed time for her blush to subside. Why would anyone cheat on Ash? The thought that he might find her attractive made her knees quiver. This whole thing was ridiculous. She was only going to be here until Boxing Day and then he would disappear from her life. What on earth was she thinking? 'Yes, Molly. It smells wonderful and how about that purple flower over there.'

'Heliotrope. That's native to Peru but gorgeous. It has a whiff of cherry pie. We just need some greenery to offset it all.'

As they set off from the house for the shore, Molly told Laura to walk ahead with Ash. 'He walks too fast for John. We'll meet you there.'

Laura had to quicken her pace to keep up with Ash's long stride.

'I really feel bad for doubting your intentions earlier,' he began.

'No need, I would have thought it odd too. I still can't believe I'm on this journey. It was a spur of the moment thing for my granny's sake.'

'John never discussed his family with me. I think he didn't want to burden me, with my parents dying so young. Molly said your mother died too.'

'When I was a toddler. I don't remember her but it's a loss that stays with me always.'

He looked down into her face. 'I was so wrong about you, I'm sorry.'

Laura shivered while the late afternoon sun played on the back of her shirt.

'I knew John had a sadness about him, but I put that down to what he witnessed in Vietnam. This afternoon, I can see that troubled look has lifted. He looks more relaxed. See how he's chatting so effortlessly with Molly.'

Laura turned her head to look back. John had his arm linked through Molly's, his other hand on his stick. They looked carefree and happy.

'How lovely to see a couple still so much in love. How long have they been together?'

'Thirty years or so. You're right. They do love each other.' Ash looked wistful.

'My long-term boyfriend walked out on me last May. I thought we were going to get married, but now I'm so pleased we didn't. I suspect we were never suited. He wanted different things.'

Ash said nothing but his fingers touched hers fleetingly. She ached to cling to his hand. They walked on in silence, but something had changed between them.

At the beach, John stood with the flowers at the water's edge. Laura had her phone camera ready.

'Rose and Alfred,' he began, then paused. 'You left the comfort of your family in Liverpool to strive for a new life and new family in Australia. You worked hard but Australia let you down. Rose, you loved your son and he loved you and never forgot you. We, your grandson and your who knows how many times great granddaughter, Laura, honour you and promise we will never forget you. I ask my adopted son to cast a flower upon the sea each Christmas Eve in your memory, Rose and Alfred.'

Laura's hand began to shake. She felt Ash's hand on her shoulder to steady her.

'I promise, John.' Ash answered. 'It will be an honour.'

'I will now sing the song my father handed down to me from his mother.' John's voice began softly before rising in a rich baritone making the hairs stand on the back of Laura's neck. The Skye Boat Song. The circle joined, Rose no longer a ghost in Laura's mind but her ancestor, one who passed down a song so familiar, one of the only memories she had of her mother. Every time Laura heard the theme tune to Outlander, it was like someone stepping on her grave. John finished singing leaving only the screech of gulls. No one wanted to break the spell.

Molly laid a hand on John's arm and lightly kissed him before saying, 'At the risk of destroying this fine bouquet, I ask each of you to take a flower and cast it into the sea,' offering a flower to each of them.

Laura chose the waratah. 'For Rose and Alfred and for you, Mum. I never got to say goodbye, but I've always missed you. May you rest in peace.' She threw her flower into the sea, watching it lie crimson on the sparkling blue water, before drifting off amidst the seabirds diving for food. Her eyes filled with tears as she lifted her mobile to take a photo for Peggy. Ash stood beside her. His heliotrope lay beside the waratah. 'I don't think there could be anywhere more peaceful on earth,' she said.

'I love it here. The first time John and Molly brought me to Orford, I began to grieve for my mother. Up until then, I had been plain angry, furious in fact. I couldn't get past it. The pain consumed me. It seems right that we can do the same for John.'

'There's a healing power here, I can feel it.'

'It's time we lit the barbie,' called Molly. Ash has brought us some barramundi fillets from Hobart. Have you tried barramundi, Laura?'

'No, I haven't.'

'You have a treat in store, especially with Ash's Asian spices.'

Laura nodded and smiled. She took one last look at the flowers drifting into the distance. This afternoon was like an ending and a beginning. She turned towards Molly, beaming. 'I'm looking forward to that.'

Chapter Forty-Two

1879 Melbourne - Alfred

Alfred stood holding the rail before walking down the gangplank. He peered through the crowd trying to catch sight of a lone woman. He had telegraphed the GPO in Daylesford with the date of his arrival, but he had no idea if she would be here. Nerves twitched in his stomach, unsure about this decision, almost taken on a whim when he reached San Francisco.

He suspected his brother had left a false trail with that handbill advertising the wealth of California left conveniently in his lodgings. There had been no sign of them in New York. Someone had told him of a family matching their description buying tickets for California, so he had blundered onwards. When he caught up with the family, their bemusement was nothing to his humiliation.

Should he have given up and returned to Liverpool when his savings were almost gone? No, Harriet's behaviour had shamed him. He had been attracted to her fragility, her pale topaz eyes peeping beneath her fluttering lashes promised much. She had enraptured him, knowing full well that his brother wanted her too. If they had fought, Thomas would have won. He had scarcely hoped that a short-sighted, balding bank clerk was any match for a muscly, handsome railway man in his wife's eyes, but it was Esther who had decided. The older brother should marry the older daughter. At the time he had been grateful while Thomas seethed until Esther paid him off. Poor Rose, she had been the consolation prize.

When was it that he realised that Harriet despised him? Not until she left - if truth be known. He had been blinded by adoration and she had acted her part to perfection Could he now feel sorry for Harriet? What choice did she have in the matter? The more he got to know his mother-in-law, the more he realised that you crossed her at your peril. Harriet had always wanted Thomas, well now she had him, along with his daughters. Alfred cursed his brother.

There was no lone woman to be seen. He turned away from the rail but then heard his name called. Looking around, he saw her, one hand aloft, beckoning, the other clutching something. What was it? He peered over the railing, the sun almost blinding him. He waved and turned to join the queue for the gangplank.

Two women greeted him as he stepped out onto land. Rose, the same sweet, shy woman, he had come to admire. If only her facial scars had not dismayed him when they first met. Now, he barely noticed. The older woman, thin with bright spots in her cheeks, but recognisably the same hazel eyes as her brother's, his father-in-law, stood a head shorter than Rose.

'You found no trace of our children?'

Alfred shook his head. 'I'm so sorry, Rose. There are no clues as to where they went.' He was riven by the hope dying in her eyes. 'You found your mother. I'm pleased for you.' He stepped forward to give Rose a brotherly kiss and stopped short as a tiny cry erupted from her shawl clad arms. 'You have a baby?' What should he say as Rose peeled away the shawl to show him a miniature version of Thomas? The breath left his body as he fought his emotions. Rose's eyes did not leave his face – was she daring him to reject them both?

The older woman stepped forward. 'My sister brought up my child. She saw it as her duty. You have both lost daughters. Look upon it as a second chance.'

'What's his name?'

'His name is Alfred White.' Rose answered in a small voice. 'Thomas Alfred but we can lose the Thomas. He can be your son. You always were a better father, be so again and I will be a better wife than Harriet.'

Alfred looked into the warm depths of her eyes and the heaviness in his soul began to lift. He smiled and ran a finger along the down of the child's head. 'Hello, Alfred, my boy.'

'Shall we go home? The train for Daylesford leaves in an hour.' Susanna felt weak with relief and coughed gently into her handkerchief, staining it with a tiny dot of red which she quickly covered.

Chapter Forty-Three

Laura 2019 Tasmania

After an early breakfast on Boxing Day, Laura took her leave, her heart heavy with regret at leaving. John and Molly had made her so welcome, giving her a Christmas to remember.

'You take care now, Laura. Have you got Ash's number?'

'We swapped numbers before he left yesterday afternoon, Molly. I'll see him for dinner tomorrow night in Hobart so I can pick up my rucksack. Goodbye, John and thank you for a wonderful Christmas.'

'No, thank you, my dear cousin. Please come back again. We've loved having you. FaceTime or whatever it is you do and watch out for those fires in New South Wales. You'd be much better off staying in Tassie. Why don't you cancel your flight?'

Laura smiled and put her arms around John. 'I may just do that, we'll see.' Her heart held a sliver of hope that Ash would persuade her. They had got on well after the initial frostiness, so much so that if her visit to Port Arthur that day had not already been booked and paid for, she may have skipped it. 'You two are the best hosts. I'd love to return one day.' Her eyes were misty. 'I missed having a family when I was young. Ash is so lucky having you two.'

Molly hugged her and whispered, 'You're just what Ash needs. If anything comes of it, we couldn't be more delighted. John hasn't a clue, of course, but that's men.'

Laura stepped back and laughed, blushing. Molly's superpowers of observation were something she had not bargained for. It was difficult to get anything past her, but perhaps neither she nor Ash had tried that hard. She had not told Molly that Ash had invited her to stay in his flat while she was in Hobart. Could she have guessed?

Crossing the bridge by the Old Convict Road a few minutes later, she smiled at the memory of their early Christmas morning walk. John had tried to educate her about the fauna and flora, while she was acutely aware of Ash walking a few steps ahead, turning every so often to look at them both. His eyes kept catching hers, a tiny grin at the edge of his mouth.

Laura drove south through the town and onward into a heavily forested area. Miles later she emerged into farmland, empty, empty roads – a thrill to drive. She stopped off in Dunalley, almost the first sign of civilisation and was delighted to find she had happened upon a monument to Abel Tasman, the Dutch explorer. It seemed apt for her ambition to delve into the history of Tasmania over the next few days. A scarlet breasted robin perched on the monument, his breast more orange and brighter than that of his English cousins. She stopped to watch him for a while before heading to the café for a quick coffee. The café next to a jetty overlooked another beautiful bay. After ordering a flat white, she stood admiring the view before turning to look at an image on the wall. Laura recognised it from a few years back although it made the hairs on the back of her neck stand up. A woman and five children sheltering in the water beneath a jetty surrounded by a demonic, orange smoke-filled sky. The inscription read Dunalley January 2013. Laura swallowed hard. Her eyes slid to the jetty outside, maybe not the same but one nearby, as she tried to imagine the fear of that family. She read the article underneath – three hours they had stayed breathing in the smoke, wondering if they would survive, an unimaginable horror. Laura had not realised that Tasmania was also at risk of bushfires. The danger felt too close as she recalled the smoke in Melbourne. Unnerved, Laura drank her coffee without lingering.

Having read *The Fatal Shore,* Laura imagined Port Arthur along the lines of Pentonville Prison in London, a gloomy, dark, foreboding edifice. She parked her car near the Visitors' Centre. Several cars and a couple of buses were already there. Intending to finish up with indoor exhibits, Laura passed quickly through the Visitor Centre before being brought up short by another reminder of life's fragility, the memorial to the Port Arthur Massacre. A vague memory resurfaced. She'd been what – twelve? She read with horror that thirty-five people had died and two dozen injured by a lone gunman with a grievance. The day was beginning to turn sour as she exited the building and entered the site.

Her mood lifted to find the dour prison buildings set at the far edge of parkland next to blue water, more holiday theme park than a London Victorian gaol, surely a sanitised image of the once harsh reality.

Set back from the attractive bay stood a sandstone church. She wandered through the walled gardens towards it. It could have been any National Trust Garden; save for the backdrop of eucalyptus trees and the Australian flowers she was beginning to recognise. Complete with a fountain and arbour, it seemed a world away from the stories of cruelty she knew she would listen to later in the day. The roofless church, itself a victim of a bushfire, retained an almost romantic feel, a grassy centre punctuated by arched windows and pinnacles and yet what stories could those stones tell? As Laura stared through the empty doorway, she again felt at odds with herself.

She wandered back through the parkland towards the bay where people were lining up to take a boat trip around the small islands. Laura looked at her printed guide, one was a burial island and the other a prison for boys as young as ten. Her breath caught in her throat, imagining Rose's son as an orphan; as unloved as these boys had been. Here was the dark edge to Tasmania, its brutal early history.

The last three days had been such a mixture of sadness, resolution and sexual tension, was it any wonder that she was on edge? Her thoughts turned to the afternoon before.

While John and Molly had rested after a huge Christmas lunch, Ash and Laura cleared away, loaded the dishwasher and stored the leftovers. Their conversation was limited to talking about work and where Laura lived in England. Outwardly it appeared light, little more than small talk. Inwardly it was more than that, Ash probed her answers, teasing out her thoughts. She felt herself shimmering under the scrutiny of his smile. Afterwards they had sat in the garden with a glass of iced coffee, and he told her about his year in London at Guy's Hospital.

'It was a great year, the year of the Olympic Games, fantastic atmosphere, but I was happy to return. This is my home, and I can't see myself ever leaving.' The look he shot was quizzical. He was sending a message about where he stood.

She responded by saying, 'From the little I've seen, I can understand why. There's a kind of beauty and peace here that is rare. You can almost touch it.'

He smiled that heart stopping smile. 'I'd like to show you more. How long are you here for?'

'Until Sunday.'

Was that a slight turn down of his mouth? 'Not long. At least I could show you Hobart. You could stay in my flat. I have a spare room. I'm on days this week but I'll see if I can swing a day off.'

It was not much, but it was also everything. Laura recognised a mutual chemistry reflected in his eyes.

'I'd like that very much,' she had said softly, although her head was telling her that the last thing that she needed was a short-lived and, therefore, doomed holiday romance.

Laura flopped onto a picnic bench to regain her equilibrium until a group of excitable Chinese tourists came to sit nearby, disturbing her reverie. Don't be foolish, she told herself. It's because I'm travelling alone that he's got to me. 'Come on,' she muttered sternly, 'You've been looking forward to this visit, put him to the back of your mind.'

A lone magpie pecking in the grass nearby, began warbling that strange endearing sound she had begun to associate with Australia. She laughed, at least John had taught her something during their pre-Christmas dinner walk. She now knew that Australian magpies were not related to British ones as much as they looked alike. She much preferred the sound of these.

Laura spent hours at the site, fascinated and appalled by the history and the stories, but by mid-afternoon, she decided to check into her accommodation nearby, intending to return for the evening ghost tour. Her cabin was only ten minutes' drive away, not especially cheap because she had booked so late.

The holiday park accommodation was spacious enough by backpacking standards and well equipped. It had direct access to yet another gorgeous bay. Laura decided to take a quick dip, grateful that she had included her swimsuit in her overnight bag.

The water was cool, and the view once again breath-taking; soft white sand, a sea verging on turquoise, and with trees the shape of parasols dotting the shore. Tiny islands, headlands and hills all added texture. She blinked trying to capture the image in her head.

Laura avoided the kayaks and swam for thirty minutes before deciding it was time to head back to her cabin and go in search of a meal, Molly's gargantuan breakfast having eventually worn off.

After a quick shower and while she towelled her hair, she looked at her phone. She had missed a text from Ash saying he was looking forward to seeing her the following day and had booked a day's leave. Could she get back to Hobart early? Laura smiled and thought that was more probability than possibility. Her skin prickled at the thought of seeing him again.

Connecting to the WiFi, Laura checked her emails. Most could be ignored but there was one from Ancestry.co.uk showing a new DNA match. It was probably nothing, just another third cousin several times removed, one of the many Thornleys. After logging on in case it was something interesting, she read it and her knees buckled as she sank onto a bunk seat, staring at the screen in disbelief.

Laura shook her head. 'It's got to be a mistake. How can they conjure up a new grandfather for me?' Her two grandfathers were called Percy and Archie. Who the heck was Rhys? Percy had died in 2016 and Archie when Laura was around eight. She remembered meeting him once or twice, a stiff ex-army guy who disapproved of his arty son, seeing it as nothing more than a pastime for wealthy young ladies and an excuse for feckless wastrels refusing to get a proper job. Flora, Archie's wife, who had died when Laura was twelve, had had artistic tendencies of her own. Laura owned a small watercolour of hers, a delicate depiction of bluebell woods. Even Laura could tell that Flora was talented. She loved the painting for its simplicity, the way the light brush strokes invoked the bluebells dancing in the grass beneath the trees. Laura remembered receiving it on her tenth birthday, Her grandmother, a wraith like figure, shy and cowed, not then by her husband but by her son's success in the advertising world. Was it possible that Flora had rebelled at some point and had an affair? Wouldn't that be delicious?

Laura's finger hovered over the link. How reliable was this DNA stuff? Her curiosity won. What harm could it do to take a peep? She clicked.

Rhys Lynton Griffiths, born 1931 in Capel-Curig, Wales. That explained her DNA being part Welsh. Little the wiser, Laura clicked on his family tree, which was sparse, going no further back than his parents, all born in the same village. He had a younger sister, Mary, but no other siblings.

Is that it? Laura wondered. A thought struck her. If Rhys was born in 1931, that would make him a lot younger than Flora, a toy-boy in fact, even more delicious. The thought of telling her father pleased her enormously. He would be beside himself with faux outrage.

Her stomach grumbled. She needed to eat. Closing her phone, Laura decided to hunt for food before ringing Ash. His shift finished in an hour. Maybe he knew what the likelihood was of false DNA results. Half of her found it impossible to believe this news.

An hour later, having feasted on the special of salt and pepper squid, she sipped her wine thinking she could risk a call to Ash, when her mobile pinged. A personal message from Ancestry lay in her email inbox. Laura's breath slowed and her heart began to pound as her finger hovered yet again over the message. The strange, unsettling feeling that had quivered in her mind all day, rose bubbling to the surface. Laura sensed that this was a moment that would live with her. Taking a deep breath, she opened it.

Dearest Laura, I can't believe this and yet I feel I must be the luckiest man alive to discover a granddaughter at my age. Can you forgive me? It must be a shock. Please, please reply. Rhys.

Laura reread the message three times, trying to guage the character of the man from these few words. He had not known about her, it was a shock, could it have been a one-night stand? She glanced at the time on her phone, quarter past five. If he were in Wales, that would make it just after six in the morning, an early riser. What should she reply?

Hi Rhys, yes, it's a shock. I'm not sure they haven't made a mistake.

Non-committal at this stage was best, she thought. Her fingers drummed on the table as she waited for a reply. Ten minutes passed.

Laura shrugged. Maybe Rhys had had second thoughts about contacting her. She picked up her phone to call Ash when that tell-tale ping happened again.

No mistake. Peggy was the love of my life. Don't think badly of her.

Laura's breath left her body, leaving a cold and empty void. Her brain refused to take it in. She had never considered Peggy for a moment. Her mother had been a honeymoon baby, born almost nine months after the wedding. Was this some kind of joke? A scam perhaps? What was this stranger trying to do, was he playing games with her? Angry, she muted her phone and went to pay her bill.

Instead of strolling back to her cabin, Laura headed to the shore walking to the furthest point away from the holidaymakers. Finding a large flat rock, she sank onto it and stared out to sea, her mind churning. Laura had come to adore her grandmother over the last seven months. To have this secret thrust upon her felt incredibly disloyal. Could it be true? Laura took out her phone to reread the email letter from Peggy which had made her embark on this trip. Everything she had written began to make sense. Regret, missed opportunities, the need to be brave – what had happened to Peggy?

Laura knitted her fingers together, twiddling her thumbs in the way that had so annoyed Jake. She wished she could hold her granny's hand and ask her. But how do you ask a question like that? Her head began to throb. Everything she thought she knew about her grandmother was thrown into the air. There was so much more beneath that calm loving surface than she understood. Now it appeared she had a new grandfather too. She shook her head. It was too much.

Her phone vibrated. It was Ash. Suddenly, she knew there was no one she would rather tell about this bewildering and unexpected news.

'Hi Laura, I'm looking forward to tomorrow. Is there any chance you could come to Hobart tonight? I'd like to take you somewhere tomorrow, but we need an early start.'

Laura considered the idea for a nanosecond.

'No problem. There's some startling news I wanted to discuss with you. It seems I have a new grandfather.'

'Wow! I can't wait to hear about it. I'll meet you at the airport in an hour and a half after you drop off your car. Is that okay?' The eagerness in his voice held the promise Laura was seeking.

'I'm on my way.' She tried to keep her voice cool, although her heart fluttered with more than a schoolgirl's crush. Did Ash feel that same instant connection she had felt?

As she walked back to the cabin to pick up her overnight bag, Laura felt like she was going through an emotional wringer. Fear, hope and not a small amount of longing made her hand tremble as she threaded the car key into the ignition.

Chapter Forty-Four

All thoughts of the ghost tour disappeared as she drove up the Tasman Peninsular. Laura forgot about stopping at the tessellated pavement after Eaglehawk Neck, she whizzed past Dunalley, turned left at Sorell with relief, only another few miles and Ash would be there, waiting for her. That thought outweighed the missed opportunities. Laura ignored the warning signs in her brain telling her that nothing could come of this, that it may leave her emotionally scarred. The only voice in her head was Peggy's willing her to be brave.

The impulsiveness of her decision to discard her plans was just one of the twists of thread knitting themselves in her mind with more questions than answers. The search for Rose and Alfred had led to a new mystery about Peggy and Rhys. Had Peggy always wanted Laura to find the truth? Insisting on Laura taking a DNA test suggested that she did.

As Laura turned left towards the airport, she looked at the clock on the dashboard, she was five minutes ahead of schedule. Would he be there? Butterflies crowded her stomach – she had not experienced those since the first days of meeting Jake.

Leaving her car at the Avis drop-off point, after only a cursory inspection, Laura walked towards the terminal building amongst a crowd of people alighting from a Hobart airport transfer bus. She caught sight of Ash before he saw her. He was scouring the Herz drop off point across the road. There was a brief moment when she paused and thought this man has the power to break my heart if I am not careful. I could flee but could I live with the regret? What would Peggy do? He turned and saw her. His welcoming smile drew her like a beacon with Peggy's voice chiming in her head. 'Take a chance, Laura.'

'I know it's only been twenty-four hours, but I've missed you,' he said, taking her overnight bag. 'Would you think me too impolite if I kissed you?'

Laura stepped forward, tilting her face, expecting a peck on her cheek, but as his mouth reached for hers, she threw away caution.

His kiss was not tentative, it was urgent, eager, matched by her. She did not mind the antiseptic scent of his skin and revelled in the taste of coffee on his lips.

'How long were you waiting?' she murmured in between kisses.

'Forty minutes,' his smile was rueful. 'I hopped in my car and drove here as soon as you put the phone down.'

Laura wondered if she ought to say that she was not the kind of girl who normally kissed someone within hours of meeting them. That was banal and unnecessary. They were both adults. In two days, she could be back here catching a plane. Why not allow herself to be caught in the moment?

'How long will it take to get back to yours?'

'Half an hour.'

'Okay. Cool.'

He looked at her, appraising her expression and then grinned. Taking her hand, he led her across the road to the car park.

Laura scarcely dared to look at his face during the drive along the dual carriageway. A few sideways glances told her enough. He drove carefully but the miles sped by until they reached a bridge across a wide river. Lights were already sprinkling the city beyond as the evening sunshine shimmered on the water.

'It's beautiful,' Laura gasped.

'You need to see it from the top of Mount Wellington.'

'Is that where you are taking me tomorrow?'

He shook his head as they headed south into the city. 'Too many tourists, this time of year.'

'Where are we going then?'

'Somewhere quieter.' He refused to be drawn. Laura sensed he was toying with an idea but had not made up his mind. 'You know, Molly said something to me before I left yesterday. She always talks a lot of sense. I haven't always listened to her.'

Laura waited to hear what he was going to say but he left it hanging, waiting for her to ask.

'She said something to me too when I left.'

After a long pause, he turned to look at her. Laura broke into laughter, and he joined in. 'I guess she said the same to us both.' His hand grazed her knee as he slowed down at some traffic lights. His tone became serious. 'Are you ready to find out?'

How should she reply? A simple yes was not enough. Laura stared out of the window towards the harbour where the sun was beginning to paint the far shore a golden red. 'John mentioned *kismet* to me before we met. I thought he was being fanciful. I have no experience of the meaning of fate. But since I set eyes on you, it's all I can think about.'

'Not all,' he said, softly. He grazed her knee again, his hand lingering a moment longer this time. 'Soon be there. It's just up the hill.'

His touch sent a heatwave through her skin. 'Can't wait.' Her voice sounded like a strangled cat rather than someone knowing she was about to embark on a love affair and incapable of resisting.

Afterwards, she lay in his arms, her cheek resting on the dark stubble of his chin, wordless as he stroked the skin of her breast until her nipple began to harden again. This time, he lingered until she begged for more. She had never felt like this, never given herself so completely, never felt every nerve ending jangle with such idiotic pleasure that left her breathless with anticipation for the next time.

'How did this happen?' he said, as he kissed her eyelids.

'I've no idea but...' The thought of this lasting only until her flight to Sydney left on Sunday made the blood drain from her head. 'I need the bathroom.' Laura sat up, clutching the sheet around her.

'That seems to be a habit with you,' Ash joked, but he sensed her sudden change of mood. 'It's through that door. 'I'll scramble some eggs. I missed out on food today.'

Laura pulled the sheet closer and walked towards the door. 'Crazy,' she said to herself. 'Where is this leading to?' She turned on the shower and stood underneath, welcoming the stream of hot water as it scoured her skin, newly sensitive to Ash's touch.

This man may be the love of her life. How could she walk away and go back to what? Daniel could never have been the answer. What they had shared was a friendship, nothing more. This was something altogether different. Rhys's message appeared in her mind. He called Peggy the love of his life. Had they spent a lifetime of regret? Had Peggy ever felt the way Laura did at this instant? And had Peggy given up passion to marry someone she did not love. If so, why?

A knock on the door. Ash poked his head through the steam. 'I came to tell you your eggs are ready. Hey what's this? Why are you sad?' Ash shucked off his shorts and walked into the shower to hold her. Her lips latched onto his. They made love for the third time with water cascading around them and Laura knew that her heart was breaking, even as Ash whispered endearments. She had no option but to return to Peggy and find Rhys for her before she died. Peggy must be told that Rhys had never stopped loving her. It was the least she could do.

Later, they surveyed the congealed eggy mess in the kitchen.

'I'll order an Indian. Whilst we're waiting, tell me your news about this new grandfather.'

As Ash ordered the takeaway, Laura strolled around the kitchen diner, picking up photos. She studied a wedding portrait, a sloe-eyed Indian woman, dressed in a sari shimmering with red and gold, a delicate shy smile adorning her face. The bride stood beside a grinning tall, bearded, brown-haired man wearing a dark blue suit. All the guests appeared white, apart from an Asian lady in a midnight blue changshan. Laura recognised Molly, red-golden tangles of curls, like a real Irish Colleen.

'Are these your parents?' Laura asked as he put down the phone.

'Yes.'

'They look so happy. Where are her relatives?'

Ash picked up the photo, his face soft with love. 'They were the happiest couple I ever knew. Ash's voice developed a sudden sadness. 'My maternal grandparents lost their first families during the Indian partition but married again. My mother was their late consolation. She looked after them until they died, then left for Australia to begin a new life. Her relatives did not approve, but she found it difficult to cope with the effects of her parents' melancholy. She wanted a new beginning. My father and Tasmania gave her that.'

'You can choose your friends but not your relatives. I don't know who said that, but it's true.'

'Harper Lee.'

'I probably should have known that. Will this new grandfather, Rhys, be worth discovering? If my grandmother loved him, I'd like to think so.'

'Tell me more.'

'I got a new DNA match today. Then I received an astonishing email from a man who claims to be my grandfather.' Laura switched on her phone and opened her email. 'Two more messages from Rhys, I assume. First, can you take a look at the DNA match, to see if it looks okay?'

Laura handed her phone to Ash. 'Your DNA test identified your grandmother, anyone else?'

'Some distant cousins on her side of the family and John. Mine said I had Welsh ancestry.'

'That seems in order.' Ash clicked on the new messages from Rhys.'

'This message says he has a photo of Peggy and him. Can he send it? His friend will do it as he doesn't understand technology. I don't think you should give him your email just yet. I'll ask him to send it to my phone.'

'Thanks.' Laura smiled at Ash's protectiveness.

'The next one says he has a note from Peggy with the date. Should he send that? I'll pass on my email. Let's see what happens.' He turned to her, 'This is quite exciting, isn't it? I can understand why this journey means so much to you. My father was always proud of his convict blood, twenty years before it became fashionable to have convict ancestors. One day I'd like to trace them back.' Ash drew her to him and kissed her, a long lingering kiss. Just when Laura thought it was about to turn into something else, the doorbell rang.

'That's the drawback of having my favourite takeout only a hundred metres away.' He drew back with a wistful grin and Laura's stomach somersaulted. 'Do you want to find spoons and plates while I find my wallet?'

Laura began to open cupboards in the spotless modern kitchen. It was sleek and masculine, all grey and white, yet felt used rather than for show. Knives and forks were already on the table from the scrambled eggs debacle, as were wine glasses. She carried plates and spoons to the table as Ash set out a variety of Indian dishes.

'I think you ordered for an army. It smells delicious.'

'Something gave me an appetite,' he winked, as he put a few containers aside. 'These will come in for tomorrow's picnic.'

'A picnic? I like the sound of that. She began spooning rice, butter chicken and lamb jalfrezi onto her plate, realising that she too was hungrier than she ought to be after her meal four hours before. 'What do you think's happening to us?' she ventured.

He looked up from serving his own meal. 'I would have thought that was obvious.'

'Why is it obvious?' Laura sat down, staring at him, wondering what answer he would give with a mixture of dread and hope.

He too sat, taking her hand into his. 'We're two people on the verge of a wonderful, glorious love affair.'

'Affair?'

Laura, I may be falling in love with you. I thought I made that fairly plain. For the first time in my life, I might add.'

'What about your wife?'

'What I thought was love was not love. I couldn't get enough of her at the time, and she knew just how to manipulate me. Does that describe you?'

He was annoyed that she had spoilt the mood. Laura shook her head. 'I'm sorry. I won't mention her again.'

'Please don't.' His look softened. 'Would you like to know when I realised that I wanted you?' She nodded, her fork half-way to her mouth. 'I'll admit, I was suspicious of you at first. You were attracted to me, weren't you?' She nodded again. 'Those signals you gave reminded me of Vanessa, her, whose name is never to be spoken again. However,' he paused and grinned. 'She would never have let her guard down enough to fall asleep and snore loudly enough to wake the devil.'

'I didn't.' Laura threw a paper serviette at him.

'You did. I watched you sleeping for ten minutes or more. No one who could look as innocent as you, with your sweaty shirt rucked up to your bra and dribble coating your chin, could be as vain as you know who.'

'You're making fun of me.'

'I am. But it made me realise that there are beautiful women who can be fun and adventurous, who don't spend all their time preening.'

He smiled beatifically, spooning rice and lamb onto his plate. 'Your turn.'

'You're just fishing for compliments. I made a complete fool of myself when I first saw you and you know it.'

Ash blew a kiss at her across the table. 'I may have. Perhaps I should make it up to you. Have you finished eating?

Laura looked at her half-empty plate. 'I have. Is it time for dessert?'

Chapter Forty-Five

Ash woke her at quarter past six.

'What time do you call this?' she grumbled. 'Let me sleep for another hour at least.'

'You can sleep in the car. We need to be on the road to catch an early ferry. Stick some clothes on. You'll need something warm. Here's a coffee.'

'I need a shower.'

He sat down beside her and stroked her cheek. 'Your skin is so soft. What do they say about English girls? Peaches and cream.'

She reached for him to pull him closer, but he resisted. 'Just clean your teeth and get dressed. You can shower later. I love the way you smell.' He nuzzled her ear before patting her bottom. 'Move.'

As the door closed, she grimaced and eased herself from the bed, slinking into the bathroom to use the bidet at least.

Laura fell asleep in the car, waking only when they joined the line for the ferry.

'Where are we?'

'Kettering.'

Her brain scrambled to make sense of it. 'Kettering's about as far away from the sea as you can get,' she said, emerging from the passenger seat. Laura found the place names in Tasmania odd. 'Why did they have this fetish for calling everywhere after random British towns?'

'Who's in a bad mood? What you need is breakfast.' He led her into the café at the ferry terminal.

She did. How much of that takeaway had she eaten last night? Only a few mouthfuls before they had abandoned it. Laura grinned at the memory before looking up. 'Oh, my God. I suspect this Kettering is somewhat more picturesque than its namesake.' She walked out onto the café balcony. The scene reminded her more of an inlet in Devon or northern Spain; sailboats and motor cruisers lining the natural marina, the sea and early morning sunlight contrasting with the heavily wooded hills beyond. She delved into her bag for her phone to take a photo. It was not there. Where was it? She always left her phone in her bag. But last night was something of a blur.

'It's not there.' Ash handed her a croissant and a cardboard cup of coffee. 'Today's for you and me. I'm not sharing you. I left mine behind too.'

'But…' Anyone else and Laura would have considered that creepy. A relative stranger taking her on a mysterious trip and removing her phone.

'No buts.' He leant to lick a flake of pastry from her mouth. 'Tonight, you can catch up. Today I want to show you why you can't leave on Sunday. Two days is not enough. We need more time together. Come on, the ferry's about to leave.'

Her hesitancy dispersed. The heavy beat of Jai Paul's *Do You Love Her* surged through her veins. The invitation to stay for longer relieved the tension that had been building at the thought of saying goodbye so soon. Laura decided to relax and enjoy the day.

Once they arrived on the island, Ash drove for twenty minutes along deserted roads. He pointed to an oyster farm and asked her if she wanted to stop.

'Not my cup of tea, I'm afraid.'

'So British,' he mocked. 'They say oysters are an aphrodisiac.'

'Do you think we need some?'

'Touché.' He squeezed her thigh until she squirmed.

'Not much further,' he promised.

After driving over a narrow isthmus of land, he turned, then followed a narrow lane to the shore. A small cabin lay a few metres from a rocky beach.

'Where are we?' Laura breathed in the scent of eucalyptus as she opened the car door, a wallaby stared at her for a moment before hopping away back towards the trees.

'Welcome to my summer retreat. It belonged to my parents. We holidayed here every summer. It's where my father died, but I still use it for fishing trips. I rent it out now, but today we have it to ourselves. Help me get the food out of the car.'

He opened the boot and handed her a cool box before grabbing a couple of bottles of red wine.

After Ash unlocked the door, Laura walked into an open plan lounge diner where a large picture window overlooked the sea. She set the cool box on the counter and wandered around the cabin. Two double bedrooms, one with an ensuite, a bathroom and an outside seating area made up the rest. Smart, chic, uncluttered, she was impressed.

'It's amazing. You're so lucky.'

Ash filled the fridge with boxes of Indian curry, a bottle of sparkling wine and fruit.

'It was just a wooden shack. My father built it himself. I had it renovated eighteen months ago. Everyone seems to be turning these into Airbnbs. I actually loved the shack, just a single room with a dunny out back, but it was badly damaged in a winter storm, and I had no time to repair it. There was an honesty and rawness about it, but maybe this is more realistic for the future.'

Laura could not help herself, 'What did she who has no name think of the shack?'

'She hated it.' He grimaced. 'Came here once and moaned about everything. That should have told me all I needed to know.' Ash took Laura's hand and kissed it. His voice softened. 'Enough of her. How about a spin around the bay before lunch? There's a kayak outside. We'll take this bottle of red wine, have a swim and then come back for lunch.'

'Oh no. I forgot to pack my swimsuit.' Laura clapped her hand to her mouth in dismay.

'You don't need bathers here, Laura. It's just you and me in this slice of paradise. I am going to do the best I can to make you want to return.'

A promise he made and delivered on, Laura thought as they repacked the car to catch the ferry. She wanted nothing more than to spend her last week in his cottage, waking up to the glorious sunrise he had described, skinny dipping in the cool but sparkling water, sunbathing in the nest of deep soft sand, sheltered from the sea and prying eyes by the tall rocks on his secret beach. She blushed at the memories of their lovemaking and wandered down to the shore for one last look.

If only we could stay longer,' she whispered to the Fairy Wren perched on a white daisy bush. 'If only Ash didn't have to work. If only the next guests were not arriving tomorrow to stay at the cottage for New Year. If only I could delay my return to England.'

'What are you thinking?' His arms slid around her, startling her, lost in the laughter of a kookaburra in a tree mocking her dreams.

'That this has been the best day of my life.'

'I think mine too, Laura. This is where my parents made me and where I want to bring my own children.' The breath in Laura's throat caught as she imagined the two of them, with a couple of children shrieking with laughter as they paddled in the turquoise water.

'When did you decide to bring me here?'

He turned her around to face him. 'I had been toying with the idea of taking you for a walk around Fern Tree Gully, but at the back of my mind was here. I wouldn't bring you here lightly.'

'So, what made you decide?'

'When I saw you in the bathroom so sad, something shifted. I knew it was the right thing to do. Why were you upset?'

'Because I knew I had to leave you. There's unfinished business at home with Peggy and Rhys, my job too.'

'You feel this too, don't you? This has to be more than a holiday fling?'

Laura stood on tiptoe to kiss him lightly, 'I want it to be more,' she whispered.

'You will stay until your flight home, won't you?' Ash gripped her hand.

She nodded. 'Yes please. I don't think anything could tear me away.'

It was almost midnight by the time they got back to the flat having stopped off to eat in Sandy Bay.

'I wish I didn't have to work tomorrow,' Ash said, 'but you'll find plenty to keep you occupied. There's a great craft market on Saturday mornings in Salamanca, close to the harbour. If you're hungry, try the Tricycle Café in the arcade there, it does great Mexican snacks. The museum's great too. They run interesting tours.'

'I'll be fine. You need to rest. Let's go to bed and sleep.'

'Are you sure?'

'Absolutely. I'm shattered.' It was not altogether a lie as she lay watching him fall into sleep, loving the way he curled into her with his hand resting on her thigh. Laura smoothed his hair back from his face so she could look at him in the light glowing from a digital alarm beside the bed. The lead up to an affair had been squeezed into hours rather than weeks. She regretted nothing. Was it possible to make this relationship work?

Laura closed her eyes, imagined herself lying on his blanket, warm sand tricking through her fingers while his wine-kissed mouth sought hers and his fingers stroked her skin.

Chapter Forty-Six

The alarm pierced the early morning light. Laura had slept soundly, and she felt refreshed enough to offer to make breakfast, even though he said he wanted to think of her tousled in sleep waiting for his return.

'My sleeping princess,' he had said, ruffling her hair. 'I don't do breakfast, just coffee.'

'Well, I want to spend every waking minute with you.' Laura clambered into one of his shirts and walked into the kitchen to try and make sense of the coffee machine.

After laying the table, she found muesli in the cupboard and milk in the fridge. Perhaps if she got everything ready, he would change his mind. Nobody should go to work without food. Laura sat at the table with her phone, realising that it had been more than a day since she had looked at it. She scrolled through her emails, nothing of any importance, then realised that Ash had sent his email address to Rhys. Perhaps Ash had received a message. She stared at his phone on the shelf where the coffee jar sat. There was no way she could pick it up. It was too early in a relationship to be caught scrolling through his private messages.

She heard the shower stop, imagined him drying himself then putting on boxer shorts, great distraction therapy while she itched to pick up his phone. He walked into the kitchen, his black hair damp, beads of moisture on his cheek, skinny jeans, barefoot.

He caught her desire and grinned. 'I wish there were time, come here.'

She stood and walked over.

'I'll never be able to wear that shirt again without thinking of you,' he clasped her bare cheek in his hand and groaned. 'Don't do this to me.'

'I'll pour you a coffee.' Laura turned away and walked to the counter, her shirt rising as she reached for his phone. She heard him groaning again and smirked. 'I want you to think of me all day. Promise?'

Ash walked over to kiss her. 'Don't worry, I will find it hard to concentrate on my poor patients.' He broke away with reluctance. 'Just give me the coffee, I've got to run.'

'Can you check if you received any emails for me?'

'What?'

She handed him the coffee and phone. 'You sent Rhys your email address.'

He took a gulp of coffee while scrolling through his phone. 'Yes, I'll send them onto you. 'Got to go. Don't forget to cancel that flight. There are keys in the flowery pot on the windowsill. Just follow Sandy Bay Road down to Battery Point and turn right down the hill. It's only a fifteen-minute walk.'

Ash grabbed his car keys, shucked his feet into clogs, pecked her on the cheek and was gone.

Laura cleared away the dishes and left her bowl and cup to drain in the sink before running her own shower, amazed at the sand still in her hair as she lathered it. All these little reminders of the day before made her smile. After dressing quickly, she was loading washing into the machine when her phone pinged.

Love you it said.

Laura choked up. Really, did he mean it? In ten years, Jake had never sent such a simple message. A couple of kisses if she were lucky. The mystery was why she ever stayed with a man who had never loved her. He was only capable of loving himself. Why had it taken her so long to realise?

She tapped out - *I love you too*, then hesitated. She had said 'Love you,' to Jake on occasion, but it had been more of an automatic response. Those words on her screen from Ash were like a tiny miracle, a promise, a miniature work of art. He did not play games. Ash meant what he said.

Her phone pinged again.

Thought u'd like these emails. Not read them. Have a wonderful day. Miss u.

Imagining his disappointment at not receiving a reply, her hesitancy disappeared. Laura clicked send – there done. A smiley face appeared, and her heart skipped a beat. How many hours was it until he returned? She forced herself to breathe deeply before dancing around his kitchen with the tune of Taylor Swift's *Lover* in her brain, imagining his lips on hers, his arms holding her tight. This feeling was thrilling, overwhelming – that it may only last for a week, Laura shoved to one side.

The spin of the washing machine brought her back to earth. Time to look at those email messages.

The first was a black and white photograph she half recognised. Peggy in her graduation gown but holding hands with a young man, a university scarf draped across broad shoulders. His thick head of hair contrasted with the balding head of the man in Peggy's wedding photo. This couple looked joyful and vibrant together. Peggy was half-turned towards him with adoration etched on her face and he stared beaming at the camera. Unlike Peggy who was gowned and holding a mortar board, he was dressed casually in an open-necked shirt. So, her graduation not his and yet pride was evident in the way his arm held Peggy close. Laura dissected his face looking for clues, but the photo was too blurry when she enlarged it.

The next image was of a postcard. *Lichfield July 20^{th,} 1959* – ten days before Peggy's wedding. It read.

Rhys, pick me up at the station 12.30 on Saturday. Talk then. Peggy.

So, they had met one week before Peggy married Percy. Did this prove Rhys was her grandfather? She forgot her doubts. That, together with the DNA test proved it, but the big question was should her grandmother be allowed to keep her secret. Peggy had buried it all these years and expected to take it to the grave, or did she? That niggling again.

There was a third email addressed to Laura.

My dear child, I hope this proves to your satisfaction that the DNA doesn't lie. I need to talk to you. Please phone me urgently, your loving grandfather, Rhys.

It was followed by a phone number; not a UK one. The coffee machine was still on. Laura poured herself a cup, then sat back at the table phone in hand, still trembling. Why, when happiness threatened to overwhelm her, did she now feel life was about to throw her a new curveball? Should she let well alone? Laura popped a grape into her mouth from the fruit bowl on the table and chewed.

Ten minutes passed. The washing machine dinged. Laura emptied it and transferred the contents to the tumble dryer, set if for twenty minutes, looked at the clock on the wall, eight thirty. She could FaceTime her grandmother. Peggy answered within seconds.

'Hi Grandma, did you get my video? You did, yes it was a lovely ceremony. Listen Grandma, that man in my video, he's someone special.

I think he's the one for me. His name is Ash. I'm staying with him in Hobart.'

She could see her grandma was typing a message. Laura waited patiently – *if so hold on. No regrets.*

Peggy's face stared at Laura from the screen. So intense was the stare that Laura understood the loneliness that Peggy had lived with all those years. Was her love of Under Milk Wood anything to do with this mysterious Welshman? Dare she ask her?

'Granny, I've found a photo. I'm going to send it to you. Don't be alarmed and if you don't want to know any more, tell me to stop, okay?' Laura forwarded the photo of the graduation.

Her care worker opened the photo for Peggy to look at. Peggy's hand moved to her heart. She looked up at Laura open mouthed, her eyes naked with longing. Laura saw a tear running down her cheek.

The reaction told Laura all she needed to know.

'Granny, I'm going to find him, I promise. Will be in touch.' Laura cut the call before she broke down. How could something so powerful have lasted that length of time? It was only since meeting Ash that Laura understood. Failure to find Rhys was not an option.

It was time to phone this mysterious grandfather. Laura punched in the numbers and waited. A long continuous dial tone began until a voice answered.

'Hello, Rhys here.' Slightly breathless with a definite Welsh lilt.

After taking a deep breath to give herself courage, Laura replied. 'Hi, I'm Laura.'

A long pause and a stifled cough. 'Thank you, thank you. I was beginning to think you wouldn't call.' His voice cracked with emotion.

'I think we should meet or FaceTime at least but I'm away from home at the moment, so can't plan a meet up.'

'I have no idea what FaceTime is. I don't own any of these gadgets. We must meet, the sooner the better, Cariad. I'm begging you. I'll pay for the airfare.'

'Where to?'

'Australia.'

Laura almost dropped the phone in surprise. 'Whereabouts?'

'Bateman's Bay, south of Sydney.'

'No way!'

'What do you mean?'

'I'll phone you back in a little while, Rhys. I have to think.' Laura cut the call, her heart splintering like the wires of a snare drum brush.

Her flight to Sydney the next day stood, but could she bear to leave Hobart so soon? Was there some other way? She googled Bateman's Bay, maybe it lay close to Sydney for her to get there a couple of days before she was due to fly home. Her face fell, over five hundred kilometres return. Impossible. Maybe Rhys could get the train up to meet her. Her finger hit google again; seven or more hours and several changes. To put an old man through that would be unforgiveable.

The best thing to do was ring the airline and check on later flights to Sydney. If only she could stay one or two more days.

'No flights at all until next Friday. I don't believe it.'

'It's New Years, they sold out days ago. I can put you down for a cancellation, although you'll have to repay. Your flight's not transferable.'

'Can I fly to Canberra? Look I need to get to somewhere called Bateman's Bay.'

'I wouldn't advise it. You have seen the news?'

News, she had ignored it for days with her mind on other things. 'What news?'

'Fires, Ma'am. I suggest you take a look.' A mixture of impatience and scorn coloured his voice.

'Thanks, I will.' Laura cut the call and began googling again. The news horrified her but that look on Peggy's face swayed Laura. She owed so much to her grandmother and if through one small act she could pay some of it back, then there was no question to answer.

Rhys picked up the phone immediately. 'It's Laura again. I'm flying into Sydney tomorrow morning from Tasmania.' She heard the breath catch in his throat before he answered.

'Is that where you live?'

'No, I'm on holiday. Look, I'll find a way to get down to see you before I leave for England in a week. Let me look into it.'

'The roads are tricky right now.'

'I know. I'll be in touch when I've worked it out.' A doorbell rang at his end and then a male voice. 'You have a visitor and I need to go. Speak soon.'

'Thank you, Cariad.' Rhys put down the phone.

Laura texted Ash. This text even more difficult than the last.

Must leave tomorrow. Grandpa in Bateman's Bay. Maybe my only chance to meet him.

Laura was removing her washing from the tumble dryer when she received an answer.

Unhappy. Only doable with utmost care. We'll talk about it before u decide. Love u xxx.

What was there to decide? As sick as it made her feel, Laura would be leaving the next day. After packing her dry washing into her rucksack, Laura picked up the flat key and set off to walk down the hill into Hobart to try and take her mind off the inevitable. What was her heartbreak in comparison to Peggy's need? Laura guessed that Peggy had been longing for some resolution to the question of Rhys. It was up to Laura to provide it. No one else could.

Chapter Forty-Seven

Ash had tried everything to dissuade her from making the journey, suggesting that she return at Easter, and they make the journey together.

'I have to do this for my grandmother now. She's not in great health.'

'But it's not safe and you're on your own.' Concern drew his eyebrows together into an almost continuous line.

'Then help me do it safely,' Laura had pleaded.

Faced with her determination, he had eventually acquiesced and spent an hour organising car hire and showing her the route, along with strict guidance on how to stay out of danger.

Ash had insisted on dropping her off at the airport before his shift, stopping for coffee until he could no longer delay. They had clung to each other before she sent him away, watching until he disappeared from the carpark, the hardest thing she had ever done.

Sitting in the departure lounge at Hobart, that they so endearingly and yet so cruelly called the 'hug zone', Laura had plenty of time to mull over her Tasmanian visit.

Twenty-four hours ago, she had longed to stay in Ash's arms, not imagining anything could drag her from Tasmania for the remainder of her trip. Closing her eyes, memories of Bruny Island filled her mind and her senses. Then yesterday's trip into Hobart where she had discovered for herself the perfect city. The city where she could imagine living her life and raising a family. It was not simply the spectacular harbour, overlooking the sparkling bay and surrounding hills. It was the atmosphere. Laura accepted that little could match the time of year and she was seeing it at its best. Her mouth still drooled over the offerings of the annual food festival which had begun that day. Her hands were still sore from clapping in a yacht competing in the Sydney to Hobart Yacht Race. And then there were the temptations of the craft market, the best she had ever visited. If her rucksack weren't already bulging, she would have crammed it with goodies.

Laura had walked the length of the harbour in warm sunshine, pausing to watch street entertainers and musicians, wishing Ash were with her to hold her hand. When she told him after organising the trip, he insisted on taking her back to the harbour as the last of the sun's rays hit the water. She struggled with the idea that they could not repeat that perfect evening later in the week.

Laura opened her eyes onto the departure lounge to see a child with chocolate corkscrew curls dancing in a private space she had found for herself. With rhythm and grace, the girl appeared bewitched by the beat of the music inside her head. No earphones, only an internal soundtrack lighting up her face and body until it was electric with movement and joy. Laura felt the performance was meant for her, both a continuation of the love she felt for this island and a promise for the future. Somehow, she would return, somehow Ash and she would work it out. Her mind calmed.

In Orford she had thought her family history journey was over with nothing more to be discovered, happy to move on to a new beginning. Now, this final piece needed to be slotted in and she would be ready for her future.

Laura stepped off the plane in Sydney and followed Ash's instructions to find the railway station. It had been a short hop from tiny Hobart airport to this vast international hub. She regretted the necessity of leaving the beauty and peace of Tasmania for the bustling throng that surrounded her as she waited for the train.

Her eyes opened wide as she stepped into the double-decker carriage. Compared with her commuter train at home, this was like stepping into a new century - comfortable, spacious, clean and super quiet.

Laura traced the shape of the words on the slip of paper in her hand, Ash's handwriting stood out clear and firm. The physical ache for him had her reaching for her phone.

On train from Sydney. Missing u like crazy. xxx, she tapped.

Wolli Creek station – Laura grabbed her rucksack. If her instructions were correct, a connecting service should be a short wait. If not, she needed to head to Central Station for a train south. For the first time since arriving in Sydney, Laura stood on a platform in the fresh air, only it did not smell fresh. There was a tang in the air, not of sea but of smoke. It caught at the back of her throat. A number of other waiting passengers wore masks. She hurried to platform four, keen to get back on an air-conditioned train. As she ran up the steps, she caught sight of the sign showing the train was due to arrive in two minutes and mentally thanked Ash once again for his work on her schedule.

This was not how she had expected to spend her precious week in Sydney, a risky journey lay ahead. Her nerves jangled as the train drew into the station. She found a seat on the left-hand side of the carriage, hoping to catch glimpses of the coastline. Opposite a chic woman of around forty, maybe slightly older, smiled at her.

'Heading south for New Year's?' Her accent still retained a British quality, despite the upward inflexion.

Laura nodded and smiled back. 'I'm visiting my grandfather for the very first time.' There, she had said it, grandfather. The woman raised her eyebrows, not sure how to reply. Laura felt bold enough to continue. 'I didn't know he existed until a week ago.'

'That can't be true. A grandfather has to have existed.'

Laura laughed. 'You're right, but he isn't who I thought he was.'

'Aah! Family secrets, eh. Got to love those family secrets.' The woman chuckled, a smoker's cough interrupting the laugh. 'How far are you going?'

'Albion Park. I have a car hire booked from there.'

'That's an hour and a half away. You must tell me the story. I'm Sheila, yeah, I know. How could my parents call me Sheila when they intended to emigrate here? Such a joke.' That throaty laugh again.

Laura warmed to the woman. You could talk to people on trains, never see them again and not worry about what you said, and Laura needed to get things off her chest. Had Sophie, although no stranger, been sitting opposite, Laura would have poured out her heart, knowing things would go no further. Sheila was a good replacement.

'Hi, I'm Laura. I'll tell you the story, but I hardly know where to begin.'

'The beginning is often a great place to start.'

How could a journey fly by as quickly? Sheila was both a good listener and engaging tour guide, pointing out places of interest and good viewing points along the way. Retelling the story gave Laura some perspective on her feelings about her grandparents.

As Laura prepared to leave the train, Sheila dug a card out of her handbag. 'Your story would make a great human-interest feature. I'd love to write it up and we could sell it to one of the Sydney papers. Let me know how it goes with your grandpa, maybe send me a reunion photo. What do you think?'

Laura glanced at the car in her hand – Sheila Porter, freelance journalist – her heart sank. So much for being an anonymous stranger she could forget after a brief encounter, Laura was annoyed. 'Don't you think you should have told me this before I told you all this personal stuff?'

Sheila shrugged. 'I said think about it, no pressure. Look, I'll be in Kiama for the next ten days. It's a pretty place and I'll be happy to show you around on your way back. Just give me a call if you want to talk some more and we can tie this up.'

Cool, calculating grey eyes stared across at Laura who fingered the card, mostly wanting to tear it up but she slipped it into her pocket before heading for the door as the train slowed. Still feeling betrayed, Laura ignored the wave from the window as she walked down the platform. What a cheek! Time to put it to the back of her mind. If all went well, she had a three-hour drive ahead, but for now she was starving.

Ash had planned her journey with precision. The car hire place was not far from the station and a mile or so from the Princes Highway. A retail park close by offered a choice of eating places and within an hour of collecting the ubiquitous hire car, yet another Toyota Corolla, Laura was on the highway driving south. She had obeyed Ash's instructions to the letter, stocking up on bottled water, energy biscuits and a mask, before tuning the car radio to pick up ABC for the latest road and fire news.

Passing the turn off to Kiama, Laura grimaced. She still could not get over the woman's audacity and imagined turning up at her grandfather's place with the news she was selling his story to the newspapers. He would shut the door in her face. Laura had avoiding thinking too much about the meeting ahead but now it was time to face it. What was she going to find? All she knew was his name, age and address. Was a resentful wife going to be lurking in the background or overly protective children wondering if she was out to make a claim on his fortune, whatever that may be? When she had spoken to him, he sounded in his right mind, a little deaf, yes – that was to be expected at eighty-eight. The conversation could be awkward, stilted, and maybe after the first greeting they would have nothing to say to each other.

A moment of doubt flickered in Laura's stomach. What was she doing? Was this a huge mistake? No, it had to be done. The image of the tear rolling down Peggy's cheek drove her on.

Fighting down her hesitation, she drove through Nowra, which appeared to be no more than a soulless out-of-town shopping area before emerging back onto the forest-lined highway. A little further on, the trees stood blackened like giant sticks of charcoal beneath the murky sky. Laura drew in her breath at the extent of the devastation.

By the time she arrived in Ulladulla, she was longing to see an image of the famous coastline. Pristine beaches, cloudless skies and blue water had filled her mind before this trip. Tasmania had not disappointed and now Ulladulla offered a tantalising glimpse of what might have been. Laura drew the car into a vacant spot overlooking a pretty bay. She stepped out of the car. The tang of smoke was stronger here, and the sky was tinged with yellow. Was it safe to travel further south? The road was open, that she knew from the traffic reports. Surely, they would close it if there were any danger? Laura glimpsed a small café at the edge of the harbour and walked towards it. She needed a flat white and local knowledge to calm her nerves.

No one was sitting outside, and Laura could sense a grittiness on her skin as she walked through the door. In normal times it would be a small slice of foodie heaven. Looking at the menu, Laura regretted that she was not that hungry.

'I'll have a veggie wrap and a flat white please.'

'Grab a seat and I'll bring it over,' the waitress said.

'Sit by us, dear. We've almost finished.' An elderly woman beckoned her over. There was not much choice.

Laura perched herself at a small table occupied by a couple of retirees.

'On holiday here?' The woman's face crinkled into a smile.

'Passing through, actually. I'm on my way to Malua Bay near Bateman's Bay. Do you know it?'

'Not well, small, pretty place as I recall.'

'I'm just a bit worried about the road south and the fires, you know.'

'Aren't we all, dear?' The woman's face clouded over.

'Never known anything like it.' Her husband chipped in, his voice gruff and angry.

'Don't start, Jimmy. Just tell her what she needs to know. She doesn't want to listen to you on your high horse.'

His shoulders slumped and he forced a smile onto his face. 'You'll be all right today, but who knows about tomorrow or the day after? There's a huge fire to the south-west. If it crosses the Princes Highway...' He rubbed the skin above his left eye where a nerve visibly throbbed. 'Our daughter has a place down that way.'

His wife grabbed his hand and squeezed. 'We want her to come to us before it's too late. Malua should be safe enough, being on the coast.'

'Make sure your tank's full in case you need to make a run for it. Top it up in Bateman's Bay.' The old man instructed, his voice stern enough to make Laura take notice.

They stood to leave as her order arrived. 'Thank you. I hope your daughter is okay.' As they walked through the door, Laura took a sip of her coffee. It relieved her itchy throat while her stomach churned. She could not face the wrap. Looking out onto the picturesque harbour, Laura considered whether she should stay for the night in Ulladulla and put off her decision until the following day. Yet forty miles was little more than her commute to work, and the man had said she would be safe to drive today. Her mind made up, Laura finished her coffee, took her wrap to the counter for it to be boxed, and opened her purse to pay. Her dollars were running low, she needed an ATM.

Back on the road, with a full wallet, Laura felt calmer. A few miles north of Bateman's Bay, she sensed that the air-conditioning was sucking in the smoky atmosphere as the sky grew heavy with haze. Laura turned off the aircon. Better heat than smoke which was thickening every minute. Either side of the highway swathes of burnt forest lined the road. Her heart began to beat faster with fear. This was worse than she had imagined. Clanking over a metal bridge spanning a wide inlet, she was relieved to find herself in Bateman's Bay. Turning east away from the smoke, her breathing began to calm. Laura had not realised how tense she had become. Straight ahead was the petrol station. Glancing at her indicator told her it was over half full, hardly worth stopping, but a niggle made her pull in. The man in the café's warning, and then seeing the devastated greenery gave her pause for thought. What had Ash told her? 'Heed the advice you're given, no matter if it seems over the top. Fire takes no prisoners, and you may need to escape at any time. Be ready, don't argue.'

With a full tank, Laura set off on the final leg of her journey. She found herself at the edge of the ocean passing through small settlements. A few hundred metres after the enticingly named Lilli Pilli, she arrived in Malua Bay. A small picture postcard type of place, she let her phone guide her to her grandfather's home.

Chapter Forty-Eight

Laura drove into the neat driveway of an older style single-storey property. Small in comparison to some of its neighbours, the kind that would be torn down and rebuilt with oodles of glamour and glitz to the full size of the plot, if other properties in the road were anything to go by. The front door opened as Laura extricated herself from the stickiness of her seat. She rubbed her neck in a vain attempt to ease the tension between her shoulder blades, her stomach awash with butterflies as she turned to face him. An elderly man, yes, tall with a slight stoop to his shoulders, too thin for his height, an arm outstretched. As she stepped close enough to see the detail of his face, shock clouded her vision. The pieces of the jigsaw slotted together.

'Laura, Cariad. You are the spitting image of my mother, bendithia hi.' He grasped for her hand.

Laura was thrust back twelve thousand miles. A voice of the hills and valleys, deep, more pronounced than on the phone. An image of Michael Sheen swam into her mind. 'What does that mean?'

'Bless her - my lovely.' A broad squat hand encased hers.

Oh, so that's who's to blame for my short stubby fingers, she thought, looking up into eyes the exact match of her own.

'Come in, come in. I've been on tenterhooks all day. I hated to think of you making that journey. The road was closed earlier in the week.'

Wordless, she followed him into an airy open-plan room. Neat, tidy, a woman's touch was obvious from the knick-knacks on a dresser.

'Does your wife mind that I've turned up out of the blue?' she asked.

'It's just me. My wife died two years ago.'

'Oh, I'm sorry.'

'No need. Her last few months were… Just say, it's better that she went. Would you like a beer after your drive?'

Laura nodded, the scratchiness at the back of her throat now more sandpaper than emery board. Rhys opened the fridge and cracked open two cans of VB, handing one to her. Gratefully, she took a sip of the cold frothy liquid.

'Sit down, please. This is your home, too.'

Laura almost choked on her beer. Like John and Molly before him, she had never expected to find such welcoming strangers on this trip. She looked across at him, weather-beaten cheeks but with a glint of pride in the eyes above.

'I'd know you anywhere, Laura. You are the daughter I imagined I might have but never did. Or do I?'

'You don't know?'

He shook his head. 'I had a son, but he died at thirty-two not long after the Bali bombings. It broke our hearts. My wife never got over it. That's when we came here. Her sister lives in Bateman's Bay and Judy needed her family.'

Laura had been around ten years old then. She remembered it vaguely, one of the early Islamic terrorist atrocities. Poor man. 'Was your son caught up in the bombings?'

'No, but his friends were.' Rhys clammed up.

Laura sensed he was unwilling to talk about it further. 'Your daughter died at thirty-two as well. My mother had an ectopic pregnancy.'

He took a step towards her, crushed with sadness. 'You can't have been very old, my lovely.'

'Almost three. My biggest regret is that I don't remember her.'

He perched himself on a small stool beside her, his arm hugging her to him. 'What about your father?'

'He was there but not there, if you know what I mean. He stopped all contact with anyone else in the family. I only found Granny six months ago. She's in a care home.'

'Peggy's still alive?' The arm around her shoulders flickered and tightened.

Laura sat back in her chair and his arm fell away. 'You loved her?'

He sighed, his right eye twitching. 'Still love her. I never stopped but I was young, selfish, maybe damaged too.' He paused. 'It took the death of my son to teach me how to compromise.'

He stood. Laura sensed a tense internal struggle.

'I was an idealistic young fool, imagined myself as an eagle in the mountains flying above the ruination of the world below. What a self-regarding idiot. Lembo, as we say in Welsh.' Rhys huffed, shaking his shoulders in annoyance with himself. 'During National Service, I,' he paused before taking a deep breath. 'Let's say I saw more destruction in Germany than I ever wanted to see again.'

So long ago, ancient history to Laura but not to Rhys. Pain temporarily creased his forehead and hooded his eyes.

'I was little more than a boy and returned home craving peace, solitude, the sound of water running through mountain streams. Instead, I chose university in a city itself torn apart from that same war and I couldn't wait to escape. Only Peggy kept me sane. I can say it now, but there was some sickness in here.' Rhys tapped his head, 'I thought Canada would cure me. I begged Peggy to join me. But what did I offer her? A life devoid of music and theatre, a solitary life in a country not of her choosing.'

'Canada? Not Australia? She let you go?'

'It's complicated. I never gave up hope until she wrote that she was marrying your grandfather. I returned from Canada to beg her not to. She's not told you any of this?'

'Granny had a catastrophic stroke when my mother died. She hasn't talked since.'

His face crumpled before shaking his head in disbelief. 'No! Poor Peggy. Her conversation was one of the many things I loved about her. We argued about anything and everything, books, politics, paintings, the state of the world, everything...' Memories silenced him.

'I'd love to hear her talk, but we have found a way of communicating. We can FaceTime later if you'd like.' Laura wished she could capture the expression on his face. It was a mixture of hope, terror and excitement.

'I don't know. Does she know you're visiting me?'

'I'm not sure. I sent her that photo of her graduation. You should have seen her expression. She may have a sneaking suspicion because there's nothing wrong with her mind. Finding out about you was more of a shock for me.'

'Do you think she knows herself, that I'm your grandfather?'

Laura took his hand, then turned hers in his. 'Look at our hands. Granny's hands are delicate, her fingers long and elegant. See my eyes.' She opened them wide. 'We have the same colour; my mother's eyes were the same. That dimple you have in your right cheek, I have it too.

Granny knows. She made me take a DNA test, it came up with Welsh ancestry. She wanted me to find you.'

'I wonder if her husband knew.'

'Did you ever meet?'

'No.'

'Why should he know? Unless Peggy told him, but he idolised my mother, so I don't think so. She was born nine months after they married. I assumed she was a honeymoon baby. Why would anyone else doubt that?'

Rhys grinned, shamefaced. 'We met in Snowdonia the weekend before her wedding. I booked us into two rooms in a guest house like she asked. We met at the station.' A shy smile curled at his lips. 'We never used the second room, just fell on each other like drowning rats. I'd bought her a copy of Under Milk Wood as a wedding present, for ours rather than hers, I hoped. I begged her to come away with me.'

Laura sensed his sadness. 'Why didn't she?'

'It was a combination, the expectation of her family, her mother especially and what I was asking her to give up. I showed her photographs of the mountains, thinking she would be impressed but she asked what the wooden shack was in the corner of the photo - my home, our home. They would call it off-grid these days. You should have seen her face!' Rhys shook his head. 'The more I waxed lyrical about life in the wilderness, the more anxious she became. I knew I was losing her until in the end she left me with a choice – her or Canada.' He sighed long and hard. 'What a fool I was. Did she have a happy marriage?'

'Again, I only found out recently that she didn't. Do you know, she listens to Under Milk Wood incessantly on the iPad I gave her? I'm pretty sure she regretted her decision.'

He slumped in his armchair before sighing. 'We can't turn the clocks back but at least I have found you before it's too late.' His smile lifted the wan pallor of his cheeks.

Tiredness, hunger and a desire to sleep hit Laura suddenly between the eyes. 'Is there a room for me? I need to lie down.'

'Of course. Let me show you.' He stood and enfolded her in his arms before showing her to a bedroom where a freshly prepared bed beckoned.

Chapter Forty-Nine

A sharp rap on the door followed by muffled voices roused Laura from a deep sleep. She stretched and rubbed the back of her neck. Perhaps a hot shower would ease the tension headache which had begun to throb above her eyes. She checked her phone first. A text from Ash.

Did u make it ok?

Guilt swam into her head. It was growing dark outside. He would be worried.

Yes- all fine – sorry, she tapped. There was a knock at her door.

'Laura, are you hungry? Can you join us?'

Who's us, she wondered before calling out. 'Yes, sure. Just give me ten minutes to shower.' Laura finished her text – *It's all been a bit emotional. Will call later. xxx*

A towel lay on the bed. She rummaged in her rucksack for a change of clothes before making for the cramped ensuite.

With her hair still damp, Laura walked into the lounge to find a man chatting to her grandfather.

'Come and meet Stan. He's the one who's been helping me with the DNA and emails.'

Laura walked towards a wiry man dressed in a clean but faded checked shirt and shorts, his hair scraped back into a thin ponytail, dark stubble covering his jaw. He beamed a gap-toothed smile at her and grasped Laura's hand in a surprisingly firm grip, the hands of a working man, hard, calloused with fingernails rimmed with ingrained dirt.

'How you going? So, you're Laura. She's a beaut, Rhys. Who'd a guessed you'd have such a stunner for a grandkid, you old goat.' His tone was gentle, mocking and his accent broad.

'Stan helps me with all sorts. He's a good neighbour.'

'I'm sure,' Laura extricated her hand before he crushed it. She smiled. 'I did wonder. You've no Wi-Fi in the house, Grandpa?' testing the word. It sounded strange on her tongue.

'I'm too long in the tooth to be called Grandpa. Call me Rhys. Everyone else does. No, I've no use for Wi-Fi. Wouldn't have a clue. Stan's a wizard with all that stuff.'

'What I don't understand is why you would bother to do a DNA test if you had no idea I existed.'

Stan looked hard at Rhys who shook his head.

'You haven't told Laura, then?'

Rhys shook his head again. 'I haven't had a chance. Look, Laura's stomach probably thinks her throat's been cut. Let's get going.'

What was going on? What hadn't she been told? Laura eyed her grandfather with a curious look. 'Where are we going?'

'To the bowls club. You'll need your driver's licence.'

Laura looked at Stan who shrugged his shoulders. 'Better do as he says.' He twiddled car keys in his hand.

Laura was invited to sit in the front of Stan's Ute as they drove up a hill and turned into a large sports club. Laura guessed it was the centre of village life judging by the number of cars parked there.

Stan showed her how to scan her licence to become a temporary member before they trooped towards the restaurant at the rear.

'You have to book this time of year. That's why I woke you,' Rhys said, as he guided Laura to the only empty table.

Laura was surprised that the menu was mostly Chinese, but after her experience in Melbourne, she hoped that it would be the same quality and her stomach began to grumble loudly.

'Hungry?' Stan smiled. Laura winced with embarrassment.

'Too right.'

'You're picking up the old Aussie dialect, then?' He grinned as the waitress came to take their order.

'So, tell me. Why did you do a DNA test, Rhys?' Laura asked, once the waitress had left them.

'I was looking for my little sister. We lost touch before she married. Stan here found out that she married a chap called David Williams. Have you any idea how many Mary Williams there are in Wales? That's if she stayed there. After weeks of blind alleys, Stan suggested a DNA test in case she or any of her children had taken one.'

'Have you found her?'

'No and it's not so important now that you've turned up.'

Laura was puzzled. 'Surely if you wanted to find her, she's still important to you.'

A look passed again between Stan and Rhys.

'Come on man, you have to tell her.'

Rhys sighed before taking his granddaughter's hand. A lump formed in Laura's throat. The noise in the room began to still as she watched his expression grow serious.

'Drinks – now it's Foster's for you, Madam, and a large VB for the menfolk. Is that right?' The waitress distributed the beers oblivious to the charged atmosphere at the table.

Rhys took a long swig of his beer then turned towards Laura. 'All good things come to an end. I'm lucky, had a good innings as they say.'

'What the old bugger is trying to say is that he's got cancer.' Stan chipped in.

'How long?' Laura's voice was quiet.

'A few weeks, maybe a couple of months. Nothing more to be done.' Rhys was matter of fact, but Laura sensed his distress.

The thought of returning to Sydney for New Year's Eve flew away. She knew she had to stay until her flight home. Conflicting emotions gripped her but the overwhelming one was of loss.

'Excuse me, I need to visit the Ladies.' Laura stood and walked from the restaurant. Once there, she found an empty stall and ripped paper from the roll stuffing it into her mouth and over her nose to lessen the noise of her blubbing.

A tap at the door. 'Are you okay in there, dear?'

Laura wiped her face with the screwed-up paper, threw it into the pan and flushed. 'Yes,' she choked.' Thank you.'

'If you're sure.' The voice was gentle, concerned.

Laura unlocked the door and stepped out as soon as she heard the door close behind the woman's footsteps. She dowsed her face in cold water and looked for a paper towel. Not finding one, she stuck her face underneath the drier for a few seconds. She looked in the mirror and smoothed her hair. It was the best she could do. Time to face Stan and Rhys.

In the three or four minutes she had been away from the table, the food had arrived.

'I asked them to hold yours,' Rhys said, as he lifted a fork to his mouth. He acted unconcerned but one look at her reddened eyes showed how the news had affected her. 'I've had a long life, been to plenty of wonderful places. Maybe I didn't make the right choices once or twice but I'm ready to go.' He spooned sweet and sour chicken into his mouth.

Laura recognised a man used to disguising his feelings and needing her to do the same. She nodded as Stan raised a hand to the waitress indicating for Laura's meal to be delivered.

'I know. I am lucky to have found you at all…'

'Let's be grateful for that and enjoy the time we have left.' Rhys took her hand and squeezed. Old age and infirmity did not disguise its strength. 'How's the tucker, Stan?'

'Bonzer, mate.'

The old buggers, they were determined to get through this awkward revelation with as little fuss as possible. Laura knew Rhys had planned it this way. She had no option but to play along. The elephant in the room was to be ignored.

Her food arrived. Not a patch on the food in Melbourne's China town, but it did its job. Conversation ceased as they ate steadily, and Laura came to terms with the news. Their glasses were refilled and after a couple of drinks she began to mellow. Stan and Rhys laughed and joked about the dire state of the 'pollies up in Canberra' as they waited for dessert, a subject Laura knew nothing about.

When the conversation turned to drought and fire, Rhys grew serious. 'I could shake them by their ruddy necks. If we don't change, this country's toast.'

'I drove through a lot of smoke and burnt-out forests,' Laura cut in.

'If we get no rain, it's only going to get worse. I feel guilty for encouraging you to come down here.' Rhys paused. 'You probably need to get back to Sydney.'

'But I want to make the most of my time with you here.'

He licked his lips and stroked his chin. 'I need to see my lawyer up in Sydney. Why don't I come up there with you until your flight back? I'd love to show you the sights.'

'That would be amazing. Are you sure? It won't be too much for you?'

'I'm not an invalid yet. We'll go on New Year's Eve. Maybe even make if for the fireworks, though they ought to cancel them this year. It's no time to celebrate with the state burning around us.'

'Oh goody, the sweets are here. The pavlova for the lady and me. The usual apple pie for Rhys, Brenda.' Stan patted his stomach.

The waitress handed out the desserts as Stan gave her a little tap on the bottom.

'Cut it out, Stan, if you know what's good for you.'

'Aw, Brenda, don't be mean. It's New Year's. One little kiss won't do any harm.'

'Not while I'm working Stan. Behave yourself.'

Laura observed the exchange at first in consternation until she realised that this banter had no doubt been going on for years. Brenda, an attractive fifty something, probably was used to having a flirty exchange with all the unreconstructed male clientele.

She winked at Laura. 'You want to watch this one, honey. Rhys, on the other hand, is pure gentleman. What's a pretty young thing doing with these two old codgers?'

'Rhys is my grandfather.'

Brenda took a step back and stared. 'Wow, yes, I can see that. Rhys, did your missus know about…?'

'No, she didn't, neither did I until last week. Laura's my Christmas present, Brenda. The best one I ever had.'

'Aw, honey. That's wonderful.' Brenda stooped down and pecked Rhys on the cheek.

'So that's what it takes,' smirked Stan. 'I wonder if any of my own ill-begotten children will turn up so I can get a kiss?'

'They'd run a mile, Stan. Enjoy your sweets.' Brenda chucked Stan under the chin and scurried back to the kitchen.

'Isn't she a beaut'. What I wouldn't do to get my hands…'

'Stan, shut it.' Rhys nodded his head towards Laura.

'Sorry, Laura.'

'All mouth and no trousers, this one.' Rhys grumbled.

Laura shook her head slowly before sinking her fork into the creamy meringue.

Chapter Fifty

Sated with food, they carried their coffees into the bar area to find more comfortable seats. Stan left to order shots of brandy at the bar for them all.

'I'm sorry about earlier, Laura.'

'No need, really.'

He's been a good mate.'

'I can see that. There's no harm in him. Brenda has his measure, I'm sure.'

'She was good to my wife when she became ill.'

Laura's phone trilled as Stan arrived back at the table. 'Oh, I have to take this.' She pressed accept and stood to move away from Rhys. Her grandmother never normally Facetimed Laura. Perhaps it was something serious. Heather's face loomed from the screen. 'Is anything the matter, Heather?'

'Only with you, Laura. Your granny's been watching TV and seen all those fires in Australia, and she's worried about you. She knows that you flew to Sydney today.'

'Put her on so I can reassure her, please.'

'Right you are.'

Her grandmother's anxious face appeared on the screen. 'Granny, I'm fine. No need to worry, okay. I'm not in any danger.'

Peggy shakily held up the map of Australia Laura had given to her before she left with her route marked out.

Heather's disembodied voice rang out. 'She wants to know if you are in Sydney and not travelling south.'

Oh dear. Should she lie? 'I'll be in Sydney for New Year's Eve, Granny.'

The map shook pointedly. Laura knew that determined expression.

'I'm south of Sydney but travelling back soon. Please don't worry about me.' Laura had to raise her voice above the noise of the crowd in the bar. Her grandmother's eyes blinked before her mouth opened. She struggled to say something, but Laura could not catch it.

'She's with me, Peggy cariad. I'll look after her.' Rhys stood behind Laura, placing his hand on her shoulder.

The map dropped from Peggy's hand as she heard his voice. A moment of sheer joy lit her face before she wagged her finger at Laura.

'Who's that with you?' Heather's voice again.

'It's my grandfather, Rhys.' Heather peered over Peggy's shoulder, her mouth dropping open in amazement. Laura ignored her. 'Granny, can you remember that DNA test? Rhys did one recently and contacted me a couple of days ago. He never knew about my mother…'

Rhys stood close to Laura, so she angled the phone allowing her grandmother to see him clearly.

'Peggy, I am so grateful to meet Laura. She's a beautiful young woman. I'll take absolute care of her. She's safe with me.' Voices around them subsided as people began to listen into the conversation.'

Laura moved away. 'Are you okay, Granny? Is it too much of a shock?' I've been worrying whether I have done the right thing.'

Peggy put her left hand to her mouth and blew a kiss at the camera.

'Look, I'll phone in an hour. It's not private here. Is that okay?'

Heather took the iPad off Peggy. 'Yes, I think that's for the best. She's all of a flutter. What on earth is going on?' Heather's face still bore traces of confusion.

'I'll explain when I return.' Laura cut the call, smiling at Heather's bemusement.

Laura walked back to her grandfather. 'I didn't want to break the news like that. I worry that Peggy's too fragile.'

'Your grandmother knows you're safe with me. We once got into trouble in the Lake District on a university mountaineering group weekend. The weather closed in unexpectedly and the leader began to panic. I led the whole group to safety. She'll be less worried about you if she knows I'm looking after you. Trust me.'

'Fire's different from bad weather in the mountains.'

'Yes, of course it is. None of us take fire lightly here.' His tone grew short. 'Let's go home, I'm tired.' Rhys knocked back his brandy.

'I won't be able to FaceTime at yours. You have no Wi-Fi.'

'We'll go to Stan's then.'

Stan's house was a typical bachelor's pad. Dishes piled in the sink, a fridge full of beers and chairs where the springs twanged against their cheeks when they sat down.

'Beers everyone? Laura, here's my Wi-Fi code.'

Laura tapped it in while Stan cracked open three bottles of Foster's. There was a FaceTime message from grandma – *Tell Rhys I made a mistake*. Laura passed the phone to her grandfather who read it and wiped a finger across his eye.

'How do I reply?'

Laura showed him but he was all fingers and thumbs on the tiny keypad. His reply read - *nwtpp*. 'What do you want to write, Rhys? I'll do it.'

'I tried to type - Me too. I don't want to use this thing. Can I talk to her?'

Laura placed a FaceTime call. Peggy answered immediately.

'Hi Granny, how are you?' She waited until the thumbs up sign. 'I'm sorry. We didn't mean to tell you that way. Are you upset?' Peggy shook her head. She pointed over Laura's head. 'Do you want to speak to Rhys?' An emphatic nod. Laura handed the phone to her grandfather.

He took it and wandered over to the doors leading outside. He opened and closed them behind him. The one-sided conversation looked intense. Laura watched her grandfather in the light of the security beam. He seemed to be coping with Peggy's responses of nods and shakes, thumbs up and down. She could not hear anything which was frustrating, but the talking carried on for minutes. At one point he wiped his eyes, then took a handkerchief out of his pocket and blew hard.

Sixty years had passed since they had seen each other. They had both married, had families, stuck together and yet, as Laura watched Rhys, emotion was playing havoc with his demeanour. She turned away, unwilling to spy further.

'He really loved the old girl, you know.' Stan drew a long draught of his beer. 'When he discovered you were his granddaughter, I asked him how come he didn't know about you. You know what he said?'

Laura shook her head.

'There was only ever one woman, apart from Judy. If I'd known she'd had my child, I would have crawled on my hands and knees back to her. I was such a fool to let her go.' Stan took another draught. 'I wish I had met a woman like that. Someone to hold on to. Have you ever been in love?'

'I thought I was, but he left me earlier this year. There's a man back in London who's keen and should be a perfect fit; intelligent, supportive and kind but-.'

'But boring?'

'Not boring, sweet, likable – just no spark.' Then there was Ash. She had no intention of discussing Ash with Stan.

'Got to be a spark, love. That's the one thing I know.'

Laura nodded agreement as Rhys returned to the room. 'How do I switch this blasted thing off?' He sounded impatient.

'Here, let me.' Laura took back her phone and switched off FaceTime.

'When do you fly back, Laura?'

'January 4th. Why?'

'Things to do.'

Laura's phone pinged. It was Ash –

How's it going?

'Do you mind? I need to make a call.' With her heart pounding, it was Laura's turn to walk outside.' The spark was there, but could you turn your life upside down for a spark? She rather hoped she could.

Chapter Fifty-One

Laura woke late. She had not slept until the early hours with her mind in turmoil. Talking to Ash had further unsettled her. How could she miss someone so profoundly after such a short time? The longing in each of their voices had scoured her heart.

Rhys looked as bad as Laura felt.

'I have good and bad days,' he said, when she questioned him.

'Rest up today and let me look after you. Are you sure you should travel up to Sydney? Maybe it's not such a good idea.' She poured coffee into a cup and handed it to him. 'Sugar?'

He shook his head. 'I've already packed thinking we could get on the road today, but yesterday's excitement has knocked me back. I'll be fine tomorrow. We'll get an early start. Go down and enjoy a day at the beach while I go back to bed.'

'Are you sure?' He nodded, his face grey and etched with more lines than Laura remembered from the day before. 'I'll make us a nice supper.' Laura opened his fridge. There were eggs and a few sad potatoes. The freezer was hardly better, just a couple of steaks, some frozen peas and French fries.

'I've been running it down. What's the point in keeping it stocked up?'

'We have enough for tonight at least.' There was bread and milk on the counter and a couple of tins of tuna in the cupboard. They would not starve for one day. Something puzzled her. It was almost New Year when the shops would be shut, why had he let his food run out? Laura turned to Rhys. 'You always intended to drive back to Sydney with me, didn't you? When did you pack? You were in bed before me.'

'Yesterday afternoon, while you had a nap.' He stared at her, considering his next words. How would she react? 'I'm lonely and I don't want to die alone. For the first time in my life, solitude is not enough. You've met Stan, he's not up to becoming my nurse. I'll need end of life care and I want to make my peace with my family most of all.'

Laura's mouth drooped open. 'You want to come back to England with me, don't you?'

'I want to go home. I want to see Peggy. I want to spend time with you.'

A mixture of hope and regret in his voice made the hairs stand on her arms.

'I should have been honest with you, I know.'

'What if we had disliked each other?'

'Laura, you're my granddaughter. I was never not going to love you. As soon as I knew about you, this was what I wanted, to end my life with my granddaughter by my side. Do you think I'm selfish? Of course I am, always have been.' He shook his head. 'I abandoned Peggy and your mother. I must make it up to you, but here I am, begging you to help me return to England, begging you to care for me. I know I don't deserve you.'

Laura laughed; the irony gripped her.

Rhys winced thinking she was going to slap him down; tell him where to go.

'If you want to know why I'm laughing, it's this. Barely six months ago, I had an almost-fiancé, no family to speak of and a life which appeared straightforward, a little tedious maybe, but I could see the way ahead. Then the boyfriend chucked me, I found both Peggy and now you who both need me. I think I have just discovered the love of my life twelve thousand miles from home, and I have no bloody idea what I'm going to do.' Laura sank onto the chair next to Rhys and put her head in her hands, howling with panic struck laughter.

'I never meant to add to your troubles, Laura. I'm sorry. Perhaps I'd better stay here.'

She gripped his hand. 'No, no. You'll come back with me. Hopefully, I can book you on my flight. You're not escaping Peggy again. She needs you. You need each other.'

'If you're sure…' A look of yearning lit his face.

Her phone pinged. She glanced at it and laughed again, this time with delight. 'It's Ash, my new love. He's booked a flight to Sydney for the day before I leave.'

'We'll work it out together, Laura. Rhys shuddered with exhaustion.

'Go to bed, Rhys. I'll go for a swim and try to clear my head. We have a few days before my flight, our flight. We'll try and figure it out. Leave me your passport and credit card and please go to bed before you pass out.'

He passed her his jacket and told her to look in the inside pocket before shuffling back to his bedroom. Oh, God, she thought, will he be fit enough for a twenty-five-hour flight?

'Don't worry about the expense,' he called. 'I've no need for money where I'm going. Upgrade yourself to business class, please.'

Wow! That will be something to look forward to. She rummaged in his jacket to find his wallet. Extracting two passports, she stared at the second, not what she'd been expecting, an unused red European passport with the British logo, lay in her hand. He must have kept it up to date, but why? Had he always intended to return home to die? It would make life simpler now she supposed.

After blithely spending thousands of dollars on two business class tickets, Laura picked up a towel, her sun hat and a bottle of water and walked down to the bay. Heat shimmered off the pavement. It was the warmest day of her trip, apart from that first uncomfortable arrival in Melbourne. A little sun, sand and water would help her mood.

The bay, small and perfectly formed with a rocky headland to the left and expensive-looking houses built onto the small cliff on the right, looked perfect for a swim. Laura walked over the strip of dry tussocky greensward to join a few stalwarts in the sun. She shrugged off her sundress, unwrapped her towel, took off her sunhat and was immediately grateful for the bathing hat which a colleague had recommended she buy for her trip. The sun pounded on her head. She skipped over the hot sand and into the water, a tropical warmth greeting her as she struck out into the bay. This was what she had dreamt of since booking her flight. Avoiding the surfboards, she headed to the rockier part of the bay and swam around, enjoying the feel of the sun on her back. It was about time that the waterproof factor fifty got some use.

Swimming in large circles while attempting to make sense of the last ten days, Laura could not allow herself to think of Ash as a holiday romance, another cliché. She accepted that her first reaction had been desire but that had deepened as she began to understand him. Yes, he was caring, attentive, humorous and honourable. The way he was with John and Molly proved that. But there was something more, something beyond that powerful attraction that had to be real. It felt like a meeting of minds, someone who almost knew her thoughts before she voiced them. Could they work it out or was it an impossible dream? Laura dipped beneath the surface to cool her glowing shoulders. Time to get out of the water before she burnt.

Chapter Fifty-Two

Back at the house, Rhys was up and about. Laura showered quickly and wrapped a towel around her hair. A strong coffee aroma hit her as she walked into the lounge.

'Did you enjoy your swim?'

'I did. You look a little better.'

Rhys nodded. 'I'm learning to pace myself. Did you book the flights?'

It was her turn to nod. 'I'll make some lunch. I bought fruit for afters.'

'I saw that, mango and kiwi with yoghurt. You've pushed the boat out.'

'We need you to stay healthy.'

Laura busied herself in the kitchen boiling eggs, buttering bread and peeling fruit. 'Tell me, how did you and Peggy meet?'

Rhys hunkered down in his favourite chair and sipped at his coffee. 'We were both shy creatures. I recognised that in her straight away. She was in her third year at university, and I'd just finished National Service. Neither of us had that many friends.'

'Sounds like me. Jake, my ex, latched on to me at a fresher's dance and I clung to him for the next ten years.

'But did you love him?'

'No, it turns out I did not.'

'I'm sorry about that.'

Rhys did look sad for her, bless him, Laura scooped the eggs from the boiling water.

'Peggy was very focussed on her studies. She was determined to do well and allowed herself little time for pleasure. I think it was a shock for her when we met.'

'How so?'

'She didn't want a serious relationship. It was too soon in her career plan, but then we cast eyes on each other one sunny autumn day in the quadrangle and we both knew something had changed.'

'You don't mean love at first sight?' Laura put down her spoon and stared at him, shivering slightly. How few days since her own gut reaction when Ash entered Molly's kitchen?

'Hook, line and sinker. We spent every moment we could together, studied, together, ate together, went to concerts together. Peggy educated me about music, books and art, and I taught her about politics and life.'

'You were friends and had a lot in common then?'

'No, Laura. The friendship came later. It was love that brought us together, the bolt of lightning kind of love, the kind that kicks you in the stomach so you can't breathe without each other.'

Laura swallowed hard, missing Ash with a sudden intensity. Her hand shook as she passed Rhys an egg sandwich. 'I don't understand. If you loved her so much, why did you break up?'

'After her post graduate teaching course, Peggy took her first job in Lichfield while I completed my final year. We only saw each other at weekends and not every weekend. Even finding time to write was difficult. We were both busy.'

'You drifted apart?'

Rhys bit into his sandwich and chewed slowly. Laura sat beside him with her own, waiting. If Rhys and Peggy had not made it, how could she expect her own new-found love to succeed with the odds so against it?

'Forced apart, more like. I planned that summer to be special. My studies were over. We both had time on our hands, though little money. We took a train to Austria. Peggy wanted to see Vienna and I wanted to show her the mountains. After a few days visiting museums and the opera, we headed to Semmering, a holiday spa. It was glorious up there. We walked for miles while I talked about our future plans. I had been promised a job in Canada at the end of September. We planned that I would go ahead, find a place for us to live and enquire about jobs for her.'

'That would have been a huge jump for Peggy.'

'In hindsight, I should have been more patient, found a job in England and made sure we moved together. Anyway, I proposed over coffee and Sacher-torte. She accepted. There was no money for a diamond engagement ring, but she found this little silver friendship ring in a shop. Openwork with patterns, I don't know what you call it.'

'Filigree,' Laura suggested.

'Yes, that's it. She loved it though it cost only shillings. I was over the moon. Everything was perfect.'

'What happened?'

'Towards the end of August, she took me home to meet her mother in Grimsby to talk about a wedding the following summer.'

'You went to Buller Street?'

'You know it?'

'Peggy's sister left it to me after she died earlier this year.' Laura could not visualise her grandfather in Buller Street. 'What happened?'

'It was a disaster from the moment I walked in the door. Her mother was determined to dislike me even before we started talking about Canada. You could have heard the row streets away. If she had forbidden her daughter to see me, it would have given Peggy the impetus to walk out the door and not look back. Doris was more subtle than that. She ladled on the guilt, the sacrifices she had made to bring her up, the promises Peggy had given. Then wheedled and whined and cried about being abandoned in her old age.'

'That's awful.'

'Something snapped in me, I suppose. I expected Peggy to stand up for herself and when she didn't, I let fly – at them both. It was unforgiveable. I'll never forget the look of horror on Peggy's face when I smashed her mother's best teacups.'

'Not the best move on meeting your future mother-in-law, I imagine. Wasn't Edith there?'

'No, I never met her.'

'Why not?'

'I walked out, left Peggy to sort out my mess. I wandered around until I found a bed and breakfast for the night. Next day, calmer, I returned to be told Peggy didn't want to see me. I let rip some more, then hung around outside for at least an hour becoming more and more angry. When Peggy didn't appear, I hightailed it back to the station. I was furious, humiliated, and not thinking straight.'

'You never made up? I don't see how you could leave it like that.' Laura's sympathies lay with her grandmother.

'Her mother never told her about my visit, of course. Peggy was out on some pretend errand. I wrote to her from Wales, but by then Peggy had returned to Lichfield. She was supposed to stay for a week in Grimsby. Her mother did not send the letter on. When Peggy didn't reply,

I sent a telegram to Lichfield begging her to meet me in Liverpool before I sailed. I looked out for her. She never appeared. The next time I wrote was from Canada.'

Laura cleared away the plates and began serving out fruit. 'I can't believe you left it like that,' she said, as she dolloped a spoonful of yoghurt into each bowl.

'You forget, we didn't have your internet and emails. The only telephones were in call boxes. None of us could afford one in our homes.'

'Even so. I would have thought you would have camped outside her home until you'd seen her.'

'There were things about my time in Germany I could not explain. Things I had buried deep. I ran back to Wales rather than confront them. I can't blame Peggy for not understanding when I hid things from myself. She wrote to me in Canada, a letter full of recrimination. I was powerless to defend myself. I simply begged her to give me another chance.'

'But you loved each other!'

Rhys sighed. 'That's why I have lived a life of regret. I understand how it all went wrong. My ticket was paid for and there was no money for a new one. Boarding that ship was the worst mistake I made in my life. I know that.'

Laura nodded.

'I should have returned the next summer to persuade her to join me, but I didn't. I'm not a good letter writer especially when it comes to feelings. I disliked my job in Toronto, so I took off on a tour of Canada and pitched up in Vancouver. When I wrote again in October, Peggy was horrified. Vancouver was even more remote from England. She didn't write again all year. I drifted further north, seeking peace and the tranquillity of the Rockies. When I next wrote, Peggy begged me to return, one last chance she called it, but I received that letter months later when I returned to Vancouver. It took time to arrange and find the money I needed, but I did go. Too late, you know the rest.'

'Why though? Why did you give up?'

'Without Peggy, something in me broke, only it took time for me to realise that it was Peggy and not peace I needed. I was confused, lost if you like. In the end I had nothing to offer her but me. It wasn't enough.'

Laura rubbed her hand across her eyes and shook her head. 'What a waste. You're not a good role model for love, you know.'

'True.'

'But you had a good marriage in the end.'

'I settled. We were fond of each other and had a son we adored. I can't complain about that.'

If you had the chance again, would you have fought for Peggy?'

'In a heartbeat.'

'I wonder if Peggy feels the same'

'She does. I asked her.'

With the story seemingly at an end, Laura took a spoonful of fruit and yogurt to eat. 'Oh, my word, this is the best yoghurt I've ever eaten. It's unbelievable. Like the best dessert from a high-end sweet trolley.'

Rhys smiled. 'That's what I meant about pushing the boat out. Gippsland yoghurt is the best, expensive but…'

'Divine,' Laura finished the sentence. 'It's reason enough to move to Australia on its own, I think.'

'Are you considering it?' Rhys cocked his head to one side.

'I don't know. I was rather hoping your story could help me decide. It's not inspired me with confidence,' Laura said, with a wry laugh.

'Learn from our mistakes. That's all you can do, Cariad.'

Laura began to clear away the dishes. How tragic for them both to have lived a life of regret. The email her grandmother had written made perfect sense to her now.

A sharp knock rattled the door.

'It's Stan. I need to give him a set of keys so he can sort the house out after we leave.'

'Are you just going to walk away from all this?' Laura asked.

Rhys walked into the kitchen and took her hand. The house can go on the market and the goods and chattels to the Op' shop. When you get to my age and stage in life, objects don't mean anything. The only thing that matters is family. Better crack open the last of the beers. Stan will expect a send-off.'

Chapter Fifty-Three

A cacophony of noise woke Laura at six the following morning, her mobile alarm, the radio alarm from Rhys's bedroom and the telephone were all ringing. Laura put the pillow over her head to shut it out. Overkill, surely. Hearing Rhys answer the phone, she stretched with a yawn. They were due on the road at seven.

'Laura, get dressed now.' Rhys shouted from the living room.

'Okay,' she grumbled and climbed out of bed.

'Now, don't ask questions, do as I say. We need to leave the house.'

'Why?' she poked her head around the bedroom door.

'Fire alarm. Don't bother showering. Collect your things and put them in the car. Let me have your passport. Quick!'

The urgency in his voice shocked her. Laura rifled through her bag for her passport and handed it to him, unsure why, then scrambled in her rucksack for clean pants. She dressed in the shorts and T shirt dumped on the floor from the night before. When she emerged from the bedroom, Laura found Rhys packing a small rucksack with water bottles, an old cigarette tin containing their passports, the remaining tins of tuna, a fork and a tin opener. Handing her an ancient woollen blanket, he ushered them from the house into a smoke laden early dawn. His suitcase for the journey was already in the car and he placed her rucksack on top. Shivering in the cool air of dawn, Laura dug into the rucksack for a sweatshirt.

'Are we going to try leaving now?' Laura asked.

'No time. We have to get to the beach.'

'Are we driving?'

'No, just move your car onto the road as far away from any trees as you can. Take what you need, sun hat, phone, wallet, and meet me on the beach. I'll set off but you'll catch me up. I walk slower than you these days.'

With her heart pumping, Laura found a spot on the road where a house was being renovated, all vegetation already victim to a digger.

Before switching off her engine, she noted the time, ten past six. Locking the car, she joined a stream of people heading for the beach.

A subdued crowd stood on the greensward by the time Laura joined Rhys. Anxious parents gathered children to them, someone carried a budgie in a cage, others had dogs on leads. All had their backs to the sea, staring at the trees to the west.

'Let's find somewhere to sit.' Laura worried about her grandfather, while wondering how long they were going to be stuck on the beach. It seemed churlish to ask. She guided him to a spot and unpacked the blanket for him to sit on, gently easing him down.

'We're in this for the long haul,' he said, answering her unspoken question. 'It's going to be hotter than ever. We should have left yesterday. I'm so sorry, Laura.'

'Shush, don't worry. It's going to be fine.'

He looked at her with stricken eyes and shook his head. 'We're safe enough here, but I've let your grandma down. Text her and that boyfriend of yours to tell her we're safe.'

'It will only worry them. Let's wait and see what happens.'

Text now,' Rhys instructed, his tone firm. 'We may lose the network if things get worse.'

Laura was shocked. She scanned the town looking for mobile masts. Could they really lose the phone signal? She could not imagine being without a phone. As Rhys pressurised her to act, she typed.

All ok. At beach. Maybe lose phone reception. Don't worry. xxx

Selecting her grandmother and Ash to send it to, she worried about their reaction. Her grandmother would be terrified. Laura sent another one to her.

Bringing Rhys home. See you next Sunday. xxx

Ash would be in bed and would wake to that message in a few minutes. She longed for a phone call.

Through the haze someone walked a horse onto the sands. Laura glanced around; the beach was filling up. Everyone looked shell-shocked, unable to believe that their worst fears may come true. Laura fought to quell her rising panic. Her phone trilled. It was Ash.

'What's happening?'

'There was a fire alarm, and everyone's come to the beach. I'm scared.'

'Is your grandfather with you?'

'Yes, but he's sick. He says he only has a few weeks.'

Laura heard Ash swear, before he took a deep breath. 'You are not to start panicking. The authorities know you are there. Do you have plenty of water?'

Ash had moved into calm doctor mode, and she forced herself to reply in the same manner. 'Yes, and food.'

'Stay near to the water. Get in if you need to. Make sure your grandfather stays warm. The firies will take you to a refuge when it's safe. They know what they're doing. Stay put, Laura. Tell me you understand.'

'I do, Ash. I love you.' She was close to breaking down.

'Love you too. Try and keep me posted. We'll be together on Friday. Hold on to that, Laura.'

She sniffed. 'I will.' The phone went dead. Laura stared at it. Ash had not cut the call and her battery was charged. She looked around and others were shaking their phones in exasperation. Laura trembled, feeling suddenly alone despite the crowd of people. She closed her phone down, then turned to look at her grandfather sitting on the blanket. He looked stricken with age and guilt. Fear about what this might do to his health overtook her. She needed to be his rock. Laura sat beside him and put her arm around him.

'I'm going to make sure you make it back to Peggy. I've made her a promise. You'll be with her on Sunday, Rhys. We'll get through this.'

He lay trembling against her. 'I'm sorry, Laura. I should have never asked you to come.'

'Enough. I'm glad I'm here to look after you. Understood?' Her words belied the fear she felt.

When Laura looked back at the twenty-four hours that followed, it was akin to being present at the end of days. From the moment that first block of trees exploded into fire, it was like her own personal horror movie had come to life. Worse than any horror movie where only her eyes and ears would be assaulted. Here smoke clogged her nostrils, greasy ash fell onto her clothes, her skin and into her mouth. The sky turned orange, the faint pink sun disappeared altogether, and the very air became a yellow soup through which the participants on the beach wandered lost, blank faces staring, disbelieving. At one point, Laura observed it as a weird Breughel painting, the human subjects in shorts and singlets, the dogs the horse and the bird in the cage, a scene frozen in time. She imagined the painting in a gallery, decades later, where people would come to marvel at the strangeness, attempting to dissect the meaning.

They began to lose the view of the town as fire jumped from one tranche of trees to another, then escaped from trees to buildings. The roar of uncontrolled fire became punctuated by explosions. Laura thought of her car with its full tank of petrol, a bomb no less, and how many other potential bombs surrounded them? She whimpered and it was Rhys who held her, his hand stroking her hair as worry creased both their cheeks. Laura clung to the comfort he offered while feeling guilty. All she had to lose was her rucksack, he and his neighbours could lose everything. Were they even insured for this disaster?

'If the fire comes towards us,' Rhys said, 'leave me, head into the sea. Don't stand in the shallows. This fire is enough to make them boil. Head further out, but only to the edge of where you can stand. If you swim too far, you won't be able to see land with all this smoke and you could become disorientated.' His voice was at first calm, but Laura shivered at his words. 'Promise me, you will leave me, Laura. You have to save yourself. Tell Peggy, I will always love her.' His voice caught on her name as he choked with a mixture of love and fear. 'That I brought you here, my lovely …' A dark powder of ash covered his cheeks.

'We'll get out of this. You have to believe, Rhys. I'll take you back to Peggy. Here, drink some water.' The plastic bottle lay uncomfortably warm in her hand as she passed it to him. He handed it back after a few glugs. Laura spat out the first gulp to cleanse her mouth from ash and grit. It tasted vile but Laura knew it was also a life saver. The temperature was soaring, but the sun's rays were hidden under the smoky haze.

At some point, Stan joined them on the beach. Laura had lost track of the hours. She was pleased to see him.

'Where have you been, mate?' Rhys croaked.

'Helping out.'

Laura thought those two words probably conveyed a master of understatement. He looked like a coal miner after a hard week down the pit.

'Bowls Club's gone, mate.' Stan passed a hand over his eyes, a gesture of defeat so profound that Laura bent her head, disguising her sympathy. 'Your property's okay so far.'

Rhys nodded and clasped his friend in a hug. Stan's shoulders shook. He turned his face to the unseen sun and howled soundlessly like a Munch painting. Laura shivered with the chill running down her spine.

At some point in the evening, they discussed whether to stay where they were. Laura thought of Ash's advice to keep Rhys warm, but where to go? Stan pointed to the concrete shell of a new apartment block facing the beach.

'That looks safe enough and the concrete will retain the heat better than sand.' They helped Rhys up, gathered their few belongings and stumbled their way across the greensward. Others followed.

Once they had settled, Laura shared out the small amount of food they had brought with them. The oil from the tuna, although unpleasantly warm, slipped across the grit on her tongue like honey from a throat pastille. Laura wished she had not rattled off that frantic text to her grandmother. She and Ash must be beside themselves. Then again, by the time news of this disaster reached Peggy, Laura could be safely wrapped up somewhere and Peggy's worry all for nought.

Surprisingly they slept, curled up together on the blanket. When Laura woke at dawn, she looked through the empty shell of the building at the pall of smoke across the sea. Apart from the snuffles of people around, there was an eeriness, something was missing, that cacophony of the dawn chorus. She wondered how many birds and animals had perished in the fires of the day before, even the month before and her heart bled. She heard a squawk from somewhere. Not all were gone. A gull flew low above the lapping waves, its wings white above the grey water. Laura rose and walked from the building, across the grass, through people still sleeping on the sand. At the edge of the sea, she dipped her toes into the water, and they came away coated in ashy slime. An older woman joined her.

'What I wouldn't give for a shower,' Laura said, aware that she stank.

'No chance of that. The fire took out the substation. There's no electricity. I'm going in.' The woman peeled off her clothes down to her bra and pants before striking out beyond the slime to clearer water beyond. As an afterthought she turned and yelled, 'Happy New Year. Let's hope 2020 is better than last year.'

New Year, Laura had forgotten. She waved and shouted back, 'Here's hoping.' What a strange year 2019 had been. What would the next year bring? She stripped off her shorts and top to follow suit.

It was a relief to dip beneath the slimy surface into cleaner water below. Laura swam underwater emerging to look back upon the devastation. Blackened tree trunks littered the horizon, thin smoke plumes rose towering into the sky. She looked high on the hill towards the bowls club but could see only smoke and the occasional lick of flame. On the headland, the houses looked untouched. A flock of brightly coloured lorikeets sat amid the leaves of a surviving tree. The sight made Laura well up with hope. They had survived, so had she and all the people stirring on the beach. Help would come and they would escape today, or tomorrow. She began to swim back to shore. Time to get Rhys home and into a proper bed.

Chapter Fifty-Four

'I'm proud of you, Laura. It must have been terrifying for you. It was for me, and I'm more of an old hand.'

They were crawling slowly forward; a snake of cars being evacuated to Bateman's Bay.

'We helped each other get through it.' Laura's eyes smarted. To have found this lovely kind man and know that she was losing him so soon, hurt more than she would have thought a week before. She glanced across at him, frail and shrunken in the passenger seat. The tension of the previous day had aged him giving her more concern for the days ahead. He would need cosseting because the thought of him dying on the journey horrified her, but he refused to stay in his house. Rhys had handed a letter of authority to Stan when they said goodbye, giving permission for someone who had lost their house to live there rent free. The option of Rhys returning to his home was ended.

The news from all over the south coast was terrible. Laura was thankful to have survived. Her hands on the steering wheel felt clammy with delayed shock.

The sports hall in Bateman's Bay offered a temporary refuge for the evacuees. Laura checked her phone, still no service.

'It's a good job you filled up your tank,' Rhys said as they settled down for another uncomfortable night. 'No electricity means no fuel. The road north is going to be jammed with motorists trying to escape. Whenever we come to a halt, turn off your engine to save gas.' He was checking his wallet and clucked at the lack of dollars.

'I have plenty,' Laura reassured him. Ash's advice had come in useful again. She wondered what he was doing. Two days without news, if the roles were reversed, she would be beside herself with anxiety. She longed to see him, to be folded in his arms, safe and secure. The experience of the last two days had taught her many things, but this was the most important. If Ash wanted her, then she would move heaven and earth to be with him. Every second of life should be treasured not wasted on unimportant things.

Laura snuggled down on the camp bed and pulled a sheet over her. She needed to sleep. Tomorrow was going to be another difficult day.

As they crawled north the following morning, they listened to the radio and realised how lucky they had been in comparison to places further south. Thousands of people waited to be rescued by sea from a town called Mallacoota on the south coast, another town, Cobargo, on the Princes Highway was wiped out. Scenes of chaos and Armageddon were being reported.

Before leaving Bateman's Bay, they had bought water and crackers with cash. None of the shops had working tills. How long was it since they had eaten a proper meal? Laura's stomach was already groaning, and the traffic queue snaked ahead, scarcely moving. The fuel indicator dipped relentlessly as the passing kilometres rose a fraction each hour that passed.

'I've been thinking,' Rhys said as they listened to more bushfire horror stories on the radio. 'Do you need the money from the house sale after I've gone?'

Laura shook her head.

'I'll donate the money to bushfire victims, then.'

'Good idea.' Laura could not imagine ever returning to Bateman's Bay.

Rhys sat beside her, silent and uncomplaining, as they inched forward along the road. Laura was thinking of the flight they were due to catch, and of her last day in Australia which she longed to spend with Ash. She was losing track of time and days. When was he likely to fly into Sydney? Her brain struggled to function after two nights of minimal sleep.

'Here is the eleven o'clock news on Thursday January 2nd …'

Laura jumped. Tomorrow! Ash was flying in tomorrow morning. Would she even be there?

By midday they were reaching the outskirts of Ulladulla and the traffic was still nose to tail. Each garage they passed had a handwritten sign, 'Closed'.

Laura turned to look at Rhys, his skin was like parchment and there was a blue tinge to his lips.

'Let's find somewhere to stop. I need a break,' she said. Laura kept her eyes peeled for a motel. Rhys needed a place to lay his head down for a few hours and her eyes were almost sticking together with exhaustion. Maybe the traffic would lessen by then. A few hundred yards further on, she saw a motor inn on the opposite side of the road and prayed that they had a room. Laura indicated and turned out of the line of cars to cross the road.

'You may be lucky. We've had no electricity for two days and a few people decided to leave this morning although the power's back now. But check-in's not normally until two.' The middle-aged woman on reception turned her head away from the radio to check her computer.

'If you have anything, I'll take it, just for a few hours, anything. My grandfather's ill. He needs rest.'

The desperation on Laura's face must have swayed the woman.

She lifted the telephone to ask if any of the rooms had been cleaned. Satisfied, she asked, 'Have you got cash? I don't think our machine's working.'

'Yes.' Laura slid a hundred and twenty dollars over the counter and was handed a key.

Laura sent a silent thank you to God. She desperately needed a shower.

The room was clean but basic, with one double bed. As soon as Rhys was settled, Laura stripped off in the bathroom and climbed under a spray of lukewarm water. She stood with it running over her head for a good five minutes as the tension began to slip away. After towelling herself dry, she slipped into clean clothes and fell onto the bed beside Rhys who was fast asleep.

It must have been four o'clock when Laura woke and stretched. Rhys was snoring. She lifted an energy bar from her rucksack and munched but it only made her hunger worse. Laura crept from the room and headed for reception. It was the same woman, still listening to the radio.

'You'll be out of luck tonight.'

'Why's that?' Laura dreaded the answer.

'Fire's cut the road north of here. There's a thirty-kilometre tailback.'

Laura wanted to bang her head against the wall in frustration. 'Would it be possible to let me know if the road opens? We have a plane to catch.'

Smiling sweetly, as the receptionist pursed her lips, Laura was sure that Sue, as her name badge said, was enjoying the drama of it all.

Sue sighed. 'I'll be off soon. I could leave a message for the night shift, I suppose,' making it sound as though it were a lot of trouble.

Laura nodded her thanks and headed out to scout for food. The carpark had filled up and a sign saying no vacancies had been moved to the entrance. With a wry smile on her lips for her wise decision, she headed to the nearby shops, noticing that the road north was solid with stationary traffic and the road south was busier too.

Australia had sounded wonderful in November with the thought of escaping some of the British winter and, without doubt, her first week had been heaven, but this second week was sheer, unadulterated hell.

With the dwindling cash in her purse, she bought some fruit, a couple of curling sandwiches, a box of cookies and a bottle of orange juice, leaving a hundred or so dollars, certainly not enough for a second night's accommodation. Laura headed back to try her mobile phone, noticing as she passed, the out of service notices on the ATMs.

Rhys was awake and his colour looked better. Laura explained the new problem as she switched on her phone, regarding the 'no service' sign with such despair that she almost flung it across the room. She tore the wrapper from her egg and salad sandwich.

'What am I going to do, Rhys?' she cried between mouthfuls. 'I'm supposed to be meeting Ash tomorrow and he still doesn't know where we are or that we made it safely out.'

'He will know that there weren't casualties in Malua Bay. Word will have got out somehow and he'll be listening to the reports on the radio. If the road opens tonight, we'll set off before dawn. Even if the driving time is doubled, it should only take four hours to drive to the car hire drop off. We could still make it.'

'I don't think I can face driving into more fire. They said the road was cut because of another one.' Her voice was becoming panicky as the shock from the previous two days threatened to overwhelm her.

'Come here, Cariad.' Rhys opened his arms and she crawled into them. He stroked her hair. 'We have the best fire fighters in the world, the most experienced. They won't open the road unless it's safe. If we have to catch a later flight, so be it. If Ash is not there to meet us, you have your whole life to make up for it. You love him, don't you? Tell me about him. I'm looking forward to meeting him tomorrow, even if just for an hour. Start at the beginning. How long have you known him?'

His soothing voice and gentle questioning calmed Laura and she began the story, going right back to the moment she received the letter about Edith's will. She lay in Rhys's arms and talked. He was a good listener, interrupting only once or twice to clarify something. As she poured out her heart to him, she realised how much she had missed him in her life.

At six thirty, the room phone rang. A man's voice, 'We've just heard that the road north is open, but the traffic is tailed back and may take hours to clear.'

'Thank you,' Laura said. 'Is it possible to get an alarm call at five a.m.?'

'To be honest, I wouldn't leave it that long. The forecast for the weekend is very bad. If there's a chance of getting out now, I would take it.'

'Thank you.' Laura put the phone down and took a deep breath. 'Shall we go for a drive, Rhys? Are you up to it?'

'Yes, Cariad.' Rhys smiled; a touch of pink had returned to his cheeks. 'Give me five minutes to use the bathroom and I'll be ready.'

They linked arms as they closed the door to the room. In the corridor, he bent to touch his lips to her cheek. 'Sorry I'm so scratchy. I reckon I'll have a beard by the time we reach London.' She laughed, her heart lighter than it had been since New Year's Eve.

The traffic, moving as slowly as a melting glacier, was escorted by the emergency services through the danger zone between Milton and Nowra. Rhys fed Laura cookies and orange juice and talked non-stop to keep her spirits from flagging and feeling drowsy. It was only when they saw the first sign to Kiama that Laura began to relax. She thought of the journalist, Sheila. If she had wanted to pay for a human-interest story, Laura reckoned she could now charge a fortune. But then there were so many tragedies unfolding in this country, Sheila must be working overtime.

Laura pulled into the next service station to fill up and catch some sleep. In an hour they could be dropping the car off, but it was too early.

Laura eased her grandfather's seat back, his eyes already closed. They managed to doze for a couple of hours before ordering their first hot meal in three days.

As they waited in the Hungry Jack for their order to arrive, Laura switched on her phone which immediately began to ping, message after message. She scrolled through, dozens, from Peggy, Ash, and even her father. What time was it in England? Peggy first.

All ok. Made it out. Will catch flight tomorrow as planned. xxx

Ash next. *Just north of Kiama. Will be at Sydney Airport sometime this morning. xxx*

Her father. *Been scary but now safe. Back in UK on Sunday. Speak soon.*

Her phone rang. Ash.

'Laura, darling, I've been out of my mind. I never should have told you it was safe to travel down there.'

'You didn't, Ash. You did your best to stop me. Then you showed me how to look after myself. Your advice kept me from harm. You and Rhys here, both of you looked after me.' Laura smiled at Rhys.

'No, Laura, we kept each other safe.' Rhys cut in.

'I'm off to the airport in an hour. I'll meet you at domestic arrivals. Have you any accommodation booked?'

'Oh no. I cancelled all my bookings before I left Tasmania. I haven't been thinking straight these last few days.' Laura answered.

'Coogee, book somewhere in Coogee.' Rhys cut in again.

'Grandpa says book somewhere in Coogee. I have no idea where that is.'

'I heard. Right O. Strange choice for someone who wants to see the sights of Sydney, but I'll get onto it. See you soon, my love.' His voice turned soft, 'I can't wait.'

Laura coloured and turned her face away from Rhys. 'Me neither, safe journey. Love you.'

Their food number was called as Laura switched off her phone, the battery almost flat.

Never one for fast food, she tucked in, moaning with pleasure as she took her first lingering sip of coffee, before looking across the table as Rhys picked at his burger. 'Everything's going to be all right, isn't it, Rhys?'

He took her hand and squeezed. 'Yes, Laura. Everything's going to be fine.'

Chapter Fifty-Five

Laura fell into Ash's arms, burying her face in his chest, before kissing him. God knew what her mouth tasted like. His tasted of coffee and mint.

'This is getting to be a habit, meeting me at airports,' she said, finally letting him go.

He put her aside to grasp Rhys's hand. 'Thank you for looking after her, Sir.' Laura loved the way Ash took both their bags and ushered them to a taxi, so solicitous, so polite. He gave directions to the driver and held the front passenger door open for Rhys.

Laura snuggled up to Ash in the back.

'You know, I am never letting you out of my sight again until you leave, don't you?' Ash said, caressing her arm. Laura watched Rhys nodding, noting that there was not that much wrong with his hearing, and she smiled. 'Why Coogee, Rhys?' Ash asked.

'He told me on the train,' Laura replied for her grandfather. 'There's a Bali bombing memorial to his son's mates there. He wants to visit one last time to say goodbye to Owen, the uncle I never met.'

Ash put a hand on Rhys's shoulder and squeezed. 'I'm so sorry, Sir.'

It was late afternoon when they gathered in the hotel reception area, close to Coogee Beach. Rhys and Laura had been exhausted after another night with little sleep. Laura had been too much on edge on the train to doze; her reunion with Ash playing over in her mind. It had not disappointed.

'Are you feeling up to this walk, Sir? It's a little bit of a trek.'

'Call me Rhys. I've never been sir to anyone. I may be slow, but nothing will stop me, young fellow.'

At twenty-six degrees, it was a perfect day as they began to walk around the bay towards the memorial on the northern cliff. They took a rest on a bench overlooking the beach where a bunch of young children were being given swimming instruction.

'There's a lovely walk from here all the way to Bondi Beach, Laura. My wife and I did it a few years before she died.'

'This place has so many bittersweet memories for you, doesn't it, Rhys?'

'Yes, my lovely. Owen was happy here. I suggested moving into his flat when he died. I thought my wife would feel close to him, but she couldn't face it. I wanted to. Oh God, how I wanted to be near him.' His shoulders shook but he was determined to do this final homage.

Laura held Rhys's arm as they stood and left the bench. Side by side they walked onto the coastal path. Rhys stopped to catch his breath and Laura passed him the bottle of water. After he had taken a sip, they set off again towards the headland.

'What a glorious view!' Laura said. The whole bay lay before them. 'It looks like a great place for families.'

When Rhys caught sight of the bronze memorial, he stopped and drew a handkerchief across his eyes. Three interlocking rings stood tall overlooking the bay and behind them, on a bronze plaque set in a wall, the victims' names were listed. Laura and Ash led Rhys to the wall so he could sit.

'This plaque is new. It wasn't here last time I came.' Rhys caught his breath.

'What happened to Owen, Rhys?' Laura asked.

'He had a great life here. He loved the liveliness after the quiet childhood, I foisted upon him. So many friends too; he was popular, you know.' Rhys mopped at his eyes. 'He should have been in Bali that week but cancelled because of work. His friends died, blown apart, their bodies smashed. Owen, well he couldn't cope with the survivor guilt. I thought because he hadn't seen it, that he would get over it. I should have known better, been there for him.' Rhys caught his breath and Laura took his hand. Ash sat next to Laura, his hand around her shoulders.

'My beautiful son gave up on life. He drowned. They said it was an accident, but he was a great swimmer. We scattered his ashes out there.' Rhys pointed out to sea where a large cruise liner sailed north towards Sydney's Circular Quay. 'There's no one to remember Owen after I've gone. His name isn't on any memorial. But those bombers killed him just the same.'

Rhys stared out to sea, before gathering his thoughts. 'I thought until a week ago that I had wasted my life but you, Laura, gave me hope. You too, young man. I can see that you love her. Don't be like me and waste time.'

'I do love this woman, Rhys, and with your permission, I would like to ask her to marry me. This week has taught me not to delay making decisions.'

Rhys smiled at Ash. 'I wish I could be there at your wedding. Go ahead, ask her.'

Laura spluttered. 'You two are talking about me as though I'm not here.' Her heart pounding to hear Ash talk of marriage.

'Best get on with it, lad, and when you're done, we can head for the nearest bar to celebrate. I need a cold beer.'

'Grandpa, you're incorrigible.'

'Then we can FaceTime or whatever you call it and let Peggy know. I've a mind to ask her to marry me too. What do you think, Laura? Are you ready to be a bridesmaid? By the way, you had better book a double room in that care home of hers.'

Laura threw her arms around him, laughing. 'I'll email Heather, the manager, and ask her. Peggy may not say yes, of course.'

'She will, just as you will. Ash is a fine young man. I'm proud of you both. Be off, the pair of you and give me some peace.' His eyes twinkled.

Ash stood and took her hand, leading her towards the edge of the cliff, before kissing her.

'I'm sorry. I respect your grandfather. He is a fine man, and I can't ask your father because he's not here. It's the way I was brought up.' He sat on the grass and pulled her down. 'Let's talk. How do you feel about moving to Tasmania?'

Laura nestled into his shoulder staring out across the bay as a jumbo jet headed for the airport. Waiting for the noise to subside gave her time to frame her reply. 'It's something I have thought much about over the last week,' she began. 'There are several times when I have shouted get me out of here! But then I think of Melbourne, which I loved, and Coogee has a really nice vibe, so maybe. But Tasmania? That's difficult.' She turned to look at him, his dark brooding eyes questioning. Laura giggled at his expression. 'Tasmania is beyond doubt, the most beautiful place I have ever been. I loved my day in Hobart. It's foodie heaven and the harbour is gorgeous, but Bruny Island, you well and truly sold me on that.'

'So that's a yes?' His eyes softened.

'It's a yes to living anywhere with you, Ash, but Tasmania is the icing on the cake. Do you think I'll be able to work?'

'We do have libraries, Laura.'

She nodded, 'I'm pleased about that.' Laura giggled again. He was being so serious when her heart felt like it was soaring amidst the swooping seagulls across this extraordinary seascape.

'I know you have to take your grandfather home. I worry about your grandmother when he goes. Does he know how long he's got?'

'He told me that he may not see the end of February.'

'How will you feel about leaving her when that happens?'

His seriousness and concern made Laura forget her giggles. 'That's also something that's been on my mind a lot. If you could have seen Peggy's face when she recognised Rhys on FaceTime; sixty years and her love was as strong. Do you think our love could survive sixty years of being apart?'

'I don't want another day apart.'

'Nor me. But their love endured. If they can spend the next few weeks together it will be worth everything we have gone through over the past three days. Granny has survived for that chance. I thought she survived for me and in part she did. She longs for me to find the same love she has for Rhys. I still don't really understand what happened between them. There's something more to it than one silly argument.'

Laura paused to look up at Ash, catching her breath as he smiled only for her. How could this beautiful man be hers? It still did not feel possible. 'Peggy would be the first to tell me to give everything up in my life to be with you and live without regret. When Rhys goes, she will slip away too. I feel it in my heart, and I'll be happy for her. Can you understand that?'

'I've seen it happen before, several times.'

'Have you?' Laura turned to look at her grandfather. He was staring out to sea, studiously avoiding her and Ash. 'I came twelve thousand miles, never having loved any man and now I have found three.'

'Three?' Ash jumped back in surprise.

'Yes, Rhys is the grandfather I wish I had always known and you, Ashwin Macauley, I have no idea why you want me, are the man I want to spend the rest of my life with. Cousin John is like the father, I never had until recently.'

'John will love that,' he said, ignoring the most important part of her answer.

'You're teasing me again. Why do you want me? It's only been a week since you were talking of beginning a love affair. Something's changed.' Laura's eyes searched his face.

Ash took both of her hands in his and grasped them tight. 'When you called from the beach, I was in shock; I couldn't breathe to think I had let you down. It was me that should have protected you, kept you safe. I have no idea how I went to work that morning and it's a miracle I didn't kill anyone. From that moment, I knew that I couldn't bear to lose you and need to spend the rest of my life looking after you. Laura, I love you with all of my heart, not for the way you look, although you are gorgeous by the way, but for your courage and the care you have for your grandparents. I respect that. It makes you someone I want to be with. Forever, I might add.'

He kissed her eyes, her nose and her mouth as Laura melted at each touch.

'Before we go any further,' he said, as he let her go. 'I need to know where I am in the culinary stakes?'

'What are you talking about?' Laura was confused.

'When we were walking around Hobart choosing what snacks to eat at the Food Festival, you were so disparaging about your previous blokes, a syrup sponge and a burnt steak, if I remember right. How would you describe me?'

'Are you serious? I'd had way too much to drink.'

'Absolutely. This can't go any further until I know where I stand.'

God, she loved his sense of humour. 'Okay, I have thought long and hard over this.' She had not but her mind scanned through the most delectable meals she had ever tasted until it settled on one. Yes, perfect. 'I once had a chicken fusion meal with spices which I still to this day don't know what they all were. The first forkful was like an explosion of flavour on my tongue. I had to savour it slowly, trying to dissect each element, from hot peppers to a strange but delicate sweetness and somewhere was the tang of lemongrass. I want to know how to recreate that dish, but it may take me a lifetime of research and experimentation until I get it right. All I know is that I want to spend my life trying.'

His lips sought hers again. 'Satisfactory answer. I can live with that, especially if you learn how to perfect it.'

After he let her go, he tapped her on the bottom. 'I think I can make an Aussie woman out of you, someone worthy of my Bruny Island shack. Do you reckon?'

'I think it's time you proposed and made my grandfather happy.' She tapped him back.

'Shall I get up on one knee?'

'I will accept nothing less.'

Ash delved into the pocket of his shorts and drew out a small wooden box. Inside, nestling on a piece of blue velvet was a silver ring set with a large oblong shell, every shade of iridescent blue. 'My father wasn't a wealthy man. He asked a friend of his to create a ring for my mother out of this abalone shell he had found on Bruny Island. Will you please marry me, Laura, and accept this ring, it would make me the happiest man alive.'

Laura looked up at Ash, and then at the ring, something old, something blue, a true match for her brooch. She held out her left hand, 'I will Ash. It's beautiful and I love it more than any other ring in the world. I can't believe you would let me wear your mother's ring.' Laura could not resist asking, 'Did she who has no name not want it?'

'I wouldn't have dreamt of offering. That should tell you something.'

'It does. It tells me everything I need to know.'

He slipped the ring over her finger and kissed her again.

'There is one condition,' Laura said after he had released her.

'What's that?'

'We call our first son, Owen, and our daughter, Rose.'

'Owen James and Priya Rose Macauley.'

'I adore our children already.' Laura caught a glimpse of them dancing in the rock pools of that special beach, both with latte coloured skin, wavy hair and dark blue, almost black eyes. 'Can we make them soon?'

'As soon as I get you back on Bruny Island. When will that be, do you think?'

Laura calculated. 'Is late March soon enough?'

He nodded. 'Book your flight as soon as you get home, promise.'

'I will, as soon as I have Rhys settled.'

'You know I think it was Owen and Rose who brought us together. If it weren't for their tragic early deaths, neither John nor Rhys would have gone looking. They are watching over us from above. As John would say, it's Karma. We should remember them both on Christmas Eve every year.'

'Rhys would like that. Let's go and tell him.'

Do you think an Easter wedding in Orford would suit? Shall I ask Molly to arrange it?'

'That would be perfect. I will ask my stepmother if my brother can be pageboy. That way my father may give me away.'

'If he doesn't, John would be honoured to give his cousin to me. Let's phone them while we walk your grandfather back to the hotel. Look at him, he needs that ice-cold beer.'

'He's not the only one. I thought you'd never ask.'

'After that, I'd better show you Sydney by night, unless there's something else you'd rather do?' He winked and Laura melted again.

She linked her arm into Ash's, the warmth of it sending a frisson of expectation through her skin.

'Sydney can wait.'

Chapter Fifty-Six

March 2020 - Tasmania

'Thank God, you caught an earlier flight.' John kissed Laura on the cheek before Molly enfolded Laura in a hug. 'Ash was beside himself with worry that you wouldn't.'

'Is he at the hospital?'

'Yes, they're hoping for the best but training for the worst.' He'll drive over to Orford for the weekend if he can.'

Laura smiled weakly. 'I'm so worried about him. Have you seen those TV images from Italy?'

'We'll lock down in time. We learnt from the last flu pandemic. Why on earth has the UK left it so late?'

What could Laura say? It seemed nonsensical to her. There had been no temperature checks, not even a question on health concerns before she boarded at Heathrow. Her temperature had been checked at Singapore and again at Sydney, where she had stayed long enough to ensure she was virus free, visited Rhy's lawyer and caught up on overdue sightseeing.

'How was the funeral, dear?' Molly changed the subject.

'It was sad, but also kind of beautiful. They had six wonderful weeks together before Rhys slipped into a coma. Peggy refused to leave his side. I was so pleased Heather arranged for them to marry while Rhys was still fit enough.'

'Ash said you were their bridesmaid.'

'I was.' Laura beamed. 'The home put on a wonderful spread for all the residents. It was full of joy and happiness. Heather even had a newspaper photographer and reporter primed.' Their love story had appeared in the newspapers after all. The Mid Sussex Times was not exactly the Sydney papers, but it seemed more fitting, somehow.

'And Cousin Peggy?' John asked.

'She died peacefully, five days after Rhys. She was ready to go.'

As they walked to the car, Laura's thoughts turned to her grandparents.

Rhys had said he would like to see his sister, Mary, before he died. Laura wrote a letter, sending it to all the Welsh newspapers and had put a plea out on Twitter to find her. It paid off. Laura had picked Mary up from Barnham Station off a direct train from Cardiff. There was no mistaking her, the same blue eyes and dimple in her cheek. Driving her straight to the home, Laura discovered she had two aunts and half a dozen cousins from Mary's nonstop amiable chatter. Mary spent an hour with Rhys, holding his hand and singing an old Welsh lullaby as he drifted in and out of sleep. Before she left, Mary spoke to Peggy. That conversation explained so much about Rhys.

'I brought the letter you sent to Rhys back in the sixties. If he had been in touch, I would have given it to him.' Mary handed an envelope to Peggy. 'I found it in Mam's things after she died together with your note to her explaining about your daughter. Did she ever reply?'

Peggy shook her head.

'I thought not. Mam never lifted pen to paper. It was always me that wrote letters for her. I'm so pleased you married Rhys in the end. You were good for him. We never blamed you for leaving him. He told us what happened at your Mam's house, how he lost his rag and smashed her tea service. He frightened you, didn't he?'

Peggy nodded.

'He never told you what happened in Germany, I suppose.' When Peggy looked blank, Mary carried on. 'Rhys was in bomb disposal. They found an unexploded bomb on waste ground and had cordoned off the area ready to blow it up safely, when two little girls suddenly wandered onto the site. The charge was already set. The men hollered at the girls, but they carried on walking towards the bomb, waving at the soldiers. In the seconds before it detonated, Rhys's best mate ran towards the children to try and save them. All three of them died. Rhys was sent home on leave. I remember him waking up at night screaming for Mam. They transferred him to a different unit when he returned. His nerves were shot, they said. I suppose today they'd call it PTSD.'

Mary turned to Laura. 'Your grandfather is a good man. He never meant to upset anyone.' She turned back to Peggy. 'Mam begged him to tell you what had happened. I think you would have understood and forgiven him for taking off like that. He just couldn't stand shouting and noise, but your mam had no call to tell him he should be locked up in an asylum.'

Peggy's cheeks flushed with pink. She nodded and reached for her alphabet sheet. – *I always wondered* -she tapped – *if only he had told me.*

Laura grasped her grandmother's hand as a mixture of guilt, pain and sadness flitted across her eyes.

'You're walking a lot better, John. The knee operation went well, I hope.' Laura said, reaching his Toyota in the airport carpark.

'It did, thank you. I've just started driving again. Molly drove here but I hope you won't mind me driving back.' He opened the back door for Laura and took her cases to stow in the trunk.

As they settled in the car, Molly turned to Laura. 'Did you manage to sort everything out that you needed to? I know it's been a rush.'

'Pretty much. At least I had finished work by the time Rhys died. They wanted me to stay an extra month, but it was impossible. I knew there would be the funeral to arrange and lawyers to meet.'

'What about your flat?'

'I took it off the market once this madness struck and rented it out furnished, which easily covers the mortgage.'

'Good, now you can relax. You've had a horrid time over the last few months, but we're delighted you've come back to us. I knew you were perfect for Ash. We're over the moon about you getting married, aren't we, John?

John dipped his head as he steered the car out of the airport traffic and on towards Sorell. Was it only twelve weeks since Laura had last done this journey? It seemed a lifetime ago. Christmas Eve was the day her life changed, the day she met Ash. Laura's hands settled on her stomach as her eyes closed with nervous tension.

She heard Molly say, 'That's right, have a sleep. We'll have you home in no time.'

Tired but with her mind still buzzing, Laura thought about Peggy's last days.

I want to be with Rhys, she had tapped in the hour after Rhys died. Laura had nodded.

'Granny, I know. I understand. He was the love of your life as Ash is mine. Don't worry about me.' Laura replied. Her grandmother had patted her hand in response.

Laura was unsurprised to receive the phone call four days later, knowing that her grandmother had been refusing to eat or drink since Rhys had slipped beyond understanding. Peggy had forbidden her to stay at night after the long vigil with Rhys. 'Don't worry about me, Laura. Rhys holds my hand at night and tells me to make haste.' It was the longest and last thing she tapped out.

Laura had rushed over to Storrington as the nurse arrived to make the final checks and was overwhelmed by how she talked to Peggy as though she were still alive.

'Mrs Griffiths, I am just going to put this stethoscope on your chest, it may feel cold.'

Mrs Griffiths, Peggy died as Mrs Griffiths and Laura had made that possible. It made her feel both humble and proud.

Heather came on duty as Laura bid her grandmother goodbye.

'Thank you for everything you did for Peggy and Rhys.'

'It was an absolute pleasure, Laura. To see them so much in love and the way Rhys looked after your granny while he could, it was special. He wanted me to give you this letter after Peggy died.' Heather handed her a plain white envelope addressed to Laura, clearly written in bold writing.

'Did Rhys know she would follow him so soon?'

Heather shrugged but with a knowing look. 'Who can know the ways of the Lord?'

Laura took the letter to read at home. How many times had she read it since? The next time it would be with Ash.

As Laura unpacked her case in the same guest room, she placed the old jewellery box on the dressing table. Smoothing out the love letter she had found wedged beneath a loose thread in the lining, she reread it. It answered some questions and gave rise to more but at least she had now found some sympathy for Peggy's mother, Doris. Who was Harry? Did Peggy know that Edith was only her half-sister? There were lines which stood out, heartbreaking and unremittingly stark. In hindsight – was that why Doris had been so cruel to Rhys? Did she see something in Rhys which reminded her of her husband's trauma?

'I have battled with my conscience. The way I see it, we were sent to war to do our duty as men. Is it not time for wives to do their duty to their husbands? John was a good soldier, a better man than me, and never let it be said that I came between a husband and wife, even if, as you say, he's lost his mind. Do not beg any more, my love. My mind is made up. Give our child your husband's surname.'

Laura refolded the note. She would never have shown it to Peggy, but it would have niggled - an unfortunate secret between them. She placed it in the box and lifted out the bluebird brooch before taking it into the lounge room to show John.

'This belonged to Susanna. It was a gift from Rose's father, whoever he was. I'm thrilled it ended up with me.'

'Molly, will you look at this?' John called her over.

'Oh, my word, it's darling.' Molly picked it up. 'A real antique brooch.'

'It's come home. Susanna had it with her in Australia until she sent it back for Rose's wedding.' Laura said.

'If Rose had had this to sell, she may not have died quite as early as she did.' John's voice sounded gruff with memories of his father's pain. 'Dad said she begged for work, but no one would take her on.'

Laura placed her hand over John's. 'Louise wore this brooch for her wedding and Peggy did for both of hers. I will wear it for mine, so Rose lives on in our memories.'

'That's lovely.' John looked up at Laura with a renewed smile. 'Now our family is united again, and Ash will not only be my adopted son but also a cousin-in-law.'

'Did Ash tell you if my father can't make it to the wedding, whenever that is now Easter seems unlikely, that I'd like you to give me away?'

'He didn't, but it would be an absolute honour. Molly did you hear that?'

Molly was back in the kitchen preparing a late lunch. 'I did,' she beamed. 'Can I pretend to be mother of the bride?'

'Yes, please.' Laura walked over to Molly and squeezed her, careful not to get stabbed by the vegetable knife she was holding. 'Will you teach me how to garden while I'm here?' Molly nodded, looking pleased.

'While I was laid up with my knee, I did a bit of digging, not the garden I hasten to add.' John said. 'I think I've found Susanna's death record. Come and see.'

Laura walked back to John where he was sitting at his laptop. 'I searched for that myself but never found it.'

'I saved it, here it is.'

Laura sat beside him to read. Susan Hornley died December 21st, 1880, Daylesford, Victoria. Father, James Hornley, cook. 'Wow. It has to be her. Where is Daylesford?'

'North-east of Ballarat, about forty-five kilometres. I sent for the death record.' John pulled it out of an envelope and handed it to Laura. 'You can see why they made a mistake when scanning. The writing is quite indistinct.'

Laura studied it. Her heart almost stopped when she saw the signature of who had reported the death. She looked at John. 'It's his handwriting, isn't it?'

John smiled. 'Yes.'

'Alfred White, son in law. That means Rose found her mother. They had a year together at least. That makes me so happy.'

'Lunch,' Molly called.

'Perfect timing. At least we now know.' John returned the death certificate to its envelope. 'Come on, we can't let Molly's lasagne go to waste.'

Chapter Fifty-Seven

By eight o'clock that evening Laura's eyes were drooping, and she took herself off to bed. She fell asleep, dead to the world, not hearing the door open, not feeling a body slip in beside her, not aware of his fingers caressing her arm. It was only when he lifted her top to let his tongue circle her browning nipple and his hand stroke the small rise below her stomach that she awoke.

'Hello, who's this?' he asked.

'Meet Owen James Macauley,' she murmured, reaching for him. 'I left my pills in Malua Bay and forgot all about them until I got home, you don't mind, do you? I didn't expect you until the weekend.'

'A Coogee baby.' Ash kissed her long and deep before releasing her. 'How very apt. Hello son. I adore you already.' He kissed the almost imperceptible mound of her belly and his fingers drifted south under her shorts until she groaned with desire. 'Did you honestly think I could stay away when I knew you were here waiting for me? You have a lot to learn, Mrs Macauley.'

'Why not start teaching me now, Mr Macauley?'

When Laura woke the next morning, he was gone. Had she dreamt it?

Molly brought her a cup of coffee. Laura took one look at it and dashed for the bathroom.

'So, it's true?' Molly handed her a glass of water as she came out. 'Ash was so stoked this morning before he left.'

'Stoked?'

'Ecstatic. He wouldn't say but I sort of guessed.'

'How?'

'The way you stroke your stomach every now and again when you think nobody's looking. I wasn't a nurse for forty years without getting to know a thing or two.' Molly patted the bed. 'You'll be needing a scan soon.'

Laura sat down beside her. 'In ten days, I'll be twelve weeks. It's what I've wanted for so long, but I'm scared too. My mother had several miscarriages and died from an ectopic pregnancy.'

'You're the picture of health and you have a nurse and two doctors at your beck and call. What more could you ask? Don't worry, Laura we'll take good care of you.'

Laura rested her head on Molly's shoulder. 'Can I tell you how much I love you and John? You're the parents I never had.'

'And you are the daughter we always wanted.'

Ash returned on Friday night for the weekend. 'That's it. No more inbound flights except for returning Australians. You made it by the skin of your teeth.' His voice trembled before he kissed Laura as she stood on the driveway to welcome him.

After drawing away, Laura could not help noticing the troubled look in his eyes.

'How do you feel about getting married tomorrow? I think I'm going to be busy for the next few weeks.'

His tone chilled Laura, but she put them to one side. 'Is that even possible?'

'Molly organised the celebrant several weeks ago, so yes, as long as she's free. Which she is because I telephoned her and explained the situation.'

'Where would we have it?'

Ash looked at her with a grin, 'In Molly's garden. If you fancied a beach wedding, tomorrow's forecast is cool and blowy, so unless you want sand everywhere?'

'No thanks. The garden works for me.' Laura threw her arms around Ash's neck. 'I have the perfect dress if I can still get into it, but only if we do away with the convention that you don't see the bride on the eve of her wedding.'

'I'm seeing you now, aren't I?' Ash held her face in his hands and kissed her. 'I want to see every square centimetre of you later,' he whispered in her ear.

Laura's skin tingled. 'There's something I haven't told you.'

'Something other than our child?'

She nodded. 'Rhys left me a letter. I thought we could read it together.'

'Nothing bad, I hope.'

'Oh no. I think you're going to like it.'

Well, let's tell Molly and John the news about the wedding first. They may have suits to press.'

Laura showed him the letter after dinner.

Our Darling Laura,

You have been such a joy in our lives these last weeks. We're so proud of you and you will have a wonderful life with Ash. He's perfect for you.

Peggy has at last agreed to join me in the wilderness. Please scatter our ashes in some remote and beautiful part of Tasmania, where eagles soar, and the Tasmanian tiger once roamed.

We wrote new wills leaving everything to you, but I have two favours to ask. The Malua Bay property should be sold, and the proceeds donated to a reputable charity to help the bushfire survivors. Owen's flat in Coogee should be given to your son, Owen James Macauley on his twenty first birthday. We wish we could have met him whenever he is born, though Peggy tells me she suspects it won't be too long. The flat's rented out now and the income should be used for its upkeep and then be split equally between any other children you may have.

All we ask is that you have a happy life filled with love.

Your adoring grandparents,

Rhys and Peggy

'Crikey! I know the perfect spot for their ashes, but did you know about the flat in Coogee?' Ash asked.

'No. Not at all.'

'Well, our son will be well off, the other children too. Do you mind if you just have me and my poor salary?'

The concern on his face was genuine. Laura smiled. 'About that, I haven't told you about Peggy's will and Percy's for that matter.'

'Who is Percy?'

'The man who thought he was my grandfather.' Laura proceeded to tell him and watched as his jaw fell further and further to the floor.

The following morning, Laura stepped into the bridesmaid's dress she had worn for her grandparents' wedding. Pale blue with long sleeves and a sweetheart neckline, the wool blend sat a little too snug over her hips and chest, but the zip coped without straining too much.

Laura took the bluebird brooch from her jewellery box and stroked it before pinning it to the dress above her right breast. 'Rose,' she murmured, 'You owned this brooch but never possessed it. Somehow, I can feel that you used it to guide me here. One day, I will pin it to my daughter's wedding dress and your story will carry on.' As she looked in the mirror, Laura half expected to see a shadowy face behind her. It would not frighten her if she did. Rose's presence was benign.

A whiff of almonds preceded Molly who knocked and walked in with a bouquet of white and yellow dahlias from her garden, as Laura slipped on matching blue ballet pumps.

'You haven't been icing a wedding cake, have you? I can smell marzipan.'

Molly looked baffled. 'No, we don't go big on fruit cakes here. I've made a sponge cake with pineapple and pecan topping.'

'That sounds scrumptious. Lovely flowers. Thank you.'

'The lavender is mostly over but I sneaked a couple of sprigs in to go with your dress. Do a twirl.' Molly instructed. 'Yes, perfect. I love the way the skirt moves. Ash will be knocked out.'

'Do you think so? It's not quite the dress I envisaged for my wedding.'

'You look gorgeous. Let's ask John. By the way, the celebrant has arrived. Everything's ready.'

John dabbed at his eyes when he saw her. 'I never had such a beautiful daughter-in-law,' he said, 'I mean that. Vanessa wasn't a patch on you.'

'John, really! What a thing to bring up on her wedding day.' Molly castigated him.

Laura was secretly thrilled and kissed him on his cheek.

'Does your father mind that I'm giving you away?'

'I texted last night. He's disappointed but understands. He thinks I'm much safer here.'

'You are. So far, the pollies here seem to be making the right choices.'

'But I worry about Dad. They say the virus is affecting older people the most.'

'Hopefully, now they've locked down in England, things will get better. We have to believe.' Laura took a deep breath and nodded; her anxieties partially alleviated. 'Ready to go?'

Laura touched the bluebird brooch for luck. It shimmered with good fortune beneath her fingers. Something told Laura that they would need all the good fortune possible over the next months.

'Yes please, John.'

Ash was waiting and she could not bear to let him wait a moment longer. Who knew what danger lay ahead for him? Every minute they had together must count.

The End

Author's Note

I began this book in the months leading up to my mother's death. She had many admirable qualities such as determination and generosity. What she lacked was education, something I am sure she regretted. I had cared for her for several years, although the last five were spent in a care home. We had a complicated relationship and didn't see eye to eye on many things. We edged around each other in stilted conversation after doing a crossword to while away the time. I realise now that Peggy became a metaphor. Laura and Peggy could not talk but had so much to say to each other whereas my mother and I found it difficult to break through the barrier that had built up over decades, worsened by her acute deafness and Alzheimer's. It's something I regret and doesn't stop me grieving for her.

Peggy is also based on a cousin who lost the power of speech and movement in her right side after a stroke. I spent one afternoon with my cousin where she struggled to convey anything, the day after I took in a notepad and a pen, and it was like a light switching on as she attempted writing with her left hand. That no one had offered this before always baffled me. Ten years later I witnessed how an iPad can also help those with speech difficulties.

The story was inspired by my three times great grandfather, James Thornton, the Steward to the Duke of Wellington. While investigating the family, I found that two of the younger James's children had swapped partners. One couple emigrated to America and began a new family. Their existing partners moved in together with the children. Divorce being almost unheard of in those days, it must have seemed a sensible option in the face of guaranteed scandal.

Essie is an invention. In no way does she resemble my actual great, great grandmother. The family did move to Liverpool where James, the younger had a confectionery shop.

Susanna, while she existed, albeit with a different name, disappears from the historical record. No husband or children have been found. I do have copies of letters sent by her father with recipes for curry and steamed perch.

My great grandfather on the other side was the skipper of the Theban which was blown up by a mine in 1919. Previously, he had been awarded a medal by the King of Norway for saving a Norwegian trawler.

In 2018, we travelled along the coast road between Melbourne and Sydney, stopping off at various Airbnb's along the way, one was at Malua Bay. A year later I watched the scenes with horror as the tragedy of the bushfires unfolded. I always intended my book to end in Tasmania, which I love and cannot help returning to, but I wrote this during 2019 to 2020 and how could I not include the most important events of the time? I apologise if readers are offended by this.

My thanks go to my editor J L Dean whose honest opinion is greatly valued and to Angela Petch, a friend and writing buddy who also gave me honest advice. Thanks also to author, Eva Glyn, who helped pull the book into its final shape. Thanks also to my dear friend Kate Sharp who worked tirelessly on my cover while undergoing chemotherapy. You are a star.

Thanks to Stephanie Dawe near Bateman's Bay, NSW, for sharing her diary of the bushfires with me and for being a proof-reader and helping me avoid errors about Australia.

Thanks to Vaughan Rees for helping me with the Welsh words.

Thanks also to other early readers who helped me achieve the final version.

Lightning Source UK Ltd.
Milton Keynes UK
UKHW012028080922
408463UK00001B/40